Allon

Book 2

Insurrection

Shawn Lamb

Allon Books

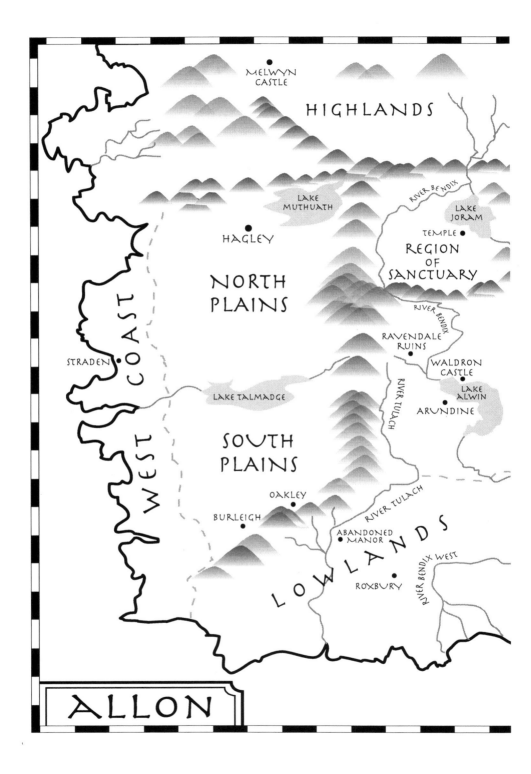

MELWYN
CASTLE

HIGHLANDS

Lake
MUTHUATH

RIVER BENDIX

LAKE
JORAM

TEMPLE •

HAGLEY

REGION
OF
SANCTUARY

NORTH
PLAINS

RIVER BENDIX

RAVENDALE
RUINS

WALDRON
CASTLE

STRADEN •

LAKE
ALWIN

Lake Talmadge

RIVER TULACH

ARUNDINE

SOUTH
PLAINS

OAKLEY

BURLEIGH •

ABANDONED
MANOR

RIVER TULACH

LOWLANDS

RIVER BENDIX WEST

ROXBURY

ALLON

Allon ~ Book 2 ~ Insurrection by Shawn Lamb
Published by Allon Books
209 Hickory Way Court
Antioch, Tennessee 37013
www.allonbooks.com

Cover design by Robert Lamb

Library of Congress Control Number: 2010911918

International Standard Book Number: 978-0-9829204-0-4

Other Books by Shawn Lamb

ALLON ~ BOOK 1
Published by Creation House
A Strang Company

Coming in 2011
from Allon Books

ALLON ~ BOOK 3 ~ HEIR APPARENT
ALLON ~ BOOK 4 ~ A QUESTION OF SOVEREIGNTY

Inhabitants of Allon

Mortals

King Ellis – age 22
Queen Shannan – age 21
Lady Arista
Wess – son of Lord Hugh, age 16
Bosley – son of Lord Hugh, age 14
Lord Hugh
General Iain
Lady Lanay
Mistress Gwen – daughter of Sir Owain, age 17
Musetta

Council of Twelve

Vicar Archimedes	Region of Sanctuary
Darius, Duke of Allon	Southern Forest
Baron Erasmus	Delta
Baron Mathias	West Coast
Baron Hollis	East Coast
Lord Zebulon	Lowlands
Sir Gareth	South Plains
Lord Malcolm	North Plain
Baron Ned	Northern Forest
Lord Ranulf	Highlands
Lord Allard	Meadowlands
Sir Owain	Midessex

Inhabitants of Allon

Immortals

Guardians

Captain Kell
1st Lieutenant Armus
2nd Lieutenant Avatar
Mahon
Vidar

Trio Leaders

Gresham	Midessex
Priscilla	East Coast
Egan	Northern Forest
Wren	Southern Forest
Jedrek	Delta
Zadok	Region of Sanctuary
Zinna	Meadowlands
Chase	West Coast
Barnum	Highlands
Derwin	Lowlands
Mona	North Plains
Auriel	South Plains

Shadow Warriors

Burris	Indigo
Roane	Bern
Nari	Cletus
Lark	

Chapter 1

FOR THE PAST FOUR YEARS, Lord Ranulf's Highland castle at Clifton served as the summer palace for King Ellis and Queen Shannan of Allon. They normally left in early autumn for the journey to Baron Erasmus' castle in the southern Delta region to hold court in a more moderate climate during winter. The royal castle of Waldron, located in Midessex, would not be completed for another year. However, the queen was heavy with the first royal child, delaying departure from the Highlands until early winter. Traveling from Clifton Castle to Waldron took nine long days on horseback and up to two weeks when traveling in a carriage with a royal procession. Given the time of year and shorter days it could take longer.

Eldric, the prominent Guardian Physician, estimated three weeks until the birth and most of that time would be spent travelling. Over the course of the journey, the remedies he prescribed to ease Shannan's discomfort grew less effective.

At twilight of the twelfth day, the royal carriage raced down the road to Waldron. Even incomplete, the castle was an impressive sight, encompassing fifty acres on a plateau set in the midst of an open plain. This gave clear visibility of an approaching enemy from any direction. Large wrought iron oil lampposts lined each side of the road for the last mile to the castle. Eventually an elaborate oak-and-iron gate would stand between the half-finished gatehouses. The planned fifteen-foot high walls rose only five to eight feet in places, with two of the four intersecting square corner turrets finished. The white marble cobblestone of the Grand Courtyard was half laid and the large marble fountain dry of water. Directly beyond the main gate stood the completed Great Hall, a stone structure of grand proportion. To the right of the fountain was located the Chapel of Jor'el with elaborate carvings, stained glass and awe-inspiring architecture.

A less ornate gate stretched diagonally between the Great Hall and Chapel. The gate separated the armory, stables, carriage house, army barracks and servant's quarters from the Grand Courtyard. Another smaller wrought iron fence and gate ran between the Chapel and the right gatehouse. This area housed the Jor'ellian Knights and priests' quarters and the gardens. Accessible to the Chapel, yet outside the main walls, lie the family cemetery and royal crypt.

A completed two-story enclosure connected the left front side of the Great Hall to the west wall. This corridor served to divide the Guest Quarters from the Family's Private Quarters on the west and south walls. The lower level served as a galleyway, while the second story housed Waldron's offices, the king's study, Captain of the Guard's office and the private quarter's of the King's Champion. This galleyway completed the final section enclosing the Family's Courtyard and Garden. Each bedchamber and guest room had a private privy, including a tub, basin, mirror, toilet, water pump and a small stove for heating the water. The army barracks and servants' quarters had communal privies for men and women that were less ornate but up-to-date innovations.

In the carriage, Ellis tried to encourage Shannan. "Not much longer."

Darius, Duke of Allon, and Lady Arista accompanied the royal couple. She was a comely young woman of twenty-three, two years older than Shannan and well certain of her mind yet discreet. Arista was Shannan's favorite of her six ladies-in-waiting. Being foster brothers Darius and Ellis bore little resemblance. Ellis' golden hair and bright blue eyes were in contrast to Darius' dark brown hair, brown eyes and more rugged features.

They focused on comforting Shannan in her growing distress. She clenched Ellis' hand while biting back another pain.

The royal carriage came to a clattering halt on the uneven pavement. Eldric jumped down from the driver's seat and almost got the door slammed in his face when Ellis exited. Darius helped Shannan climb down. Arista came from the opposite side of the carriage to help. Instead of hurrying upstairs, Eldric lifted Shannan in his arms and vanished in a flash of white light of dimension travel, the common method used by Guardians.

"Captain! General!" Ellis shouted before he, Darius, and Arista rushed inside with Vidar, the queen's Guardian protector, at their heels.

At age forty-four, General Iain was a strong athletic figure with dark red hair and whiskers, dressed in his royal blue and silver uniform. "Secure the castle," he ordered soldiers and Knights.

Like all Guardians, Kell was extraordinarily handsome and tall at seven and a half feet. His hair was midnight black and his eyes a brilliant gold. "Elgin! Sorrel!" He summoned two vassal Guardians. They were shortest of Guardians at seven feet tall, lesser in strength compared to Kell and other warriors, and wore no weapons while the uniforms were steel-blue and silver. "Prepare messengers for immediate dispatch to the Council once the child is born."

Both saluted with a clenched right fist striking the left breast before hastening to follow orders.

In a sumptuous royal apartment still in the process of decorating, Eldric reappeared with Shannan. She was unconscious. Dimension travel wasn't easy for mortals, often causing them to faint or become sick, but in this case it was necessary to ensure the safe arrival of the child. She woke when he placed her on the bed.

"It's time, Majesty."

"You're telling me?"

Ellis, Arista, Darius and Vidar entered. Two maidservants and another female Guardian accompanied them. She was dressed similar to Eldric in professional robes with a skirt reaching her ankles.

"Majesty, you remember my assistant, Phoebe," said Eldric.

Shannan nodded, biting back the pain.

"Sire, Your Grace." Eldric motioned toward the antechamber door.

"Leave?" chided Ellis.

"For the good of Her Majesty and the child." Eldric's violet eyes were prompting. Guardians not only had unusual colored eyes, but with a glance could compel or command.

Vidar took Ellis by the arm and escorted him to the antechamber. Darius followed them. Kell and Armus were already in the room. They stood three inches taller than Vidar. His appearance reflected his station as the premier Guardian archer with clothes of forest brown and green that complimented his auburn hair and vivid copper eyes. Armus was Kell's lieutenant since the Beginning over two millennia ago. He was strong and brawny with ruggedly good-looking features, brown hair and bright chestnut eyes.

Iain entered. "All is ready, Sire." When Ellis only gave him a preoccupied and passing nod, he moved to stand beside the Guardians. His six-foot athletic frame appeared puny next to them.

Ellis winced in anxiety at hearing Shannan's cry. "She sounds like she's dying!"

"She's just having your baby. The one you wanted to be born here, remember?" said Darius.

"As if I'd forget. Prophecy says the Royal Child will be born at Waldron."

"Indeed, Sire. But is this the child to be born here?" said Kell.

"What does that mean, Captain?"

"I sense there will be more royal children."

"I should hope so."

Darius took the two mugs of the mulled cider brought by a servant and handed one to Ellis. He wryly smiled at Kell and spoke. "The stress is making him edgy. He's never been a father before."

Ellis flashed a teasing smile. "Neither have you. You're not even married. Or is there something I should know about, brother? Lady Arista, perhaps?" Darius choked on his drink and Ellis laughed. "I jest. I could never image you fathering a child out of wedlock."

Darius recovered quickly and spoke in a deadpan tone. "I could never image you as king, but it's reality." Hearing another cry from Shanna, he soothed Ellis. "Easy. Eldric will see she and the baby are well."

For the next hour Ellis paced the antechamber. Darius also manifested nervousness, crossing to a window then back to his seat near the hearth. A servant brought food, but Ellis ignored it while Darius picked at some morsels.

Hearing an infant's cry, Ellis bounded for the antechamber door and met Eldric in the threshold. The Guardian smiled and said, "You have a fine healthy son, Sire."

"Shannan?"

"Tired, but well."

"A son. Congratulations." Darius thumped Ellis on the back.

"Aye, Sire," agreed Iain.

Ellis proudly smiled and entered the bedchamber. Shannan reclined against the pillows, her hair matted to her forehead, appearing pale and tired, but smiling. Phoebe and Arista tended to the babe, wrapping him in blankets after wiping him clean. Arista carried him to Shannan. He grew fussy at movement then quieted in his mother's arms.

Ellis tentatively touched his son's face. "He's so small."

"But handsome, like his father, and with the same blue eyes," said Shannan.

"Dark of hair, like his mother. I didn't know babies had so much hair. It's fine and soft."

"Since his hair is dark, born at night and Jor'el has heard our prayer for a son, he shall be called Nigel."

"Nigel," Ellis repeated and smiled with approval.

"Hail, Prince Nigel," said Darius. Iain, Kell, Vidar, and Armus mimicked his speech and bow.

"Sire, Her Majesty and the prince should rest," said Eldric.

Ellis kissed Shannan on the forehead. After looking at his son again, he, Darius, Kell, Armus and Iain returned to the antechamber. Vidar remained with Shannan.

"This a fine day. I haven't felt this proud and happy since Shannan and I were wed," said Ellis, although his frown didn't match his words.

"But?" asked Darius.

"I hope Nigel's birth will solidify the unconditional support of the Council."

"Ellis, the Council pledged their allegiance. For any of them not to recognize Nigel, they would be foresworn and disgraced."

"I understand that. My hope is they will see the symbolic meaning. Even with the walls of Waldron not yet complete, the House of Tristan is reestablished."

"Zebulon and Gareth must acknowledge that." Darius clapped an arm about Ellis' shoulders. "Do not let this interfere with your joy. You and Shannan are blessed with a son."

"Ay." Ellis glanced slyly at Darius. "What about you? I saw the smitten grin as you watched Arista when she held Nigel."

Darius roguishly smiled. "I won't deny I have taken a fancy to her."

"But have you told her?"

Darius grew sheepish. "I'm getting around to it."

Ellis laughed. "You can bravely face battle, stand up in the Council and confront Zebulon, but you can't tell a woman that you're in love with her."

Darius waved a brotherly scolding finger at Ellis. "You can be irksome." Ellis' laughter increased, making him grumble. "Very well. I'll tell her. In my own way and time."

"Come. Now I can eat. Gentlemen, spread the word: Prince Nigel, heir to the throne of Allon is born." He steered Darius from the antechamber.

While Iain left to comply with the order, Kell detained Armus. "Stay close to Nigel. I'll dispatch Elgin and Sorrel," he said, his face and voice were less than enthusiastic.

"As his Overseer or is something wrong?"

"I don't know about an Overseer yet. Like Ellis, I'm hoping this does quiet the tension among some of the mortals."

"You're not certain."

Kell snorted an ironic chuckle. "You and I both know how fickle mortals can be even when good things happen. You and Vidar stay extra vigilant until I'm certain all is well." He left the antechamber and Armus returned to the bedchamber.

Over the next two months, Waldron Castle became a hive of activity. The Council of Twelve arrived to pay homage and celebrate Prince Nigel's birth. Feasts, private banquets, gaming and merrymaking of all kinds happened at Waldron and across Allon. Vicar Archimedes pronounced blessings upon the infant prince. Foreign monarchs sent gifts in honor of the royal heir.

After another long day Ellis and Shannan paused by the nursery on their way to retire. As usual, Vidar followed. Armus and Lady Faline, a mother of four, were in the room while Nigel slept in his crib.

"How is he?" whispered Shannan.

"He is well, Majesty. He has a healthy appetite and sleeps soundly once fed," replied Faline.

Shannan kissed her son and softly said, "Sleep. Jor'el is watching over you."

Kell entered, accompanied by Avatar, a Guardian warrior. He was leaner in bulk than Armus with bronze hair and a small goatee framing his lips. Vibrant silver eyes reflected his mood, which at present was jovial.

"Avatar? Is all well?" asked Ellis.

"Ay, Sire."

"I asked Avatar to accompany me," said Kell.

"And where have you been all day, Captain?"

"I was summoned to the heavenlies for instructions concerning the appointment of Prince Nigel's Guardian Overseer."

"Overseer?" asked Shannan.

14

"What I have been doing in watching over the prince," said Armus.

Kell explained. "According to Jor'el, each royal child will have a Guardian Overseer. It was the same with your ancestor Tristan and his family. Armus had the privilege of being assigned to Tristan. Other Guardians served in the similar capacities. If you recall, Wren kept close vigil over you in Dorigirith."

"So Armus is to oversee my son the same as he did my ancestor."

"No, Avatar is."

"Avatar?" asked Armus in surprise.

"It is Jor'el's will." Kell's glance shifted from Armus to Avatar then back again.

"Then it shall be done."

Shannan noticed Avatar was thoughtful and looking at the crib. "You dislike your assignment, Avatar?"

"No, Majesty. I've never been an Overseer before. Although I've seen many mortal infants and children over the centuries, I only interacted with them on a casual basis."

Armus chuckled and clapped Avatar on the shoulder. "It's not too difficult when this small. It grows more complicated as they get older. Mortals call it a *nanny*."

Kell smiled, shaking his head at Armus but speaking to Avatar. "You make certain no harm comes to the child, either from an enemy or of their own making. Sometimes you offer advice, but mostly, you blend with the background and stay alert for trouble."

"I know you'll do well, Avatar. Shannan told me how you lead the rescued Guardians from Ravendale. And I saw you rally the flank during battle. Your wounds didn't stop you," said Ellis.

Avatar bowed to the compliment.

"Is that all of Jor'el's instructions?" Shannan asked Kell.

"A few minor points dealing with the Guardians, but nothing more of royal concern."

She tried to suppress a yawn. "Good, because I'm tired." She and Ellis left with Vidar.

15

"You may rest also, my lady. Avatar will summon you when needed."

"Thank you, Captain." Faline wearily smiled before speaking to Avatar. "I'll be in the antechamber."

A smirk at Avatar, and Armus followed Kell in leaving.

Once alone, Avatar approached the crib. For a long moment he watched the sleeping Nigel. He was so small and helpless, yet with a look of innocence. Carefully, he reached down and used a finger to brush Nigel's cheek. The babe stirred, making a soft contented mew. Avatar smiled and gently laid his hand on Nigel, nearly covering his entire body.

"According to my heavenly charge, my sword, my friendship and my loyalty belong to you as your constant companion and protector. No harm shall come to you from friend or foe, mortal or Guardian for as long as I have strength and breath. This I pledge in Jor'el's name."

In the hall, Armus laid hold of Kell, slowing the pace, but not stopping their course. "Why Avatar?"

"Do you object to his selection?"

"No, although I had grown accustomed to the child, and, well, I expected it to be me. I did it before."

Kell cocked a brow. "You sound jealous."

"I am not," Armus insisted louder than intended as told by the curious eyes of guards and servants turning toward them. He lowered his voice. "I'm surprised. Avatar is our Trio Mate, a mighty warrior and one I'm proud to serve with, but watching an infant? That takes patience, understanding and ... " Kell's laughing stopped his protest and he scowled.

"I asked Jor'el the same about your temperament on your first assignment. It did wonders for your patience."

Armus' scowl changed to a smirk. "Well, if Nigel inherits any of Ellis' impatience and Shannan's stubbornness, Avatar will have his hands full."

"Perhaps sooner than later."

"Why?"

Kell looked about before replying. The royal guards returned their focus to duty but a few servants lingered so he drew Armus into the shadow of a doorway to speak privately. "Nigel's birth may have stilled some voices, but there is a growing uneasiness."

"Zebulon and Gareth are always contentious. I sometimes wonder why Jor'el allows such mortals to exist."

"It goes beyond them. There is darkness to this unrest. Remember, I couldn't find Dagar's talisman after the battle."

Armus' brow leveled in concern. "Have you told Ellis and Shannan?"

"No. I want to wait until I get a better sense if the talisman is involved. I ordered the Trio Leaders to do a search of their provinces."

"Any word yet?"

"No, only I won't leave anything to chance. Keep alert and spread word to the others."

A soldier hastened up to Kell. "Captain, the king sends for you. He's in the bedchamber." He pointed down the hall.

Kell wasted no time in making his way to see Ellis, Armus at his heels. Ellis wasn't alone; Darius, Iain and Baron Erasmus were with him. Erasmus was the lord of Delta region and member of the Council of Twelve and a merry individual who kept his curly blonde hair close cropped for manageability. Rarely did he wear gray or black clothes, rather lively colors to suit his personality. However, at the moment he looked troubled.

"Good, Kell. The time of celebrating has brought out the worse in some people. Erasmus received a report of an uprising in Chandler," said Ellis.

"What kind of uprising?" Kell asked Erasmus.

"Rabble-rousers, yet causing significant damage and fright to warrant the sheriff employing the militia to quell it."

"What does Jedrek say about it?"

Erasmus shrugged. "I've not heard from him."

Ellis keenly regarded Kell. "Do you think there is more to this than a celebration that got out of hand?"

"I'm always suspicious of any trouble, Sire."

Armus glanced at Kell upon hearing the cryptic reply and discreetly said, "Captain."

Ellis' gaze shifted between the Guardians. "Kell, is there something you're not telling?"

"No, simply asking questions to make an assessment."

Armus tried to be casual in averting his eyes from Ellis's probing glance but Ellis confronted Kell. "Armus isn't convinced by your statement, nor am I. Not to mention the fact Guardians are supposed to be above lying."

Kell kept his voice benign when replying to Ellis. "I'm not lying, Sire. I'm truly not aware of any specific trouble, merely a sense of disturbance. I asked the baron about Jedrek to determine whether it is solely of mortal making or otherwise."

"You mean the Dark Way?" asked Darius.

Armus fought to keep from reacting upon catching Kell's warning eye. Their attention was brought back to Ellis when he spoke.

"There haven't been reports of Dark Way activity in years."

"I know," began Kell. "As I said, I am always suspicious of trouble. Since the night of the prince's birth the sense has grown stronger, so I instructed the Trio Leaders to search their provinces."

"Which Jedrek would have reported if he found any," said Erasmus.

"Ay. However, since neither of us have received word from him, it may well be mortals squabbling, or as the king said, a celebration that got out of hand."

Darius gave an ironic laugh and spoke to Ellis, "If we hear of trouble from the Lowlands then it could just be in response to Nigel's birth, which solidifies your authority, and Zebulon's already surly about it."

Ellis rolled his eyes concerning the most gruff and mean-spirited Council Member. "General, have you received any reports of trouble?"

"No, Sire," replied Iain.

"You may be right about Zebulon, and where he goes, Gareth will follow," Ellis spoke to Darius.

"Allard would remind you of Owain."

"He doesn't have to, I remember well what he did." Ellis scowled and waved a finger at Darius. "And I'll be watching for any misstep."

"The Vicar vouched for him, Sire," said Kell.

"Ay." Ellis paced while considering out loud. "Erasmus says the situation in Chandler is under control, Kell can't sense anything specific and there hasn't been word of trouble from the Trio Leaders or to Iain's knowledge." He stopped and looked at Kell. "You're right to be suspicious of everything with too many possibilities to be certain of where the trouble lies."

"Your orders, Sire?"

"Stay alert and report to me if anything else should happen."

"Should we tell the other Council Members?" asked Erasmus.

"Not yet. Why encourage the likes of Zebulon and Gareth to even think about causing trouble when they are capable of doing it themselves?"

Darius chuckled. "I hope someday to hear you say that to Zebulon."

"Indeed," agreed Erasmus.

Ellis smirked in ironic annoyance. "Goodnight, gentlemen."

In the hall, Armus confronted Kell. "Why didn't you tell him about the talisman?"

Instead of answering, Kell led Armus to his private chamber located off the galleyway and away from prying eyes and ears. "I don't want to cause undo alarm. And where was your discretion and support?"

"I was surprised by your lack of forthrightness. Notice I didn't say lying."

Kell scowled. "You know I speak when I'm certain and not before."

"Well, you made Ellis suspicious."

"Maybe I should have left you with Nigel and appointed Avatar my new second-in-command."

Armus laughed. "Never happen."

Despite his irritation, Kell smiled. "Go. Tell the others to keep alert."

Chapter 2

THREE MEMBERS of the Council of Twelve took advantage of a clear winter's morning and left Waldron, heading south. Approximately thirty servants, men-at-arms on horseback and carriages transporting their families followed them.

Sir Owain of Midessex was thirty-eight with a ruddy complexion, trim body, and rough hands that showed his love for the outdoors and farming life. He rode a placid mare between the others. Lord Zebulon of the Lowlands was eldest of the trio at forty-nine, gruff-looking with a salt and pepper beard and dull brown eyes. His brother Sir Gareth of the South Plains was ten years younger, stout, with coarse whisker stubble that serve as a beard. The spark of youth in his hazel eyes began to fade.

"That went better than I expected," said Zebulon.

Gareth snickered. "How? Did you expect Ellis to have a girl?"

"Wouldn't be his first mistake."

"Why are you so critical of the king?" asked Owain.

"Because in my esteemed brother's eyes, Ellis is a young whelp who is wet behind the ears," said Gareth.

Zebulon grew terse. "It takes one with experience and knowledge to rule. You don't get those playing in the forest all your life."

"Angus did well raising him," said Owain.

"Angus isn't here to advise him, Darius is."

"Darius is more like Angus than you want to admit," said Gareth.

"That's the problem."

"I suppose he would do better to have someone older, wiser, and more cynical as advisor. Yourself, perhaps?"

"Ay."

"He has the Council, and often seeks advice, together and individually."

Zebulon laughed, loud and mocking. "Ned isn't old enough to grow a beard. What wisdom can he offer?"

"Growing a beard doesn't make one wise. And I'm beginning to wonder if being old does," grumbled Gareth.

Zebulon snarled and had to look past Owain to glare at Gareth, which made Owain check his mount and venture into the argument.

"My lord, if you were less critical, your advice would be better received."

Zebulon's glare changed from Gareth to Owain, causing the mild-mannered lord to repine.

"Don't be offended. He's only speaking the truth," Gareth chided Zebulon.

"You're all incorrigible! Ellis is a boy pretending to be king, Owain a sniveling lack beard willing to lick anyone's boots while you nip at people's heels like a annoying little dog without backbone to stand up face-to-face." Zebulon kicked his horse and rode ahead.

"How do you put up with him?"

There was a heavy pause before Gareth answered. "He's my brother. It's just his way."

Silence fell between them for the rest of the morning. The few comments exchanged dealt with directions or the weather. By midday, they reached the crossroads where Owain and his family took leave of the brothers.

With an icy rain falling, Owain joined his wife, Lanay, and their eldest daughter, seventeen-year-old Gwen, in the carriage. Gwen favored her mother in looks with dark blonde hair and hazel eyes. She stared out the window watching the departing brothers.

"Why is Lord Zebulon always in such a foul mood?" she asked.

"Not all men are soft-spoken and generous like your father," said Lanay. She noticed Owain frown at her comment. "Did he say something to upset you?"

"Let's just say, not everyone shares your opinion of my attributes."

Lanay huffed. "The nerve of him."

He patted her hand. "Now, my dear, Zebulon has many faults, but he is still a fellow Council Member."

"The king tolerated him when he grew too loud and boisterous last night, claiming it was good to keep an enemy closer than a friend," said Gwen.

Owain raised a brow at her. "I thought you retired early?"

She blushed. "I—I ..."

He kindly smiled. "I understand. Being your first trip to Court, you didn't want to miss anything so you went exploring on your own."

She smiled in relief then continued, "Why doesn't the king discipline Lord Zebulon for his disrespectful attitude?"

Discretion and deliberation made him slow to reply. "That is a question asked by others. The king replied it is better to know about open hostility then be caught off guard by a friendly hand." He chuckled. "Quite a wise statement coming from a whelp who is wet behind the ears according to Zebulon."

Gwen gaped in surprise. "He said about the king?"

"Among other things. Ellis keeps him on the Council for political reasons."

"What about Lord Zebulon's statement concerning an enemy?

He fidgeted in his seat, his expression growing annoyed. "That is an entirely different matter."

"Why? It sounded much like what the king said about him."

He abruptly turned away, the irritation on his brow changing to discomfort.

Lanay placed a supporting hand on Owain's arm while speaking to Gwen. "Enough political talk."

Gwen wouldn't be put off and lashed out. "That's not what troubles me, it's how I was treated."

Her statement brought his focus from the window to her. "What do you mean? Did Zebulon say something to you?"

"No, but most barely spoke to me, especially after learning I am your daughter."

He growled in anger.

Lanay attempted to calm him. "It doesn't have to mean anything."

"No? I'm only mildly tolerated now they treat my daughter with contempt."

Lanay flashed a cautious glance to Gwen then back to Owain. "Most of the nobles at Court are arrogant and self-righteous, you know that. Zebulon and Gareth are the worst."

"No, it was Lord Allard and Baron Mathias," said Gwen.

To this Owain grew red-faced, muttering unintelligible words.

Lanay scolded Gwen. "Enough. You're upsetting your father."

"So you accept my ill treatment?"

Lanay hissed in outrage, but Owain replied, "No, she does not and neither do I. However, I will handle it at the appropriate time."

Lanay regarded him in surprised concern. Seeing her expression, he gave her hand a reassuring squeeze. "Leave it for now." He could see she didn't agree, but yielded with a nod. When he looked to Gwen for the expected answer, she scowled and turned to the window without speaking.

Presley Manor, a fine sturdy home of wood and stone, stood in the southeast part of Midessex eighty miles from Waldron Castle. The two younger girls, twelve-year-old Candice and ten-year-old Katlyn, were eager to hear about Court; so after greeting their parents, pressed Gwen for details.

Owain sat to relax in his favorite chair by the hearth while the girls moved to another side of the drawing room to talk. They were a lively trio and brought a smile to his lips. It pleased him that they inherited their looks from Lanay, all having various shades of blonde hair and hazel to blue eyes.

Despite only being twelve, Candice considered herself knowledgeable in the ways of the world, while ten-year-old Katlyn's independent streak made for many clashes. Gwen had a brooding nature, but all more talkative and argumentative than he liked. Lanay dealt better with conflict.

Still, quiet simplicity was more to his liking than the grandeur and complexities of Court. However, what Gwen said about her treatment disturbed him. Since being reinstated to his position, he kept a low profile, tending to estate and provincial duties rather then meddling in the affairs of Allon. He hoped it would be enough to quell the voices of objection to his reinstatement. Apparently, it did not.

His considering gaze passed to Lanay upon hearing her speak to Wade, his valet, about supper. She was a well-organized and accomplished woman. In his case, he saw the wisdom of an arranged marriage. Instead of repelling each other, her strengths countered his weaknesses and she found his soft-spoken manner to be refreshing and calming. Not that they didn't clash, only those times were rare. He didn't like being harsh with her in the carriage, but the discussion had to end. He didn't want to deal with the vexing subject. However, learning the focus changed to his daughter, he would have to.

Images of the conversation with Zebulon and Gareth flashed through his mind. Although he disliked confronting bullies, he would sooner deal with the brothers than Allard or Mathias. Allard's shrewd intellect was capable of talking rings around even the most astute scholar. He felt inferior and intimidated by Allard. At least he knew Zebulon's mind by what he said while Gareth always agreed with his brother. He never knew Allard's mind and motive.

Mathias was a swaggering and dashing man whose handsome features belied the cunning mind of a trained sailor and soldier. Where Allard used words and reason to deal with people and situations, Mathias employed charm and craftiness. Against these two he faced his greatest challenge. For Gwen's sake, he had to find the fortitude and means to confront them.

Loud laughter drew his attention to where the girls sat chatting.

"Oh, it must have been grand seeing all the lords and ladies in splendid dress," said Katlyn.

"Of course. You don't expect them to wear country rags at Court." Candice tugged on Katlyn's dress sleeve.

"These aren't rags," said Gwen. The girls wore rich, fine day gowns with higher necks on the bodices for decorum. "Besides, I saw the queen and her ladies dressed very similarly during the day."

"The queen wouldn't be seen in these," insisted Candice.

"The queen is more modest and practical than you are."

Katlyn giggled and Candice stuck her tongue out at Katlyn. The youngest fumed and stuck her tongue out in retaliation.

Gwen huffed in disapproval and rolled her eyes. "Children."

"Listen to you! Just because you're old enough to go to Court doesn't mean you're better than us," chided Candice.

"I never said better. I simply know how to behave. You must practice your manners before you are presented at Court next year."

"I know my manners."

"Do not," rebuffed Katlyn.

"Do too!" Candice mercilessly pulled one of Katlyn's hair curls, making her cry out.

Gwen seized Candice. "Stop it! You won't impress anyone with your temper much less attract a husband."

"Father says he's put enough money aside in dowries to pay for whomever we want."

"He told you?"

Katlyn sneered at Candice. "He didn't tell her. She was sneaking around and overheard he and Mother talking." When Candice went to smack her, Katlyn jumped out of the way. "He'll have to buy you a husband. You're too mean to get one by yourself."

"That's enough!" Lanay snapped, stepping between the girls. "Such talk is inappropriate. Your father will make the decision when the time comes. Now go to your rooms until supper and let him relax."

"But …"

"But nothing, Candice."

25

Candice stomped her foot and marched out of the room, a pouting Katlyn followed her.

Gwen paused in leaving to speak to Lanay. "I hope whoever Father chooses for Candice will be strong enough to tolerate her."

"Or love her enough to temper her behavior." Lanay nudged Gwen on her way. She waited until the door closed before approaching Owain. He stared strangely at her. "What are you looking at?"

"You, my dear. I marvel at how you handle them. At times I'm at a loss to understand what they're talking about much less what to do."

She softly smiled and took a seat beside him. "After all these years, you still don't understand women?"

The door opened and Wade entered, accompanied by a blonde-haired, blue-eyed nobleman of twenty-five. "My lord, Baron Erasmus."

Erasmus removed his hat and handed it to Wade.

"Erasmus? This is surprise," said Owain.

"I was on my way home and I didn't think you'd mind."

"Of course not. Wade, food and drink for the baron."

"Drink only. I won't be staying long enough to eat."

"Where is Erin?" asked Lanay.

"At a nearby inn."

"Yet you came here, why?" she asked in suspicion.

"Council business, for which I beg your pardon to speak with Owain in private."

She frowned at the request, yet withdrew.

"Did something happen after I left?" asked Owain.

"Ay. Word reached Waldron of civil unrest."

"Unrest? You mean rebellion?"

"No, not outright rebellion," Erasmus quickly replied then frowned. "It began when some hot-heads took to the streets of Chandler –"

"In your province?" said Owain in surprise.

"Ay," grumbled Erasmus. "But the day after I reported the occurrence to Ellis, word came from Malcolm, Allard and Hollis of rumblings in their provinces. Ellis ordered us to take charge of the situation and report our findings by the end of the month."

"So much for the prince's birth quieting matters."

Erasmus appeared pensive in his observation of Owain and asked, "Have you experienced any trouble?"

"No," he answered before seeing Erasmus's expression. "You have a problem with that?"

"Not I. However, others do."

Owain scowled in annoyance. "Allard. He objected to my reinstatement."

"He wasn't the only one voicing concern."

"Mathias."

"And Ranulf."

Stunned at hearing of the formidable Highland lord's involvement, Owain repeated, "Ranulf? Why would he join Allard and Mathias?"

Erasmus titled his head and cautiously replied, "You have a reputation."

Agitated, Owain crossed to the hearth and glared at the fire. The tense and unsettling situation with Gwen was worse than his originally thought. Learning of Ranulf's involvement told him the suspicion and mistrust was spreading. What more could he do to counter it than he already has? Befuddled, his shook his head and spoke aloud his frustration.

"I have done nothing these last four years. I've been a model of obedience to the Vicar and king."

"With what is happening, it is natural for suspicion to be raised and questions asked. Darius mentioned Zebulon."

He glanced over his shoulder to Erasmus. "Did he mention me?"

Again, Erasmus hesitated in answering. "We spoke of many possibilities and options."

Not satisfied by the evasive answer, Owain turned to face Erasmus and forcefully repeat his question. "Did he mention me?"

Erasmus sighed and gave an affirming nod. "Ay."

Owain swallowed back his concern to ask, "What did Ellis say?"

"I came to tell you about the unrest along with conveying his orders."

Owain seized Erasmus. "Stop avoiding the issue! I must know."

He steadily looked at Owain. "Ellis didn't comment on any single possibility, only everything must to be investigated and the source of this unrest discovered and stopped."

Owain roughly released Erasmus and began to pace, momentarily gnawing on his lower lip. "So you came here to warn me I am one of those possibilities. I don't think the others will be pleased about it. I'm already condemned in their eyes."

Erasmus stopped Owain to speak to him directly. "Answer me truly and I will defend you to the others, including the king. Do you know anything about what is happening?"

"Before I answer, tell me why, when all the others are lining up against me, you are taking this risk to warn me?"

"Because I believe everyone deserves a second chance. You said yourself you have behaved properly the last four years and done nothing to arouse suspicion. And," he said, growing a bit reticent. "I observed unwarranted and rude behavior toward Gwen."

"Was it Allard or Mathias?"

"It doesn't matter who. Whereas I understand questions based upon the past in regards to you, it was troubling to see your daughter treated in such a manner." He grew reflective and melancholy. "Erin endured such base treatment because of Kemp betraying Ellis. It took much patience, love and care to soothe her wounds. I don't want that to happen to your wife and daughters."

"Nor do I, which is why I have behaved."

"I know. Now, answer me. Do you know anything about what is happening?"

Owain squared his shoulders. "I swear to you, I do not."

Erasmus smiled in relief. "Ellis wants our reports in one month." At that moment Wade returned bringing refreshment and Erasmus greedily drank. After a sigh of satisfaction he said, "Now I must leave. I told Erin I would return promptly after speaking with you."

"As you wish." Owain escorted Erasmus to the door.

"Will there be anything else, my lord?" asked Wade.

Owain shook his head and waved for Wade to leave. Alone, he sat in the chair beside the hearth. Although a generous offer by Erasmus to defend him, he didn't believe it would help to shift the rising tide against him. Zebulon and Gareth confronted everyone. Ranulf joining Allard and Mathias left only Darius, Malcolm, Ned, Hollis and Archimedes. The Vicar would not choose a side, so he could be eliminated. Beside, he recommended Owain's reinstatement. Malcolm had been ill since Marcellus summoned the Council only to spring a trap to prevent them from joining Ellis. He was among those captured and thrown in the dungeon where he contracted his illness. Ranulf managed to escape. Erasmus' father and Hollis' father died incarcerated. This move only briefly silenced the Council. Ranulf's short imprisonment cemented his determination while Hollis and Erasmus wanted to avenge their fathers' deaths. Weakened and infirmed in body, Malcolm was sent home to the North Plains to serve as an example of Marcellus' power. However, when given the opportunity, he joined Ellis. The only ones who did not offer immediate fidelity were Kemp and Owain.

Despite his betrayal, Kemp died trying to protect his sister, Erin, during the coup. Ned, Kemp eldest son, denounced his father in favor of Ellis and assumed the Northern Forest seat on the Council. Owain didn't believe his forced cooperation with Marcellus went as far as Kemp, but others did. Then again, his attempt to capture Ellis ended with him being taken prisoner and used by Ellis for surety in leaving Midessex. During the botched prisoner exchange one of Ellis' men died. Not a way to ingratiate yourself to a future king, although he felt he had no choice to protect his family. Ellis' mercy in granting the probation surprised him. Ellis claimed he didn't want any more bloodshed and hoped his action would unite the Council of Twelve and help Allon to heal.

So engrossed in his pondering, he didn't realize Lanay entered until she spoke to him.

"I heard Erasmus left. Is everything all right?"

He didn't look at her when replying. "He told Erin he would return after delivering the king's orders."

She sat opposite him. "What are the orders?"

He still didn't look at her. "The Council is to ferret out the source of unrest and send him a report in one month."

She was surprised. "There has been trouble?"

He nodded, staring at the fire. With a resigned sigh, he admitted, "Some believe I'm the source of the trouble. That was Erasmus' true reason for coming, to tell me."

She grew angry. "You? What could make the king think you're the cause?"

"Not Ellis. Allard, Mathias, and Ranulf. I have a reputation, and it is hard to argue the past."

She reached over to take his hand. "Courage. Do as the king orders and still the voices that wrongly accuse you."

For the first time, he looked at her, his eyes determined. "For your sake and the girls, I will do what is necessary."

<hr />

The next morning and with great zeal, Owain dispatched his militia to scour Midessex for any signs of trouble. Erasmus' report gnawed at his brain. However, he couldn't let the opinion of others sway him like it did in the past. The only way to still the private gnawing and silence the voices raised against him was to prove not to be the weakling and coward they branded him. Thus, for three-and-a-half weeks he coordinated the search from Presley, receiving, compiling, and sifting through the reports. He barely slept, ate little and fretted much.

The night before his report was to be dispatched to Waldron, he worked on the final draft by the light of a solitary oil lamp and dying fire. The lack of personal care showed in his scruffy face, ruffled hair and unkempt clothes. Food was brought and left on the corner of his desk. Only the bottle of wine was consumed.

Lanay entered. She wore a heavy winter dressing gown and carried a small candle. He hadn't noticed her arrival. "Owain. You can't keep this up."

He replied without looking up from his work. "I'm almost done. Come the morning, I'm off to Waldron."

30

"What? Not in your condition. Send Wade or Lieutenant Milner."

Owain looked up. Although tired and pale, his resolve was unmistakable. "Nothing short of my personal appearance and effort will satisfy."

She could not argue. "Very well. Still, you must sleep and have a good breakfast before you leave. At least humor me in that."

He wearily smiled. "Ay. I have only to sign and seal the report to be finished."

Clean, fed and a bit refreshed from a few hours sleep, Owain ordered his driver to leave. With the bad weather it was wiser to take the carriage than ride on horseback. Wade accompanied him.

"Do you believe your report will please the king, my lord?"

"Ay. Although it's not Ellis who concerns me."

"Lord Allard."

Owain looked side-ways at Wade. "Ay. I must maintain my wits and not let myself be rattled."

Wade slyly smiled. "Have no fear, my lord. I will keep a sharp eye and ear."

Owain chuckled. "I know you will, only I am the one who must stand my ground. Allard is clever, Mathias a swaggering braggart, Ranulf a stubborn Highlander. I can only hope they haven't convinced Zebulon and Gareth against me."

Chapter 3

THE KING'S STUDY was located on the upper galleyway between the Great Hall and the Family's Private Quarters. The construction of the room only required some finishing touches on plaster moldings, curtains and furnishing remaining. Departing workers, both mortals and Guardians, tried not to disturb Ellis, who sat at his desk reading through the reports from the Council.

Kell stood in his customary place not far from the king observing all activity. He heard Ellis sigh for the fourth time. "Something disturbing, Sire?"

"I can't find a single thread to give a clue to this unrest. Oh, they mention various reasons of discontent. Some claim they were financially better under Marcellus and Latham. Others are rabble-rousers who make trouble at any opportunity." He shook his head in consideration. "There is more. I feel it. So does Shannan. Only it's indistinguishable. At least before we knew the source."

Kell pursed his lips in consideration before speaking. "There is something else."

Seeing the expression, Ellis leaned back in his chair to give Kell his full attention. "What?"

"After Dagar vanished I searched for his talisman. Latham wore a copy made to act as a conduit for power. Unfortunately, I couldn't find it.

"Why haven't you told me this before?"

"Because I don't know if it still exists. Despite the recent trouble, there is no proof of the talisman. It may have been destroyed along with Dagar."

"That hardly accounts for our sense of disturbance."

"Which is why I haven't said anything, because I don't know for certain yet."

"Did Jor'el mention it?"

"No."

Ellis snatched up a report and flipped through the pages. "Malcolm's men ran across remnants of the Dark Way, although the place appeared abandoned. Ned mentions relics. Can someone trained in the Dark Way be using the talisman?"

"Ay, Latham and his predecessors did. The extent or potency of the power without Dagar is the unknown."

"Just Dagar, or any Guardian?"

Kell brows grew level at the disturbing question. "I'm not sure since Dagar infused it with his powers to defeat Jor'el. The Guardian would have to possess equal strength, power, and desire. I can't think of anyone who fits the description."

"But it's still possible?"

"I suppose. However, the mortal wouldn't have access to the nether dimension and the creatures of infrinn since I sealed it."

"Creatures of infrinn? You mean kelpies and the like?"

"Those are nuisances and can easily be manipulated by a mortal well-trained in the Dark Way. However, other creatures are more fierce, and terrible and require great power and energy to control which no mortal can achieve."

Ellis was baffled. "Could Dagar access these creatures?"

"Ay, he enhanced them, which is how he gained the upper hand in the Great Battle." Kell's face grew harsh and somber in remembrance of Dagar's rebellion and the banishing of Guardians from Allon.

Wary of the captain's reaction, but curious, Ellis asked, "Why didn't he use them against us?"

"Why should he? He was free, believed he killed you and Shannan was poised to marry Marcellus. In his mind, he defeated Jor'el's Promised One, prevented our complete return and could rule unchallenged. Only after Erin was revealed did he realize the deception. Her single act of bravery turned the tide. By then we were fully restored. When you arrived, it became a battle for survival."

"Ay, the consequences are too horrid to imagine if Erin had not acted." Ellis grew melancholy in recalling his cousin's daring and dangerous risk by switching places with Shannan. Only a thin veil kept her identity hidden. The Guardians' arrival prevented Dagar from killing her once she was discovered. Ellis' eyes narrowed at the reports scattered upon his desk. "Now remnants of the Dark Way remain. I should have been more forceful in stamping it out."

"You're not responsible. All mortals have a choice of whom they will serve."

Ellis shook his head, glancing up at Kell. "I am king. The responsibility of Allon's security lies with me."

"True, but the spiritual well being of a mortal lies within each heart. For that you bear no responsibility."

"Perhaps, but I have been lax in creating a country that honors Jor'el. No longer." He stood. "Inform the Council we will inaugurate the Council Chamber in the morning. For now, I'm going to the Chapel."

The interior of the Chapel was complete with finely crafted wood and highly polished marble columns and floors. Two female servants bowed to Ellis. He waved them out and walked to the bottom of the altar step. He crossed his arms over his chest, got down on one knee, and his head bent.

"Hear your servant, Jor'el. Help me to understand if this new threat is of the Dark Way or of some other making. Grant me the wisdom and strength to defeat it like you did before." He sat on the front pew, staring at the altar.

Images and conversations came to mind, beginning with the day after the battle four years ago. Those most responsible for aiding the enemy where executed while others imprisoned, banished, or given probation. Further opposition to his ascension proved minor. For too long the House of Tristan had been absent and the Dark Way allowed to rule.

He received no word any of those banished had returned to Allon, while the handful released from prison for medical or merciful reasons had not caused trouble. Allard reminded him of Owain's past duplicity and personal reservations about allowing him to be reinstated. True, Owain was weak-minded, but Archimedes vouched for him. Ellis didn't want to point the finger of blame without proof. Besides, Owain wasn't clever, Allard was.

Could he be diverting attention to Owain to keep suspicion from himself? He used his wit and intelligence to bargain with Tyree when Marcellus ordered his men to hunt me down.

Ellis thought about each Council Member. Darius' loyalty and mettle went without question. Archimedes was Jor'el's devoted servant and Allon's spiritual leader. Ranulf and Erasmus were also eliminated by virtue of their closeness to the royal couple.

Zebulon. He would be more likely than Owain. Hollis is quiet, almost secretive. Ned is too young, he thought with a smile, but it soon faded. Perhaps Ned's age was his weakness, easily swayed by an elder. He tried to dismiss the nagging thoughts. *He is Kemp's son.*

Remembrance of Kemp's betrayal rattled Ellis. Kemp grew brooding and cynical when outcast and hunted during the merciless search for Ellis. Marcellus attempted to thwart him by taking Shannan for his wife and Dagar killed Kemp in his attempt to save Erin after her discovery of posing as Shannan.

"No, Ned was ashamed of Kemp and disowned him," Ellis disputed himself.

Gareth came to mind. Sometimes he pulled against Zebulon's tyrannical hold, at other times he acted like a whipped puppy. Darius told him Gareth felt obligated to Zebulon for raising him after their parents died, and didn't always agree with him. He was a possibility, more due to his association.

That leaves Mathias or Malcolm. Malcolm only has half the strength he once did because of me. Ellis' brows furrowed at recalling Malcolm's long debilitating illness caused by spending time in Ravendale's dungeon. Still, he had not seen or heard any remorse, regret, or resentment from Malcolm. Mathias was amusing with his swaggering manner, yet a cunning sailor and trained warrior. He and Hollis commanded the Royal Navy.

Ellis sat up and looked at the altar. "Hugh? Could he have waited all these years to avenge his brother's death and regain the throne for Unwin?" He shook his head. "He killed Marcellus. He killed his own brother." He recalled the worn, hopeless expression on Hugh's face after killing Marcellus. *He believed everything was lost to him. His life, his children.*

He jumped at feeling a hand on his shoulder. Shannan sat beside him.

"Kell told me you were here and why."

"Unfortunately, my mind isn't any clearer. How could any of the Council even think of betrayal?"

"Who says anyone has? Is there proof?"

"No, although a few mentioned findings related to the Dark Way."

"Then take the search in that direction."

She spoke in simplistic certainty that Ellis blinked at her then chuckled. "I've been racking my brain and you speak the obvious." Seeing her smile, he added, "The thought did cross my mind. The problem is how to do it discreetly and where to begin."

"Include the Council about your intention."

"I told them some things when I sent them back to ferret out this trouble."

"But not in a formal setting. Tomorrow you are calling the first official meeting of the Council at Waldron. It is time to take full command."

Ellis nodded and slightly frowned. "Darius expressed similar sentiments. I admit, I have been hesitant to impose my will, preferring to ease them into liking the idea of our reign."

"You won't convince Zebulon or Gareth by reason. The only thing they acknowledge is unquestioned authority. Letting the Council debate and arrive at a consensus may work in times of peace, but not under threat or times of danger."

"Agreed. Still, I must have a clear direction in my heart and mind before I proceed."

"Naturally. Why do you think I delayed coming to see you?" When he laughed with realization, she continued. "I arrived at the conclusion before you did. Besides, do you think I will let someone or something threaten our son?"

"No." He kissed her forehead. "I wouldn't bet against a mother's protective instinct. I remember the female boar that tried to gouge me when I accidently ventured too close to her brood." She just stared at him, making him snicker before adding, "Ay, and your shot to save me."

"It is the same immovable attitude you must show the Council: that you will not tolerate any threat. You are king and ordained by Jor'el. On that fact alone, you can make your will known."

Ellis put an arm around her shoulder and pulled her to him. "Ay."

***

The design pattern of the Council Chamber resembled the Temple of Jor'el only built of the castle gray stone and not marble. Beautiful stained glass windows depicted the provinces in their unique manners. Under each window stood a handsome, carved, wooden, cushioned chair. The chair to the right of the platform was for the Region of Sanctuary in whose window was the Temple of Jor'el. Next came the Highlands, with mighty mountains dominating its window. Beside the Highlands was the North Plains, flowing fields of grain colorfully depicted in the window. Its sister province of the South Plains was known for its abundance of vegetables. The West Coast proudly displayed its naval contributions in bold colored glass. A large figure of cattle from the Midessex completed the west wall.

Opposite the Region of Sanctuary, and to the left of the king's chair, was the Northern Forest whose quarried marble and stone helped construct Allon's Temple and Waldron. The Southern Forest window displayed massive timbers and woodcraft. The Meadowlands was renowned worldwide for fine horses and the best wool. The Lowlands took the wool and boasted of extraordinary tapestries. The East Coast imported and exported high-quality goods. Many Allonians and foreigners flocked to the Delta for its spas and mineral deposits. Down the middle of the tile floor, a multicolor patterned carpet led the way to the king's high chair.

Several of the Members entered. Lord Allard's strawberry-blonde hair made him hard to miss in a crowd. His green eyes told of a witty and intelligent person. Baron Mathias and Lord Ranulf accompanied him. A peer of Allard at age thirty-four, Mathias was a brown-haired, hazel-eyed man of dashing good looks that matched his swaggering reputation down to the way he meticulously trimmed his goatee. At fifty-four years old, Ranulf appeared as most Highlanders, dark, brawny and fit.

Servants arranged the chairs and cleaned the dust of construction when Zebulon and Gareth entered.

"Not ready yet?" Zebulon's growling voice slightly echoed in the chamber.

"We're leaving now, my lord," said a servant.

Darius, Ned, Malcolm and Hollis arrived. For a young man of twenty-six Malcolm appeared pale, his gray-blue eyes weary. Ned was a fresh-faced eighteen-year old with dirty blonde hair and wide hazel eyes while Hollis a clean-shaven, plain-looking man in his thirties.

Zebulon scowled at the departing servants. "This was an ill-conceived move."

"The move was to insure the fulfillment of Prophecy concerning the birth of the royal heir at Waldron," said Darius.

"We're all aware of that. I meant meeting in this incomplete chamber."

"You expected the king to move one meeting to Deltoria?"

"Would have been warmer."

Allard became distracted from the conversation at seeing someone enter. "Owain. When did you arrive?" His speech made the others turn to Owain.

"Last evening after supper."

"What of your report?"

"I gave it to the king before he retired."

38

Allard and Mathias exchanged dubious glances. Zebulon snorted in annoyance. Gareth frowned while Ranulf and Darius grew thoughtful. The rest were subdued in their reactions, although due to illness it was hard to tell Malcolm's mood since he appeared sickly most of the time.

"My lords, good morning," said Archimedes. He was well advanced in years at one hundred and sixty. Since Ellis' victory his health rapidly declined, bent at the shoulders with heavy lines crisscrossing his face. Master Uriah, an able-bodied priest of twenty-nine, assisted Archimedes.

"My Lord Vicar, you look well this morning," replied Darius.

Archimedes wryly smiled. "One more day Jor'el has granted me. Though they are long and painful days."

"Come, sir, sit." Uriah led Archimedes to the Region of Sanctuary chair.

"I wonder how much more pain he must endure?" said Erasmus.

"It would be merciful for Jor'el to call him home," said Mathias.

"Don't be so quick to judge. I understand the will's desire to fight against pain," chided Malcolm.

"I didn't mean that. Archimedes is a loyal and faithful servant who deserves his eternal rest."

Zebulon sarcastically snickered at Mathias. "Will you listen to the dandy? Got religion all of a sudden?"

Insulted, Mathias stiffened. Allard and Darius stepped between he and Zebulon to forestall any confrontation.

"Lords of Allon!" Kell's voice boomed through the chamber. "By the order of His Majesty King Ellis, the Council of Twelve will assemble." At his call to order, the Members moved to stand before their respective chairs. Smiling, Kell held up a hand when Archimedes reached for Uriah's help to him rise. "No, lord Vicar. The king bids you remain seated." Seeing everyone ready, he announced, "By Jor'el's will and His Divine appointment, His Majesty King Ellis."

Bedecked and wearing his crown, Ellis entered. The men bowed and remained bent while he assumed his seat. "Be seated, my lords."

Archimedes spoke with all formality. "What is the will of the king? Speak, and we, the Lords of Allon, will obey."

Ellis kindly grinned. "I'm glad you are well enough to attend us, Vicar. For indeed, this day I shall speak my will without discussion or alteration." He noticed Zebulon's angry glare at Gareth. "Do you object, Lord Zebulon?"

Zebulon cleared his throat, caught off guard by the question. "No, Sire."

"Really? Your behavior in previous Council meetings shows you value none but your own opinion."

Gareth's brow knitted and his gaze shifted between his brother and Ellis. Darius coughed in an attempt to stifle a laugh. Mathias stroked his goatee to hide his amusement. Others also show various forms of amusement, satisfaction and surprise at the confrontation.

Ellis observed the reactions, yet kept his primary focus on Zebulon. "Well, my lord? Have you nothing to say?"

"That would be a first," Darius couldn't help but say.

"Indeed," agreed Mathias, attempting to suppress a snicker.

Zebulon stirred at the insult. "Sire, surely the reason for this summons was not to humiliate me."

"Humiliate isn't the word I'd use. Educate, would be a better choice."

Darius bit his lip to contain his laughing, but was unsuccessful.

Ellis turned a rebuking eye to Darius. "My Lord Duke."

"Sire," answered Darius, his voice strained with control.

Ellis proceeded. "My lords, after reviewing the reports I am convinced the Dark Way is again rising to threaten Allon." His statement brought a measured, stunned reaction.

Archimedes sat forward in his chair. "Are you certain, Sire?"

"Ay. Almost all reports mentioned some form of a reemergence of the Dark Way." Ellis cast a quick side-glance at Owain, catching his eye while replying to Archimedes.

"The king is correct, Vicar," said Mathias.

"Ay," agreed Hollis.

Gareth murmured a low agreement. Malcolm, Darius and Erasmus also gave verbal assent. Even Zebulon snorted and nodded.

"What of you, Owain? Does your report agree with ours?" asked Allard.

Owain hesitated to reply. "I found no such evidence."

"Interesting that we have and you have not."

Owain abruptly turned away.

"What we can do, Sire?" asked Ned, trying to contain his anxiety.

"In light of a possible threat to Allon, there will be no discussion, no debate, no advice." Again Ellis saw Zebulon's displeasure and continued speaking. "You will promptly return to your provinces and destroy any form of the Dark Way. There will be no exceptions. Allon belongs to Jor'el and will be completely purged. If you have trouble, I will come to deal with it— in arms, if necessary."

To this, Zebulon sat forward glaring at Ellis. Gareth also moved, yet was not as bold in his regard of the king. Most displayed shock at the announcement of arms while Darius wore a pleased expression.

Ellis returned Zebulon's stare and firmly spoke, "My lords, to your duty. For Allon and for Jor'el."

Darius stood. Allard, Ned, Mathias and the other followed his lead. Zebulon stood, shoulders square and proud, his eyes never leaving Ellis. Darius spoke, "For Allon and for Jor'el." The others repeated his words.

Ellis descended the platform and left.

"I suppose you enjoyed seeing me humiliated, Your Grace," chided Zebulon.

"I did enjoy it, though not for the reason you said. The king is Jor'el's appointed, and we," Darius spread his arms at his companions, "are his servants. All our positions, possessions, and honors come from him. For too long we have presumed to tell him our will."

"Ay," agreed Erasmus, Mathias and Ranulf.

Seeing Gareth's resigned expression, Zebulon asked, "You agree with them?"

"Ellis is the king; and if Allon is being threatened, we have sworn fealty to obey him."

"Why do you continue to rebuff him? His right to rule is undeniable," said Owain.

Zebulon was hot to dispute. "What of you? You made an agreement with Tyree to capture him and hand him over to Marcellus. Only Allard's arrival stopped you."

Owain winced at the rebuff. In doing so, he noticed the way Allard, Mathias and Ranulf scrutinized him, harsh and unforgiving. He forced a response. "I made amends for my folly."

"Yet with trouble all across Allon, your province is quiet."

"That isn't my doing!" Owain lashed out then stammered defensively. "I mean the trouble. The quiet in my province is because I manage better."

"You manage better?" Zebulon laughed with mockery and cast a glance to Allard. "Oh, come, Allard, that requires a response from the man who tricked Tyree and saved his province."

Allard's gaze shifted to a nervous Owain. "I have already stated my opinion."

Owain found Erasmus, hoping for some form of the promised help. Erasmus appeared indecisive and kept silent during the bombardment. *So much for defense.* Now, he truly felt alone. He set his jaw and turned on his heel to leave.

Zebulon shouted after Owain. "Ay! Return home to the rest and quiet of your better managed province while we defend Allon!"

Owain was agitated. He told himself repeatedly he had to stand up to Allard, Mathias, and Ranulf. Although he wondered about Zebulon, he hoped confrontation with the gruff and mean-spirited lord would not happen. Alas it did. Despite questioning him during the meeting, Allard was subdued in his reply to Zebulon. A thought struck him in recalling the way Ellis regarded him when speaking of the reports.

What must he think of my province's lack of trouble compared to the others—surely, not the presence of the Dark Way? This disturbed him more than backing down from the others. He had to learn the king's mind.

With purposeful steps he went in search of Ellis. A burly Guardian stood before the door to the king's study. It took a moment for him to recall

Armus' name. He met only a few Guardians over the years but none as impressive as Armus or Kell.

Armus bowed to his approach. "My lord. May I help you?"

"I wish to speak with the king."

"Do you have a scheduled audience?"

"No. I came in regarding to the Council meeting. I am …"

"Lord Owain of Midessex. I will see if the king is available."

Armus knocked on the door. Kell answered and a few low words were exchanged before Armus was admitted. Kell glanced at Owain before closing the door. Although a brief glance, Owain flinched at the deep scrutiny in the golden eyes. Guardians made him uncomfortable, unnerving creatures with unnatural colored eyes capable of reading a mortal's soul.

After several moments, Armus emerged. "The king will see you, my lord."

Owain flashed a nervous smile and passed Armus to enter the study. Ellis sat on the corner of his desk reading what appeared to be his report. He bowed and spoke. "Sire. Thank you for seeing me on short notice."

Ellis glanced up from reading. "I was about to send for you. Your report is the only one that does not mention the Dark Way."

"I found no evidence within my province."

"So you told the Council. What I want to know is why?"

Owain's mouth wet dry and he licked his lips before answering. "I don't know, Sire."

Ellis sent a skeptical glance across to Kell. The Guardian captain turned his attention to Owain, who avoided the golden eyes to watch Ellis put down the report and begin to pace, hands clasped behind his back.

"You must admit it is strange, considering your past actions."

Any hope Owain had concerning Ellis' favorable opinion began to fade only he couldn't back down. "Sire, I have made every effort to make amends." When Ellis nodded, yet said nothing in reply, he continued. "Vicar Archimedes vouched for me, and on his word, you graciously reinstated me. For that I am grateful, Sire."

Ellis stopped pacing, and for a long moment regarded Owain. Under the eyes of royal scrutiny, Owain's nervousness increased. He clenched his fits in an effort to keep his wits.

"Your gratitude is about to be tested. Your ability to withstand the test is what I must consider."

Despite his effort, Owain's nervousness got the better of him and he lashed out. "What of Zebulon and Gareth? They openly criticize your sovereignty yet I don't see their loyalty being questioned."

Kell stepped forward at Owain's raised voice and open challenge. Ellis stopped Kell, although his attention remained focused on Owain.

"How I conduct affairs of state and deal with individual Council Members is at my discretion and not answerable to you. However," Ellis' voice grew low and he approached Owain, "it was not their actions which cost the life of a trusted servant and the wounding of another."

Owain flinched in fearful apprehension.

"Did you think because of the Vicar's recommendation and your reinstatement, I have forgotten the deadly consequences of your cowardice?"

"No, Sire."

Ellis' narrow stare made Owain repine. "Go. Do as I have instructed."

Owain bowed and withdrew.

For a moment, Ellis stared at the door then shifted his gaze to Kell. "Well? What sense did you get from him?"

"Difficult to say. He was already nervous before you frightened him. Push that fear too far and he may act rashly again."

"Perhaps. The problem is how to balance that against eliminating this trouble. Too much is at stake for me to let my guard down or be gentle."

"Agreed, and you made your point. It's up to Owain how he responds. Should I send for Zebulon?"

Ellis chuckled and returned to his desk. "No. I think his public education will serve better than a private tongue-lashing. I'm sure Darius has said something. In this case, let the Council corral their own."

Kell smiled in approval. "You've learned well when to apply direct and indirect pressure."

"Time will tell how affective I've been." Ellis grew thoughtful. "What about Hugh? Or Iain?"

"Iain took the Jor'ellian vow. He would dishonor his position and place himself under Jor'el's wrath for taking action against you or toying with the Dark Way."

Ellis nodded in agreement. "Do you think Hugh would want to regain the throne for Unwin?"

Kell titled his head in consideration. "Difficult to say. Mortals sometimes tend to be fickle in their allegiances. Although blood kinship is strong, I have witnessed family members turn against each other."

"Blood isn't the only form of kinship," said Ellis with a fond smile.

"Ay. Over the centuries I've seen a few bonds as strong as you and Darius."

"All the same. Is Hugh still here?"

"Ay. Wess is considering joining his uncle in your service."

"Wess is old enough?"

"Sixteen and itching to test himself. Not unlike another youth a few years ago." Kell grinned.

Ellis laughed. "What of Bosley?"

"Fourteen, and not taken with soldiering like Wess."

"His twin daughters?"

"I don't know. They are not yet of age to attend court."

For a moment, Ellis chewed on his lower lip. "Send for Hugh so we can get a sense of him."

In the completed barracks of the royal army, Iain told of his exploits to his nephews. Wess was a strapping youth of sixteen just shy of six feet tall with a thick head of dark hair and brown eyes, focused in rapt attention on his uncle. Bosley was bored. At fourteen he had similar color hair and eyes to Wess, but their mannerisms were opposite. He sat at the table making invisible traces on the wooden top. He jumped at hearing a voice in his ear. It was his father.

"War not to you liking?" At forty-one years of age, Hugh was a distinguished looking man with hazel eyes and brown hair beginning to grow gray around the temples. Bosley grew sheepish and Hugh smiled. "It's not to my liking either."

"What are you two conspiring about?" quipped Iain.

"Nothing," replied Hugh. He winked at Bosley, making the boy smile.

A royal squire entered and approached Hugh. "My lord, the king awaits your pleasure in his study."

"At once." He glanced to Iain, who heaved an ignorant shrug.

"Something wrong?" asked Wess.

"Doubtful," said Iain, with a reassuring smile. "Still, a summons from the king is not an honor to be taken lightly." He sent a prompting look to Hugh.

Hugh mimicked Iain's' encouraging smile. "I'll back shortly."

He and his sons came to Waldron to celebrate the birth of Prince Nigel and visit Iain. He did not expect to have a personal visit with the king. He spoke a few times to Ellis when he inquired about Marcellus' dealings while king during the first year of Ellis' reign. Since then contact was limited to letters of correspondence. He and his family were left unmolested to live a normal life, a welcomed change from the uneasy life at Court during Marcellus' reign. He couldn't dwell on the past too long without the old feelings of guilt and despondency gripping him. Focusing on the present situation raised a new sense of apprehension regarding the unusual summons.

Perhaps there was no connection rather Ellis learned of Wess' desire to join the army and wanted to speak to him. After all, they were of the rival royal family Ellis defeated, and having an heir wear his uniform was a bit unusual. However, Ellis never treated them with contempt or threatened them. In fact, he granted mercy and provided for them.

Hugh took a deep steadying breath when the squire knocked on the study door. Whatever the reason, he would meet it head on and with dignity. An impressive Guardian answered the knock. He recognized Kell and balked at meeting the golden eyes.

"My lord." Kell motioned Hugh inside. "Sire, Lord Hugh."

Ellis stood in front of the hearth warming his hands. "Ah, my lord, good of you to come so promptly."

Hugh bowed. "I'm at your command, Sire."

"Are you and your sons enjoying the visit with General Iain?"

"Very much. In fact, I may be leaving Wess with his uncle to begin training for Your Majesty's service. With your permission, of course," said Hugh, voicing one of his concerns to gauge Ellis' mood.

"Granted," said Ellis without hesitation, in fact, he smiled.

Hugh inclined his head in acknowledged gratitude.

"What of Bosley?"

"I'm afraid, my youngest son doesn't lean toward war."

"It can be a nasty business. How old are your twin daughters?"

"Eleven. They stayed home since they are not yet of age."

"So your family enjoys retirement on your estate?" Ellis continued in his pleasant manner.

"We lead a quiet, peaceful life thanks to Your Majesty."

"Your gratitude is appreciated, but it is I who owe you a debt," Ellis spoke with great sincerity.

Thus far the meeting proceeded cordially, but being reminded of the past made Hugh wince, his voice a bit halting in reply. "You owe me nothing, Sire."

"It still pains you?"

Hugh nodded, the words difficult. He hoped the past would not be a part of the summons. Yet a day didn't go by that he didn't think about it, about killing his brother. It still hurt. Ellis glanced to Kell, whose golden eyes focused on him. The Guardian's eyes were more unnerving than when he arrived. Thankfully Ellis' voice brought his attention back. The king's pleasant features gave way to serious consideration, which reflected in his voice.

"Could that pain cause you to consider any action?"

Hugh became guarded at the change in tone and question. "Sire?"

"Have you been told of recent events?"

"I have, only I fail to make the connection."

"Then I'll speak plainly. The recent unrest is stirred by the Dark Way."

Hugh immediately understood. "Sire, Marcellus and I constantly clashed over Latham." Ellis sent a sideways glance to Kell. This time Hugh braced himself against the Guardian's stare to continue. "Sire, I swear, I would never align with the Dark Way. Latham killed my wife! Iain's sister."

Ellis stared at him a moment before speaking, his voice benign. "Perhaps. However, your family once ruled so you should understand the reason behind the orders I now issue. Until this unrest is dealt with, you and your sons will remain at Waldron."

Hugh paled. "We're under arrest?"

"No, under supervision, and within the castle walls."

Despite his disturbance that one of his fears was realized, Hugh maintained enough dignity to bow. "We are at your command, Sire."

Ellis turned back to the hearth and Kell opened the door. Hugh saw a discernable warning in the Guardian's eyes before leaving.

When the door closed, Ellis asked Kell, "Do you believe him?"

"Do you?"

"I believe he believes he is sincere. How far that sincerity extends remains to be seen."

"Agreed. I'll instruct Mahon of his assignment." Kell left.

Ellis began pacing to consider. At a window he noticed activity in the courtyard and stopped to observe. Owain approached his carriage. His departure could be good or bad. Good in showing Owain being diligent in following orders, or bad, in that the haste to depart could once more indicate his involvement with the Dark Way. Again, Ellis didn't want to ascribe blame prematurely. His brow wrinkled in curiosity at seeing Erasmus hurry and intercept Owain. With the window closed, he couldn't hear the conversation, and opening it could alert them to his interest, thus he observed the exchange. By their body language the conversation was terse. In fact, Owain appeared to be getting the upper hand and Erasmus on the defensive. The conversation abruptly ended when Owain entered the carriage. Wade got inside just before driving off.

The door to the study opened and Ellis was slow to turn from the window since the only people who entered without being announced were Kell, Shannan or Darius. Out of the corner of his eye, he saw Kell and Darius.

"Mahon will be discreet," said Kell.

Ellis chuckled. "A Guardian warrior discreet in observation? Reconnaissance, naturally, but watching someone at Waldron? His size will be enough to catch Hugh's attention."

Kell grinned. "You'd be surprised what a warrior can do to go undetected."

Ellis laughed and shook his head. "No. You are amazing creatures, whereas we mortals tend to be confusing at times. Which leads me to a curious incident in the courtyard." He motioned to the window. "Owain was leaving when Erasmus rushed to catch him. I couldn't hear what was said and didn't want to be indiscreet in my observation, but by their body language and Owain's abrupt departure, the exchange was heated and he got the better of Erasmus."

"Owain bested Erasmus?" said Darius in surprised interest.

"Ay. Rather odd considering Owain is the one easily intimidated and Erasmus rarely backs down. Do you have any idea what it could be about?"

"No, but it doesn't mean I can't find out."

"Do. Discreetly."

"Guardian or mortal discretion?" quipped Darius.

Ellis cocked a grin at Kell but spoke to Darius. "In your own unique manner, brother ferret."

In the barracks, Iain still held Wess' attention, while Bosley kept pretending to draw on the tabletop. Bosley noticed Hugh's return.

"Father. What did the king want?"

Hugh tried to lighten his mood by ruffling Bosley's hair. "The usual politics. You and Wess run along. I need to speak to uncle." Bosley eagerly left with Wess sluggishly following. "Stay inside the castle walls!" he called after the boys.

"Something wrong?" asked Iain.

Frowning, Hugh sat at the table. "The past is coming back to haunt me. This latest unrest stems from the Dark Way."

"So? Latham's dead and Dagar vanquished by Kell."

Hugh heaved a hapless shrugged. "Ellis hinted that I may be a threat since my family ruled. He's ordered the boys and I to remain here under supervision until this is over. With my luck, it'll be a Guardian watching us."

"Guardians aren't so bad. Remember I told you Avatar saved the children and I."

"I know. I just thought we were past this."

Iain patted Hugh's shoulder and sat beside him. "I know this seems harsh, perhaps unreasonable, but Ellis has a good heart. This is a precaution. Keep your head down and all will be well. I give you my word."

"You're that certain of him?"

"I pledged my life to the Jor'ellian cause and the Son of Tristan is Jor'el's chosen. I would die for him."

"You would have died for Marcellus."

Iain wasn't offended by the jab. "In the line duty, not from a heart of loyalty. You're aware of the difference so why question me?"

Hugh scowled in frustration. "It's not you. It's the children. They are finally becoming whole again and I don't want this to upset them."

"The girls are at home and blissfully unaware. Wess is hardly disappointed since he wants to join the army. Bosley needs to stop daydreaming and focus on his future."

"He took Lida's death the hardest so I've not pressed him, rather encouraged him in areas other than the military, only he's reluctant. He doesn't know what he wants."

Iain pursed his lips before speaking his mind. "I understand allowing him time to grieve. I miss my sister. However, Bosley is past the age of childhood. He needs firm direction. Being here will do him some good." Seeing Hugh's brow furrow to the contrary, he continued his argument. "Soldiers aren't all who are here: Jor'ellians, priests. While here he can witness the inner workings of the king and Council in a crisis. He can experience things he wouldn't at home. Maybe he can find his direction."

Hugh looked cross. "Did you forget he's seen court, as a royal prince?"

"As a child. And why are we arguing? We want the best for the children. Now cheer up. Let's find the boys and get something to eat."

Chapter 4

THE DRIVE FROM WALDRON to Presley took two days. Owain ordered the driver only to stop for a change of horses. What little food he ate was consumed on route. True, Erasmus' failure to uphold his pledge of defense infuriated him, but more irksome was believing that another would help. His mind turned from the Council to his conversation with Ellis. All hope of silencing the speculation against him by a favorable report was dashed. *"Did you think because of the Vicar's recommendation and your reinstatement, that I forgot the deadly consequences of your cowardice?"* The question echoed in his ears.

The premature capture of the Son of Tristan would have proven disastrous for Allon. All he thought about was protecting his family and surviving. His capture as a result of his failed attempt was unfortunate. However, Lieutenant Horton arrived and said Lanay sent him offering two of Ellis' men in a prisoner exchange. How did she know? He did not inform her of his plan. He recalled Ellis instructed his soldiers of the intention to use Owain for surety in leaving the province, but how were Ellis' men captured? Only after returning home from the fateful encounter did he discover Captain Tyree and the Shadow Warrior, Witter, were at Presley. They told Lanay of his involvement and ordered her to act with the prisoners Tyree captured. Oh, how he regretted drawing her into danger. Still, the prisoner exchange would have succeeded and no one killed if Allard and his forces not arrived.

Why should I be held responsible for the man's death? Lieutenant Horton killed him before retreating. I never wanted bloodshed.

The memory made Owain's anger against Allard grow. He used his clever wit to convince Tyree to spare his province of the Meadowlands by providing the king's army of Shadow Warriors with all the supplies they needed and no one condemned his ingenuity. How could actions motivated by a desire to protect be considered brilliant for one person, but cowardice for another?

Allard's actions spared death, mine caused death, or so the king reminded me. I didn't mean it!

The brooding thoughts only served to agitate his anxiety. He resolved in his mind that this time Lanay and the girls must be kept safe. He would endure whatever scorn or accusations Allard and the others chose to inflict, but not his family, not again.

The jolting of the carriage stop woke Wade. Owain remained awake the entire time and he appeared pale, tired and troubled. When Lanay emerged from the house wearing a smile of greeting, he snatched her hand to go back inside, ignoring her questions. In quick strides he led her to the study and closed the door.

"Where are the girls?" he asked.

"Finishing their studies. Why? Does this concern them?"

"I just don't want them overhearing." He moved nearer to speak more confidentially. "The other provinces reported finding remnants of the Dark Way. The one exception is Midessex."

"Why? I don't understand the connection."

"Others do. Including the king!"

She paled, speechless at the implication.

The emotions propelling him suddenly drained away and he sat in a chair beside the hearth.

She knelt next to him, her tone compassionate. "It's not your fault what the others find. You should be happy the Dark Way is not here."

"Why is Midessex spared when the others experience trouble? That is the question Ellis asked and I couldn't answer."

With sobriety in her tone and regard, she asked, "What will you do?"

"He ordered the Council to destroy it—no exception."

She was confused. "How can you do so with something that doesn't exist here?"

He shook his head. "I don't know."

She stroked his cheek. "You look tired."

"I must get to work immediately."

"Will you at least eat?"

"Ay. Also, send in Wade as you leave."

Later, after most had retired, Owain and Wade were in the study. Owain sat at the desk shifting through papers. Wade warmed his hands over the fire, fighting to stifle a yawn.

"My lord, it'll be daylight in a few hours. Please, get some sleep."

Owain stretched out the muscle kinks in his shoulders and neck. "Ay. Prepare my bed."

Wade smiled in relief and left.

Owain yawned and ran weary hands over his face. He jumped at hearing an unfamiliar female voice from behind saying, "You knew they wouldn't believe you." A short, slender, cloaked and hooded figure stepped out from a shadowy corner.

"Who are you? How did you get in?"

The woman removed the hood to reveal a pretty face with fair-hair and captivating green eyes, perhaps in her mid-thirties.

His brows furrowed in concentration of remembrance. "I think I know you."

She pushed back the cloak from her shoulders. A raven-crested medallion hung around her neck.

His eyes went wide at seeing the medallion. "Latham's talisman!"

She smiled. "I'm glad you recognized it."

He stared at her in great apprehension. "Latham's mistress. I once knew your name ... Musetta. You made Kemp betray Ellis."

Mockery filled her laughter. "I didn't make Kemp do anything he wasn't willing to do. Same as Tyree did not make you do anything you weren't willing to do. The Son of Tristan was a nuisance, causing trouble, disturbing your peaceful life and threatening your station. If you didn't help, Marcellus would reconsider your position on the Council, if not your life."

"How do you know?"

"I know much. For instance, how Allard has been against you all these years. He insulted you in the Council meeting, while your faithful valet is a royal spy, sent to keep you in line."

"What?"

"Do you really think the Vicar or Son of Tristan trusts you?"

"Wade served me during my probation."

"Are you so naïve to believe it is a coincidence?"

Wade returned, startled to find Owain wasn't alone. "My lord? Who –?"

"Ask him," she interrupted. "Dare him to deny it."

Wade appeared confused at her accusation, but Owain said, "You told me the Vicar appointed you to aid me during my probation and then my reinstatement. Is that true or were sent as a spy?"

"I told you the truth, my lord. The Vicar appointed me to serve—"

"That's a lie." Musetta looked directly at Wade and clenched the talisman.

Wade swallowed, a wave of fear crossing his face.

"Well?" demanded Owain.

Wade had difficulty turning from Musetta to reply. "The Vicar wanted me to help you maintain a proper attitude and asked I inform he and the king the moment there was trouble." When Owain glared in chagrin, he grew insistent. "It is was for your good, my lord. To avoid any weakness from reoccurring."

She scoffed. "Do you hear him? For your own good."

"My lord, I told the king you were diligent in following his orders."

"Did you?" Owain rebuffed. "Well, he reminded me how I was responsible for the death of one servant and the wounding of another. Doesn't sound like you made a favorable report."

"Dismiss me, and they will me become more suspicious."

"Not if you can't tell them." Musetta grabbed the talisman, glared at Wade and said, *"Thu a' marbh."*

Wade seized his chest, terror and pain filling his face. He became ashen with death and collapsed.

Owain watched in horror. His face slowly turned from Wade to Musetta, and his voice barely above a whisper. "What do you want?"

"The same as you: to correct the past. You, so you can finally live peaceful and unhindered, and I to take revenge for what was taken from me."

"I don't understand."

"It's not important you understand. It's important you finish what you started and show everyone you have courage and are a man to be reckoned with."

"That's why I must root out the Dark Way and prove—"

"No! You must snatch the throne from the Son of Tristan."

He was thunderstruck. "A coup? You're mad!"

"Not mad. Only by taking bold action can you silence them. And by his downfall I will fulfill a promise and have revenge."

He vehemently shook his head and waved his arms. "Get out!"

She touched the talisman, her eyes narrowing with effort. He began laboring for breath. "At any time I can strike you down. Or perhaps your wife, or daughters?"

"No!" he gasped.

She released her hold of the talisman and he fell against the desk taking loud gulps of air. "My method of persuasion should not be your sole motivation. Wouldn't it wonderful to be put Allard in his place, to repay Zebulon for all his insults? By seizing the throne you would have the means to strike back."

He regarded her from under shrouded brows of recovery, his breathing slow to return to normal. "I don't want to be king. I want to be left alone."

She sneered at him. "You're a pathetic, mealy-mouth wimp who doesn't deserve the title of 'sir.' Tell me, how did you become a knight?"

His lips pressed together, arms rigid at his side, fists clenched as she continued in high ridicule.

"Oh, I know. Your father paid for the title to keep you from disgracing the family by your lack of courage. His actions saved your family then, but your wife and daughters have suffered since because of your cowardice."

He crossed to the hearth, slamming his fists on the mantle. "Enough!" He pushed himself off the hearth. In doing so, he saw Wade's body. Swallowing back the bile, he said, "Can he be disposed of?"

She snapped her fingers and a sudden flash of white light filled the room. A tall, large being with dull gray eyes dressed in black appeared from the fading light. He wore an identical talisman.

Owain paled in fear. "A Shadow Warrior!"

She waved the Warrior toward Wade. "Remove him."

In another flash, the Warrior and Wade were gone.

Her grin was tainted with sarcasm. "Seizing Waldron in its incomplete state won't be too difficult. Now prepare your men. The time to move will be very soon." Again she snapped her fingers and another Warrior appeared. Taking his arm, she nodded, and she and the Warrior disappeared.

Overcome, Owain fell into a nearby chair. He just agreed to a coup against the king. Once again, he had no choice to protect his family. Only this time, the consequences would be worse if he failed. Things needed to be different. He couldn't be the meek whipping boy others believed him to be. No, he must rely on his own wit, intelligence and mettle like never before. He couldn't expose his family to what was about to happen.

In haste, he stood, grabbed the lantern off his desk and hurried upstairs to the bedchamber. Lanay slept and he hated to disturb her, but he had to act fast. She woke with a start to his urgent voice and shaking.

"Quickly! Take the girls and go the Fortress at Pickford. Remain there until I send for you."

"What? Why?"

"No questions, woman. Do as your told," he snapped, and tugged on her arm to draw her out of bed.

She regarded him in surprise. "Owain? What's come over you?"

"There is no time for discussion. You must make haste." He took clothes out of her wardrobe. "Move, woman!"

She snatched the clothes he tossed at her. "Has something awful happened?"

"Ay, now hurry!" He ushered her to the dressing screen. "I'll wake the girls."

From behind the screen she called, "Leave me some light."

Owain lit a candle before hurrying down the hall to Gwen's room. She was groggy and not easily woken. It wasn't until he jerked off the covers exposing her to the cold night air that she awoke.

"Father?"

"Get up, get dressed and pack a day bag. You, your mother and sisters are leaving."

"Where are we going?"

"No questions. Do as you are told." He lit the lantern for her. "I'm going to wake your sisters. I expect to see you dressed and downstairs in fifteen minutes, no longer, Gwen."

In the winter, Candice and Katlyn shared a room. They snuggled together in bed sleeping. He moved quickly to secure his family, yet at that moment, he realized he might not see them again. Thus, for a brief moment he watched their serene faces. He placed the lantern on the nightstand beside the bed and was gentle in this waking since Candice was a light sleeper. To the sound of his voice, her eyes opened.

"Father."

"Wake Katlyn and get dressed, pack a day bag and come downstairs for departure."

"We're going some place?"

"Ay." He lit the room's lantern. "It's cold so dress extra warm. And hurry."

Owain rushed to the stable and woke two grooms, giving orders for immediate departure. He returned to the house and up to the bedchamber. Lanay was dressed for travel and putting on a sturdy pair of boots. A packed day bag and heavy woolen cloak were beside her on the bed.

She stood to put on her cloak. "Does this have to do with the unrest?"

"Ay. More than that I cannot say." He held her by the shoulders, compassion filling his face. "This is for your own safety and that of the girls." He embraced and kissed her then, a bit roughly, separated and snatched her hand.

"Wait, my bag."

He grabbed the bag. In the hall, he shouted, "Gwen! Girls!" while heading downstairs with Lanay. He heard the voices of affirming replies.

He dropped the bag to make certain Lanay's cloak was secure and she wore a hat he took off the rack near the door. "I told Stoddard to have extra blankets in the carriage. It's a cold, bitter night and I'm sorry to send you out in this, but I must."

Lanay took his hands to stop his fussing of her cloak. "What about you? What are you going to do?"

"Do what I must to protect my family."

"Owain, you're frightening me. Only once before were you like this."

"Do you trust me?"

"Of course."

He held her face in his hands. "Then no matter what happens know that I love you and I love our girls."

She embraced him, sniffling back tears of fear.

He winced, his face screwed in anguish. "Please, I need you to be strong."

She stood on her own, wiping her eyes.

Gwen hurried down the stairs carrying two-day bags. Candice held the hand of a groggy and slow moving Katlyn while also carrying a bag.

Owain regarded his daughters, his gaze lingering on Gwen. "You are the oldest. I expect you to help your mother and take care of your sisters."

"Of course. But, Father, what is this all about?"

"I asked your mother and now I ask you. Do you trust me?"

"Ay."

"Then do as I have said without question."

Outside they heard the jingling of harness and horses near the front door. Stoddard appeared and gathered the luggage. "Ready to leave, my lord. My lady."

Snow fell heavily. Stoddard secured the bags on top of the carriage. The girls quickly climbed inside and bundled themselves against the cold. Lanay hesitated. Worry furrowed her brow when she took hold of Owain's arm, trying to search his face.

"You will not tell me anything?"

He shook his head. "This might sound strange, but you must walk the last part of the journey. It would be best that no one knows where you are heading."

"Very well." She hugged him.

He kissed her then helped her into the carriage. He spoke to Stoddard. "Take them to the Meadowlands border and direct them to the post house."

"You want them to walk unescorted?"

Owain grew stern. "For their safety, there must be as little of a trail to follow as possible. Do you understand?"

"Ay, my lord."

"Now go!" For a long moment he stood watching the departing carriage until the swirling snow obscured his view. He hastened to the stables.

A gasp of surprise escaped as Gwen sat up and stared out the carriage window.

"Something wrong?" asked Lanay.

"I saw a strange flash of light near the back of the house."

"There's no lightning with snow," chided Candice.

"I didn't say lightning."

Katlyn snuggled up against Lanay. "It's cold. Why did Father send us out in the middle of the night?"

Lanay tried to contain her emotions. "He has his reasons."

Gwen closely watched her mother. "Did he tell you why?"

"Enough to agree we should leave."

Candice frowned and tried to get more of the blanket she shared with Gwen. "Where are we going?"

"To where your father said."

"Where's that?"

"Some place a good distance from here."

"But where?"

Lanay looked sharp. "Enough! I have answered you."

Candice scowled and tugged on the blanket, which nearly exposed Gwen to the cold. She pulled back to cover her lap. In a huff, Candice hunkered down. "It's not fair."

"This isn't about fair," began Gwen, turning from Candice to Lanay. "This is about what happened at Court."

Seeing Lanay's pricked frown, Katlyn asked, "What happened, Mama?"

"Father probably tried to buy Gwen a husband only he refused and now we're disgraced," grumbled Candice.

When Gwen pulled the blanket off Candice in angry response, Lanay intervened, her voice and eye stern "It's not about marriage or your sister. And we haven't been disgraced. Not yet. That is what he is trying to avoid."

Candice sat up in surprise and fear. "Something did happen!"

"It deals with the Council," Lanay reluctantly admitted. When the girls bombarded her with questions, she clapped for silence. Once they quieted she spoke. "I'm unaware of the details, but you saw his agitation so the circumstance is dire."

"Ay. He didn't sound or act like himself," said Gwen.

"He's very worried and is sending us to safety." Lanay grew misty eyed, looking out the window. "I'm frightened for him."

Gwen took her mother's hand for comfort. "I'm sure he knows what he's doing."

Lanay wiped her eyes. "Ay. We must trust him. Now, no more questions. Let us do as he asks."

Kell sat alone in his room across from the king's study. The light of the oil lamp turned low for meditation. His eyes sprang open when the light of dimension travel appeared. A male Guardian with white hair and violet eyes appeared. His wore a vassal's uniform of russet with modest ornamentation, including a jeweled hilted dagger. Kell stood.

"Gresham?"

"Something's wrong, Captain. There's a disturbance in the province."

"Have you spoken to Owain?"

"The disturbance is at Presley, only when I got there neither he nor his family were home."

Kell became concerned. "Were they taken by force?"

"I sensed nothing to suggest kidnapping or foul play. In fact, the housekeeper was unaware of their absence until I arrived."

"What of Wade?"

"Probably with Owain, who's avoiding me, like usual,"

"You've had problems with him?"

"Owain isn't a cooperative mortal."

"He cooperated with Archimedes."

Gresham scowled. "Archimedes isn't a Guardian. Toward me, he is overly nervous and easily frightened, so he takes to dodging issues. His prompt compliance to the king's orders gave me hope this time might be different. I was wrong."

Kell frowned in annoyance at the side issue. "What about the disturbance?"

"It's a coldness I haven't felt since Dagar, which is why I reported to you rather than look for Owain."

The answer was both disturbing and puzzling. "Yet you said you sensed no compulsion or force?"

"No. As I said, he probably left to avoid me. There maybe no connection to the disturbance."

Kell's earlier annoyance returned. "This deals with the Dark Way. Considering the king's orders and his warning to Owain, the disappearance doesn't bode well."

"True." Gresham heaved a resigned shrug. "Then again, it is Owain."

Kell's glare grew hot. "Archimedes vouched for him. Any deception or misstep on his part would reflect badly upon the Vicar's judgment. That will not set well with Archimedes, the king or myself. Can you think of where they went?"

"Perhaps to stay with family or friends. Only I didn't want to waste time before reporting to you."

"Find them and learn what you can. If not from Owain then his wife or Wade."

"At once." Gresham disappeared.

Despite the late hour, Kell considered informing Ellis of Owain's disappearance. He warned Ellis about pushing Owain. Had Ellis' threat done that? Wade reported Owain's diligence. What suddenly happened to change that? And is it connected to the dark, cold disturbance he and Gresham sensed? Or was Gresham right, and Owain withdrew because the pressure proved too much? Being Trio Leader of Midessex, Gresham knew Owain best from working with him on provincial matters. There were too many unanswered questions to discern the cause or meaning of the turn of events and Ellis would want answers. At present he had none to offer. Thus, he chose to wait until Gresham returned with more information.

Chapter 5

THE NEXT DAY, Ellis and Kell crossed from the armory to the main building. In the exercise yard, Ellis paused to observe Iain instructing Wess and Bosley in swordsmanship. He noticed Hugh's description in each boy by the way they responded to Iain. Wess possessed an impressive degree of skill for his age while Bosley had to be coerced. When Bosley let the sword point touch the ground, Iain firmly took the boy by the shoulders.

"You must give your full attention to what I'm telling you. Someday your life may depend upon it."

"I don't want to be a soldier."

"Learning how to handle a sword isn't only for soldiers. All men must be skilled in arms to defend themselves and those in their care." Seeing Bosley frown, Iain's temper grew short. "When you turned thirteen you became an adult, yet for the year since you're done nothing but complain. You are of royal blood and have duties! One is not to shame your father or your mother's memory with irresponsible behavior." Bosley winced in pain at mention of his mother, but Iain didn't back down. "Now pick up your sword and listen well."

Although sneering in reluctant compliance, Bosley did as told.

"On guard." Iain crossed swords with Bosley. "Disengage and come at me." Bosley did so and Iain slapped the sword aside. "Keep a firm, yet controlled grip. Again." Bosley repeated the move and again was batted aside. "Again!" For a third time, Bosley acted and was thwarted. "Again! This time like a man and not a boy!"

Bosley angrily snarled and came at Iain, but when Iain parried, he held fast and immediately riposted. Iain widely smiled.

"Good. You can do it. Wess." He motioned for Wess to take his place, to which Bosley rolled his eyes. "Now spar."

Ellis caught Iain's eye and grinned before turning to leave. He spied a clean-shaven, blonde-haired Guardian warrior standing to one side trying to act casual. He knew Mahon tried not to be too obvious. By nature the Guardian was unpretentious and jovial, with bright, sky blue eyes set in a youthful face that betray his thoughts and moods.

Ellis chuckled. "I don't think pretense is Mahon's style."

Kell's grin was sly and cunning. "His skills in battle are keen and precise. Avatar trained him."

"All disguised behind a baby face."

"Mahon is over fourteen hundred years old."

Ellis laughed, shaking his head. They entered the main building by a side door where they met Armus and Darius. "Now, that's the face of warrior," he said to Kell concerning Armus.

"Thank you, Sire," Armus said, although showing ignorance of the reference.

Darius held out several dispatches. "These just arrived."

Ellis took them. He continued his trek while opening a dispatch to read. "Ranulf reports minor resistance, yet is making progress." Handing it back to Darius, he opened the other report, never pausing in his step. "Mathias reports some trouble but feels certain he can handle it."

"Mathias believes he can handle anything."

"Let's hope he can. I don't want to carry out my threat of arms if I don't have to."

"Do you regret saying it?"

"No. I will do what is necessary. Only it's taking too long to recruit my army. Several on the Council have larger forces than I do."

"Sire, Archimedes reports the Jor'ellians number ten thousand," said Kell.

"Excellent." He paused upon reaching the stairs. "Has General Barlow returned?"

"An hour ago," replied Armus.

"Fetch him. Along with Iain."

Armus saluted and departed while they went upstairs.

"Ellis, are you certain about Iain?" asked Darius.

"Why not? Just because I ordered Hugh to remain, doesn't mean I question his loyalty. If not to me, then to his Jor'ellian vow. Has he said anything?"

"No, he's been supportive of your decision."

In the study, Ellis reread the dispatches. He finished when Barlow and Iain arrived. Barlow was a bear of a man in his fifties with a full black beard and dark brown eyes.

"You sent for us, Sire."

"I want a status report on the royal army."

"Two thousand foot soldiers, five thousand five hundred and twenty horsemen, two hundred small pieces of artillery."

"Two hundred and ten. The others arrived from the Highlands yesterday," Iain corrected Barlow.

Barlow growled in dispute. "The effectiveness is still in question."

Ellis observed the exchange. Adding the new form of weaponry was a source of contention between the generals. Stoker, a Guardian metal smith and weapons specialist, along with Master Rhys, a well-known inventor, convinced Iain about the usefulness of the cannons. Barlow remained skeptical. He only yielded when Ellis became involved.

"Archers?" Ellis asked to appease Barlow.

"One thousand. Masters at long and short range."

Iain didn't flinch at the dig.

"With ten thousand Jor'ellians that makes a total force of nearly thirty thousand," said Darius.

Ellis pursued his lips. "Zebulon and Ranulf have as many men. Hollis and Mathias command the marines and navy. Several other countries have armies two or three times our size. How many are here?" he asked Barlow.

"Roughly one thousand in and around the castle. Four thousand more are stationed throughout the province with the rest at their assigned outposts."

"You fear some on the Council may be behind the unrest?" asked Iain.

For a brief moment Ellis regarded Iain before answering. "I'm considering all possibilities and options."

"As you should, Sire."

A ruckus from in the Courtyard drew them to the window. Three battered and bleeding men arrived on two horses. One man appeared in very bad shape, being held in the saddle by a companion. Several royal soldiers, Mahon, and another Guardian warrior aided the men to dismount.

Ellis opened the window. "What's going on?"

"Lord Malcolm's men, Sire," replied Mahon.

Ellis and the others rushed to the Courtyard by way of the outer galleyway stairs. Along the way, Ellis sent for Eldric. When they arrived, two men sat on the ground with the third lying next to them in great pain. One tried to stand at seeing Ellis, only to stumble and fall back.

"Be at ease. What happened?"

"Hagley was attacked, Sire."

"By whom?"

The men exchanged quizzical glances and shook their heads. "We don't know. It happened so fast," said one.

"Some wore black and were heavily armed, others looked liked farmers," began the second, growing upset. "We tried to fight, but we couldn't tell from where the next attack would come! Lord Malcolm dispatched us to plead for help before the North Plains falls."

Eldric arrived and Ellis instructed him to attend the wound. He waved the others to return inside. "Barlow, how long to get a force ready to march to the North Plains?"

"If I dispatch messengers immediately, by tomorrow morning."

"Do so, only keep a small detachment here. Also send to the outposts nearest the North Plains to gather at key points along the border for reinforcements and containment."

Barlow and Iain saluted before departing.

Ellis passed the Great Hall and Council Chamber, heading toward the rear of the main building. "What do you make of it, Kell?"

"Hard to say. The individuals dressed in black may be mercenaries, disbanded soldiers from Marcellus' army—"

"Or Shadow Warriors," said Armus.

Kell frowned at him in annoyance. "I didn't want to jump to that conclusion."

"I thought the same," began Ellis. "Have half the Jor'ellians remain here along with Mahon, Vidar, and Avatar."

"Should I remain also?" asked Armus.

"No. Go to Archimedes and take charge of any Jor'ellians he can spare. Also instruct him to dispatch messengers to the Council to go on full alert. If it is just mercenaries, we can handle it, but if the Dark Way is involved, we'll need their full support."

Darius laid hold of Armus' arm to stop his departure, yet spoke to Ellis. "If they are mercenaries, Mathias and Hollis should take immediate control of the ports to protect against escape. Also send a vassal to Garwood and tell Jasper to have my forces meet at Welford."

"Ay. Include that in the orders. Go."

Armus saluted, stepped back and vanished in the white light of dimension travel.

"Once all is settled here, I'll inform the Trio Leaders and placed the Guardians on full alert," said Kell.

Ellis, Kell and Darius arrived at the family salon. Shannan was there along with Arista. Nigel lay in a bassinet made so he could be with the family during private times. He contently cooed. Avatar stood behind the bassinet. Vidar sat on a window seat cleaning his crossbow.

Shannan smiled and rose to greet Ellis. His serious features alerted her to trouble. "Something wrong?"

"The North Plains has been attacked by unknown forces. Malcolm sends for my help."

"When do you leave?"

"Tomorrow morning. Barlow and Iain are assembling the troops. I sent Armus to Archimedes to release more Jor'ellians." He drew her away from the others. "There is an underlining disturbance I can't place so I'm uncomfortable about leaving you and Nigel here. Perhaps the Guardians should take you both to Melwynn."

She was kind in her rebuff. "How would it appear if I leave during a time of danger? I'm not afraid for myself or Nigel." She glanced toward the bassinet. Avatar and Vidar were attentive.

"Along with Mahon," said Kell.

"And solders and Jor'ellians," added Darius.

She smiled with confidence. "We shall be safe."

Ellis kissed her hand. "Now, I have to prepare. Pray for me."

"Always." She embraced him.

After embracing her, he crossed to the bassinet. "Don't give your mother too much trouble while I'm gone." He leaned down and kissed Nigel. He sent a cautious look to Avatar and Vidar and quietly spoke. "Guard them well."

"We will, Sire," replied Vidar. Avatar gave an assenting nod.

Ellis sent a friendly smile to Arista and Darius while passing to leave.

Darius lingered. "I'll look after him," he reassured Shannan.

"I know you will." She embraced him

"Who will look after you?" asked Arista.

He held her gaze. "Hopefully, you will include me in your prayers."

Arista blushed and replied, "Always."

Shannan spoke after Darius left. "When will you two finally admit your feelings?"

Arista's blush deepened. "I didn't want to presume."

"Presume. It is obvious how you both feel."

"Perhaps, when they return."

"If not, I will presume."

In his chamber, Iain packed for departure.

Wess watched, frustration filling his face. "Why can't I go? Father said the king gave permission for me to join the army."

"You're not trained for battle and until you are you will remain here."

"I can handle a sword and sit a horse. The rest I can learn."

Iain paused in his packing to send an admonishing glare to Wess. "You are not ready and I won't argue the point any further."

"Uncle …"

"General to you, Recruit!"

Wess was first surprised then came to attention.

Iain sized up Wess. "That's better. All new recruits are subject to the orders of their commanding officers."

Hugh and Bosley entered. "I told you he was here," said Bosley.

Hugh didn't appear pleased, staring at his eldest son. "I've been looking for you."

Wess didn't answer, staying at attention.

Iain spoke. "He tried to convince me he's ready to march with the army." He put up a hand before Hugh could voice his protest. "He didn't succeed. In fact, I was about to issue orders." He turned to Wess. "You are to remain at Waldron. With the king away, the garrison will have to protect the queen and prince."

"You think they'll attack Waldron?"

"Unlikely. Still, protecting the royal family is just as important as marching against the enemy. Continue to sharpen your skills for next time the army is called upon."

Wess frowned in displeasure.

"Do you question my orders, Recruit?"

"No, sir."

Iain steered Wess to the door. "I need to finish packing."

Hugh motioned for Bosley to leave also. "I was concerned when I couldn't find him and glad you convinced him to stay."

Iain smiled and shrugged. "You heard me pull rank. Now, I do need to finish."

"Keep your head down," said Hugh.

❧

Arundine, Council Hall of the Guardians, stood in the most central part of Allon, deep in a forest of Midessex, a magnificent, six-sided, domed shrine of white marble, similar to the stone used in building the Temple of Providence. The interior was larger than anticipated by the exterior. Six pillars held up the dome with twelve marble chairs arranged in a semi-circle. The marble floor formed a map of Allon, naming each province in front of its respective chair. Here the Trio Leaders met. These were the Guardian counterparts to the Council of Twelve.

Three Guardians were appointed over each province, responsible for the spiritual oversight and protection of the mortals. They commanded thousands of Guardians in their respective duties within the provinces, and ultimately Allon. Kell, Armus and Avatar formed the top-ranking Trio in the Guardian hierarchy. Each provincial Trio had a leader who dealt directly with the mortal lord and represented the Trio on the Guardian Council.

Priscilla, Guardian of Fair Winds, watched over the East Coast. Her beautiful face was accented with long, pale-yellow hair, part coiled in a crown-like braid on her head, and sky-blue eyes. Her flowing gown of shimmering sea foam and dark green was fastened about the waist with a shell buckle. Sight of her made a lasting impression on mortal sailors. Zinna was a skilled archer from the Meadowlands. Auriel's strawberry blonde hair and fair features were in stark contrast to her warrior status and the sword strapped to her back and chakram hanging from the belt at her right hip. Wren and Mona completed the female contingent of the Guardian leadership. Only Mona was absent.

Barnum of the Highlands equaled Armus in brawn with a grizzled beard and good-natured sneer. He replaced the much-admired Valmar, who perished during the battle with Dagar. Jedrek was a fair-haired youthful Guardian of the Delta with fiery amber eyes, whose appearance belied the mind and heart of a cunning warrior. Chase, a mild-tempered sea Guardian, commanded the West Coast. Derwin of the Lowlands had a temperament directly opposite Chase, fiery and outspoken. Although a warrior with the stubbornness of a mule and sword of iron, Zadok possessed a surly manner, full of retorts and complaints. Hardly the type one would consider for Leader of Allon's most treasured province, the Region of Sanctuary. He and Derwin got along well. Egan of the Northern Forest rounded out the Guardian leadership. A quiet and unassuming warrior by nature with black hair and deep piercing blue eyes, decisive actions spoke for him. Gresham's seat was empty.

Kell waited for the Leaders to take their seats before calling the meeting to order.

"Captain. How can we begin? Gresham and Mona are absent," said Auriel.

"Both are occupied."

"What about Armus and Avatar? They are not here either," said Zadok.

"Avatar is now Prince Nigel's Overseer. Unfortunately, my caution in warning you to possible danger proved correct. The North Plains is under attack by unknown forces. Malcolm sent to Ellis for aid. He leaves at dawn and dispatched Armus to the Fortress to take command of the Jor'ellians and meet him at the border."

"Any word from Mona about who?" asked Jedrek.

"No. Gresham is investigating the disappearance of Sir Owain and his family."

"You think there's a connection?" asked Derwin.

"Unknown as of yet. This may be mortals rebelling or a resurgence of the Dark Way. Until we know for certain Allon is on full alert. Any hint of trouble from the mortals or sense of evil, deal with it immediately and inform me." Kell stood, drew his sword and held it out. "For Jor'el and Allon!"

In unison, the Leaders rose and drew their swords or daggers to mimic Kell's motion and battle cry.

The following morning Shannan stood on the steps to the Great hall wrapped in a fur-lined cloak. Arista was in faithful attendance. Ellis wore the Golden Armor and Sword of Allon. Kell's daily uniform was replaced with the splendor of his Guardian battle armor. Iain, Barlow and Darius were also dressed for conflict.

When Archimedes concluded the blessing over Ellis and the troops, Ellis mounted his warhorse. Horses were not necessary for Guardians, although for this occasion, Kell sat upon a magnificent white spirit stallion.

Darius surprised Arista by kissing her hand, his long look in her eyes unmistakable in their meaning. The blush rose to her cheeks and she smiled while watching him mount. A private look of satisfaction passed between Ellis and Shannan before he turned to lead his troops from Waldron. Darius rode by his side, followed by Kell, then Iain and Barlow.

The momentary gratification turned to sobriety. Shannan felt a supportive hand on her shoulder. She didn't look back, knowing it was Vidar. When the last soldier was through the gate, she took Arista's arm and went inside.

Outside, snow swirled in the howling wind. Inside the cottage, Musetta sat in a chair near a roaring fire. She wore a black doublet and breeches with her hair now cut to shoulder length. Two Shadow Warriors flanked her, one male and one female. The male was the same one she summoned to remove Wade's body, still wearing the talisman. The female was an imposing figure in black breeches and tunic, close-cropped black hair and almost colorless eyes with only a trace of blue. She wore a short dagger at her hip but no sword.

The door opened and Owain entered. His hat and cloak were covered in snow. He stopped upon seeing the Shadow Warriors, concerned etched on his brow.

Musetta noticed his apprehension and privately smiled. "Shut the door. It is too cold to leave it open."

Owain did so yet remained near the entrance, cautiously eyeing the Warriors.

"You remember Burris. This is Nari."

Burris and Nari coolly regarded Owain.

Owain turned his attention to Musetta and noticed her attire. "Clever. At first glance, and from a distance, you'd pass as a man."

"That's the idea. Is all ready?"

"Ay. I've brought a force of two thousand."

"Only two thousand?"

"It's all I could muster in a day."

Her disappointment turned to consideration. "Well, combined with sixty Shadow Warriors that should do for now."

"I thought you said this would be easy?"

"If all goes according to plan."

A white flash of light filled the small room. Owain and Musetta shielded their eyes. Another male Shadow Warrior appeared.

"Roane? Is there trouble?" asked Burris.

"The king and his army left Waldron."

"How many remain?"

"We counted twenty Jor'ellians, two hundred soldiers, and two Guardians: Vidar and Mahon. Cletus and Indigo are standing watch."

She laughed. "Excellent."

"Vidar is the best Guardian archer who ever existed," warned Burris.

"Ay. Like Kell and Armus, he is from the Beginning," said Nari.

"They won't be expecting us. Besides, his lordship will lead the initial strike force of two thousand against a little over two hundred. It should be easy." Musetta turned to Owain while speaking.

"Ay, with those odds. How did you get Ellis to leave Waldron?"

"An uprising in the North Plains required his immediate attention."

He snickered. "You forced him to keep his word of using arms. Well done."

"I have kept my end of the bargain. I suggest a night assault to completely catch them off guard."

Owain formulated a plan out loud. "It will take seven days of long, hard marching to reach Hagley. Strike too soon and Ellis will make a hasty return. Since he left this morning, we must give him more time."

"We can always bring the fight to him," said Burris.

"Ay. Once engaged in battle he would risk much to leave the field and return to Waldron," agreed Roane.

Owain was nodding. "Good. Wait until he reaches the border. In four nights we'll coordinate our attacks." He saw the way Musetta stared at him with a mixture of confusion and surprise. "What are you looking at?"

"You do have some courage."

"I'm not totally devoid."

Chapter 6

FOUR DAYS LATER, as dusk settled over Waldron, servants went about their task of lighting the castle's torches and oil lamps. In the exercise yard, Mahon watched Wess coax a reluctant Bosley into more sword practice.

Wess broke off the bout, frustrated by Bosley's lack of effort. "You're never going to improve if you don't try."

"It's late, and I'm cold and hungry."

"Remember what uncle said, we may be needed to defend Waldron. Only a garrison remains and the walls are incomplete."

"We're not soldiers. So stop pretending to be one."

Wess squared his shoulders. "The king gave permission for me to join the army. Besides, uncle's right, we have duties." Angry, Bosley turned to leave and Wess seized him. "If the castle is attacked every able body must help defend it before the king can return."

Bosley jerked away. "You're not Uncle or Father, so don't tell me what to do."

"I am the oldest."

Mahon stepped between them. "Peace. Brothers should work together, not be at odds."

"Tell him, he's trying to be some kind of general!"

"I'm trying to help you be a man."

Mahon took Bosley by one shoulder. "He's right, you need to start acting more mature. However," he added, and took hold of Wess by the shoulder. "You should be more diplomatic. He's your brother, not a servant."

Subdued, Wess nodded while Bosley scowled.

"Now, it grows late. You can practice tomorrow. If you wish, I'll demonstrate a few Guardian moves."

Wess smiled in excitement at the offer. "I'd like that."

"So would I," agreed Bosley.

Mahon chuckled. "We'll start after breakfast. Now go freshen up and I'll see what food I can scrounge from cook since you've missed dinner."

The boys moved off, chatting about the morning.

Hugh joined Mahon. "At least one of us can convince them. I couldn't get Wess to stop and eat. I returned to make him stop."

"He's very determined."

"Always has been. I wish Bosley shared some of that determination."

"In time he may."

With a hint of skepticism in his face and voice, Hugh's confronted the Guardian. "Was your offer genuine or in the line of duty?"

Mahon was taken back by the question. "My lord?"

Hugh cocked a sarcastic smile. "Don't pretend, Mahon. I know the king assigned you to guard us. Granted you've tried to be discreet, but let us not play games."

"I don't play games with duty."

"Then I'll speak plainly. What reason was given for guarding us? Or should I say, how concerned is the king about our possible interference?"

"I was asked to keep watch for your safety."

Hugh scoffed. "I'm sure that's what you were told."

Mahon grew offended, bright sky blue eyes direct on Hugh. "My lord, the Son of Tristan is honorable. He does not deal with innuendos and veiled threats. He is concerned for the safety of all those he left behind."

A Guardian's eyes were commanding when needed and Hugh stared at Mahon for a moment before speaking. "Iain said Ellis has a good heart.

However, you must understand, the way he deals with his Court is far different than what I was used to."

Mahon features relaxed. "I'm certain it's been a challenging adjustment for you and your family."

Hugh uncomfortably shifted his weight from side-to-side. "I am grateful for his mercy in sparing my children." He shrugged. "Why me, I still haven't figured out."

"Your action helped to save Allon." When Hugh turned away, Mahon laid hold of his arm. Hugh slowly turned back, eyes shrouded in timidity when glancing up to the Guardian. In those eyes, Mahon saw deep hurt and pain. "It's not the king's mercy that troubles you, it is the fact you cannot forgive yourself for killing Marcellus."

Hugh spoke in a low, choked voice. "You told them brothers should work together and not be at odds. I took my brother's life."

"Marcellus yielded to the Dark Way and ruthlessly used it to his own ends. If you must find blame, it is the Dark Way at fault and not you. So you can forgive yourself like the king has already done."

Once more Hugh stared into Mahon's eyes. This time the Guardian's expression was sympathetic and soothing. "You truly mean that. Ellis has forgiven me."

Mahon kindly smiled. "Ay. You are not prisoners and I am your protector. Why make such an offer to an enemy? Besides, I'm a Guardian of Jor'el. It goes against my spirit to defend anyone of the Dark Way. As for your sons, I sense no evil between them or in them. Be at peace, I don't believe they will repeat your painful history."

Hugh swallowed back his rising emotion.

"Now, I told the boys I'd fetch dinner. Have you eaten, or did your fatherly concern lessen your appetite?"

Hugh chuckled in relief. "I can eat now."

"Good. Join them, and I'll be back shortly."

Hugh stopped Mahon's departure. "I never had the opportunity to know a true Guardian. Learning Latham's Shadow Warriors were Guardians turned to evil skewed my view of your kind. I'm beginning to see things differently. Thank you."

"You're welcome, my lord." Mahon smiled and left.

Shannan stood in the private salon, dressed in her old forester clothes of breeches and jerkin, posing for an artist. Her hair was loose and she held an old bow. She had been standing in one position since supper and now it was nearly time to retire.

"How much longer, Master Carlton?"

A large easel stood near the window to use daylight. At night, two oil large lamps provided light. Carlton made a few minor strokes of the brush and smiled in great satisfaction. "I'm finished, Majesty."

She stretched after holding one position. "Well?" she asked Vidar, who sat on the window seat behind Carlton.

"It looks very good."

She came to view the painting. The portrait depicted she and Ellis prior to defeating Marcellus and Dagar. Also in the portrait were a large wolf and giant eagle. She smiled in fondness. "It brings back so many memories."

"Your Majesty is pleased?" asked Carlton.

"Ay." Her voice a bit choked.

"All I need to do is a few finishing touches around the edges, allow the paint to dry and set it in a frame. I should have it ready in three days."

"Very good." She waved to several servants at the door. They promptly came to help Carlton. She and Vidar left the salon.

"He is a masterful painter," said Vidar.

She paused in the hallway and looked back at the salon. "Ay, only it feels too personal to hang in the Great Hall like Archimedes suggested."

"Then don't."

She chuckled and continued her trek toward the family's quarters. "Ellis will agree it belongs in the family salon."

They stopped in the nursery. Faline wore a dressing gown ready to retire. Avatar stood in his usual place a step from the crib. Shannan approached and saw Nigel sleeping. She bent down and kissed him. When she straightened, she noticed Avatar wryly grinning.

"I suppose you find it boring guarding a mortal infant who only eats and sleeps."

His grin widened. "At least he's less trouble than other mortals."

She laughed. "Good night."

"Good night, majesty," said Faline and Avatar.

After midnight, shadows crept toward Waldron. All markings on their muted red uniforms were covered in black cloth. With only two hundred soldiers remaining to guard the castle, only fifteen stood watch at one time. The task was almost too easy.

One royal soldier raced to the alarm bell. He managed to ring the bell four times before being slain. Hundreds of men rushed through the breeches in the wall and the front gate.

In the barracks, Hugh emerged from the room he and the boys shared, partially dressed and armed with his sword. The boys wore heavy woolen nightshirts, leggings and slippers. Enemy forces fought their way inside.

Bosley stared in fear. "Who are they?"

"It doesn't matter. Stay down!" Hugh ordered the boys before racing to join the fighting.

"Father!" Bosley shouted and reached to grab Hugh but Wess snatched his hand.

"Come on!" Wess pulled Bosley toward a door at the rear of the barracks.

"Where are we going?"

"To the armory for weapons."

"What?" Bosley stopped.

"Father and the others need help. Now, come on!" Again he pulled Bosley by the arm. At the armory, he threw open the door and shoved Bosley through.

"It's dark."

Wess didn't respond to Bosley's complaint but left the door open for light. He grabbed a sword and scabbard off the wall and handed it to Bosley. "Take this."

"Why?"

"Do as your told!" Wess put on a thick padded blue and silver doublet before tossing one to Bosley. "Put it on." When Bosley hesitated, he began to dress him. "For protection." He placed the sword around Bosley's waist then buckled a sword about his own waist. He shoved a pair of boots at Bosley. "Now put these on."

"Why?"

"You can't fight in slippers." Wess hastily pulled on boots. He frowned with impatience at watching Bosley fumbled putting on the boots. "Hurry! Let's find Father."

Bosley fussed with the large doublet while following Wess. "It doesn't fit—" His eyes grew wide at seeing the fighting. Wess shoved him behind some barrels and construction debris. "Who they are?"

"I don't know. I can't see a badge." Wess spotted a group heading toward the Family Private Quarters. "The queen!" He bolted away.

"Wess! Wait!" Bosley called. Wess ignored him and ran after the enemy soldiers. Reluctantly, he followed.

From across the courtyard, Mahon saw the boys heading for the private quarters. Dealing with six enemy soldiers prevented him following them. He caught a glimpse of Hugh engaging the invaders. Fighting in the defense of Waldron was hardly the action of a man with questionable intentions. In short order Mahon finished the soldiers and rushed to Hugh's aid. His arrival prevented Hugh from being blind-sided.

"Thanks, but I'd appreciate it if you get the boys to safety," said Hugh. The sound of battle grew near. "Go! I can handle myself." He raced off to rejoin the battle while Mahon headed in the direction Wess and Bosley went.

Startled from sleep, Shannan sat up, her heart racing. Vidar stood in the threshold, his crossbow armed and ready. "What's wrong?"

"The alarm bell—" He fired. "We're being invaded!" He shut and barred the door.

She bolted out of bed. "Who? How?"

"No time for questions. I must get you to safety."

She grabbed the breeches and tunic she wore earlier from off the chair beside the bed. "Alert Avatar and get Nigel. I'll be there in a moment." She hurried behind the dressing screen.

"I'm not leaving."

"Go! Get my son!" she commanded in the Ancient.

Vidar growled in frustration and left by way of the antechamber door. In the hallway, he encountered half a dozen enemy soldiers and fired his crossbow.

Avatar emerged from the nursery. One swing of his sword and two soldiers fell. In short order the Guardians dispatched the enemy. "Who are they?"

"Don't know. Shannan sent me to have you bring Nigel." Hearing approaching feet, Vidar whirled about with his crossbow aimed and ready.

"No!" Wess shouted, throwing his hands up, Bosley hiding behind him.

Avatar grabbed Vidar's bow in time to stop him from shooting the boys. "What are you two doing here?"

"We came to help the queen. They've breeched the front gate."

"And the barracks. Father went to help—but they're outnumbered," said Bosley, upset.

They heard Nigel crying. "Take care of them," Avatar said to Vidar before heading back to the nursery.

Vidar herded the boys towards Shannan's room when she emerged, dressed and armed with a dagger. "What's happened?"

"They're everywhere!" Bosley said, trying not to cry.

Wess held a steady hand on Bosley's shoulder. "We came to warn you, Majesty. Protect you, if we must."

She curbed an impulsive smile. "I accept your help, Master Wess. Master Bosley."

Vidar became alert. "Go to the nursery and stay with Avatar. I'll hold them off." He raced toward the sounds of battle.

Arista appeared from the other end of the hall wearing a fur-lined robe over her dressing gown and sturdy slippers. "What is happening?"

"We're under attack." Shannan nudged them toward the nursery.

Avatar held Nigel wrapped in warm blankets when Shannan, Arista, and the boys entered. "Where's Vidar?"

Shannan shook her head, trying to maintain her composure. "He went to divert the enemy. Faline?"

"I haven't seen her." At the sound of approaching battle, Avatar handed Nigel to Arista then drew his sword. "Come. I must get all you out of here."

"Are we going to dimension travel?" asked Arista, trepidation in her voice.

"No. There are five of you and I can only take two at a time. And I won't leave any of you vulnerable."

"What about Vidar?" asked Wess.

"He'll find us." Avatar peeked out the door. The battle sounded fierce. He heard a couple of bowshots, but the hallway was clear. "Quick! Down the back stairs." He watched them follow his instructions but also kept alert for trouble.

When Bosley looked over his shoulder, he ran into someone. He started to cry out when a hand covered his mouth.

"Easy, young master," said Mahon. The boy's expression showed uncertainty whether to be relieved or concerned. The others arrived.

"Five," Avatar told Mahon.

"Vidar?"

"Covering for us."

"The way to the postern gate is clear."

"Follow Mahon," Avatar told them.

From the stairs, they made their way out of the family's quarters, through the back garden and to the rear parade grounds. Seeing a dozen soldiers, Mahon signaled them to take cover.

"You there!" shouted a soldier.

Mahon and Avatar immediately confronted the enemy. Six soldiers fell in the first assault. Some cut down by the Guardians' swords, others sent flying by a wave of a Guardian's hand. In a moment twelve soldiers were either dead or wounded. The victory was short-lived when another enemy soldier spotted them and called for reinforcements.

"Go! I'll hold them off," said Mahon.

"Jor'el be with you."

"And with you."

Avatar urged the others to the back gate. He quickly looked for signs of the enemy and saw no one. He estimated several hundred yards to the woods at the rear of Waldron and the snow fell heavily. On his signal, they all left the gate, racing for the trees.

Arista clung to Nigel, shielding him while running. Bosley tripped and fell headlong into the snow. A hand pulled him up and began moving before his feet could touch the ground. Avatar nearly carried him to the trees and there set Bosley down.

"Keep going until you can't run anymore," he said.

With the sounds of battle echoing in their ears, they moved without looking back. Bosley and Arista were the first to tire, Bosley because he was the youngest and Arista because she carried Nigel. Avatar gathered them into a semi-protected hollow. Arista wearily sat on a log to catch her breath. Bosley collapsed beside the log laboring to breath. Wess bent over, hands on his knees, gulping for air.

Shannan sat next to Arista and reached for Nigel. "Is he well?"

Arista nodded, still breathing heavy.

Nigel fussed from all the jostling but appeared in one piece. She hugged her son while looking back in the direction of Waldron. "Who would do this?"

"I don't know," replied Avatar.

"I couldn't see their badges because they were covered in black cloth," said Wess.

"Did you see the color of their uniforms?"

"I think they were red or some form of the color, but it's dark. Sorry, Majesty."

"You have nothing to apologize for. You're both very brave to come help me. Thank you."

Bosley sniffled. "I hope nothing happens to Father."

Wess approached Avatar. "Is there a place nearby we can take them to safety?"

Avatar grinned at the mortal lad. "Ay. Only give them a moment's rest."

Mahon saw Avatar and the others pass through the gate. He just finished dealing with five soldiers when something stuck him hard from behind and he went sprawling. He got to his knees only to be struck again and sent flying backwards, crashing into a building where he hit his head, almost blacking out. Through hazy vision, he saw a burly Shadow Warrior standing with his feet braced and hands on his hips, snarling. He wore something around his neck that looked familiar only he couldn't focus clearly

"Puny warriors. When will you learn, you're no match for us?"

Mahon gritted his teeth against the pain in his head and body. He attempted to rise and again went flying through the air and into the postern gate. This time he collapsed, semi-conscious, his ears ringing and head swirling from being struck a third time. He did have enough sense to notice the arrival of a second Shadow Warrior and one he recognized, Roane.

"Burris, what are you doing?"

"Having some fun."

"Well, finish him and report to Lord Owain."

Mahon grimaced. He had to make defense rather than simply be killed. At Roane's departure, Burris briefly took his eyes off him. Mahon snatched a heavy plank from a construction pile, and swung at Burris' head. The Shadow Warrior staggered sideways. Dropping the plank, Mahon stumbled out the postern gate. He heard Burris' shout from behind. Using his remaining energy, he vanished in dimension travel. He only managed to go far enough to avoid detection before reappearing and collapsing into unconsciousness.

In the midst of battling three mortals, Vidar barely recognized the flash of white light to one side and the arrival of four Shadow Warriors. One immediately fired a small crossbow, the arrow catching him high in the right shoulder just under the collarbone. Wounded, he could only raise his crossbow to his hip and fire, striking one Warrior. He stumbled backwards trying to reload when another arrow grazed his left side, bringing to his knees. A Warrior raised his sword to strike. Vidar did the only thing he could; he vanished.

He reappeared in Shannan's room. The Warriors could easily follow his essence since he hadn't left Waldron, but until he knew Shannan was safe he had to remain. Gritting teeth, he pulled the dart from his shoulder and stifled an outcry so as not to be heard. He took a pillow out of its cover to use the cloth to wrap his wound and stem the bleeding. The wound in his side was painful, but not as bad as his shoulder

Hearing sounds in the hall, he vanished again, this time reappearing in the lower kitchen. He swayed, trying not to faint. Any use of power when wounded drained precious energy. When the sensation passed, he closed his eyes and stretched out his senses, searching for Shannan. She wasn't at Waldron. That meant Avatar got her and Nigel away safely. Still, the appearance of Shadow Warriors wasn't good.

Ellis is away and he has the Armor and Sword. His eyes snapped opened. "But not the Golden Bow."

For a third time he vanished. This time, he reappeared on his knees exhausted and clenching his wounds. He was in a vault beneath the armory. The room housed the Armor of Allon, Golden Bow and a quiver of golden arrows. Few knew of the vault's existence. One look told him the bow was there. He sighed with relief and closed his eyes.

"Thank you, Jor'el. Now grant me the strength to find the Daughter of Allon and confront what enemy has dared to invade Waldron."

He pushed himself to his feet and readjusted his crossbow to a more comfortable position across his back. He took the quiver and carefully placed it over left his shoulder, grimacing in pain since any movement hurt. Once he had the bow in hand, he glanced upwards, and said, "*Seach do an luths mi ragh, Jor'el!*" The room filled with bright white light and he disappeared.

Burris arrived at the gathering in the courtyard. Nari, Roane, Cletus, Bern, and Indigo were with Musetta and Owain. He flinched in pain and anger, rubbing his head where Mahon struck him with the plank.

"Did Mahon get away?" demanded Roane.

"You let a Guardian escape?" chided Musetta.

"I didn't let him! He cracked my skull."

"He can't get away!"

"If he does, he will warn Ellis," said Owain. His irate gaze passed between she and Burris.

"He probably dimension-traveled beyond our sensing distance of a mile. That would require tracking him, which would take me from Waldron."

Musetta's eyes narrowed upon the Warrior and she clenched the talisman. Burris fell to his knees in distress, yet it was obvious from the sweat on her brow that her action against him was taxing. She broke off her concentration. "Let that be a lesson. Give the talisman to Roane."

Burris sneered in anger and relief, taking large gulps of air to recover and sting of demotion. He did as commanded, yet Roane hesitated to take the talisman so Burris slapped it into his hand.

Roane put it on and tucked the talisman under the neck of his uniform then spoke. "Two of our numbers were vanquished and one Jor'ellian escaped."

"What? More failure? And why are you hiding it?"

"Because if Mahon is able to warn Ellis, he could also tell Kell about it."

Her scowl passed to Burris. "Perhaps I should have given Roane the talisman and authority to begin with. At least he has some discretion."

Burris didn't reply. His withering glance at Roane was enough to show his anger.

Musetta ignored the exchange to inquire of Indigo. "What about the queen and young prince?"

"I don't know. I secured all the servants in basement as you ordered."

"The postern gate was open when I waylaid Mahon," said Burris.

"You let them escape too?"

"I didn't see anyone escape only Mahon."

Her anger rose to fever pitch. "Take a dozen Shadow Warriors and find them! Do not let the Daughter of Allon reach the Son of Tristan."

"Nari, with me. We'll take Orin and his group."

"If they have escaped—" Owain began to protest.

"They won't elude Nari and Burris for long," said Roane.

"What about the royal soldiers and the rest of the Jor'ellians?"

"Many are dead, others badly wounded and the remainder taken prisoner."

"Owain!" a loud, angry voice shouted.

A bloodied and battle soiled Hugh was in the custody of several soldiers. The wounds were minor and he strained against their hold, trying to lunge at Owain.

"Bloody coward! Double traitor!"

Musetta confronted Hugh. "It is you who are the traitor for killing your brother and allowing this pretender to steal what was promised to me and my son!"

Hugh wasn't intimidated. "Latham's whore. I should have known."

She slapped him. "I could kill you where you stand." She reached for the talisman and Hugh braced himself.

Owain seized her hand. "He is of the royal line of Unwin. By way of him you can legitimize your claim."

"Never!" declared Hugh.

She wickedly smiled. "Guard him well."

Hugh fought being drug away by the soldiers.

Musetta moved toward the Great Hall and Owain followed, his brows furrowed in guarded curiosity. "You mentioned your son. Was Latham the father?"

"Ay."

"Where is the boy?"

"He is safe. Which is more than I can say for the infant prince."

Sudden, fearful comprehension show on his face and he stopped her. "Wait! This whole scheme is to kill a child?"

"The royal heir. That is only a part of it. We'll seize his throne and kill his son, all in one night."

The evil delight in her eyes sent a shiver through him. "You're mad."

"Call me what you will, but it does not change your involvement." She turned upon her heels and continued to the Hall, leaving Owain thunderstruck by her declaration.

Mahon awoke with a start at hearing something and scrambled to his knees. He reached for his sword only to discover he was unarmed. His eyes darted about searching for the source of the noise. He heard it again and rose to his feet and swayed at feeling dizzy. Again the noise sounded. This time he realized it was familiar and saw an owl on a nearby branch.

"Ooohh," he groaned, feeling horribly dizzy and queasy. He carefully lowered himself to sit on the ground. Slowly he recalled what happened. *Attack. Waldron. Shadow Warriors.* Images flashed across his dazed mind of the boys, Shannan, the prince, Arista and Avatar. "Must help." He could only get to his knees. He tried again and stood, bracing against a tree to stop swaying.

For a moment he considered which way to go, then stumbled through the trees. He pulled to a staggering halt upon hearing noises and catching a glimpse of movement through the trees. He crouched in the brush to observe. The postern gate was now closed and men wearing muted red uniforms occupied the battlements. The invasion succeeded. He could do reconnaissance inside, but that required all his skill and power to go undetected. With Shadow Warriors around reconnaissance was out of the question since they could detect Guardian activity mortals could not. The longer he remained the more likely the Shadow Warriors would sense him.

He looked back at the wood, thoughtful and considering. If he honed in on Avatar's essence he might be able to find them. A sudden bout of dizziness and nausea seized him. He swallowed back the sensation. Who was he kidding? In his condition and unarmed, he would be of little help to Avatar in protecting his charges. He couldn't do reconnaissance, and he couldn't help protect the queen and prince. The only choice left; find help. He used a tree for balance and stood.

"Jor'el, guide my steps," he prayed before retreating back into the wood.

———✦———

Meanwhile, on the border of Midessex and the North Plains, the royal camp was in an uproar. Ellis emerged from his tent armed with his sword, wearing boots and a heavy doublet thrown over his shirt and breeches.

Jasper raced up to Ellis. The forty-year-old master-at-arms of Garwood lost his left eye helping Ellis defeat Marcellus and Dagar. He held a bloody sword.

"We were attacked on the north side of camp. A raiding party, perhaps. We lost two soldiers but it's under control." Jasper led Ellis to the attack point.

Along the way, they witnessed wounded soldiers being treated, while others dealt with the dead. At what appeared to be the main point of conflict, soldiers and Jor'ellians surrounded a group of twenty men sitting on the ground. All showed signs of battle. Darius, Barlow, Iain and Kell were present.

Ellis angrily eyed the men. "Who is the leader?"

"Him." Barlow pointed to a roguish looking man of thirty.

"What is the meaning of this?"

The man set his jaw, not replying.

Jasper jerked him to his feet. "You will answer the king!"

Still, the man refused to speak.

Ellis stepped forward to look the man straight in the eye. "Whether you speak or not, your action is treason, and you will pay the penalty. Will you die with a clear conscious having confessed or face Jor'el's eternal wrath for raising rebellion?"

The man winced, the question having its intended impact. He whispered, "Not here."

Ellis turned on his heels. Darius, Iain and Kell followed with Jasper and Barlow escorting the man. Just out of view of the other prisoners, Ellis stopped to confront him. "Well?"

He was edgy. "I don't know why they're doing this. All I know is it has something to do with Dagar and Marcellus. They told us your claim to the throne is not true and it was promised to another."

"Who said this?"

"And who is the other?" added Darius.

The man's anxious glance passed between Darius and Ellis. "I don't their identities but one was like him," he pointed to Kell, "only dressed in black and cold gray eyes."

Ellis grew rigid with indignation. "A Shadow Warrior? Why agree to help one of the Dark Way?"

Ashamed, he stammered. "I'm not sure, Sire. I guess I allowed myself to be persuaded because of my circumstances."

"What do you do?"

"I'm an armor maker. Since the war, I haven't had steady work. My family—" He fell to his knees, repentant. "I'm sorry, Sire! Forgive me. Don't let me die unforgiven."

Ellis' features softened at seeing the genuine sorrow. "I forgive you. General Barlow, secure him until his fate is decided."

"He is a traitor, Ellis," said Darius.

"Ay. But is his story an exception, or is he one of many displaced? Will his execution add fuel to their cause, or could mercy still some voices? Come. I want to interrogate the prisoners and perhaps learn if it is isolated or not."

The interrogation provided mix results. Some were disillusioned like the armor maker, others lifelong malcontents, still others told how they were threatened if they didn't help. Except for the malcontents, the majority was genuinely sorry when confronted by the king. After two hours, Darius, Kell, Barlow, and Iain accompanied Ellis back to his tent. Jasper set about reestablishing the watch and guards for the prisoners.

Armus waited outside the tent. Four Jor'ellians were with him. "It appears we missed the excitement, Sire."

Ellis sarcastically grunted and waved everyone inside. "Well?"

"Archimedes released twelve hundred Jor'ellians. These are the commanders. Ferrell, Hardwin, Kasey and Roarke."

They clasped their swords and spoke in unison. "Sire."

"Gentlemen. I'm afraid we have discovered a new and disturbing development. According to the prisoners from tonight's raid, they were persuaded into rebellion by a Shadow Warrior."

Commotion interrupted their conversation. The flap flew open and Mahon stumbled in, falling to his knees. Blood covered the front and back of his head and he was pale. Armus knelt beside him for aid only Mahon pushed him away to look at Ellis.

"Waldron is taken."

Dumbfounded, Ellis said, "What? How?"

"Soldiers, hundreds, thousands perhaps. And Shadow Warriors."

"Shannan and Nigel?"

"Arista?" asked Darius, anxious.

Mahon grimaced back pain before answering. "With Avatar. I was protecting their escape when I was blindsided by a Shadow Warrior named Burris. He wore something around his neck. Perhaps a shielding medal, I don't know, I didn't see much." He winced and grimaced in pain.

Armus whispered to Ferrell, who nodded and left, then Armus helped Mahon to sit in a chair, the younger warrior wobbly.

"How do you know it was Burris?" asked Kell.

Mahon's glare was irate. "I heard Roane call him by name, and speak the name of who is responsible—Lord Owain."

Ellis went rigid, blue eyes flashed like fire. Darius cursed under his breath. Kell gripped the hilt of his sword, golden eyes narrow with intense anger.

"Shadow Warriors caused trouble in the North Plains. That points to someone schooled in the Dark Way and not Owain," said Darius.

Ellis' deadly look stopped any further speech from Darius.

Kell spoke with authority. "He has abused the Vicar's judgment and Jor'el's mercy."

"Ay," agreed Ellis, his voice thick and deadly. "No clemency this time. He will deal with the full measure of royal and divine retaliation."

"Say the word, Sire, and we ride to Waldron," said Barlow.

Iain refuted. "That leaves the North Plains open for the taking. He did this to distract you, Sire."

"Which one? Is the North Plains the distraction to draw me from Waldron, or is Waldron to stop me from securing the North Plains?"

"From the interrogations, I would say the North Plains is the distraction with Waldron the main objective. These men had no heart for rebellion."

"Perhaps. If I leave now, I risk losing the North Plains, and that could threaten the stability of the kingdom."

"At least Shannan, Nigel and Arista escaped with Avatar," said Darius.

"Along with Lord Hugh's sons. They came armed to help the queen," said Mahon.

Ellis flashed a smile but quelled it to see how Iain took the news. Even though he appeared stoic, a small grin showed at hearing of their bravado.

"What about Hugh?" asked Iain.

Ferrell returned with Eldric, who tended to Mahon. The warrior didn't immediately reply, rather hissed in pain when Eldric examined his wounds.

"He asked me to protect the boys. I was going to do that when I found them helping the queen to escape."

"What of Vidar? Wasn't he with Shannan?" asked Ellis.

"I didn't see him. Avatar said he was providing cover."

"You're lucky to be seeing anything after these cracks," said Eldric.

"Vidar wouldn't abandon Shannan," said Kell.

"Where will Avatar take them, Melwynn?" Iain asked Kell.

"Doubtful. The most mortals a Guardian can dimension travel with are two. He is protecting five. He wouldn't risk leaving the others while Shannan won't take it well that someone has invaded her home and threatened her son."

Ellis chuckled under his breath. "She'll tell Avatar to take Nigel to Melwynn then try to join up with me."

"She wouldn't risk Arista and the boys. She'll take them to safety first. Garwood is closer than we are," said Darius.

"Ay. Take Hardwin and some Jor'ellians and find them."

"I'll go with them," said Mahon.

"You're not going anywhere," refuted Eldric.

Mahon fiercely scowled at the physician. "I was hindered from my duty once, you won't stop me."

Kell nodded at Eldric, who grumbled under his breath and tied off the bandage around Mahon's head.

"General Iain, since your family has become involved, take Ferrell and a scouting party to do reconnaissance of Waldron."

"Take Auriel," said Kell.

"That leaves Hagley. Will you continue there?" asked Barlow.

"No. You and Armus take half the army and the Jor'ellians to Hagley. Determine who is causing trouble and send me word. Owain is being used, but is the person responsible at Hagley or Waldron? Once I know which, I will move." Ellis spread his arms. "May Jor'el bless all of you in your tasks." When they began departing for their assignment, he said, "General Iain, Mahon, remain." For a moment Ellis regarded Iain. "General, I wanted to explain why I asked Lord Hugh and his sons to remain at Waldron."

"There's no need, Sire. I understand it was done out of safety and precaution."

"In part. However, when I spoke to him, Kell and I became concerned by his defensive and nervous demeanor. Mind you, I realized it's not an indication of treasonous activity. However, under the circumstances his behavior was troubling."

Iain' jowls flexed, more with concern than offense. "He expressed some disappointment about the interview. He thought everything was in past, and disturbed to learn otherwise. Perhaps that is what you and Kell sensed."

Mahon shook his head. "No. He is grateful the king spared his children, but wonders why he was spared."

"He told you this?"

"Ay, during a conversation regarding my assignment. His words made me realize he had yet to forgive himself for killing Marcellus. Because of that he has difficulty accepting mercy for himself."

Kell pondered the statement. "That would explain the conflict we sensed."

Mahon was stout in his rebuttal. "There was no conflict in confronting the invaders. I believe he finally forgave himself and could act without reservation on your behalf, Sire."

"Due to your conversation?"

"Ay."

Iain gripped Mahon's arm, a look of gratitude on his brow unable to verbalize.

Mahon gave Iain a grin before speaking again. "Sire, I don't want to keep the duke waiting. For Lord Hugh's sake, I will find the boys along with the queen and prince."

"I should be leaving also. Perhaps at Waldron I can learn what's become of Hugh." Iain and Mahon saluted Ellis and departed.

For several moments, Ellis paced, his brows etched in deep thought.

"You are troubled about Lord Hugh?" Kell asked at length.

"The contrast between he and Owain is stark. Both committed acts they admittedly regret, yet where one embraces restoration, the other has difficulty accepting mercy. Not from arrogance, rather deep pain. If I had known what Mahon reported of Hugh, I would not have ordered them to remain."

"If you hadn't, his forgiveness would still be in doubt. You acted right in your mortal reasoning, only there is more at stake in Jor'el's reasoning."

Ellis glanced with suspicion at Kell. "Did you know that before?"

"No. Whereas I couldn't discern the source of his conflict, I knew it was deep and personally painful. You provided the opportunity while Mahon the means, but it was Hugh's choice. Now he has embraced the mercy given him."

Ellis grew angry. "Heaven have mercy on Owain and whoever else is responsible if I lose my wife and son. I will not be merciful this time."

"You are not alone, Son of Tristan. Using Shadow Warriors shows this is also an assault against Jor'el's sovereignty."

"Ay. Fetch bread and wine for meditation."

Outside, Kell met Armus and Gresham. The latter was agitated.

"I'm sorry, Captain! I thought I acted quick enough."

Kell gave a rough, dismissive wave. "You are not to blame for the choices a mortal makes."

"If I had discovered his plan I could have stopped him."

"Have you found his family?"

"No, I was in midst of searching for them when I felt an overwhelming compulsion to go to Waldron. Seeing what happened, I honed on your spirit and came here."

Kell didn't look pleased and snapped in annoyance. "Find them! They may hold to key to why he turned."

Gresham vanished in dimension travel.

During the conversation, Armus took note of Kell's unusual agitation, and when Kell moved off, he followed. "What about you?"

"What about me?"

"Don't avoid the issue. Shannan is on the run and you're here."

"If I found the talisman none of this would be happening."

"Now you're going to take the blame?"

Kell pulled to an abrupt halt. "Why aren't you seeing to the Jor'ellians?"

"Shannan has been your charge since the day she was born. Don't let your concern for her cloud your judgment."

Kell's gaze narrowed with insult. "You think I'd do that?"

"You counsel other Guardians about how mortals allow emotions to rule their actions, especially when love is involved."

"I'm not in love with Shannan," insisted Kell in a low, harsh voice, his eyes darting side-ways. No one was paying attention.

"Parental love. And don't deny it. I've known you too well and too long," replied Armus, in the same low voice with a tone of certainty.

Kell glared at Armus. Their association from the Beginning created a bond that allowed Armus to speak to him in ways other Guardians would not dare. He sighed long and deep, giving a short nod of ascent. "I consider her my daughter in spirit. Don't tell anyone." Armus kept looking at him, which made him snicker. "I should know better than to say that. Thanks. Go. Tend to the Jor'ellians, I'll be fine now."

"About Shannan. What about Owain?"

Kell drew to his full height, his features fixed and eyes reflecting the authority of his station. "To whatever extent his plan succeeds or fails, I will make certain he answers for his rebellion. Without personal prejudice."

Armus cocked a satisfied smile. "Now, I'll tend to Jor'ellians, Captain," he emphasized the rank then saluted and departed.

Kell closed his eyes and became still. A moment later Elgin arrived on foot.

"You summoned me, Captain?"

"Go to Garwood. If Shannan is heading there she may arrive before Darius. Once you hear anything, report back. Although we might be on the move, so hone in my essence."

Elgin saluted, stepped back and vanished in dimension travel.

Chapter 7

LEAVING THE HOLLOW, Avatar led them to a small cave on a hill further north from Waldron. He stood guard at the opening while the others rested. Wess joined him.

"The wood is too damp to start a fire for food and warmth," said the youth.

"We're not spending the night. Whoever invaded Waldron will come searching for the queen and prince, if they haven't started already. Daylight will be shortly and we should get as far as possible in the dark."

"Avatar. How far to the North Plains?" asked Shannan.

"Too far. In order to intercept the king, we would need to double back or take another route around Waldron. Either option is too dangerous at present. Garwood is closer."

"Doesn't it take four days on horseback to reach Garwood from Waldron?" asked Wess.

"Ay, and possibly double on foot in this weather."

Nigel grew fussy so Shannan wrapped the blankets tighter around him. "Eight days out here is too long for him. You should take him to Melwynn while we go to Garwood."

"No, I won't leave the rest of you vulnerable."

"We'll protect the queen and Lady Arista," Wess said indicating Bosley.

Avatar grinned at the bravado. "Of course. However, something is wrong. I sense a darkness similar to what Dagar once commanded." He turned to Shannan while speaking. "I won't leave. Nor should we stay here much longer."

"The snow is still falling," complained Bosley.

Avatar glanced outside the cave. "Not as hard, and it will help cover our tracks."

"How will Vidar find us?"

Shannan smiled and Avatar chuckled before replying. "Vidar is the premier Guardian archer and hunter. He doesn't need tracks to follow. Time to go."

Shannan pulled up her cowl, stood, and readjusted Nigel to a more comfortable position for carrying.

"Bosley can carry the prince, Majesty," said Wess.

When Bosley tossed an annoyed side-glance at Wess, Shannan smiled. "I'll ask if I need help. Thank you for the offer. Both of you."

Wess formally nodded and Bosley gave an uncertain smile. "I'll keep the rear," Wess said to Avatar. Wess detained Bosley when Shannan and Arista followed Avatar. "Stay with the queen and prince."

"Who made you captain to you tell everyone what to do?"

"We all must help if are to survive, so stop being childish and selfish. Now go." He nudged Bosley after the others. Bosley hastened to catch up to them while Wess kept a proper rear guard.

Since he had to react and think fast during the invasion, Wess did not have time to fully consider the situation. Now he took time. He enjoyed listening to his uncle's stories of army life and was eager to join him. However, those stories and the limited training he received in arms, horsemanship and military strategy, did not prepare him for this. Still, he boasted of his abilities and desire. He couldn't show fear or indecision, not for the fact Bosley would tease him; he expected that no matter what he did, rather the lives of the queen and prince were at stake. Their only hope was Avatar. The Guardian rescued him, Bosley, his sisters and Iain from Ravendale's dungeon when Latham captured them to use as blackmail against Hugh. Avatar's presence was of great comfort and a boost to Wess' confidence.

Even if he weren't here, it is my duty to protect the others.

Wess slipped in the calf deep snow, yet managed to catch onto a tree and keep from falling. He glanced around to get his bearings. The whiteness of the ground helped with night visibility. New snow filled their tracks. Avatar was right about helping to cover their escape, yet made for slower going and uncertain footing. Arista's gait was unsteady, so he picked up his pace to join her.

"Footing is treacherous, my lady. I just slipped."

Arista hugged her arms close for warmth while trying to keep her balance. She glanced down to Wess' feet. "At least you're wearing boots. Slippers and stockings aren't much good in the snow. Nor is a robe."

"I wish I had something to help you keep warm." He wore a doublet, but no cloak.

"Aren't you cold?"

"I'm trying not to let it bother me."

Although it was almost too cold to smile, she did. Ahead, Arista observed Bosley walking beside Shannan. He tightened his belt to bring the large doublet closer to his body. He clenched the longer sleeves in his fists to keep his hands warm.

"Your brother is following your example of managing with what he has." Arista slipped and Wess caught her. "I wish I could say the same."

"Slippers are notoriously slick. Next time we stop, I'll find something that can grip better. In the meantime grab hold of me when you have need."

Weather didn't affect Guardians like mortals. Being on the run with five mortals, Avatar kept one eye out for danger and the other on the progress of his charges due to the extreme conditions. Occasionally he heard grumbling from Bosley and noticed Arista holding onto Wess' arm to keep her balance. Shannan tried using parts of Nigel's blanket to warm her hands, but it was more important to keep Nigel warm. He had to find a place for warmth and shelter.

Two hours later, he gathered them in a small grove of evergreen trees for a temporary rest, and to hide them from view. There was little snow under the trees and the rays of the morning sun grew stronger. Soon the temperature would climb and at least chase away the night's chill.

"Are you sure we should stop?" asked Shannan.

"For a little while. You must get the warmth back to your arms."

Nigel grew fussy, demanding Shannan's attention.

Bosley sat on a log. "I'll take him, Majesty."

"My arms could use a rest." She gave Nigel to him. She blew on her hands and rubbed her arms to increase circulation. Wess aided Arista to a large rock next to the log. Even with his help, a muffed cry of pain escaped. "Arista? Are you hurt?"

"No," she grunted. She reached down to rub her feet.

"Her slippers aren't holding up well against the cold," Wess explained to Shannan then asked Avatar. "Any suggestions?"

Avatar briefly thought before replying. "I have an idea." He used his dagger to cut off a portion of the hem of his uniform. He knelt in front of Arista. Taking one foot at a time, he carefully removed each slipper, and wrapped half the cut cloth around the foot before putting the slipper back on her foot. "The cloth should help."

She nodded, biting back the pain his administration caused.

"Can we build a small fire? The prince is cold," said Bosley. He arranged the blankets closer around Nigel while holding him as tight as he dare.

Avatar looked sympathetically at Nigel. "Unfortunately, no. The light and smoke can be seen and smelled for miles, alerting those who may be looking for us."

"How long before we move again?" asked Wess.

"When Lady Arista can walk."

"I can walk. We must get the prince to safety." She reached for Avatar to help her stand yet stumbled and clung to him.

"I can carry you."

She shook her head. "You're our only means of defense." She gingerly stood by herself.

Wess found a sturdy fallen branch for Arista. He then spoke to Avatar. "Take the queen, prince and Bosley and go on ahead, I'll help her."

Bosley carried Nigel. This was the first time he held an infant since his younger twin sisters were born. He was three years old and his mother made him sit in a chair before placing Cassie in his arms. After a few moments, she took Cassie and gave him Callie. He wasn't sure what to think at the time being so young. He remembered a sense of pride and responsibility. At least that's what his mother said because he was now an older brother like Wess and they were small and helpless and in need of his aid and protection. Eventually, that gave way to sibling rivalry. Now he held another infant, and one as helpless and in need of protection. Only this was the royal prince.

He recalled Wess scolding him about growing up and being responsible. He didn't like the way Wess spoke, commanding and mean. But was he being mean? Bosley glanced back at Wess helping Arista. He always took his responsibility seriously, and Bosley made fun of him. Now that he was charged with a serious task, he wasn't finding it funny. Nigel grew fussy.

"Hush, little prince. I'm here. I'll keep you warm and safe."

"You're doing very well with him," said Shannan.

Bosley was startled by her voice then smiled. "He's no trouble."

"No, but we are in trouble. I'm grateful for you and your brother's help."

His smile widened, then faded. "What do you think has happened at Waldron?"

"I don't know. Once we reach Garwood, I will find out and get word to the king we are safe."

Hearing a strange, echoing creature-like noise halted the conversation. Bosley nervously glanced up while Shannan became wary. "Stop and wait for the others, I'm going to speak to Avatar." She didn't wait for an answer.

The Guardian stopped to look up through the trees, a hand on the hilt of his sword.

"What do we do?" she asked.

"Find a place to hide before being spotted." He surveyed the forest while speaking. "That looks good." He pointed to a carved-out hollow beneath a massive oak tree on the far side of the large creek some fifty yards away. Unfortunately, the side of the embankment they were on was twice as high as the far side, perhaps thirty feet.

"The creek is running fast. There's no ice on the edges."

"We have no choice."

The others reached them when they heard the noise again, only closer and not echoing.

"Quick!" Avatar took Bosley by the shoulders and started down the creek embankment, holding him so he wouldn't slip with Nigel. Once at the bottom, he nudged Bosley towards the water's edge. "Cross to the hollow."

"How deep is it?"

Avatar waded out part way to where the water depth reached just below his knees. Hearing the creature, he hurried to shore. "Shallow enough to cross without swimming and the current isn't too strong. Now, go!"

Avatar helped Shannan when she slipped on the embankment. She then hastened to join Bosley, who was in the middle of the cold water and nearly chest deep. He struggled to keep Nigel from getting wet. She took his elbow to steady him.

The branch broke, sending Arista falling down the slope. Avatar caught her. This time the screeching sounded dangerously close, startling them.

"Hurry! Join the others," Avatar told Wess. He lifted Arista in his arms to carry her across.

At the hollow, Avatar set Arista on her feet. The hollow was large enough for the mortals to stand erect, but he had to kneel to fit. An ear-splitting cry frightened Nigel and he cried. Bosley tried to calm Nigel. A massive shadow passed over the creek and hollow.

Avatar placed a hand on Nigel and leaned close to whisper in the Ancient. *"Bi samhach agus cadail. Mise bheir dion sibh."* Nigel grew quiet.

Amazed, Bosley went to question Avatar, but the Guardian put a finger to his lips. They heard the creature again, and the shadow appeared from the opposite direction.

Wess dared to take a glance. A large grotesque-looking, black vulture with rotting flesh and feathers circled overhead. He recoiled and cast a fearful look to Avatar. "What is that thing?"

"A *sealgair-hagan*. A hunter-hawk. Once unleashed it won't return until it has killed its prey."

"Avatar," Shannan whispered in warning. The hunter-hawk landed on the embankment opposite the hollow. From head to the tip of its lizard like fantail, the hunter-hawk was nine feet with a wingspan twice its body length. It screeched at them, head reaching, wings spreading.

"When I engage it, run for your lives."

"I can help you," said Wess.

"No. You keep them safe." Avatar moved to the creek bed and drew his sword. "Be gone, creature of darkness, before you feel my blade!"

The hunter-hawk leapt off the rock toward Avatar. Instead of waiting to repel the attack, he raced into the water, his sword swinging. It tried to avoid the blade, only was too close to swerve away completely and Avatar slashed its body in passing. The hunter-hawk made a sharp bank up and away from the oak tree.

"Run!" Avatar shouted over his shoulder while watching the hunter-hawk arch up. Any moment it would make a steep fast dive at him. At the apex of the arch, he saw the others running along the water's edge, looking for a place to climb out.

Hearing the hunter-hawk's cry, he turned back in time to see the dive. He stood in the middle of the creek, braced his feet, sword ready, intent on dodging the talons and wounding it again. Only his plans weren't what the hunter-hawk had in mind.

At the last possible second it pulled up, talons outstretched toward him and made a vertical climb, whipping its tail and knocking him sideways into the water. His head came up in time to see the beak snap at him and dove underwater to avoid having his head bitten off. He surfaced a short distance away. The hunter-hawk circled the creek ready for another strike. He groped for his sword underwater, keeping a sharp eye on the creature. His hand gripped the hilt just as the hunter-hawk dove. Something struck the side of the creature's head and it banked away. Wess stood on top of the embankment near the oak tree preparing to throw another rock.

"I said run!"

"Look out!" Wess threw another rock at the hunter-hawk.

This time the creature avoided the rock and headed for Wess. The hunter-hawk positioned itself to snatch Wess, exposing its back to Avatar. The Guardian threw his dagger, striking where the neck and wings connected to its body. The force of the throw sent the hunter-hawk past a ducking Wess and smashing into the oak, collapsing into a huddled position at the base of the trunk.

When Wess approached the hawk, Avatar seized him. The Guardian plunged his sword through the creature's head to make certain it was dead.

"Where there is one hunter-hawk there could be more. We have to prevent whoever sent it from discovering the carcass or they'll know we were found."

Avatar pulled his dagger out of the creature and wiped it, and his sword, clean on the feathers before sheathing both blades. He grunted with effort to lift the hunter-hawk and throw it down into the creek. The carcass sank before bouncing to the surface and floated away on the current.

"You're supposed to be looking after the others," he scolded Wess.

"The queen ordered me to come back. She said if anything happens to you who would watch over Prince Nigel?"

Avatar shook his head and grunted in frustration. "She is a headstrong mortal."

"She's the queen."

Avatar couldn't help a chuckle. "Where are they?"

"Not far ahead." Wess led the way to where the others waited in a small shelter alcove.

Bosley sat on the ground holding Nigel, speaking softly to him while Nigel made noises between fussy and cooing. Arista sat next to Bosley unwrapping her feet. Shannan paced and whirled about in anticipation when Avatar and Wess arrived.

"Thank Jor'el you're both safe," she said in relief.

Avatar cocked a reproving brow. "You took a risk sending the boy back."

"I couldn't let anything happen to you. Who would take care of Nigel?"

"That's what I told him, Majesty."

"At the moment, my responsibility is to protect all of you not just an individual," Avatar said to Wess, before drawing Shannan a few steps away to speak in private. "I appreciate your concern and desire for your son's safety, Daughter of Allon, but would you have me forfeit the lives of everyone?" He purposely used the Prophetic title linking her to the Guardians, rather than her mortal title of queen.

"I used that excuse to get Wess to obey. He was reluctant to leave."

"And well he should. I gave him a charge."

With a firm, stubborn expression, she regarded him. "You called me Daughter of Allon, so you know I will do what I can to protect the lives and welfare of Guardians. Your life is as important to me as my son."

"I appreciate that more than I can say. And I remember our dangerous venture into the nether dimension. However, if a life is too be sacrificed, let it mine and not Nigel, or anyone else."

His silver eyes showed the sincerity and unction of his words and she sighed in resignation. "I pray that choice doesn't happen."

"So do I," he said, a smile growing as he glanced back to Bosley entertaining Nigel. "There is a certain appeal to a mortal infant I've found surprisingly pleasant."

She chuckled, her humor short-lived. "Right now he's uncomfortable and fussy." She went back to Bosley and took Nigel. He squirmed and his lips were blue so she wrapped the blanket closer for warmth. "He's getting cold," she said to Avatar.

"I tried to keep him warm," said Bosley. He stood and stomped his feet trying to get warm, but his pants and boots were wet. "My feet are cold."

"So are Lady Arista's." Wess indicated Arista, who vigorously rubbed her bare, red feet.

"No, stop!" Avatar knelt and seized her hands. "Frostbite only gets worse by rubbing. You must leave the wrappings on."

She picked up the wrappings from off her lap. "These are wet and cold. What good are they?"

He took the strips and cupped his hands around them. "*Blath de Leus*," he spoke in the Ancient then blew on the cloths for well over a minute. When he was done, he bowed his head and closed his eyes, deeply breathing for recovery.

"Avatar?" asked Shannan.

"I'm all right. The cloth is dry now." He wrapped Arista's feet.

She marveled. "They're not only dry, but warm. How?"

He wryly smiled. "Something I've picked up over the centuries."

"Is there anything you can't do?" asked Bosley, impressed.

"Ay, I can't dimension travel all of you safety at once. Otherwise I would have done so and avoided all of this."

"How many can you take at one time?"

"Two. Which leaves the rest vulnerable, and after our encounter with the hunter-hawk, that is out of the question. Everyone must do what is told, without question or complaint." Gravity filled the silver gaze passing between the youths.

Wess straightened, his hand resting on the hilt of his sword. "We won't fail the queen or prince." He slapped Bosley's arm at seeing his brother frowning.

"Ay."

"I know you won't," Shannan spoke with certainty.

"We've talked and rested enough. There may be more hunter-hawks." Avatar took the lead. Shannan carried Nigel. Bosley and Arista followed with Wess kept the rear guard.

Her feet warm and wrapped, Arista kept up with the others. However, further northeast they traveled the hilly and more densely forested the terrain became. This helped to stay out of clear view of hunter-hawks, but more difficult for navigating the five inches of snow covering even the most shaded of ground.

Rest became infrequent, and only done for water and a few moments to catch their breath after a difficult climb or descent. Every time they considered stopping for a lengthy rest and to search for food, Avatar sensed danger and pressed their journey.

By mid-afternoon, Arista again lagged behind. Wess slowed to stay with her. Bosley took Nigel so Shannan could rest her arms and get some warmth back in her hands. However, Nigel's fussiness grew more frequent.

"Avatar, we have to stop and get Nigel warm," said Shannan.

"I know. I'll scout ahead, you wait for Arista and Wess."

Avatar discovered an abandon bear's den that would serve to shelter the mortals. Upon returning to the others, he caught the disappointment in Arista's eyes. The bandages were only a temporarily help. He spoke to Shannan.

"I found a bear's den."

"Won't the bear return? They hibernate in winter," said Bosley.

"It's been abandoned for a some time." Avatar took Nigel from Bosley and headed for the cave.

With help from Bosley and Wess, Arista entered the cave and sat.

"The bear made a decent nest. Judging by the size, I'd say she had three cubs," said Shannan. She sat and received Nigel from Avatar.

"Can we start a fire?" asked Bosley.

Avatar shook his head. "No. One spark and this old nest would go up like kindling. You'll be fine soon. It must be five to seven degrees warmer in here." He cocked a brow at Bosley upon hearing a gurgling and growl.

The boy held his stomach, his voice sheepish. "I'm hungry."

"So is the prince," said Arista. She tried to help soothe Nigel.

"Unfortunately, I can't help the prince. I'll try to find something for the rest of you to eat. If a bear made a den here, there must be some winter berry bushes nearby."

Wess took up position at the entrance when Avatar left. *What a contrast the brothers are, one most willing to help, the other reluctant. Still, when pressed, Bosley does comply.* All the same, he wouldn't leave the safety of the queen and prince to the youths for long and quickly gathered berries and pine nuts.

Bosley accepted the nuts and berries. "Will there be enough for everyone to eat?"

Avatar handed a portion to Wess while answering. "Guardians do not need food like mortals. We can survive without eating. Our physical bodies are only to facilitate serving in our duty." He gave a portion to Arista then took Nigel from Shannan before giving her the remainder.

"But I've seen Guardians bleed and heard of some who died in the battle that defeated Uncle Marcellus," said Wess. He slowly ate his portion.

Avatar sat between Wess and Shannan. He laid Nigel on his lap, and folded part of his uniform over the infant for added warmth. "Our physical bodies are just as fragile as yours, and mortals can injure us, but not kill us. And we heal very fast. Those Guardians who died where killed by Shadow Warriors, Guardians who turned to the Dark Way."

"How?"

Avatar's face grew taut, his eyes narrowing. "Many endured torture for centuries before succumbing. Others willingly joined Dagar. Either way, they betrayed Jor'el and our station."

Wess watched Avatar's reaction with concern. "Were you tortured?"

"No!" Avatar's sharp tone startled Nigel, who cried. Avatar spoke the Ancient in a soothing tone, laid his hand on Nigel and calmed the infant.

"What do you say to make him quiet?" asked Bosley.

"Words of reassurance and a touch for comfort."

"For not being a Overseer before, you're doing very well," teased Shannan.

"What's an Overseer?" asked Bosley.

Shannan sent a quick, mischievous side-glance to Avatar. "A nanny."

Avatar chuckled. "You've been around Armus too long." His attention went back to Nigel, when Nigel began sucking on the tip of his little finger stained by berry juice. A few times Nigel screwed up his face but continued to suckle. "Are the berries sour?"

"No. All he's had is milk. Here." Shannan mashed her remaining two berries onto Avatar's fingertip. He, in turn, let Nigel take the juice.

"Won't it make him sick?" asked Arista.

Shannan frowned with regret. "Right now it's better than nothing."

Arista tried to be reassuring. "We'll find a nurse when we reach Garwood."

After a brief silence, Wess spoke, sheepish, but curious. "Avatar." He waited to get the Guardian's attention from Nigel. "About what I asked you earlier. I'd like to know. I need to know."

For a moment Avatar regarded Wess. At sixteen, he experienced more than many his age. Born into royalty, he witnessed his aunt afflicted with disease by the Dark Way for confronting evil; an uncle using the Dark Way to secure his reign; his mother killed by Latham to ensure his father's cooperation; and survived the coup that took down his family and restored the House Tristan. Now, the Dark Way returned and he was again entangled in a desperate situation. He deserved an answer.

"After our escapade from Ravendale, I was able to offer intelligence concerning the castle and Latham, which we used in freeing others from their imprisonment. Mahon and Vidar were among those Dagar tortured." His brows furrowed in concern. "Both of whom I hope and pray are well."

Shannan gave him a supportive clasp on his arm. "I know they are."

He looked directly at her. "I can sense Vidar, but Mahon's essence is faint. I am more concerned for him."

"Is Mahon your friend?" asked Wess.

"My friend and protégé. I trained him centuries ago when he was a new young warrior."

"How old are you?" asked Bosley.

"Over eighteen hundred of your mortal years."

Bosley and Wess gaped in wonder. "And Mahon?" asked Wess.

"Fourteen hundred."

"I didn't know Guardians live so long."

"Kell, Vidar and Armus are over two thousand years old and among the Originals. The first groups of Guardians created. Kell was the first of all of us, then Jor'el created the rest in two hundred year intervals, ending after eight hundred years."

"Why? He couldn't have created you all at once?"

He chuckled. "Of course, but this way we were eased into dealing with mortals."

"Don't you mean so mortals could grow accustommed to sarcastic Guardians?" quipped Shannan.

He heaved a shrug and smiled. "Consider it mutual in becoming acquainted."

"So you grow up?" asked Bosley.

Avatar heartily laughed. "No. We are created fully-grown and capable of performing all our duties. Kell instituted apprenticeship to help in learning how to deal with mortals since our character and natures are vastly different. Kell and Armus mentored me and then I mentored Mahon."

"Has he mentored anyone?"

"No, and he won't since no new Guardians have been created in over a thousand years."

"How long did you train him?" asked Wess.

"Almost three hundred years. The length of time varies depending upon the caste to which the Guardian belongs. Warriors take the longest since much is required of us."

"So how long do you live?" asked Arista.

"Our spirits are immortal while in physical form only a Guardian can kill another Guardian. When that happens our spirit returns to our former station in the heavenlies."

Wess' features were pensive, his voice glum. "Then Guardians kill each other like mortals."

Avatar's response was emphatic, but controlled in volume so as not to disturb Nigel. "No! Taking another Guardian's physical lifeforce is forbidden. Those who do, face unthinkable, eternal consequences. Dagar knew this when he made the others turn."

"So Shadow Warriors kill without regard for those consequences," Wess concluded, staring mercilessly at the ground. "Witter was a Shadow Warrior. What about Tyree? I remember he was a ruthless, cold man. I hated him and I feared him."

"Tyree was mortal."

Avatar felt a grip on his arm. Shannan shook her head in a gesture of sympathetic caution. In profile, Wess' jowls tenses and eyes narrowed. Bosley retreated against the wall. Avatar's tone grew light.

"Speaking of mortals, have the berries and nuts settled your growling stomach, Master Bosley?"

"A bit."

"Good. And do you feel warmer?"

"A bit."

"Even better since we should be leaving."

"Can't we stay the night? After all it is warm and sheltered. Who knows when and where we'll find something else to rest or food to eat."

Avatar's considering gaze passed to Shannan, to which she said, "His reasoning is sound."

He looked out of the opening to see the colors of twilight. "Very well. There isn't much daylight left anyway."

"I'll take the first watch," said Wess.

"No need. Guardians don't require sleep. You can all rest." He gave Nigel to Shannan and moved to the opening. He drew his sword and sat cross-legged with the sword on his lap.

Later in the night, Nigel cried in pain. Avatar took Nigel from Shannan to quiet him so he wouldn't wake the others. Again, she expressed her frustration at being unable to feed him. Since a nurse took over the duties of feeding, she was incapable of helping her own son, and that upset her.

Nigel grew quiet, although he remained awake. Avatar coaxed Shannan to go back to sleep while he kept Nigel on his lap, the sword on the ground beside him. He sat with his back to the entrance to shield Nigel from the cold. Nigel squirmed and screwed his face in discomfort. Avatar laid his hand over his charge.

He leaned down and whispered, "If I could do more for you, I would, but for now I can only help you sleep. So do so in Jor'el's peace."

Avatar's hand remained on Nigel. It was gratifying to see Nigel's face now peaceful in sleep. After eighteen hundred years of observing, interacting and protecting mortals, in only few days, he felt closer to Nigel than to any mortal.

He heard a soft stirring. Shannan moved, but did not wake. At that moment he understood Vidar's dedication and Kell's diligent concern for her went beyond duty, it went to their heart. There was private teasing and snickering about experiencing mortal 'parental love,' which was taken in good humor. Well, at least Vidar did. No one dared to say too much to Kell. Not for fear, rather out of respect for his position. Of course Armus said anything to Kell. Being Kell's aide, he could speak more freely than others. Still, he chose to be discreet about certain subjects, and labeling a Guardian with mortal feelings could be considered an insult. Guardians controlled their emotions and didn't let them interfere with duty. Now, his duty to Nigel took on a more personal meaning.

When a sleeping Wess moved, he inadvertently kicked Avatar's sword out of reach. To retrieve his sword, Avatar removed his hand from Nigel. Almost immediately, Nigel grew fussy. Avatar put the sword back within reach, and replaced his hand on Nigel.

"Easy, my dear one. I'm still here."

Nigel settled down, only Avatar would not remove his hand again.

At the first gray light of dawn, Avatar roused his charges. They were groggy and hungry. He foresaw the hunger and gathered more nuts and berries prior to dealing with Nigel. Bosley frowned, yet ate without comment. That was some improvement in attitude.

Avatar readjusted Arista's bandages. Her feet were redder than the day before. When he finished tending her, he insisted on inspecting everyone's feet for signs of frostbite. The others wore boots with wool socks and Nigel was tightly wrapped in blankets. Their feet showed some signs of being affected by the cold. He would have to keep a close eye on their progress, yet move quickly if they were to reach Garwood without further suffering.

Avatar led them from the den heading northeast. No fresh snow fell overnight but the morning was bitterly cold. After two hours, Arista lagged behind. Wess aided her, only this time her pain was obvious and her gait slow and uneven. She grimaced, and her grip on Wess was hard, making him wince, though he never complained.

Unfortunately, Avatar couldn't do much to alter the situation. They had to reach Garwood. His eyes narrowed in consideration and he prayed under his breath. "Jor'el, direct my steps to be sure and swift in bringing them to safety."

Up ahead, the trees ended at a clearing. He waved the others to stop before carefully making his way to the tree line. He crouched down to avoid being seen. Shannan joined him. His attention was on the field. The morning light reflected off the pristine blanket of snow.

"Do you sense something?" she asked.

"No. Staying in the trees is better than venturing out in the open."

For a moment she too studied their surroundings, comparing the length of the field to the tree line. "If we stay in the forest it will take too long to go around and I don't know about adding time. Nigel's already cold and hungry and I don't believe Arista's feet can take much more."

"Ay, but I want to get everyone to Garwood safely." He again studied the field against the trees. "We have no choice. We must cross in the open." He glanced back to see Bosley about five yards behind them with Arista and Wess ten yards further from Bosley. "I'll have to carry her again. How is Bosley doing with Nigel?"

She grinned. "Very well."

When the others reached them, Avatar told of his plan. "Take the lead. I'll follow with Lady Arista," he said to Wess.

"I don't know if this is a good idea," said Arista.

He turned his back to her and got down on one knee. "Climb on. If there is trouble, I can set you down quickly." He felt her comply by placing her arms on his shoulders. He wrapped his arms about her legs, hoisted her up and stood. "Hold on, I intend to move fast."

The others reached the halfway point when Avatar, with Arista on his back, left the wood. Guardians could outrun horses with ease, so Arista gasped in surprise when he started running. What happened next, happened quickly.

Ear-piercing screeches filled their ears. Eight leathery, winged, reptile creatures attacked them. Avatar tried to ease Arista to the ground. Unfortunately, in dodging one of the creatures, he slipped and both fell. A creature leapt at her, and with a swipe of his arm, Avatar knocked it aside. As he reached for his sword, another sank its teeth into his right side. He cried out, seized it by the neck and squeezed, trying to choke it into releasing him. His right knee buckled, but he kept squeezing. The creature made horrible gurgling sounds before its neck finally snapped and it went limp. He tossed it aside and collapsed to his hands and knees, grimacing in painful annoyance.

"Look out!" Arista warned.

Still down, he whipped out his sword and cleaved the creature in two. He fell back to all fours.

She knelt next to him for support. "How badly are you hurt?"

He growled in frustration. "My feet and ankles are numb." He watched the scene unfold. Wess was knocked aside by a creature. Shannan fell to her knees trying to avoid one leaping at her. Bosley had Nigel and was running for the far trees. Avatar used his sword to try to stand, but was unsuccessful. "The numbness is growing up my legs."

Bosley pulled up in fearful surprise. Holding Nigel protectively against his body, he turned and ran back toward the others. A large wolf bounded from the trees. The wolf leapt. He dropped to his knees to shield Nigel. The back legs of the wolf brushed passed his head. He dared to look up. The wolf jumped over him and snared one of the creatures out of the air by the neck.

Twang! Whiz! An arrow shot over his head and struck another creature. He was uncertain where the arrow came from and balked when someone appeared next to him say, "Are you all right?"

He blinked at seeing a stunningly beautiful woman kneeling beside him. She had long auburn hair and bright green eyes in a flawless complexion and wore a forester-brown jerkin with a green cowl and leather belt. The breeches were of identical color to the jerkin and tucked into knee-high leather boots. A plain-sheathed dagger and leather pouch hung from the belt.

She carried a crossbow and quiver of arrows. He could only nod when she helped him stand. At that moment he gaped at her height, seven feet by reckoning.

"You're a Guardian."

She smiled. "My name is Wren, young master, you are in my province." Her attention was diverted to Nigel, who grew fussy. "He appears unhurt."

A flash of white light materialized behind Wren. She became alert the instant a large hulking Shadow Warrior appeared. His backhand sent her flying sideways. He drew his sword to hack at her and she used her crossbow to intercept his blow. He pressed his weight down on her. She sneered in angry determination and locked her arms only he was gaining the advantage.

"*Kato, ionnsaigh!*" she called in the Ancient. He knocked her bow away and stunned her with a glancing blow to the head.

The cry of an eagle sounded before its talons clipped the Warrior in the head. He tumbled to one side to avoid another attack. The diversion worked, he left Wren to deal with Kato.

Two more Shadow Warriors appeared near Shannan and Wess. One was Nari, the other a male with a grizzly beard and sneer. Twang! A shot from behind struck the male and he vanished in a flash of grey light. The distraction was all Shannan needed to throw her dagger, which lodged in the back of Nari's left shoulder. She staggered, reaching to dislodge the dagger.

Vidar joined Shannan and Wess and handed her the Golden Bow. Before Nari retaliated, Shannan was armed with the weapon pointed at her. Nari hissed in anger.

"Not so fast, Daughter of Allon!" called Burris.

When Shannan turned, Nari took advantage of the distraction to retreat into the trees. Shannan's aim faltered at seeing Burris holding Nigel in one arm and Bosley on his knees, doubled over in pain. Nigel cried.

"Shoot and your son dies."

"No!" Bosley shouted and launched at Burris.

Burris caught Bosley by the throat, the boy struggling and gasping for breath. He laughed with hauteur when Bosley went limp. "Pitiful using a boy

116

to defend your son." He tossed Bosley aside like a rag doll. The boy landed fifteen away, unmoving.

"Bosley!" Wess fearfully exclaimed. He received no answer and with painful anger, gripped his sword, pointing it at Burris. "You killed my brother!"

"He's alive!" said Vidar.

Bosley remained on the ground heaving in large gulps of air.

"You think you can do better, boy?" Burris bared his teeth at Wess.

"You'll deal with me if any are harmed," said Vidar.

Burris laughed, loud and mocking, making Nigel cry louder.

Avatar sneered in fierce anger at seeing Burris toss aside Bosley and taunt Shannan, Wess and Vidar. Making a quick scan of the field, he estimated a dozen Shadow Warriors surrounded them. The numbness now reached past his knees, but he had to act. He drove his sword point into the ground and used the pommel to push up and stand, bracing his balance. The Warriors reacted to his movement. He jerked his sword out from the ground using both hands and raised the pommel in front of his face, the blade pointing skyward.

"*An dealanach siuthad!*" he shouted and thrust the sword above his head. A sudden clap of deafening thunder resounded over the field. Shafts of blinding light flashed from his sword in all directions.

Wren shaded her eyes against the flashes. Vidar snatched Shannan, turning his back to Avatar to protect her. Wess leapt aside to shield Arista while Bosley lowered his head. In the trees Nari just dislodged the dagger when she heard the thunder and dove for cover.

The creatures let out loud screaming cries when struck by lightning before exploding and vanishing. Some Shadow Warriors turned to run while others attempted to shield their eyes from the light. None escaped the bolts. When all the creatures and Shadow Warriors were gone, the lightning stopped and thunder faded. The clearing grew still and quiet.

Shannan peaked under Vidar's protective arms and saw nothing. No Shadow Warriors, no creatures. Standing away from him, she noticed Avatar on his knees leaning against his sword in great distress. Nigel laid on the ground next to him. She rushed over and fell to her knees, scooping up Nigel. She examined him for sign of injury. He was unharmed however, Avatar was ashen, his eyes half closed.

"Avatar?"

He barely lifted his head to look at her. "Is he hurt?"

"No, he's fine."

Avatar collapsed to the ground. In fear she watched Wren and Vidar determine Avatar's injuries.

Wess helped Arista to join them. Bosley scrambled though the snow to them. "Is he dead?" he asked.

"No, unconscious," replied Wren, much to everyone's relief. She eyed Vidar's injuries. "Can you help me get him to the trees?"

"Ay." Vidar positioned himself to lift Avatar using his left arm and not his injured right shoulder. However, he flinched in pain when moving.

They placed Avatar on the ground and leaned him against a large oak. He woke, groggy and a bit disorientated at first.

"Avatar? Are you badly hurt?" asked Shannan.

"I can't feel anything below my hips."

Wren examined his wound. "The bite is deep and nasty."

"What were those creatures?" asked Wess.

"Kelpies, demonic creatures of the Dark Way. Their poisonous bites are deadly to mortals but a nuisance to Guardians. It'll take a while for the feeling in his legs to return."

Avatar's voice was weak. "Where did the Shadow Warriors come from?"

"They must have been among those who took Waldron," replied Vidar.

"Is that how you got wounded?" Wren asked Vidar, who nodded.

Despite his injured and weakened state, Avatar rubbed his legs in an attempt to stimulate sensation. "We can't stay here."

"You can't go anywhere, and that's not going to work," said Wren. Avatar growled in determination and more vigorously massaged and smacked his legs in hope of regaining sensation. She seized his wrists to stop him. "Your wound has to be medicined for the numbness to go away."

"She right," said Vidar.

Avatar sighed in resignation and sat back against the tree. Wren reached into the pouch on her belt and pulled out two vials. She sprinkled a cream colored powder from one vial onto Avatar's wound. He winced, gritting his teeth.

She sent a small, satisfied smile to Vidar before pouring some of the contents of the second vial on a cloth. It was a dark thick liquid with a rather pungent smell. She placed the wetted cloth against Avatar's side and he hissed. She put one of his hands over the cloth. "Hold it in place while I bandage it."

His face screwed up when he leaned forward so she could wrap the bandage around his waist. She finished and he gingerly rested against the tree. "You enjoyed that," he grumbled before closing his eyes.

Wren grinned and went to tend Vidar.

"How long until Avatar can move?" asked Arista.

"With a bite that bad, a few hours at least. I suggest you get some rest," replied Wren.

"Can we build a fire?" asked Bosley.

"Ay," replied Wren, but "No," refuted Avatar at the same time, his eyes opening.

Wren sternly looked at him. "I can shield them. You are in my element now, warrior."

Avatar's disputing glance found Vidar, who said, "She can. We both can."

"You're also injured."

Vidar moved for Wren to put powder on his side wound. "Not as badly as you, I can still function."

"Avatar, you must rest or you'll be no good to any of us," said Shannan.

Without further protest, he closed his eyes.

Bosley shied when the wolf nudged past him to stand next to Shannan. "It could have killed us."

Shannan chuckled and patted the wolf's head. "Torin won't hurt you."

"Torin? Didn't he help you against Dagar?" asked Wess.

"Ay. He roams the forest around Waldron." Torin's nose reached toward Nigel. "My son." Torin sniffed Nigel then gently licked his cheek.

"Amazing," said Arista.

The cry of an eagle came from a nearby branch. "That's Kato. He also helped Ellis and me," said Shannan. "I wasn't ignoring you. I didn't know you were here," she said when Kato squawked and flapped his wings.

Wren chuckled. "Kato, keep watch." The eagle gave a reply before taking off. "Now, if the young masters will fetch wood and start a fire, I'll find food after I finish tending Vidar."

"Go with them, Torin," said Shannan. The wolf hesitated, so she added, "Vidar will remain." Torin followed Wess and Bosley. Shannan turned her attention to watching Wren's administration of Vidar's shoulder. He grimaced. "You functioned rather poorly. Normally you would have taken down three in the time you got off one shot."

"At least I can walk." He hissed louder than Avatar when Wren put a bandage soaked with the thick liquid on his shoulder.

"Sorry. Hold it while I secure the bandage."

He didn't relax until she was done. She packed up her pouch and headed out to hunt.

Shannan gave Nigel to Arista and sat next to Vidar. "How bad were things when you left?"

"I suspect Waldron has fallen. Whoever is behind this is determined to destroy you, Ellis, and Nigel."

Her brows furrowed in deep thought. "I should have Avatar take Nigel to Melwynn and you take the rest to Garwood while I join Ellis."

"No, he won't be recovered enough to dimension travel, and it would be foolish to go by yourself." He squirmed in discomfort. "We'll get everyone to safety, then decide how to reunite you and Ellis."

Wren returned carrying two rabbits. "Are the boys not back yet?"

Vidar snickered. "Mortal boys can't compete with a Guardian huntress who cheats."

Her smile grew teasing. "I could have been quicker." She set about preparing the rabbits to cook.

It wasn't until she was done that Wess and Bosley returned. Wess built a fire and tried to use flint rock to ignite the wood.

"*Teine.*" Wren flicked her fingers at the wood. Immediately, fire appeared. When she set the spit with the rabbits over the flames she noticed Bosley's baffled expression. "Something troubling you, young master?"

"I'm not used to seeing Guardians use their powers, though I remember Avatar rescuing us from Ravendale. I thought he was the most powerful being I'd even seen. How did he do what he did today?"

"His name means *He of the Lightning Sword,* but it only happens when he uses his full power."

"Full power?"

Vidar replied. "Jor'el created us with strength and power equal to our task. Since warriors have the greatest responsibilities, they are the strongest. Still, it is dangerous for us to use our full power in physical form and only done in extreme circumstances."

Wren continued, "Normally I can command four animals simultaneously. Going beyond that, requires a great deal of my energy." She soberly glanced to Avatar, who slept. "The first time I witnessed him use his power was at the Great Battle after Dagar seriously wounded Kell. Forty Shadow Warriors surrounded those of us who remained. I was certain we would be defeated. Avatar stepped between them and us. Again acting the heroic fool, or so I thought," she said with a small, wry smile. "When he spoke the Ancient and raised his sword I didn't know what to expect. The force knocked everyone down. When it was over, they were gone, the same way as earlier. We survived, but he almost drained his entire lifeforce to save us."

Bosley listened, concern on his face. "Will he die now?"

She shook her head and kindly smile. "No. His color is returning and he is sleeping peacefully." Arista grimaced and rubbed her feet. "Are you in pain, my lady?"

"Because of frostbite, Avatar was carrying her when we were attacked," said Shannan.

"I can help with that." Wren proceeded to tend to Arista's feet.

"I'll arrange sleeping pallets and make certain the fire is prepared for the night." Vidar cleared the ground surrounding the fire of remaining snow, rocks and debris. He also spoke the Ancient to dry the wet areas where snow melted from the heat then arranged soft plucked winter grass and weeds for pallets. "No blankets, but we'll keep the fire a good temperature to compensate," he said when completed.

Wren finished tending Arista's feet and packed her supplies into her pouch. "I'll take the prince so you can sleep." She took Nigel from Shannan.

"He is fussy from hunger and activity. Avatar tried to keep him calm and help him sleep. Unfortunately, we couldn't find any ginger root to soothe his stomach."

Wren smiled. "I will. Now, get some sleep."

Shannan moved to the pallets. Bosley's eyes were already closed. Wess helped Arista to lie down. Any movement caused her pain. Shannan lay with her head toward Arista and watched Wess move to his pallet.

"Truly, you are in great pain," she spoke in a low private voice.

"I'll manage."

"Perhaps you should have remained at Waldron."

"No," Arista's voice rose, disturbing Wess.

"Is there a problem?" he asked.

"No. Go to sleep," replied Shannan with a kind smile. She waited for him to settle down and close his eyes to continue the conversation. "Your loyalty and friendship is appreciated but I wish I could spare you suffering."

"Having painful feet is a small price to pay to see you and Nigel safe. My only regret is I didn't listen to you and tell Darius—" she couldn't finish, her voice choked by emotion, tears swelling.

Shannan moved to comfort Arista. "Don't fret. I know Darius loves you. Besides, once Ellis learns about Waldron he will dispatch Darius to find us."

"You think so?"

"I know he will. There is no man Ellis trusts more. And with Darius will come Jasper, who won't let Darius go into danger alone. Kell might come, but I'd rather Ellis kept him close to face battle. Our task is to survive until we are either found or reach Garwood. But whichever happens," her tone grew teasing, "you will tell Darius or else I will."

Arista began to laugh yet stifled it to prevent disturbing Wess and Bosley. "Ay."

"We'll make sure you survive to do just that," said Vidar. He sat on the log nearest Shannan cleaning his crossbow and not looking at them. "Now, get some sleep."

Chapter 8

ALTHOUGH A MORTAL inflicted her wound, Nari chose to make her way back to Waldron on foot rather than dimension travel. Any impairment compromised abilities and dimension travel required a great deal of energy and control. She held her left arm close to her body and growled in annoyance when Cletus confronted her.

"What happened to you?"

"Where's the mistress?"

"In the hall. Why?"

Nari didn't reply and headed to the main building, Cletus following. Musetta was in conference with Owain and Roane. Nari bowed, wincing in pain. "I'm sorry to report that we failed."

"What? How?" demanded Musetta.

"Something unforeseen, and I've never encountered," began Nari in contrition. "We had the Daughter of Allon surrounded and Burris held the prince when *he* stood and spoke in the Ancient."

"Who?"

"Avatar." Her fellow Warriors scowled at the name, but Musetta became angry and Owain concerned, thus she hastily continued. "He is a powerful Guardian warrior, mistress. A kelpie bit him, yet he managed to rise and speak the Ancient to invoke his power. Thunder and lightning came from his sword, striking down the kelpies and destroying the others."

Owain was skeptical. "And how did you survive?"

"The Daughter of Allon wounded me before he acted and I retreated to the trees to tend my wound. I dove for cover. Seeing none left, I returned to tell you."

Owain spoke his displeasure to Musetta. "If your Shadow Warriors can't withstand her and Avatar - "

"Wren and Vidar appeared. Although Vidar was injured," said Nari.

"One Guardian or three doesn't matter. If you and your supposed invincible companions are ineffective, we will fail!"

Musetta grasped the talisman, making Owain stiffen. He didn't flinch in pain or withdraw. Instead she spoke. "We are not defeated yet. We hold Waldron and can cause more diversionary trouble for him until the Daughter of Allon and prince are dealt with."

"Do you even know where they are now?" Owain demanded of Nari

"A meadow two days northwest of here."

"I'll send out a patrol immediately."

Roane took offense. "Mortals only?"

The question stopped Owain's departure, the mortal lord very angry. "Your kind failed!" He marched from the hall.

"How can mortals succeed when we have failed?" Cletus chided.

"Burris was arrogant, taunting the Daughter of Allon. That's when Avatar acted. If Burris had taken the boy and not shown off, the situation might have ended differently," said Nari. She grimaced in pain, holding her arm.

Musetta fingered the talisman. "There will be other opportunities. We need Owain and his mortal forces—for now. Any word on where his family is hiding?" she asked Roane.

"They are not with friends or family. They maybe at a Fortress." He spoke the last sentence with reluctance.

"So? Shadow Warrior's helped Tyree to clear the Fortresses when searching for the Son of Tristan."

Roane squared his shoulders and glared down at Musetta. "I was among them. Jor'el prevented us from trespassing or harming anyone inside the Fortresses. We could do nothing until they were outside."

"How did you get them to leave?"

"They were ignorant of what power we did or didn't possess and our reputation greatly feared. Tyree was free to act. He set fire to a few of the Fortresses."

Musetta's eyes narrowed in consideration. "Continue the search, but quietly. The longer Owain believes we know their whereabouts the more sway we have. Tend to your wound." Cletus, Nari and Roane turned to leave. "Not you, Roane, I have a special task for you." She fetched her satchel, opened it and carefully pulled out a box shrouded by a black cloth. The box was about eight inches high by five inches wide. "Take this and follow Owain's patrol. Once they have found the Daughter of Allon and her son, unleash it."

He reached for the box. "What is it?"

She held onto the box while replying, "A *tardundeen.*" He balked, staring in wide-eyed apprehension. "I thought Shadow Warriors weren't afraid of anything." She released the box so he had full possession of it.

"I thought they were all destroyed after the Great Battle."

"Except this one. Dagar kept it should his plan to destroy the Son of Tristan fail. Unfortunately, he didn't have a chance to use it."

The explanation did little to ease Roane's uneasiness.

Her grin grew caustic. "It's perfectly safe until you throw the box and speak the Ancient command. *Lor-*"

"I know it!"

She still smiled. "Good. Then you know to run. Now, go. Follow the patrol."

A nagging sense of futility gnawed at his brain as Owain dispatched the patrol. He knew the outcome of this business would be deadly, only he never envisioned the scope of Musetta's plan until after they seized Waldron. This went beyond a coup; she wanted to destroy the royal family.

You're only fooling yourself if you claim ignorance. You just didn't want to acknowledge the truth. Ellis will never accept defeat. You did not think past the impulse of the moment. That is Lanay's strength.

He gripped the hilt of his sword when pain racked him at the thought of his wife. He couldn't show inner turmoil to the departing patrol. After the last man left, he headed toward the hall. He didn't see Roane rush to follow the patrol, nor the shrouded box tucked under his arm.

A captain of the guard saluted Owain. "Sir, Lord Hugh requests to speak with you. He says it's very important."

This was the last thing Owain wanted to hear. He couldn't imagine what Hugh could say that was so important. He followed the guard to the barracks where Hugh was being held in one of the dormitory rooms. While the door was being unlocked, Owain braced himself for the encounter as the word *traitor* echoed in his ears. Hugh spoke with such vehemence he couldn't forget the voice or face. The door opened and he saw Hugh lying on the bed. He only took one step into the room.

"You asked to speak with me?"

Hugh's eyes narrowed in caustic surveillance of Owain. "You look no different. How did the witch get you to betray him?"

Owain jowls tightened with insult. "I didn't come here to discuss myself. So speak your piece, I have business to attend."

Hugh sat up and swung his feet over the side of the bed. "Appearances can be deceiving. I don't think Ellis or anyone thought you had the backbone to raise rebellion."

Rigid with insult, Owain turned to leave.

"Wait!" said Hugh while quickly rising. Owain turned back and Hugh drew closer to speak privately. "You have a chance to reverse your fortunes and maybe even convince Ellis of the reason for your actions."

"What reason?"

"To kill the witch."

Owain stared at Hugh, the words startling.

"Shouldn't be too hard, you can get close enough."

"You mean like you did with Marcellus?"

Hugh winced and grew defensive. "For the better good! My brother was controlled by Latham and the Dark Way, just like this witch is doing to you."

Owain's hands balled into fists to stem the rising tide of guilt and frustration. He abruptly left, ignoring Hugh's string of supplications. The words startled him at first then became frightening as they sunk in.

Can it be that simple? Would I be viewed a hero like him? His mind scoffed. *What hero? Ellis ignores him.*

Hugh said rightly that people didn't think of him having backbone. Would killing Musetta change their opinion? His thoughts became a tangled mess of warring thoughts regarding the possibility. Yet whatever argument vied for his attention it always came back to how he was viewed in comparison to others. He and Allard made almost the same in bargain with Tyree. He suffered punishment while Allard became a close advisor of the king. Hugh killed his brother and received a pardon, never once given any punishment for his crimes while Duke of Allon. If the past was any indication, Owain doubted he would escape any consequence should he kill Musetta.

"Is the patrol dispatched?"

Owain jerked from his deep consideration at hearing Musetta's voice then seeing her standing before him.

"You seem troubled, my lord."

"Thoughtful."

"Have you slept? A few hours of sleep may ease your mind," she said, a pleasant smile across her lips.

He warily regarded her. "I'll consider it."

"As you wish." She feined a yawn; stretching in fatigue. "I might take advantage of some sleep myself. I'll be in royal bedchamber if you need of me."

Any further thought about Hugh's suggestion vanished.

Vexed and frustrated, Hugh paced the chamber. What made him think he could convince Owain?

128

Just because he's finally shown some backbone, doesn't mean he'll listen to reason. Reason? He's invaded Waldron. What is he thinking? He's not, not with Latham's witch around.

True, Marcellus and Latham blackmailed Owain into trying to capture Ellis. What coercion did Musetta use to motivate him now? His family is alive and he's been restored to his position on the Council. A sudden flash of insight struck.

"Ellis suspected Dark Way activity and tried ferreting it out. He probably questioned everyone not just me. After what happened he may not have thought Owain capable. His mercy is coming back to haunt him."

A sudden shiver ran down his spine at hearing his own word, *mercy.* Marcellus would have executed Owain immediately upon suspicion, seized his property and imprisoned or killed his family. Mahon's words echoed in his mind, *"If you must find blame, then it is the Dark Way at fault and not you."* Yet once again the Dark Way imprisoned him; only this time real bars stopped him and not threats to his family. He winced at the thought of his children. Callie and Cassie were safe, but what of Wess and Bosley? Did Mahon find them and take them to safety?

"Jor'el, protect them. And help the king."

Chapter 9

AVATAR STIRRED at hearing something. It sounded like the voice of a small child or a woman. He smelled smoke. His eyes snapped open. It took a moment to recognize his surrounding. Shannan, Bosley, Wess, and Arista lay around a fire. Were they hurt or dead? And where was Nigel? Bosley turned and he saw the boy was asleep. Vidar sat between he and the others, a loaded crossbow in his lap. Avatar heard fussy protesting, the same sound that woke him. Wren stood nearby holding Nigel, speaking softly to him only unable to calm him.

"Having trouble with a mortal infant?" he teased. She smirked in annoyance at him. "How long did I asleep?"

"Five hours. I think the kelpie bite along with your antics made you feebler than you realize. Shhh," she said when Nigel grew louder.

Vidar moved to join Avatar and waved Wren toward them. "Give him to me before he wakes the others." Wren did so, but it soon became apparent he couldn't calm Nigel either.

Avatar took Nigel from Vidar. "You both have a way with animals, but not mortal infants." He moved the blankets to see Nigel's face. Using a finger, he caressed Nigel's cheek. "Easy, my prince. I'll have you safe soon, I promise." Nigel grew quiet.

Vidar grinned, watching Avatar interact with Nigel. "He knows you."

Avatar shrugged, still caressing Nigel's face.

Vidar continued, "He responds to you because Jor'el appointed you his Overseer. The bond formed for both of you the moment of his decree. Why else risk your existence the way you did?"

Avatar wryly smiled.

Vidar cocked a brow at realizing Avatar toyed with him. "Warrior arrogance."

"Now you're sounding like Wren."

"Ha, ha, very funny. All joking aside, how are you feeling?" she asked.

"My legs tingle with sensation. But I thought you said you could shield them while I recover?"

"I am. However, the dozen Shadow Warriors and the kelpies you dispatched shows whoever is behind this commands the Dark Way."

"Ay. How many were at Waldron?" Avatar asked Vidar.

"Four attacked me."

"Sixteen. That's not good," she groused.

Avatar ignored her comment and continued to question Vidar. "What about Mahon? He was holding the gate for us."

"I didn't see him."

Avatar closed his eyes, his brows furrowed in concentration. He winced and rubbed his eyes. "That wasn't good. My senses couldn't get past the woods."

She placed her hands on her hips in mock outrage. "I told you I was blocking our presence. This entire grove is shielded from prying senses."

Vidar laughed. "I think you need more rest for your brain than your brawn."

Avatar's attention went back to Nigel when he grew fussy. "Don't worry. I won't let them annoy you like they do me." Nigel giggled, stretched and yawned. "Sleep, my little prince. No one will disturb you."

"Ay. We'll keep watch." Vidar returned to his post, so did Wren.

Shannan woke and saw Vidar standing off to one side. Wren stood watch opposite of him. The sight and surroundings brought back so many

131

memories. For years she and Ellis explored and trained in the forest of Dorgirith preparing for the day they would eventually face Dagar, Marcellus and Latham. Unknown to them, Wren was diligent in her duty of shielding Dorgirith. When it came time to leave to start her part of the plan, Wren accompanied Shannan. En route, they met Vidar. He suffered cruelly in Dagar's netherworld before his orchestrated escape. True, Dagar planned for Vidar to get close to the Daughter of Allon and turn her over to him, but Vidar found the strength to break Dagar's hold and became her most loyal and trusted Guardian. Had it really been four years since then? Dressed in forester clothes and sleeping in the woods, it seemed like yesterday. So much had changed, but their loyalty remained. Now, they were called upon to protect her and her son against a new and unknown foe who controlled the Dark Way. Even wounded, Vidar kept to his duty. So did Avatar. She turned to where he slept. He was gone. Concerned, she sat up.

"Something wrong, Majesty?"

Her head jerked about at hearing a voice beside her. Avatar sat on the log and he held Nigel. She swallowed back her surprise. "I thought you were still sleeping. Are you better?"

"Ay." He smiled and stomped his feet. His movement woke Nigel who made a fussy groan.

She reached for Nigel and Avatar gave him to her. "I hope he didn't give you too much trouble."

"Trouble from an infant who only sleeps and eats? No, but he is hungry. And he feels a little wet."

She chuckled. "I can remedy the wetness with a small piece of your hem." He looked baffled, to which she added, "For a diaper."

"Oh." He stood, took out his dagger and cut from the portion of his uniform hem he used for Arista's bandages.

Shannan heard Wren and Vidar snickering. "Don't laugh, you two. I'll take a swatch from one of you next time." She laid Nigel on the ground to change his diaper.

Arista and Wess were next to wake.

"Avatar, you're sitting up," said Wess. "Hey, he's all right." He prodded Bosley awake, who was sluggish at first then smiled in relief upon seeing Avatar.

The Guardian grinned at the boys. "Indeed. How are your feet, my lady?"

"Better. Wren used some ointment to relieve the pain. Is it much farther to Garwood?"

"Three days."

"Unless we take the Guardian way now that there are three of you."

Avatar was about to reply when they heard Kato. The eagle swooped down from the trees to land on a branch. For a brief moment, Wren listened to Kato before speaking.

"Trouble. A mounted troop is heading this way."

"We should leave with the Guardians now," said Arista to Shannan.

"No, injuries limit our abilities," began Vidar. "It's a risk for us even to attempt a dimension travel. I had to call upon Jor'el to help me."

"We stay together for safety and defense," said Avatar. "Douse the fire and cover any signs we've been here," he instructed the boys.

Wren motioned Vidar and Avatar to move away from the mortals to speak in private. "The remedy doesn't work that fast. Are you recovered enough to fight?" she asked Avatar.

"I'm recovered enough to walk, and moving is more important. Can you keep them from following us or do you need Vidar's help?"

Insulted, she glared at him then spoke in the Ancient to Kato. The eagle took off. "Jor'el help you, warrior."

"Vidar needed help, I'm standing on my own."

"Can I shoot him?" she groused to Vidar.

"No, you already wasted medicine, no need to squander a good bolt."

"We're ready, Avatar," they heard Wess say.

"Better hurry to catch up to Kato before you get lost," said Avatar.

Wren traveled two miles when she saw Kato circling. Hearing a horse, she crouched behind an outgrowth. Through the trees, she spied twenty men dressed in muted, dark red uniforms with black cloth over their identifying crest.

"Over here! I found something," a man shouted

She watched the man dismount near an overhang. The others changed course and headed in his direction.

"Well?" demanded a man on horseback.

"They stayed here for awhile." The man pointed to the ground inside the shallow cave. "Then went that way."

"How long ago, can you tell?"

"Within a day."

The mounted man smiled with satisfaction. "Let's go!"

Wren moved to follow when she heard Kato's call. The eagle made one circle before moving in the direction the group came from. She thought about whether to pursue the men or follow Kato. At another call from Kato, she made up her mind and followed him. She pulled up sharply at seeing a dark figure dart behind a large rock formation. Crossbow ready, she carefully approached the rocks. Kato's warning screech made her look up. That was enough time for something to knock her back fifteen feet and into a tree where she hit her head. Stunned, she tried to shake off the impact. Her ears rang with Kato's constant call. She caught sight of a blur passing by her head.

Kato dove at a Shadow Warrior. Roane. He batted at Kato with one hand while holding something black in the other hand. It was a confusing scene, but all that concerned her was locating her crossbow. It lay nearby and she saw it the same time Roane noticed her movement. She lunged for the crossbow, only he was faster, and his foot came crashing down on the bow, dislodging the arrow. Again Kato dove at Roane, this time knocking the box from him. Roane dove and caught the box just before it hit ground.

Wren snatched up her crossbow, only in her injured and dazed state, fumbled trying to reload. When she was armed, she swung around to take aim. Roane kicked the crossbow from her grasp and in doing so caught her under the chin, snapping her head back and rendering her unconscious.

Hearing Kato's angry screech, Roane grabbed the crossbow and fired off a quick shot. Kato barely avoided the arrow and soared up and out of range.

He tossed the weapon aside and raced in the direction Owain's men had taken.

⁂

Darius pressed his group day and night since leaving camp, pausing long enough to refresh themselves and their mounts with food and drink. The situation was too desperate and the thought of Shannan, Nigel, and Arista driven out into the cold and defenseless, gnawed at him. True, Mahon reported Avatar accompanied them, but the enemy was employing Shadow Warriors. What were the odds a lone Guardian could stand against a large group of Shadow Warriors?

Showing signs of fatigue after three sleepless days in the saddle, Darius and Jasper checked their mounts next to Hardwin to watch Mahon squat and examine the ground.

Hardwin dismounted. "Are we on the right track?"

Mahon didn't immediately answer, his focus on the ground, hand resting on the hilt of his sword. Suddenly, he cried out in pain, swaying and grabbing his head.

Hardwin seized Mahon to keep him from falling over. "What's wrong?"

"Shadow Warriors," he muttered in pain. His head snapped up. "Avatar!"

"What about him?"

"There's been a great depletion in his lifeforce. We must be quick. They're in danger." Mahon ran off. Guardians could easily out run horses.

Hardwin vaulted into the saddle. He, Darius, Jasper and the others hurried to follow since Mahon could quickly lose them. He was already a half-mile ahead in a clearing.

An eagle cried out and swooped dangerously close to Darius. He jerked the reins. His horse skidded and protested the sudden stop. Hardwin and several others drew their swords. The eagle turned toward them again. Instead of attacking it landed on a nearby branch.

Darius got his mount under control. "Put up your swords. I know this eagle. Kato. Did Shannan send you?" Kato responded and spread his wings,

135

his head making a nodding motion. "Take me to her." Kato took off. Darius and his group followed.

For several miles they rode until Kato landed on a rock formation. Darius and his men halted. "Is Shannan here?" The eagle leapt off the rock to the ground and disappeared behind the formation.

Darius dismounted and went around the rocks. He balked at seeing a body half-hidden behind the rock and a large tree. "Shannan?" He knelt, but saw it wasn't her. "Wren." The Guardian groaned at being roused. "Easy. You're badly hurt."

She wiped her vision clear. Blood stained her fingers. "Your Grace?"

By now Jasper and Hardwin joined them. Jasper held her crossbow. Hardwin and Darius helped her sit against the tree.

"What happened?" asked Darius.

"A Shadow Warrior," she chided.

Hardwin stood, sword in hand and alert for danger.

"I think he left," she said to his reaction. "But he had a black box. That's all I saw before being knocked out."

"There are hoof prints," said Hardwin.

She was slow to answer while another Jor'ellian tended to the gash on her head. "I just spotted a troop of men before he attacked."

"Can you identify them?" asked Darius.

Annoyed, she waved off the Jor'ellian and stood. "No, but they were looking for the Daughter of Allon."

"Do you know where she is?"

"With Vidar and Avatar heading for Garwood."

"Nigel, Arista, and the boys?"

She grinned. "Also with them."

"We need to find them before those men and that Warrior do," said Hardwin.

She took a deep breath, her head bowed and grimacing back pain. "I'll take you to them."

"Are you well enough?" asked Jasper.

Wren straightened to her full height. Her green eyes determined as she took the crossbow from him. "As long as I have breath and my crossbow, I will not fail the Daughter of Allon."

Kato flapped his wings with an affirming cry.

"*Cuileag et lorg se Nighean de Allon, Kato. Cuileag et lorg se Nighean de Allon, mi ite-carads!*" Wren commanded. Kato was first to acknowledge and take flight, followed by a chorus of birds responding and taking to the air. "We will find them."

Avatar tried to urge speed in their flight to put as much distance between them and danger as possible. However, with two boys, an infant, Arista's impeded pace, and the injuries he and Vidar suffered, the pace was frustratingly slower than he would have liked. They only covered nine miles in five hours. He hated to admit Wren was right, but he knew recovery usually took two days. Sensation returned to his legs to allow him to walk. Moving swiftly in battle would be difficult. He hoped Wren could stall long enough for full recovery.

Ahead through the trees was a clearing. Not good. He couldn't carry Arista again. He told everyone to stop and rest before proceeding to the tree line to do surveillance. This meadow was larger, perhaps a mile across then dropped off on the other side.

Vidar and Shannan joined him. "That may be a ravine on the other side. Scout ahead while I stand guard," he said to Vidar. "We'll remain in the safety of the trees until he returns." He ushered her back to where the others rested. She sat next to Bosley on a large flat rock and checked on Nigel

Avatar approached Arista, who sat on the ground adjusting the wrappings. "How are your feet?"

"I'll manage."

"That's not a direct answer." He knelt to tend to her feet.

She stopped him. "How they are doesn't matter. We must get the others to safety." Nigel cried and Shannan tried to quiet him. Arista nudged the Guardian's shoulder. "Tend to your charge, I'll take care of my feet."

Avatar crossed to Shannan and sat beside her. Her gaze was fretful. "He's too cold and hungry to stay out here much longer. You must take him to Melwynn."

"I cannot and will not leave."

"Vidar—"

"Vidar's courage is without question, but he can't stand alone against Shadow Warriors. You saw what I did." Hearing the neighing of horses, he stood and made ready to draw his sword. Torin moved beside him, snarling. "Be still, Torin," he whispered in harsh command.

"Over there!" a man shouted, pointing toward them.

"Run!" Avatar took Shannan's arm to help her stand and run only his legs were sluggish while she carried Nigel.

They reached the clearing, when the sounds of horses and shouting could be heard in pursuit. Several horsemen emerged from the trees a hundred yards from them. Across the clearing, Vidar ran toward them.

"Keep going to Vidar," Avatar told Shannan before stopping.

"But—?"

"Go! I'll do what I can." He drew his sword to make a stand. "Get them to the ravine!" he shouted to Vidar.

From over the treetops a flock of birds appeared, their shrilling calls echoing all around. The birds dove at the men.

"Good girl, Wren." Avatar grinned in approval. "Keep going!" he shouted at Vidar and moved to join them when …

"Log agues milled!"

The shout brought Avatar to a halt. He turned in time to see a black box fly through the air and land in the snow between he and the horsemen. The box began to shake. Growling noises came from within. Suddenly, the box exploded, making the earth violently shake and sending a black cloud of smoke thirty feet into the air.

The shaking was so violent that Bosley and Arista fell head first into the snow. Wess collapsed to all fours. Vidar caught Shannan to keep her from falling. She held Nigel close. Horses shied, throwing some riders and the birds broke off their attack.

Avatar staggered back, struggling to maintain his balance. He just righted himself when the shaking stopped. He squinted to make out the large hulking shape in the thinning cloud. The shape moved, the ground lurching with each step. A loud roar startled men and beast. Avatar flinched, warily watching the cloud vanish. The shape become more distinct and his eyes went wide with alarm.

"A tardundeen!"

The black hairy beast stood fifteen feet tall with the massive head of a raging bull and the curved horns of a ram. The torso was manlike with bulging arms and enormous hands holding a huge axe. The legs were also that of a bull with cloven hooves. The beast swung the axe at Avatar, who dove under the blade to avoid being cut down.

Whiz! Whiz! The sounds were followed by two quick impacts when arrows from Vidar and Shannan's bows struck its body. It yanked out the arrows.

During the distraction, Avatar managed to get to his feet, only the creature swung at him again, forcing him to dive to avoid being struck. He barely got to his feet a third time when another swipe caught him in the back of his shoulders and sent him sprawling, sliding some ten feet in the snow.

"Hey, you ugly beast!" a voice shouted.

The tardundeen turned in the direction of the call and immediately, a dagger struck the base of the neck making it stagger back. Mahon dashed around the beast to Avatar.

"Would have been nice if you arrived before it clipped me."

Mahon smiled and gave Avatar a hand up. They joined the others. Vidar and Shannan stood ready to shoot.

"Why didn't you shoot it again?" Avatar chided Vidar

"You kept getting in the way then your cohort arrived. You wanted us to shoot him by mistake?"

"Glad to see they're unharmed, despite the archer," said Mahon.

"Let's keep it that way." Avatar and Mahon stood shoulder-to-shoulder in front of the mortals armed and ready.

The tardundeen finished pulling out Mahon's dagger and tossed it aside. Instead of turning back to them, the men became the focus of the beast's attack. They tried to avoid the swinging axe while attempting to kill the beast. Birds also attacked but nothing seemed effective against the tardundeen. The axe separated men and horses, killing some while scattering others. It snatched two birds out of the air in one hand, crushing them in its fist.

"Quick! To the ravine," said Avatar.

Most heeded his order, except Shannan. She balked at seeing Kato dive toward the beast. The axe rose in another attack at the men, and in the arch of the swing, Kato was too close and plummeted helpless to the ground.

"No!" she cried. She fired at the beast, striking the left shoulder blade. The distraction was over. The beast turned, reaching for the arrow and spotted them.

Avatar pulled Shannan toward the ravine. The beast's advance made the ground shake and both fell. He tried to stand, but the ground shook worse as the beast neared. Seeing the raised axe, Avatar lay on top of Shannan to shield her.

"*Seah Jor'el's ordugh, stad!*" a loud female voice commanded.

The beast snarled; the axe suspended a few feet from striking Avatar.

Again the voice ordered, "By Jor'el's command, stop!"

The beast reared back and with a mighty roar of rage, turned toward the speaker.

"Wren!" Mahon pointed across the clearing.

She stood with her crossbow ready, Darius and the others behind her. The beast roared again, striking its chest before advancing toward Wren.

Wren shouted, "Vidar!"

Vidar armed his bow. "Shannan, your bow!"

She scrambled out from under Avatar to stand beside Vidar.

"Aim for the base of its skull. Wait for Wren's signal, repeat her command and fire," he instructed, aiming his bow. Shannan mimicked him.

"Shield the others!" Avatar said to Mahon. They took up position between Vidar, Shannan, and the others. Behind them, Bosley turned his back to protect Nigel while Wess shielded Arista.

Across the clearing, Wren stood rock still with her crossbow aimed, watching the beast bear down on her. The ground shook.

Darius, Jasper, Hardwin and the soldiers steadied their nervous horses. "Wren?" Darius questioned when the shaking grew violent.

She didn't move or reply, then, "Now!" She released her shot. So did Vidar and Shannan, all shouting, "By Jor'el's command, stop!"

Wren's arrow struck the beast between the eyes a mere second before two arrows stuck the base of its skull. The beast reeled back from the first impact then jerked forward. With a throaty growl it swayed and collapsed. The earth jolted, sending a mix of snow, rock and mud everywhere.

Vidar and Shannan turned aside in time to only be partially splattered. Avatar brushed the muck from his hair and shoulders while Mahon wiped his face.

"I suppose things could have been worse," said Mahon. He just finished speaking when a low rumbling sound came from all around the clearing. "I spoke too soon."

"It's not dead!" Jasper drew his sword.

"Wait," said Wren.

The splattered snow, rock and mud began to move back, covering the beast. As it gathered on top, the mound disappeared into the earth until the clearing looked like did before, a perfect and pristine blanket of white snow.

Wren put up her crossbow. "It's dead."

"Your Grace, some of the men are still alive," said Hardwin.

"Secure them." Darius sent his horse across the clearing. "Shannan. Thank, Jor'el you're safe." He dismounted before the horse stopped and embraced her. "What of Nigel?"

She waved Bosley forward. "Hungry and out of sorts, but unharmed." She placed the bow over her shoulders to take Nigel.

"We are all well thanks to Avatar and the others," said Arista.

Darius drew Arista to him and passionately kissed her.

"I didn't know they liked each other," Bosley said to Wess.

Shannan chuckled, although focused on a fussy Nigel.

141

Jasper sheathed his sword and moved to look over her shoulder to inspect Nigel. He moved the blanket to get a better view. Nigel's face was screwed up in discomfort and annoyance. "You look like your father when he's in a ill-tempered mood." Nigel started crying. "Sound like him too."

Shannan laughed and gave Jasper a good-natured jab with her elbow.

Hardwin and the soldiers easily secured the men. In fact, only two were healthy enough to put up a fight but chose otherwise. Fourteen were slain by the beast and four wounded.

"Majesty, it's a relief you and the prince are unharmed," said Hardwin. The four Jor'ellians with him kept hold of the two horsemen.

She acknowledged Hardwin, her focus on the men. "Who are you?"

The men remained silent so Hardwin ripped off the black cloth covering the crest from the sleeve of one man. "Lord Owain's men."

"Owain?" she repeated, astonished.

Arista covered her mouth in dreadful surprise, a muffled gasp escaping. Darius comforted her. "You're safe now."

Shannan struggled to maintain her temper. "Why were you pursuing us?"

Again they didn't reply, only this time Jasper whipped out his dagger and placed the blade against one man's throat. "The queen asked you a question. Answer her."

The man remained stubbornly silent.

Darius confronted him. "I would be within my rights to let him to kill you for treason. What were your orders?"

The man winced when Jasper's blade nicked his throat, drawing blood. "To find the queen and prince," he grunted through gritted teeth of anger and reluctance.

"And do what when you found them?"

Jasper's blade again nicked his throat, only this time deeper and drawing more blood. The man briefly cried out in pain. "Kill them!"

Arista's distress was visible and she seized Darius. He held her while ordering, "Sir Hardwin! Take them to the king, quickly and quietly."

"Ay, Your Grace. Giles." He signaled the eldest of the Jor'ellian to take command of the prisoners.

In angry disbelief, Shannan watched the departure. "Ellis will be furious. Owain abused his mercy and the Vicar's grace."

Jasper sheathed his dagger. "What about the dead and wounded?" he asked Darius, only Avatar replied.

"Leave the wounded to tend to the dead then fend for themselves."

Bosely was visibly disturbed. "Leave them?"

Avatar looked directly at Bosley, his voice compassionate yet authoritative. "You heard they were ordered to kill the queen and prince. That is treason and a violation of Jor'el's law in raising rebellion. This way, Jor'el decides their fate in the wilderness. It is divine justice."

Darius placed a hand on Bosley's shoulder to get the boy's attention. "If taken to the king, they would hang."

Bosley's expression showed he struggled to comprehend.

"You, your brother and Arista were also in danger. And no doubt many were killed at Waldron, not to mention Kato . . ." Shannan's voice faltered.

"I'm sorry I didn't arrive sooner," said Wren.

Torin rubbed against Shannan's leg. "At least you're alive."

"We must get you all to safety," said Darius. "Horses," he called and two of his soldiers came forward and dismounted.

"Horses for the young masters. They have earned my gratitude for their bravery," said Shannan. She gave Nigel to Jasper to mount then received him back.

Avatar lifted Arista into the saddle. Two Jor'ellians heeded Shannan's command and yielded their horses to Wess and Bosley. Hardwin and his group left the meadow heading west; the rest headed east. Darius rode beside Shannan with Jasper accompanying Arista. The soldiers and Jor'ellians who gave up their mounts rode double with their companions. The Guardians took the lead.

Avatar glanced at Wren. There was dried blood on her head. "What happened to you? Trip while trying to catch up to—" He stopped upon realizing he was about to say Kato then hissed when Vidar sent a warning jab to his wound. No need to ask the archer why since he checked his humor.

Hurt and anger filled her glare at him. "I ran into a Shadow Warrior."

Forgeting the jab and bad humor, Avatar's face immediately hardened and he demanded, "Who?"

"Roane. I noticed he carried a black box."

His fierceness increased at hearing the familiar name. "The tardundeen."

"I know that now, not then. I thought all were destroyed after the Great Battle." She glanced in skewed annoyance at Mahon. "I guess you missed something in clearing Dagar's cavern."

"No, I didn't. Even Kell approved of the job my team did."

"Then how did Roane get it?"

"The talisman," said Vidar. "No Shadow Warrior would willingly handle one."

Avatar looked with curious concern at the archer. "Owain has the talisman? He's not trained in the Dark Way."

"I don't know for sure, although that would explain where he got the courage to be so bold and to command Shadow Warriors, kelpies and a tardundeen."

"Or someone is using the talisman to force him," said Mahon.

Wren chaffed at the argument. "What does it matter? He seized Waldron and gave orders to kill the Daughter of Allon and her son. He bears responsibility."

"In our present duty, nothing. However, knowing who is behind this may help in putting down the revolt," said Vidar.

"First thing's first. We take them to Garwood," said Avatar.

Wren nodded then left.

"Where's Wren going?" asked Darius.

"To scout ahead."

"Amazing she can move after her encounter with the Shadow Warrior."

"Although she fared better than Mahon," teased Jasper.

Seeing Mahon scowl, Avatar asked, "How many?"

Mahon's irritation increased. "One. I was blind-sided at the gate. What about you? I sensed a serious drain in your lifeforce."

"We were surrounded and I was forced to use my power."

"How many?"

Avatar widely smiled. "Twelve Shadow Warriors and eight kelpies."

"And he was wounded by a kelpie beforehand," added Vidar, making Mahon snarl at him.

"That occurred after I defeated a hunter-hawk."

To this, both Vidar and Mahon were surprised.

Jasper laughed while Darius smiled and spoke to Shannan. "Because of Mahon's report, Ellis dispatched us to find you. We thought you would head to Garwood for the safety of the others."

"Ay. And after they are secure I intend to join Ellis."

"We knew you'd say that."

She smiled. "I didn't realize I was so predictable."

"This is one time I'm glad your were."

Chapter 10

THE HEAVY SNOW finally tapered off. Lanay and the girls walked along the road from Pickford to the Fortress. Not many traveled that day leaving few compacted tracks to use and make the journey easier. Each carried a day bag. Actually, Katlyn dragged her luggage, lagging behind the others.

"Come on, keep up!" called Candice.

"I can't! This is heavy. And I'm tired. Oh, why couldn't we take another carriage?"

"I've already explained everything," Lanay said in exasperation. She handed her bag to Gwen before going back to help Katlyn. Once she had the girl's luggage, she nudged Katlyn forward, only the girl stumbled.

"My feet are cold."

"Stop complaining. We're all cold," chided Candice.

"All of you stop where you are!" Lanay glared at them. "How many times must I explain this is what your father asked us to do?"

"To travel in the snow and cold for days?"

"Ay! For our safety."

"A carriage would be safer," Gwen groused, drawing a look of ire from Lanay. "Well, it would have."

Lanay sighed in agreement. "I know. However, because I trust him, I will do as he asked." She began walking again.

"Like last time?"

"Mind your words, Gwen," Lanay warned, motioning toward the younger girls.

"They know. Or at least they should."

"Ay, we went to a Fortress before," Katlyn said in remembrance.

"You were six, what do you remember?" asked Candice.

"I remember the priests were funny."

"Priests funny? I didn't find them funny at all. Too strict and sour-faced." Candice made faces, which amused Katlyn. "They kept talking about the Dark Way like Father was responsible."

Lanay's voice turned sharp. "Beware, Candice."

"Why? It's true," insisted Gwen. "I heard similar talk at Court. Some think what is happening now is because of Father again."

Angry, Lanay stopped Gwen. "No! He wouldn't. Not after last time."

"Then why send us away?"

"To protect us."

"From what, Mother? From the Dark Way? From the king? What?"

The question stymied Lanay and she became frustrated. "I don't know!" She impatiently waved for them to move. "And it's too cold to argue." She carried Katlyn's luggage while Gwen held two bags.

"Mother."

"No, Gwen! I'll speak of it no more," Lanay said without looking back.

Being the eldest, Gwen remembered more of that dreadful time than her sisters. Royal soldiers escorted them from Presley to the Fortress of Barton for safekeeping. At the Fortress, Master Colter informed them of King Ellis' wish they be made comfortable for the duration of their stay. When asked how long, Colter only said they would be well cared for.

Two weeks later a Guardian by the name of Kell arrived and spoke privately to Lanay. Gwen managed to hide behind a curtain in the room to listen and learned the real reason: Owain's involvement with the Dark Way against the king. Naturally her mother defended her father while expressing concern for her safety and that of her daughters. The Guardian dismissed her concerns and when he spoke about the probation and its reward or consequences depending on Owain's conduct, Gwen made a point to remember him. His black hair and height made him imposing, while his golden eyes were cold and indifferent. She recalled not liking him from the first moment and his image sprang to mind when Candice mentioned the Dark Way and her mother's quick reaction.

Just like back then, they were sent to a Fortress. True, it was at her father's orders and not the king's, but the similarities were too striking to ignore. *Is the Dark Way again involved? What trouble has he gotten into now? Or is he truly taking a stand to protect his family?* Knowing him, the last question seemed unlikely. Oh, she loved him, but his mild-mannered character was not given to feats of courage or acts of bravery.

Her mother walked ahead of her. True, she complemented his character, was devoted to him and aided him during the probation. However, her delicate nature could not withstand those who actively sought to ruin him. This is where she and her mother differed. If she had remained behind, she would have helped. After all, he often commented how she had the strongest will and was the most level-headed of the family. Unfortunately, he charged her with helping her mother and taking care of her sisters. Once they were safe and settled, she would find a way to leave and return to help him.

Gwen scowled when the snow started falling again. Going to a Fortress was one thing; having to walk in the cold and snow was entirely different. *Father may have thought it for safety, but how safe can it be walking on a deserted road to an isolated Fortress in such weather?*

"This is where we leave the road," said Lanay.

The statement brought Gwen from her dreary brooding. Lanay appeared to be pointing at nothing more than a small path with tracks half filled with snow.

"That can't be right. It's a cart path," she insisted.

"According to the directions we are to turn right at first path we come to. The Fortress is another half-mile."

148

"Mother." Gwen grabbed Lanay's arm to stop, but Lanay jerked away and moved off the road.

Candice tugged on Katlyn's sleeve to get her moving. She cast an annoyed sneer at Gwen when passing her older sister. Katlyn didn't seem to notice anything, listlessly pulled along by Candice. Gwen followed her sisters. Her mother may avoid talking on their trek to the Fortress, but once there, she would get her to speak.

After a half-mile they arrived at the Fortress. Three priests who worked outside the gate, rushed to their aid, relieving them of their burdens.

"My lady? What are you doing here on foot?" asked one priest.

"It is a long story for which we seek sanctuary."

"Of course." He called to another priest near the gate, "Fetch Master Quentin."

Several assisted in ushering Lanay and the exhausted younger girls into the hall. Still others rushed to fetch blankets, warm food and hot drink. By the time Master Quentin arrived, they were given blankets and mulled cider. The food would take a little longer.

Quentin was a middle-aged, rotund man with a kind face and pleasant smile. "My lady? What dire circumstances brings you here in such condition?"

Lanay drank and paused to catch her breath before replying. "I am Lady Lanay, my husband is Sir Owain of Midessex."

"Of the Council of Twelve."

She nodded, again taking a drink. "At his request, my daughters and I seek sanctuary. The circumstance of which I would speak with you in private."

"Of course, after you have rested." Quentin waved at the priests. "See rooms are prepared."

She just nodded, more interested in the cider and getting warm.

An hour later Quentin responded to Lanay's summons. Although the guest rooms were sparse of decoration and noble amenities, they were comfortable and spacious. Alone, Lanay sat in an ample cushioned chair before a large fire, her clothes supplemented by a priest's fur-lined cloak and fingerless, knit gloves.

"You sent for me, my lady."

She indicated a smaller chair opposite her. "Please, Master Quentin."

He sat. "I hope the food and rooms are to your satisfaction."

"Ay, thank you." She drew a deep thoughtful breath before proceeding. "Please understand we speak in the utter most confidence."

"Naturally."

She briefly chewed on her lower lip. She had to know if he was familiar with the past. Then again, it was common knowledge, but would that affect how she and the girls were treated this time? "How much are you familiar with my husband's history?"

Quentin tempered his reply. "Since Vicar Archimedes was in charge of Sir Owain's probation, he sought prayer from the Fortress Masters on his behalf. Only the Masters," he emphasized at seeing her become upset. "So I know more than the general public about his state of mind and progress."

She tried to contain her disturbance at the answer. "This is very difficult for me, Master Quentin."

He leaned forward and asked, "Why did your husband send you to a Fortress?"

She stirred with offense. "You ask that with suspicion. Could it be due to prejudice because of your knowledge?"

"No, my lady. There is unrest, which have many concerned about a resurgence of the Dark Way."

To this statement, she couldn't argue, but did he too suspect Owain? "Have you any specific information about what is happening?"

His smile was discreet yet kind. "Enough to pray for the king to protect Allon and for the Council to have wisdom to aid him. However, being the wife of a Council Member you should know more than I, the master of a remote Fortress."

She plaintively sighed, her brows furrowed with indecision.

"My lady, you may speak confidentially. What you tell me will stay between us."

She glanced at him from under shrouded brows. "Therein lies part of the problem, I don't know. All I do know is Owain was afraid because of the unrest and sent us away for our own safety."

"Then you must trust his judgment."

She became apprehensive. "That is easier said than done."

"Because of the past?"

Her sharp expression faded to a frustrated frown. "I am wrong to doubt him?"

He observed her for a moment before replying. "Included in the Vicar's concerns was how you and your daughters suffered. Knowing that, I cannot fault you for being guarded about the current situation. As for doubting your husband, only you can answer that question. Perhaps while you are here, you can find the answer, and take rest from your concerns."

"Thank you." She turned away not wishing to say anymore. He offered no new information.

By her obvious reticent action, he rose, bowed and withdrew.

In the hall Gwen noticed Quentin emerge from her mother's room. "How is Mother?"

"She has much on her mind and I counseled her to rest."

"Did she tell you why he sent us here?"

"I am not going to betray a confidence. Be assured he is concerned for your safety."

Gwen's frown deepened into a painful sneer when he steered her from the door to Lanay's chamber. She balked at being prevented and stopped. "She did tell you why. No one trusts him."

"You are jumping to conclusions."

"No, I'm not. Everyone at Court was standoffish and smug. At first I believed it was because I was young and inexperienced, then learned the truth. I'm his daughter, so they treat me with distrust and contempt."

"You were told this?"

"Not directly. I overhead enough talk about holding the past against him. Maybe even the king."

151

He grew stern. "You shouldn't base conclusions on hearsay and assumptions. Upon Vicar Archimedes' recommendation the king reinstated your father."

"Nothing has been the same since!"

"Of course not. What did you expect?"

She heaved an exasperated shrug. "Lord Zebulon said it was wise to keep an enemy closer than a friend."

"When did he say that? And how did you hear?"

"At the banquet to celebrate the prince's birth. Political talk about the Council but even the king agreed! Father was stricken by the exchange. So don't tell me it has nothing to do with their lack of trust."

His eyes were steady and probing, making her stiffen in annoyance. Oh, it was bad enough being at the Fortress. Dealing with a priest is insufferable. Angry and frustrated she looked away. His voice brought her back.

"What you heard is true in the political sense and not necessarily personal. Or that Lord Zebulon was speaking specifically concerning your father or the king agreed."

"It's happening again! You can't deny that."

"Child, like your mother, you need rest," he said in an attempt to comfort her, or more rightly steer her back to her room, but she jerked away.

"I'm not your child. I'm his!"

Quentin's agreeability altered. "While you are here, at *his* direction, I will do as he wishes and help to protect and provide for all of you. Despite your disrespectful attitude." This time his hold was firm, with the intent of not accepting any resistance, thus she went. "I'll have supper sent up."

She flashed a tight, unfriendly smile. "Thank you, Master Quentin."

Their eyes met, his scrutinizing gaze infuriating. She quickly entered the room and shut the door. For a moment, she listened to his departing footsteps.

Candice was awake but Katlyn slept. "Well, did you speak to Mother?"

Gwen sneered at the door before answer. "No, he wouldn't let me. He said she is resting. I believe he doesn't trust Father."

"He said that?"

"Shhh!" warned Gwen, motioning to the bed. She drew Candice toward the fire to speak. "Not in so many words. He's evasive and annoying, like all priests. You remember how they treated us last time."

"Ay, like we were traitors along with Father."

"Mind your tongue. Father was tricked and paid the price. We all did. Now it's happening again."

Candice became fearful. "You think he sent us away because he's become involved with the Dark Way?"

"The circumstances are too similar to ignore. Besides, it's not like him to withhold anything from Mother."

"What will happen?"

Gwen shook head. "I wish I knew. For now all we can do is stay here, shut up again."

"You may be wrong."

"You weren't at Court. Father is not well liked, nor are we. It could be very bad this time if he doesn't succeed."

Candice stared in disbelief. "You want the Dark Way to succeed?"

"No! I want Father to succeed or we might face a worse fate than before."

Candice began to cry. "I hope you are wrong."

"There is only one way to find out." Gwen carefully peeked out the door and saw the hallway empty. "Stay here and be quiet until I return." She stepped out and eased the door closed. She hurried to Lanay's room and entered without knocking, startling her mother.

"Gwen? Is something wrong?"

"Don't make excuses, Mother. Tell me what Master Quentin said about Father and why we're at a Fortress again."

"That is a private matter between Master Quentin and I, as well as between your father and I."

"Mother," she insisted, seizing her Lanay.

"Mind yourself, Gwen!" Lanay jerked free.

"I'm not a child to be scolded or sent away. I have a right to know."

153

Lanay's visible deliberation was momentary. She motioned for Gwen to follow her to the chairs near the fire where they sat. "According to Master Quentin, there is a resurgence of the Dark Way."

"Is Father involved again?"

"All Master Quentin said is the king and Council are in the process of quelling it."

Annoyed, Gwen sat forward on the edge of her seat. "Why didn't you press him? You are the wife of a member of the Council of Twelve, he's just a priest."

"Priests deserve respect."

Gwen snorted to the contrary. "What have priests done for us?"

Lanay became angry. "Vicar Archimedes aided your father during his probation. Which helped him to keep his station and afford us to continue living the life we are accustommed."

"Some life! We are scorned on all sides."

Lanay waved in frustration. "You're making it worse than it is."

"We're trapped in a Fortress again!"

"We're not trapped. We're here at your father's request."

Infuriated, Gwen bolted up. "Why? If he's not involved with the Dark Way then why didn't he tell you so? Why not say he is helping the king? Father tells you everything." Lanay shied away in discomposure. "Mother? What did he say that you're not telling me?" When Lanay didn't answer, she positioned herself to be seen. "What did he say?"

In distress, Lanay clamored, "He didn't tell me anything!"

"Then why are you so despondent? Why avoid telling me?" Gwen gasped in concern. "You *do* believe he is involved with the Dark Way."

Lanay tried to stifle her emotion, a muffled sob escaping. "I'm afraid for him. I'm afraid for us."

Gwen knelt beside her mother's chair. "Why would Father do that again? I know he loves you, loves us."

Lanay wiped her eyes. "I don't know. I have nothing upon which to base my fear, only he's so changed."

"You mean because he commanded us to leave?"

"Ay. The last time he acted like this was the day he agreed to help Captain Tyree and that awful Shadow Warrior to capture Prince Ellis."

Gwen's face grew resolute. "If he is involved then we should be at home supporting him, not hiding like animals."

Stunned, Lanay stared at her. "Are you saying you approve of the Dark Way?"

"No. I'm saying we should support him to make certain he doesn't fail."

"We don't even know what he is doing. I could be completely wrong and he truly is helping the king."

Gwen stood, her anger coming out in her tone and short, agitated gestures. "Does it matter when our lives are at stake? The king's justice will be brought on us if he fails, not the Dark Way."

"That's what frightens me."

Again Gwen knelt and held her mother's hand. "We need to stay strong in our belief he will succeed in whatever he is doing."

Lanay gripped Gwen's hand, a sorrowful smile on his lips. "You are the strongest in will and determination. Owain claims I give him strength, but that's only because I love him with all my heart. Dealing with others, I'm as weak as he is."

"Then let me lend you my strength for when Master Quentin speaks with you again."

"Ay. Only who summoned him. I don't know if or when he'll return."

"I'll stay here with you. I'll fetch my things and be back shortly."

For several days, they were left to themselves. Gwen thought about approaching Quentin, but lack of attention gave her the opportunity to explore the Fortress for a means of leaving.

During the course of her daily wandering, she made mental notes of the locations of windows along with the number of grates used for fresh water or sewage. Whenever she tried to get near the front or rate gate, a priest, guard or servant stopped her from going outside. She gave various excuses, but the orders were strict they remain inside for their own protection.

Some protection, she thought after the fourth time of being denied at the front gate. *Well, if I can't get out the regular way, I'll find another.*

She leisurely made her way back to her the room she shared with Lanay. Candice and Katlyn were with their mother and working on needlepoint. "Where did you get those?"

"Master Quentin was kind enough to supply us everything we need to keep ourselves productive and occupied," replied Lanay. "There's a hoop and cloth on the side table for you, or you can use the stand and I'll use the hoop."

Gwen frowned in vexation. "How can you do needlepoint?"

"What do you expect us to do while we wait, twiddle our thumbs?"

Gwen picked up the extra hoop. "This isn't much different."

Lanay put down her needle to stand and confront her. "You must learn to channel your energies to more productive things than brooding."

"She's been touring the Fortress every day," said Candice.

"You have?" asked Lanay. "I didn't think you approved of being here."

Gwen gave Candice a scolding glance while replying. "I don't, but walking in the fresh air is better than sitting cooped up inside pricking my fingers with every stitch."

"She even tried to go out the front gate," said Katlyn.

After a disapproving scowl at Gwen, Lanay herded Candice and Katlyn out of the room. "Take your hoops and continue practicing in your room. I want to speak with Gwen."

"There's no fire in our room and it's cold," complained Katlyn.

"Candice, send word to Master Quentin and you'll have a one soon enough. Now, shoo." Lanay pushed the girls out the door. She suspiciously regarded Gwen. "What are up to?"

Gwen tried to act casual by taking a seat and pretending to concentrate on the hoop she still held. "Nothing."

Lanay crossed to the chairs. "Don't lie to me. Why are you touring the Fortress?"

Gwen didn't look at her. Instead she worked on adjusting the hoop. "I told you it's better than being cooped up."

Lanay snatched the hoop. "I know you, my girl. Both you and your father tend to shy away when telling a falsehood."

Gwen boldly glared at Lanay. "You mean like you did when you refused to talk to me the other day?"

"That's different. I have nothing upon which to base my suspicion so how could I answer you? But you have a purpose, I can see it."

Gwen stiffened, her lips tightly pressed together.

Lanay scowled. "You don't have to tell me, you said it the other day; you want to support him. To do that you have to leave."

Gwen started to turn further away then boldly faced her mother. "So? I love him effort to support him without question."

Lanay hissed in offense. "You think I don't? How dare you!" She began to pace in agitated steps. "I kept him going during the probation and held our family together. Now, I will do the same, not you!"

Gwen bolted up. "How, Mother? By staying in a Fortress?"

"Since that is his wish, ay!" She seized Gwen by the shoulders. "You have no idea how to handle such situations, the various complications, ramifications and consequences involved. By staying here we are supporting him in the best way possible."

"I don't agree."

Lanay roughly released her. "Your agreement doesn't matter, obedience is important to hold this family together!"

Gwen huffed and began to leave when Lanay's words stopped her.

"You think me weak for not taking such a bold stance as you would, but sometimes boldness and strength are not the answers. Proper humility and contrition can turn away wrath, just like it did before."

Gwen whirled about to face Lanay. "What if it doesn't, Mother? Will you stand mute before the king and accept unjust punishment?"

"Gwen, we don't know what he is doing! To speak of punishment is premature."

"Under the circumstances it is a strong possibility."

"Ay. Yet until I know for certain, the best action is to do nothing!"

Gwen again turned to leave and once more Lanay's words halted her.

"Have you considered that any action you take may harm rather than help him?"

With furrowed brows, Gwen looked back. "No."

"If he is again acting on impulse, how will your acting on impulse help him?"

Gwen grew sober and thoughtful. "I don't suppose it would."

She approached Gwen, her face and voice compassionate. "No. Besides, by remaining here, safe and sound, we give him peace of mind on our behalf." She tenderly stroked Gwen's hair. "Now, isn't that worth something? To ease his concern for us?"

Gwen bit her lower lip to stop the quivering. "I'm so worried for him."

"Of course. We all are. Candice and Katlyn are scared. Remember, he asked you to look after them. Don't disappoint him."

"No." She wept and hugged her mother. "I'm sorry."

"You don't need to apologize for loving your father. Rest assured, when I learn what is happening, I will aid him as diligently as I did before in whatever way necessary." She softly smiled at Gwen. "We all will."

Gwen wiped her eyes.

"Now, have I put your notion of leaving the Fortress to rest?"

"Ay. I guess I misjudged you. You do have some inner strength."

Lanay grinned. "I need it to deal with you." She fetched the hoop, smiled and held it out to Gwen. "I had Master Quentin bring extra thimbles for you."

Gwen took the hoop to begin working. Lanay fetched the girls and they all sat doing needlepoint. Although she used the thimbles to protect her fingers, Gwen's mind wasn't on her work. The conversation kept replaying in her mind, warring against her impulse. Intellectually, she acknowledged her mother's sound reasoning and if staying here eased his mind why did she still feel such a strong urge to leave? Was this the overwhelming desire spurring him to action? If so, there was a dangerous, reckless side she found confounding and a bit frightening. Fear never stopped her before. *You have no idea how to handle such situations, the various complications, ramifications and consequences that are involved.* Her mother's words echoed in her mind. Even the warning did not quiet the increasing urge. In fact, the more she worked on the needlepoint, the stronger the urge became. Thus with purpose and a determination, she remained silent for the remainder of the day. Come the night, she would act.

Past midnight, Gwen carefully rose from her bed. Lanay slept soundly, which was fortunate, because if she remained with Candice and Katlyn, Candice woke at slightest noise.

She went to bed with a dressing gown placed over her clothes. She slipped on her shoes, and tiptoed across the room to where the cloaks hung on pegs beside the door. She exchanged the dressing gown for the cloak before carefully opening the door and exiting.

She eased the door closed then glanced up and down the hall. Several wrought iron oil lamps attached to opposite sides of the wall, illuminated the hall. Seeing no one, she quickly put on her cloak, fastened it and raised the hood. Dashing down the hallway, she paused at the top of the stairs. Two lamps were attached on either side of the stairwell. It looked dark partway down the steps, but dim light shone from around a bend so the stairs were not too long or dangerous to navigate without a lantern. Her pause was brief before glancing again for signs of anyone in hall. Seeing no one, she made her way downstairs. At the bottom, she heard voices and darted into the shadow of a doorway. A priest spoke to a Fortress guard. When they passed, she continued on her course.

Since leaving by the front and rear gates were impossible, she headed for the stables. She noticed a chute opened to the outside. Perhaps used to bring hay from a storage shed outside the wall or for waste after cleaning out the stalls. Either way, didn't matter, she intended to use the chute to leave. She stayed in the shadows and out of the scope of lamplight. However, upon reaching the corner of a building, she would have to cross into the open to reach the stable. At first all appeared empty and quiet. When she stepped out of the shadows, someone grabbed her.

"Going some where, miss?" asked a guard.

She tried to jerk free but he held fast. "Just getting some air."

"Really? After midnight?" he asked in disbelief. "Come, I'll take you back to your room."

She kicked him, barely missing his groin and bit his hand to break free. She ran toward the rear gate, thinking only of escaping.

"Stop! Don't let her out!" he shouted.

Two guards moved to intercept her and she darted away. The one she kicked hobbled over and snatched her cloak, pulling her off her feet. She landed hard on her buttocks and back. All three surrounded her with two pointing their pikes at her.

"Enough, miss," scolded the one she accosted. "For assaulting a Fortress officer I'm taking you to Master Quentin. You can explain your actions to him." He pulled her to her feet. Another guard took hold of her other arm. "Fetch her mother and bring her to Master Quentin's room," he told the third guard.

Although struggling was useless, she offered resistance, which proved futile when she stumbled. Only their hold kept her from falling.

The officer loudly knocked on Master Quentin's door, calling for the headmaster. After a moment Quentin appeared in the threshold looking like he just woke from a deep sleep.

"What it is, Captain Durant?"

"We caught this one trying to escape."

Seeing Gwen, his fatigue vanished, replaced by sternness. "Why, young lady?"

She pressed her lips in a refusal to answer.

"I sent Harris to fetch her mother," said Durant.

Quentin's eyes never left Gwen. "Take her to my study. I'll be along shortly." He shut the door.

This time Gwen didn't resist when Durant and his companion followed Quentin's instructions. While Durant maintained hold, the other guard lit several of the study lanterns. The wait wasn't long. Quentin and Lanay arrived together. He put on his robes of office while Lanay wore a dressing gown, not looking pleased.

"Why?" demanded Lanay.

Once again Gwen didn't answer.

"She refused to answer me," said Quentin. "Do you know about this attempt?"

Lanay frowned and nodded. "She wants to help her father. I thought I talked her out of it earlier today. Apparently, I was mistaken." She cast a scolding glare to Gwen, who stiffened, yet remained silent.

"Why do you feel that way, child?" Quentin asked Gwen.

"I'm not your child, so stop patronizing me!"

"I'm not patronizing. Your action is an abuse of our hospitality and sanctuary. And you owe your mother and I an explanation."

"You call this sanctuary? We're prisoners unable to come and go."

"For your own protection. And don't argue! You have been headstrong and contrary since arriving." When Gwen set her jaw, he continued. "You think I've been unaware of your little reconnaissance trips around the Fortress?"

To this statement, she looked surprise but Lanay was more vocal. "You knew what she was planning?"

"Of course. We had a rather contentious exchange after I called upon you that first day. She questioned me about the nature of our conversation. From that point on I had her watched."

Gwen's temper exploded. "You say we're not prisoners, yet you have me watched!"

"Your own words and behavior made me suspicious. I took the necessary measures to ensure you did not place yourself, your mother, your sisters, or this Fortress in jeopardy by impulsive and reckless behavior. My caution proved correct."

Lanay stepped forward in Gwen's defense. "I'm certain my daughter didn't mean any harm to the Fortress."

"Who cares about the Fortress?"

"Gwen!" Lanay warned.

161

Firm features and harsh eyes, Quentin stood in front of Gwen. "Beware such talk, Child. The Dark Way is at work and must be resisted if it is to be defeated."

Her eyes narrowed in resentment and she lashed out. "I'm tried of being mistreated because you and everyone else believe my father is in league with the Dark Way! So what if he is?"

Shocked and concerned, Lanay laid hold of Gwen. "Mind your tongue! You are speaking to a Fortress headmaster, a servant of Jor'el."

Quentin's eyes never left Gwen. "She has no fear of Jor'el."

"That's not true, Master Quentin," refuted Lanay. "Tell him it's not true," she urged, jerking Gwen's arm.

Gwen turned to her mother. "It is true. I don't fear Jor'el and I don't fear the Dark Way either. I only want to help Father."

Lanay was flabbergasted and Quentin irate.

"You are a naïve foolish child. However, since you have spoken so blatantly against Jor'el and this Fortress, I have no choice but to place you guard until the situation is resolved."

Lanay gasped in horror, her voice barely audible. "No, you can't."

"I'm afraid the actions and admission of your eldest daughter give me no alternative. This is as much for your protection and that of your other daughters along with the integrity of the Fortress. Captain Durant, escort Mistress Gwen to a room on the upper floor." He motioned for the third guard. "Take her ladyship back to her chamber and see to whatever she needs."

"Ay, Headmaster."

Gwen jowls flexed when Durant escorted her from the study and up narrow stairs to a very small room. Inside were a single bed, a nightstand, personal brazier for heat and a candle. The window was high off the floor and very narrow. Doubtful even a child could fit through the opening.

"If you're thinking of escaping by the window, don't. It's a sheer drop of one hundred feet," said Durant. He lit the brazier and candle. "The coal should last the night. You can blow out the candle when you're ready to retire. If you need anything, speak to Harris, he'll be your guard tonight," he said about the second guard. Both left and Gwen heard the key turning in the lock.

In disgruntled anger, she plopped on the bed. This had to be the same overwhelming impulse that drove her father. She hoped his action would have better results than hers.

Chapter 11

THE CASTLE OF GARWOOD sat perched on the highest peak in the Southern Forest, overlooking the town which bore its name. It stood like a sentinel protecting the town and the road leading to Jor'el's Fortress of Garwood. The ramparts offered a commanding view of the countryside. Upon arrival, Darius ordered rooms and food prepared for the queen, prince, and others. Being a bachelor, no room was available for an infant. In fact, the steward brought Darius' crib out of storage.

"That's the best I can do," said Edmund, his graying auburn hair and hazel eyes set in a ruddy complexion. A groomed beard and mustache framed a stout chin and thin lips. He wore the brown and gold livery of the house he served. "The nurse will be here shortly."

Shannan smiled warmly. "It will do fine, Edmund."

He grinned as he observed Nigel, who was out of temper. "He may look like you, but he acts ornery like Ellis."

She laughed. "I'll tell him you said that."

He shrugged. "He'll ignore me like he and Darius did as boys."

The nurse arrived and Edmund left. While the nurse tended to Nigel, Shannan bathed and changed into the best clothes the housekeeper could offer. By the time she was done, Vidar returned, accompanied by Avatar and other servants bringing food. Wren treated their wounds and helped replace their torn and soiled uniforms.

The nurse left once Nigel fell asleep. Shannan sat at a table to eat; only her mind too preoccupied and she picked at the food.

Avatar sat next to the crib. After a few moments of observing her preoccupation, he spoke. "Owain isn't capable of this on his own."

"Or perhaps he is, and we underestimated him all these years," she argued. Passion made her stand and pace. "Aligning with the Dark Way he seized Waldron and chased Nigel and I into the wilderness—where we could have lost our lives several times over! Not to mention your wounds and Kato." Her voice cracked, but she continued before Avatar spoke. "Forced Ellis to take up arms. I can only hope the rest of the Council won't be divided by this and stand with us."

Vidar dryly snickered to Avatar. "There is no point arguing with her when she's like this."

She ignored the comment. "I'm going to speak to Darius." She left the chamber. Vidar accompanied her while Avatar remained in the room.

She went to the salon, a common place for gathering in the evening. Wren and Mahon stood guard inside the room. He didn't wear a head bandage and the injury was visible. Wren's wound was clean, but also not bandaged. Arista, Wess and Bosley were with Darius. She wore a modest dress, and the boys wore clothes from when Darius and Ellis were younger.

"The rest of you couldn't sleep either," said Shannan.

"Rather difficult under the circumstances. I feel much better having bathed, changed and eaten," said Arista.

"I'm sorry the clothes are not of royal quality. Father gave away Mother's gowns after she died, and well—" said Darius with a rakish smile and shrug.

"There hasn't been a female to take her place as Lady of Garwood," said Shannan, concluding for him.

"Ay."

"Have you been looking?" Shannan sent him a prompting nod.

"I haven't had the desire to look."

"What?" she said in surprise, a quick, impulsive glance to Arista.

165

Darius balked at his miscue. "I mean—I don't have the desire to look any further." He approached Arista. She blushed upon meeting his eyes. "All I thought about is how awful it would be not to see you again and tell you my heart. Please do me the honor of marrying me and becoming Duchess of Allon, Lady of Garwood."

"Ay." She embraced him, softly weeping in his arms.

"I still didn't know they liked each other," said Bosley.

Darius and Arista laughed and separated. She wiped the tears from her cheek and he spoke. "We had not voiced our feelings before."

Bosley flushed with embarrassment.

"The subtly of relationships are wasted on the young. They say what they mean," said Shannan.

"That being said, what now, Majesty? Does the king have a plan to put down Lord Owain's rebellion?" asked Wess.

Darius replied, "He does. Yet before fully committing to the plan he wanted to be assured of the queen and prince's safety."

"Now that we are safe, I intend to join him and together, confront Owain."

"I too will join the king."

"That is not necessary, Master Wess."

"With all due respect, Majesty, I gave my word to protect you. When you leave Garwood you will again be vulnerable and I would be untrue to my word if I let you go alone."

Shannan fought to keep a smile from her face while regarding Wess. "You do your father and uncle credit by your gallantry. I accept your offer."

"I too must go and for the same reason," said Bosley.

Her gaze shifted between the brothers. Wess was determined from the moment they left Waldron, but Bosley had been reluctant. Now she neither heard, nor saw, reluctance from Bosley. In hindsight, his reluctance faded after fleeing Waldron and resolve manifested itself in confronting the Shadow Warrior to save Nigel.

"Very well. Find Captain Jasper and tell him I instruct you both to be outfitted as my escorts."

Wess and Bosley bowed and departed.

Arista smiled. "You realize this means we're all going?"

Shannan chuckled, squeezing Arista's hand. "I wouldn't dare try to stop you."

"Why not?" asked Darius.

Both women turned to him with staunch, fixed features. Arista spoke, "I have seen war. I was at the battle with my father and uncles. They are all Jor'ellians and were with General Iain's force."

"I was with Iain and I don't recall seeing you."

"I served in the field hospital where one of my uncles died from his wounds." She became sober in remembrance. "Although women are forbidden from becoming Jor'ellians, Grandfather believed we can serve in other ways. He passed the belief onto his sons and grandchildren, of which I am the only girl."

Darius grinned, taking her hands to kiss the knuckles. "I'm glad." He turned to Shannan. "What about Nigel? If we are all going to join Ellis will you leave him here?"

"No. He'll be sent to safety." She rose and left.

Upstairs, she quietly entered the bedchamber. Avatar sat with his back to the door, elbows on his knees and chin on his hands. He bolted to his feet when she touched his shoulder.

"Peace. It's only me."

"I didn't hear you come in. I guess my meditation went deeper than usual."

"You are still recovering, and I didn't want to disturb him." She watched Nigel sleeping. "I'm glad he is too young to understand the situation."

"Are you sufficiently rested to join Ellis?"

She looked up at him, a sarcastic grin appearing. "You aren't taking Vidar's advice about not arguing with me."

He smiled and bowed his head is submission. "What would you have me do, Daughter of Allon?"

Her sarcasm gave way to genuine gratitude. "First, I praise Jor'el's choice of my son's Overseer. Well done, Avatar, and thank you. Now, you must continue your duty elsewhere, and no argument this time." She picked up Nigel. He barely squirmed. "Take him to Melwynn. If we cannot stop Owain, he is the only hope for Allon's future."

"Jor'el will be with you and the Son of Tristan."

Her tender smile grew uncertain when she looked from him to Nigel. "Be good for Avatar, my son." She kissed him and handed him to Avatar who stepped back, and in a flash of white light, disappeared.

Shannan left to rejoin the others and met Arista in the hallway. She was fretful, even hesitant, as she asked, "May I speak to you in private?"

"Of course." They returned to the bedchamber and shut the door.

In the armory, Jasper and a sergeant selected uniforms for Wess and Bosley while boys waited.

"What made you change your mind?" asked Wess.

Bosley shrugged. "Taking care of the prince, I suppose. He's so small and helpless. Like Mother said about Cassie and Callie when they were born."

Wess smiled, wide and sarcastic. "She told me the same about you. And I haven't had a moment's peace since." Bosley poked him, which made him laugh. "I'm kidding. You did well with the prince. I'm proud of you."

Bosley looked skeptical. "You are?"

"Ay. Father and Uncle will be too, when I tell them how you attacked a Shadow Warrior to save the prince."

"I don't know what I was thinking."

"You don't think when you're defending a charge. You act, quick and decisive," said Jasper. He and the sergeant carried the uniforms. "Here, try these on for size."

With the armory being cool, they quickly changed clothes. Bosley smiled. "This fits. How come? Isn't this a soldier's uniform like the other I wore?"

"It belongs to a page about your size. The uniforms are similar, with a few exceptions for arms and armor," replied Jasper.

The sergeant examined the fit of Wess' uniform. "A little wide in the shoulders and arms. A few years of training and growth, and you'll fill out. Captain?"

"Ay. You'll make a fine looking soldier someday, Master Wess."

Wess straightened, an expression of pride on his face. "I hope to be as good as my uncle."

"From what I've seen and heard, you're on your way. In fact, I fought side-by-side with the general the day Ellis confronted Latham and Marcellus."

"You did?"

"Ay. He helped to position the Jor'ellians and Lord Darius' troops in the forest surrounding the Temple. Our original assignment was to prevent the enemy from escaping, but during the battle it became obvious no one thought of fleeing, so we fought."

Bosley looked curiously at Jasper. "If you don't mind my asking, Captain, how do you fight with only one eye?"

The sergeant laughed. "Don't let the patch fool you. Captain Jasper has been Garwood's Master-at-arms for over fifteen years."

"I was born here and squire to Sir Angus, Lord Darius' father and the king's foster-father, before becoming master-at-arms. And I didn't always wear this patch. I lost my eye helping Ellis escape Latham's men." He made a sudden playful attack move at Bosley. The boy jumped back. Jasper laughed. "Proper training, daily practice and a gut intuition can make up for some disabilities."

"I'll try to remember that, Captain," Bosley said, a bit embarrassed.

Jasper steered the boys to the armory door. "Now, get some rest."

Wess and Bosley returned to the house and up to the room they shared. Bosley moved toward the bed. Wess went to survey his reflection in the mirror. He tugged at the shoulders and sleeves, examining himself at various angles.

"You're not going grow that fast," teased Bosley. He sat on the bed and pulled off the boots.

"I didn't get a chance to see how the king's uniform fit me. Everything happened so fast." His voice grew somber and soft. "I didn't even see Father."

"What did you say?" asked Bosley. He reclined on the bed.

Wess turned from the mirror to face Bosley. "I didn't see Father."

Concerned, Bosley sat up. "Do you think something has happened to him?"

Wess sat next to Bosley. "When we were supposed to be resting, I overheard the queen ask Vidar about Waldron. He said it is fallen. It could be very bad."

Bosley grew fearful. "You mean Father may be dead?"

"Possibly. And why I want to return, to find out." Seeing Bosley upset, Wess gripped his shoulder to steady him. "We can't fall apart now, we've come too far with too much at stake."

"If he's dead …"

"Then we are the men of the family. Cassie and Callie will need us like never before."

Overwhelmed, Bosley vigorously shook his head. "Why is it happening again? Why can't they leave us alone? They killed Mother, and Father isn't involved with them anymore."

"He was never involved with the Dark Way! Grandfather and Uncle Marcellus listened to Latham. But this isn't about us, it's about the Son of Tristan and Daughter of Allon—same as before. We're caught up in it because of who we are, heirs to the House of Unwin. Because of Uncle Iain's defection, Father's actions and King Ellis' mercy we are alive."

Confused, Bosley stared at Wess. "I don't understand."

Wess sighed, long and deep. "You were too young then, but you need to know everything now."

"I know Latham killed Mother using his power and imprisoned us to blackmail Father," said Bosley, angrily.

"More than that. Do you recall Uncle Iain telling us how Jor'el sent Avatar in response to his prayer for help in rescuing us?"

"Ay."

"Then took us to safety?"

Bosley nodded.

"He did so because he was joining the Jor'ellians to fight against Marcellus, to avenge Mother and rescue Father if he could."

"I kind of guessed that. After all, he is a general and Mother was his sister."

"You don't know what Father did!" Wess drew a deep steadying breath before continuing. "Marcellus and Ellis were locked in battle, with Ellis winning. To stay alive, Marcellus pretended to surrender. When Ellis took his sword, Marcellus struck with a hidden dagger, only it broke against the Golden Armor."

Bosley made a sour frown. "He always lied and cheated."

"Ay. Mother didn't trust him, and he and Father constantly argued."

"So what did Father do?"

"With Marcellus focused on Ellis, Father came up from behind and killed him." Wess made a quick stabbing motion to the back of Bosley's neck for illustration.

Bosley flinched, his eyes growing wide in fearful surprise. "What?"

"Father didn't know about our rescue. He knew Mother was dead and believed we were prisoners. Marcellus allowed Latham to use the Dark Way against his own family! Don't you understand? Marcellus approved of Latham's plan to hold us hostage; kill us if needed. Father did the only thing he could: killed his brother to stop the Dark Way from destroying us and Allon."

Bosley was stunned speechless and grew paler.

Wess placed a comforting arm about Bosley's shoulder. "It was because of Uncle Iain's bravery in battle and Father's actions that Ellis pardoned them and allowed us to live. Think, Bosley. What king would allow a rival royal family to remain alive after taking the throne? Only a merciful king."

Bosley shook his head in bewilderment. His voice hushed and choked. "I never thought much about it. I didn't want to remember."

"I don't blame you. I asked questions afterwards, but Father kept putting me off." Wess shrugged. "I can't imagine the depth of despair driving a man to kill his own brother."

With a hurt, angry frown, Bosley said, "You've threatened to kill me before."

That stung and Wess recoiling, clamoring, "I never meant it! I'd just get frustrated with you. When I was your age, Father overheard me lash out at you. He harshly reprimanded me and told me the story. Since then, I've tried to hold my tongue when we argue. I'm sorry I ever said it!"

"So am I." Bosley wept and Wess comforted him.

"We can't let the Dark Way win! No matter what happens. Which is why I told you everything."

Bosley wiped his face on his sleeve.

"Now, let's try to get some sleep."

"I don't think I can."

"You have to try. The queen is depending upon us when we leave tomorrow." Wess took Bosley by the shoulders and without any resistance, put him to bed. "I love you. I know I've never said that before, but I do."

"I love you too. Even if you do try to act like a captain."

Wess chuckled. "Go to sleep."

Sometime later, Bosley quietly left the bedchamber. Wess slept, but he couldn't sleep. He didn't like hearing about the past. He remembered the difficulty accepting their mother's sudden death. Everything about that time was painful, and he avoided thinking about it. Unfortunately, the current situation made it impossible to avoid any longer. Another desperate escape, Avatar's involvement, his father again in danger; it was all too familiar to dismiss. He must face reality. He must make grown-up decisions.

In truth, the process began while caring for and defending Nigel. This made him consider Ellis and Shannan. Despite what Wess said about allowing them to live, he did not feel threatened by Ellis and thought he appeared every inch a noble king with a kind, generous smile. Ellis greatly contrasted Marcellus. He never understood why he disliked Marcellus, being too young to give voice to his feelings. Something about the way he acted toward to his mother bothered him. But from the first moment he met Ellis he sensed a difference. Ellis' smile immediately placed him at ease, something he never felt with Marcellus.

Queen Shannan was a courageous woman. The sight of her fighting beside the Guardians against the beast was a sight he would never forget. Perhaps the most personally touching part was her expressed confidence in him and how sincerely grateful she was for their help. His mother had the same quality of reassuring conviction. Since her death he wasn't certain of himself, much less of his future. After their life-and-death adventure, he couldn't imagine disappointing the queen anymore than disappointing his mother. *Oh, why would anyone on the Council betray them? Why would anyone want to return to those horrible days?*

Hearing voices and laughing, he realized he had wandered downstairs. He stopped to listen. Along with laughter he head footsteps behind him and was startled by a hand on his shoulder. He sighed in relief at seeing Mahon.

"Where did you come from?"

"I didn't mean to startle you. I've been following you since you left your room. I'm supposed to watch you, remember?"

"Nothing will happen to me here."

"No, but you are troubled. What's wrong?"

"Everything! Father, Sir Owain, the Council. How could they allow him to do this?"

Mahon glanced to the drawing room. "The duke can better answer you about mortal motives and choices." With a hand on Bosley's shoulder, he guided the lad inside. Darius, Jasper, and Edmund sat near the hearth conversing. "Your Grace."

"Mahon. Bosley? What are you doing up this late? I thought you'd be fast asleep after your ordeal."

"I couldn't sleep, Your Grace."

"His mind is troubled about Sir Owain," said Mahon, his eyes direct on Darius. "I told him you could answer his questions."

Darius beckoned Bosley to them. He came and he sat on the footstool in front of Darius' chair. "I have wondered about Owain and racked my brain to find a reason. The thought of betrayal is deplorable, while his order to kill the queen and prince is reprehensible. Not worthy of a member of the Council. A man's true heart is told by his actions not his words, yet nothing Owain said lead me to believe him capable of this."

"I heard Father and Uncle Iain speak about something similar he did in the past."

Jasper snarled with a throaty growl and poked at the fire.

"Ay," began Darius. "However, Owain fulfilled his punishment and the Vicar declared him repentant."

"That's a mild way of putting it and avoiding the subject," chided Jasper.

"Easy, Jasper. No need to upset the lad," said Edmund.

"Upset? He faced Shadow Warriors and an attack by a tartundeen. I don't think hearing about Owain's duplicity comes near to that level of upset." Edmund squirmed in his seat and frowned as Jasper continued. "And your wound still troubles you on cold nights."

"Wound? Does it have anything to do with Sir Owain?" asked Bosley.

Edmund's vexed glance found Darius while Jasper made defense to Darius. "The lad has a right to know. After all, what he endured was a result of Owain's actions."

Edmund still appeared cross, but Darius nodded and acquiesced. "Jasper's right," he said to Edmund then to Bosley. "Owain was persuaded by Tyree and Witter to aid them in trying to capture Ellis to stop him."

"Let me. You don't know how Brody and I were captured or the bargaining to use us against Ellis," said Jasper.

"Is that how you lost your eye?" asked Bosley.

"No. This happened before, but my eye patch was used to convince Ellis of my identity. Along with Brody's hunting knife. Our lives in exchange for Owain."

"How?"

174

Darius answered, "Owain attempted to capture Ellis only he ended up becoming Ellis' prisoner. Ellis thought to use him as a bargain for us to leave Midessex alive then he'd be freed. We didn't know about Jasper and Brody."

Jasper took up the story. "In repayment for her kindness, Ellis had Brody and I escort an elderly woman to her grandson. After safely leaving her, Tyree's men surrounded us. I tried to be inconspicuous and let Brody do the talking since Tyree knew me. Even with gaining the eye patch and new clothes, it didn't take for him long to recognize me. Witter arrived, and he and Tyree argued. We couldn't hear clearly, but the next thing we knew, we ended up being taken to Presley—Sir Owain's manor house.

"Astonished and intimidated by our arrival, Lady Lanay, Owain's wife, claimed no knowledge of his agreement with Tyree and Witter." Jasper shrugged and scowled. "Of course it didn't matter to them what she did or didn't know; only success in capturing Ellis mattered. The situation quickly turned ugly when Owain's men returned and reported the capture went awry and he was now Ellis' prisoner. I thought Tyree would kill us in fit of rage. Lanay's quick suggestion of using us in exchange for Owain stopped him. It took some convincing, but in the end, she won the argument."

"Did you or Brody say anything?"

Jasper snorted an ironic chuckle. "Brody tried and was clouted for his effort. I kept silent. If I opened my mouth, Tyree would kill us. We clashed a few times before."

"I'm surprised you kept your other eye," said Edmund.

Bosley surveyed Edmund. "Did Tyree wound you during one of his clashes with the captain?"

"No. It happened during the exchange to save his ornery hide." Edmund jerked at his thumb at Jasper.

"What about the king, Owain and Brody? Were they hurt?"

"Ellis placed me in command. At the exchange point, Owain used the guise of asking me to cut him loose from his bounds. I wasn't prepared for his attack."

Jasper gave Edmund a clap on the shoulder. "You're a steward not a soldier and no match for Owain." He continued explaining to Bosley.

"Owain's man freed me and I was able to make defense of Edmund after he was wounded, but that left Brody vulnerable." His features grew harsh yet regretful. "His hands were still bound and defenseless when Owain's man struck him dead."

Bosley gasped in horror.

"By that time, Ellis, Allard and I arrived and Owain and his men fled," said Darius.

Bosley was having difficulty comprehending. "After killing one of the king's men he's still on the Council?"

"Owain's man killed Brody, he wounded Edmund. Despite Brody's death, Jasper was rescued, Edmund recovered and we left Midessex."

Bosley's brows knitted in confusion. "I thought a lord was responsible for the actions of his servant? Uncle Marcellus always blamed someone else and used Witter and Captain Tyree as punishment. People were frightened of them and they scared me." He shied away and bit his lower lip.

Darius touched Bosley's shoulder for the boy to look at him. "Ellis isn't like Marcellus."

"I know. But why didn't he punish Sir Owain?"

"He did. At the coronation, Owain recanted his allegiance to Marcellus, apologized for his misguided actions, and pledged fealty to Ellis. As punishment, he was removed from the Council and he spent four years on probation under the watchful eye of the Vicar."

"Remember my story. Tyree and Witter were hard to refuse," said Jasper.

Bosley shivered at Jasper's comment. Darius gave the boy a comforting squeeze on his shoulder. "They aren't alive to cause any more harm. Witter was defeated by Kell and Tyree executed shortly after the coronation."

Relief passed over Bosley's face. "How did Sir Owain return to the Council?"

"He successfully completed his probation, and upon Archimedes' recommendation, Ellis reinstated him."

"So the king showed Sir Owain mercy," said Bosley, more to himself than them.

"Ay. Just like he did your father, you, your bother and sisters," Mahon spoke for the first time.

Bosley gazed up at the Guardian, the light blue eyes sincere and penetrating. "My uncle ruled by fear but King Ellis rules with kindness." He turned from the Guardian to the others. "Why would Sir Owain, or anyone on the Council, turn against such generosity?"

Darius momentarily stared at Bosley. So simplistic and powerful was the assessment and question. "I'm afraid the ways of politics aren't always clear-cut. Diplomacy and subtly can often mask a man's true intentions. Owain followed Ellis' instruction like the rest of us. Perhaps it was Zebulon's meanness that pushed him too far. He was merciless to Owain after our last meeting."

"Why? Did he suspect what Sir Owain was going to do?"

"No. Zebulon is mean to everyone while Allard is too clever to be pinned down on anything. They both made their feelings known about Owain."

"But no one did anything to stop him!"

"As I said, there was no indication of trouble," chided Darius, then sighed realizing how harsh he sounded. He patted Bosley's shoulder. "I'm sorry I don't have a clear answer for you. I don't have one for myself."

"Men on the Council should know and act better than petty politics."

Edmund and Jasper chuckled.

Darius grinned. "Ay, we should. Maybe you can teach us."

Embarrassed, Bosley blushed. "I didn't mean to scold, Your Grace. I just find the difference between my uncle and King Ellis surprising. I can't imagine why any one would want to hurt him, the queen or the prince when all they've shown is kindness. I saw too much of what fear and hate can do," he said, a catch in his voice and his face growing stern.

Mahon lifted Bosley's chin. "Don't let the past make you bitter."

"Mahon's right," began Darius. "It may be some lingering bitterness guiding Owain's actions. More importantly, neither Hugh nor Iain have let bitterness take root. If anything, they are your examples. Loyalty and trust begin in the heart." He lightly poked his finger against Bosley's left breast.

"You saw with Marcellus how a strong man earns grudging respect and obedience from fear. But no one can place full, untainted loyalty and trust in a heart that doesn't already have it. Your father and Iain didn't let the Dark Way overtake them, which is why Ellis trusts Iain as his general and provides for your family."

"What made you and Wess come to the queen's aid?" asked Mahon.

Again, Bosley glanced up into the Guardian's kind yet probing eyes. "I'm not sure. I followed Wess and ran for fear."

"The entire time?"

He shook his head, growing thoughtful. "No. When the queen spoke with confidence in me and I held the prince, I wanted to help. The Dark Way did so much harm in the past. It killed my mother and I didn't want to see anyone die again." His voice cracked in anger and he looked down to regain his composure.

"The same desire to protect and made you charge a Shadow Warrior, is the same feeling guiding your father and uncle in their actions."

"I think I understand now."

Darius smiled and patted the boy's leg. "Good. Now try to get some sleep. We have a long journey starting tomorrow."

Bosley left with Mahon.

"I hope the conversation helped you," said Mahon.

"A bit. Yet everything now is so much like the past."

Mahon stopped Bosley at the door to the chamber, placed his hand over the lad's heart and said, "Only under great testing and trial can what is inside come out." He softly smiled. "So far, you and Wess are both passing the test. Continue to trust Jor'el and you will completely succeed."

"What about Father? I'm afraid for him."

"He was alive and unharmed when I left. I will do all within my power to reunite you." Seeing Bosley relieved but fighting a yawn, Mahon led him into the chamber. Silently, so as not to wake Wess, he helped Bosley climb into bed. Placing a gentle hand on Bosley's head, he spoke in the Ancient, "Be at peace and sleep," and Bosley closed his eyes.

For security, Shannan and Arista wore the brown and gold uniform of Darius' soldiers and were armed with their hair tucked under hats. The Golden Bow was hidden in a cloth sheath and attached to the saddle of Shannan's horse. Wren, Vidar and Mahon were dispatched to keep secret surveillance of the group since the sight of Guardians might cause suspicion. Torin went with them.

Darius, Shannan and Arista rode in front of the group of fifty soldiers and twenty Jor'ellians. Darius tossed his fourth look at Arista.

"Why do you keep looking at me? Is it the clothes?"

With a teasing smile and light voice, Shannan spoke. "Whereas it is perfectly acceptable for me to dress like this and ride out to do battle, he takes exception to you doing the same, now that there is an understanding."

"Is that why?" Arista asked Darius. "Just as your loyalty and duty to the king moves you to his side in a time of crisis, so does mine to the queen."

The response soothed Darius and he grinned. "Well said."

"You expected less from Archimedes' granddaughter?" Shannan continued in her merry humor.

"No, I need time to get used to the idea of my future wife facing battle."

"Courage and loyalty are traits you both have in common."

"Subtly isn't one of your traits."

"I'm queen. I don't have to be subtle."

Wess and Bosley rode beside Jasper a short distance behind Darius and the others. "How long till we reach the North Plains?" Bosley asked Jasper.

"Depending on the route, perhaps five days to the border."

Wess glanced skyward before making his assessment. "No, we won't be able to travel a full day today. It's nearly noon. Add a day, which makes six. Unless we take the pass through Somerset Valley and cross the river at Redford Crossing, then four days."

Jasper arched the brow of his good eye. "How did you come up with that?"

"I studied a map and calculated the distance and traveling speed of roughly seventy mounted men."

Jasper smiled and waved toward Darius. "Come." He and Wess moved forward. "Your Grace." At his call, Darius turned but didn't check his horse. Jasper pulled along side. "Have you determined a route?"

"I was considering taking the road to Alford, crossing the river and then through Cahill. Why?"

"Six days," said Wess, making Darius turn further to see him.

Jasper wryly smiled. "I think Master Wess has a better and shorter route."

"Really? Come and tell me."

Jasper drew his horse back so Wess could move along side Darius. "Your Grace, I believe it would be best to take the pass through Somerset Valley and cross the river at Redford Crossing." When Darius just looked at him, Wess continued, howbeit a bit apprehensive. "The elevation is lower so there shouldn't be too much snow and far enough from Waldron we should pass undetected. If we pick up the pace we can make it in four days."

Darius looked askew to Jasper. "You told him this, didn't you?"

"No."

"I examined a map and calculated speed and distance based on the seventy of us."

"I told you he and Bosley were very helpful to me," said Shannan.

"I didn't choose that route since I was more concerned for safety than speed, but it is well thought out." Darius studiously regarded Wess and said, "We'll alter course and head for Somerset Valley."

"You will ride with us," said Shannan.

Wess beamed with pride. "Ay, Majesty."

By sundown they put a good distance between themselves and Garwood. Ten men led extra horses with supplies and canvas for a tent. A grove of evergreens proved a suitable campsite. Some soldiers erected the tent; others fetched wood for cooking and warming fire; and still others formed a defensive perimeter. Being off the main road and safe from prying eyes, the

Guardians rejoined the group. Wren and Vidar downed a large buck, dressed the carcass and roasted it, and in less than two hours.

Beside one of the smaller warming fires near the center of camp, Bosley contently stretched out on a blanket, his head resting on a saddle. "I don't think I've ever had such good venison."

"Thank you, young master," said Wren, smiling. She and Vidar sat on a log next to the well-devoured carcass, which rested on a spit for easy serving.

Suddenly they were on their feet, loaded crossbows in hand. Mahon drew his sword and moved to protect Shannan. She and Arista sat on campstools near the fire. Torin growled in warning.

"What's wrong?" asked Shannan.

"Someone is trying to enter my defensive perimeter," said Wren.

"Mahon, stay here. Torin, come," said Vidar. He signaled Wren to the left before dashing off into the darkness with Torin.

Swords drawn, Darius and twenty men formed a protective circle around the women. Bosley and Wess joined the men. Jasper and the rest made a larger defensive perimeter. For several tense moments they waited. Only the crackling of the fires and several nocturnal animals broke the silence.

Then …

"Be at ease, it is Elgin," called Vidar. He appeared from the darkness with the vassal Guardian.

"Your Grace—Majesty!" Elgin said in surprise when Shannan moved from the circle. "It is good to see you are unharmed."

"Thank you, Elgin. What are you doing here?"

"Captain Kell dispatched me to Garwood to wait for either you or the duke. Since neither of you were there when I first arrived, I took a little detour to locate you."

"And got lost in the wilderness as a result of your dereliction, I suppose," chided Mahon.

"No," said the vassal defensively. "It wasn't dereliction of duty. I sensed evil and followed it hoping to locate the queen and prince. Only I arrived at meadow with a lot of horse tracks. I traveled back to Garwood and learned of your departure and intent to join the king."

"You were told the queen was with me?" asked Darius in displeasure.

"No, Edmund was very discreet. Vidar told me."

"How is Ellis?" asked Shannan.

"Well, but worried for you and the prince."

"Nigel is safe with Avatar."

Elgin smiled in relief. "That's good to hear."

"We shall be rejoining Ellis in three days."

"Captain Kell said they might be on the move and to hone in on him when I return with news of you and prince. When I did so, I felt Vidar's essence was closer. Although Kell has moved, east, I think. I didn't focus too long on him, more wanting to find you, Majesty."

"Waldron," said Jasper to Darius.

"I hope you're right."

"Stands to reason. He stopped to await word then dispatched you, which he wouldn't do if he were going in battle. He must have discovered the North Plains was the diversion, which I always suspected since seizing the seat of power is more important than a province."

"We left him five days ago. He could have returned to Waldron by now."

"Doubtful since he learned it after our departure. I'd say three days at the most, which could place him near ..."

"Riverton," concluded Darius with a growing smile. He called for Wess. "Your Grace?"

Darius placed a hand on the young man's shoulder. "The route you chose was not only well-conceived in the mortal sense, but divine inspiration. Instead of going through Somerset Valley, we'll turn due south and intercept the king in two days. Well done."

"Thank you, Your Grace."

"Now, get some sleep."

"I'd like to stay on watch."

"As you please."

Wess moved to take up position in front of the tent for Shannan and Arista.

"He's extremely conscientious of duty. Much like Iain," said Shannan.

"It's more a matter of proving himself," said Mahon.

"What makes you say that?"

"Marcellus was also his uncle. Two more drastic contrasts cannot be found than he and Iain. One is honorable; one submitted to evil and inflicted evil on others. When faced with a choice Iain and Hugh made the right decision. Wess and Bosley face that same choice. Bosley spoke to the duke about the Council, expressing concern on matters of loyalty in government."

"He did," affirmed Darius. "He has a good heart and the right attitude."

"Wess fights against his family's past. It is a difficult battle to prove himself to himself," said Mahon.

She turned to where Wess stood. He didn't appear to notice. "He has nothing to prove. He was a child and not involved while Hugh and Iain have more than convinced Ellis and I they are honorable men."

Mahon cocked a contrary brow. "The king ordered them to remain at Waldron under my supervision until this situation is over."

"Over concern for their well-being."

Darius shook his head. "Precaution because of Hugh's heritage. However," he said, forestalling her protest, "when Mahon told us what they did, Ellis admitted his reasons for the initial order turned out not to be the ultimate reason for their staying. He commended them to Iain and those in attendance."

She grew resolute. "He won't doubt them again. I won't let him."

Darius grinned. "He won't. Now, it's late. You best get some sleep. Wess will stand guard."

Chapter 12

HAGELEY WAS A FORTIFIED CITY of roughly ten thousand inhabitants. Barlow, Armus and their forces arrived four days after leaving the main army. Before dawn, on a knoll overlooking the city, Barlow sat upon his mount, surveying the terrain through a spyglass. The light of oil lamps and tower torches were being extinguished for the day.

Armus stood beside the general's horse. "All appears quiet."

"Unusually quiet," said a female voice.

Mona, the Guardian Trio Leader of the North Plains, stood six inches shorter than Armus, but still the seven-foot height of a Guardian. Aquamarine eyes beautifully complemented her rich brown hair. She wore breeches and a tunic with only a dagger for a weapon.

"Can you tell us what's going on?" asked Armus.

"I sensed a disturbance. Before I could approach Lord Malcolm, the city was shut. I tried to dimension travel inside but was repelled."

"Repelled by what?"

"I don't know. I was about to report to Kell when I learned of the message Malcolm sent Ellis and decided to await his arrival."

Barlow again looked at the city through the spyglass. "No sentries. Which is strange, since they must know we're coming."

"Not if this is the distraction and someone is using the Dark Way to keep us from discovering that," said Armus.

"Well, I see nothing stopping us from approaching the gate to demand admittance. Unless this repelling force extends to mortals." His gruff voice matched his challenging regard of Mona.

She shrugged in uncertainty. "I don't think so, but I can't be sure."

His scowl showed his displeasure. "Hagley isn't a city to be taken by force; it has to be sieged. Not something the king will want to hear."

"Easy, General. Mona may not have been able to get in, but I can."

"How? You're both Guardians. If the Dark Way can stop her, it can stop you."

"I'm a warrior, Mona's a vassal—granted a highly positioned vassal as a Trio Leader," he added at seeing her sour reaction, "but I'm still the stronger."

"Rather than brute force, I have an better idea. One that will accomplish both determining who is using the Dark Way and if the city has to be sieged," she said.

Intrigued, Barlow leaned forward. "I'm listening."

Mona took a deep breath and closed her eyes. A moment later two Guardians arrived in a joint flash of white light. They were identical in appearance with black hair and dark yellow eyes wearing gray tunics and breeches. Armus chuckled upon sight of them and Mona made the introductions.

"General Barlow, the night twins of the North Plains, Daren and Darcy."

"General," they said together.

"Who is who?"

"We can never tell, but they know," said Armus. He spoke to the twins. "Someone is employing Shadow Warriors against the king and queen."

"We heard there was trouble," said Darcy.

"Why have you summoned us?" asked Daren.

Armus told them what was reported about Hagley and Mona added her observations and recounted the inability to dimension travel.

185

"Since they haven't posted sentries, we need quick reconnaissance of the city," Armus concluded.

"Why them? I have good scouts and Mona was repelled by the Dark Way," said Barlow.

The twins widely grinned while Armus answered, "With their special powers of stealth, it can be done quickly and without anyone's knowledge, including Shadow Warriors."

"Then go to it," said Barlow to the twins.

Instead of vanishing, they made a dash of incredible speed from the knoll toward the city. Barlow quickly raised the spyglass to watch.

Armus laughed. "You won't see them."

Neither did the local guards at the main gate. Not that the twins weren't visible to the naked eyes, rather Darcy lowly spoke the Ancient to summon their special power. They walked right by the guards, who didn't so much as blink.

"It'll be quicker if we split up," said Daren.

"Ay. Take the west and north sections, I'll take the east and south."

Speed worked in the open, but for navigating the city streets, they used short dashes from place to place, keeping to the shadows. Being pre-dawn not many mortals wandered the streets, except local soldiers on patrol. Fifteen minutes later they met again at the front gate, shook their heads at each other and left.

Impatient, Barlow tapped the spyglass in his open palm. He flinched in surprise when the night twins appeared in front of his horse.

Armus and Mona didn't react to their return. "Well?" asked Armus.

"Nothing," said Darcy.

"Not even a trace of Shadow Warriors," said Daren.

"What? I was repelled," she insisted.

Armus didn't answer, rather stared at the city; chestnut eyes narrowed with scrutiny.

"Could the repelling force prevent you from sensing anything?" Barlow asked the twins.

"Doubtful," said Daren.

"Unlikely," said Darcy in near unison.

"What about mortal soldiers?"

"The normal garrison," said Darcy.

"Ay, only Lord Malcolm's soldiers," agreed Daren.

Barlow deeply frowned and pursed his lips in annoyance before speaking in a begrudging tone to Armus. "You were right, this is the distraction and they use the Dark Way to keep us guessing. Time to pay the city a visit." He gathered the reins, intent on moving but Armus seized the horse's bridle to stop his departure.

"Shadow Warriors would not simply abandon a place they had taken, nor would Malcolm send for help if there wasn't real trouble."

"I will order the city elders to allow the army to enter and do a more thorough search." Barlow attempted to turn his horse's head, but Armus wouldn't let go.

"First let me take a dozen Jor'ellians and act as envoy."

"No! This is not a time for diplomacy."

"Something's not right, General. Let me do as I have said."

"No! We haven't much time. They must see the king's standard and submit. We can soothe over ruffled egos later." He stuck the Guardian's arm to release the bridle and turned his horse toward camp, ending the discussion.

"That didn't go well," she groused, drawing Armus' ire, to which she added, "I mean there aren't many mortals who can resist you, Lieutenant. Your charming demeanor," her voice trailed off at seeing her attempt to correct her errant comment only sounded worse and irritated him more.

"Go back and make certain there are no Shadow Warriors. I don't like this," he told the twins.

In an instant, they were racing toward Hagley.

"What do you want me to do?" she asked

"Watch our backs," he grumbled before returning to camp.

With the army deployed five hundred yards from the city, Barlow, Armus, Roarke and a dozen Jor'ellians approached the main gate. The mortals were mounted, Armus on foot. One knight carried the Jor'ellian banner, another, the royal standard. The group halted fifty yards from the walls.

"Hello, the city! I am General Barlow. I am here by order of King Ellis to reclaim Hagley from those who have oppressed you."

"You must be mistaken, General, we have not been oppressed," called the guard.

"What of Lord Malcolm? He sent a plea to the king for aid."

One guard spoke privately to another. The second guard ran off and the first spoke to Barlow. "We are sending for the city elders, General."

Shortly, two men in prosperous clothing appeared on the rampart. One was middle aged the other older. The older man spoke. "There has been a terrible mistake, General. Please convey our apologies to the king, but you have ridden all this way for nothing."

"What of Lord Malcolm?"

"His lordship is spending the winter in Kirkwood," said the second

"Who sent for help using his name?"

The two men exchanged sheepish glances, unable to answer.

This did not set well with Barlow. "Open the gate!"

"General, we—" the first began to protest.

"Do it! We shall see if all is in order as you claim. If all is well, we will withdraw. If not—?" Barlow motioned to the army. "You see my army."

In fretful consideration, they surveyed the army. The older man motioned to the guards barking an emphatic "Go!" The guards disappeared from view of Barlow and the others.

Wary, Armus gripped the hilt of his sword. "I don't like this, General. Let me go in alone."

"No, I said we do this together."

The sound of mechanism stopped Armus' reply and allowed Barlow to move his horse away from the Guardian and toward the city. He slowed the

188

animal until the gate opened wide enough to permit entry. He was the first to enter, followed closely by Armus, Roake and the Jor'ellians.

Just beyond the gate lay the city square. Although dawn was long past, the shops and houses remained shut. Considering the time of day, this was unusual. Armus viewed the square with a critical eye.

Roarke also noticed the oddity and signaled the Jor'ellians to stay alert then spoke to Barlow. "No one is out and about yet, General."

At that moment the city elders and guards appeared. The men were more nervous than on the rampart.

Barlow observed everything and confronted the elders. "What trap is set?"

"No! No, trap," insisted the older man. "There are things better said in private." He indicated the closest building.

"Please, General," said the second.

Barlow dismounted. His feet no sooner touched the cobblestone …

"Faileas!" Armus exclaimed the Ancient word for shadows.

Immediately, twenty Shadow Warriors appeared. No light, just appeared.

"For Jor'el and for Allon!" Roarke shouted the Jor'ellian battle cry and drew his sword.

The Jor'ellians fought from atop their horses. Soon some animals were either killed or knocked down by the Shadow Warriors forcing the knights to battle on foot. Daren and Darcy quickly arrived and sent a jolt of temporary blindness to halt the Warriors, then aided the fallen Jor'ellians. Barlow did not have Jor'ellian training and was not fairing well against Shadow Warriors.

Armus intercepted a Shadow Warrior about to hack at Barlow. "Get out of here!"

"I don't run!" Barlow ducked when another Warrior attacked. The mortal general fought his best, but was struck dead.

Snarling fiercely at seeing Barlow's death, Armus turned aside the Warrior's blade. He was about to launch his counter attack when the Warrior shouted, *"Dorchadas a buail!"*

The Jor'ellians doubled over in pain or collapsed in distress. Daren and Darcy fell to their knees, holding their head. Armus staggered back, gritting

189

his teeth to withstand the pain. Three incapacitated knights were cut down before Armus could regain his footing. With determination, he assumed the Jor'ellian stance; his sword poised level next to his head.

"By Jor'el's strength, I fight his enemies!" he declared in the Ancient and launched himself at the Warriors.

The power and speed of Armus' attack was impossible to stop. In groups of three and four, the Shadow Warriors fell, gray light signaling their demise. After a few moments, all twenty were gone.

Armus stopped in mid-motion, his sword wielded to one side, brightened chestnut eyes alert and looking around the square for more of the enemy. Seeing movement, he turned, ready to strike.

"Armus!" Mona said, raising her hands in defense.

He clumsily stopped himself from striking her and stumbled back, exhausted. She caught his arm only he was too heavy for her to hold up, so she helped him sit on a nearby crate.

Stunned, Roarke glanced about. "What happened?"

Armus couldn't speak, trying to catch his breath, so Mona replied. "Armus used his power to defeat the Shadow Warriors."

"The general is dead," said a Jor'ellian. "I found this." He showed Roarke a square shaped medallion.

Armus waved him over and reached for the medallion to examine it. He looked aside to Mona and the twins then spoke to Roarke. "This is why we didn't sense them. It's a shielding medal. It protects whoever wears it from detection."

"I wonder if there are any more of those or Shadow Warriors."

Armus shook his head. "My declaration would have driven them into the open."

The elders fell to their knees. "Mercy!" cried the older one. "We had no choice."

"Ay! They threatened our families."

Armus stared at the mortals, bright chestnut eyes direct and probing. "Do you swear in Jor'el's name?"

"Ay," said the first.

"In Jor'el's name," added the second.

"They speak the truth." Armus leaned back against the building to rest.

"What about Lord Malcolm?" asked Roarke.

"He is in the dungeon. They forced him send to the king for help by harming Lady Matrill when he initially refused," said the oldest.

Roarke stiffened and Armus sat forward, piqued by the answer.

Mona was first stunned, then angered. "Where is she now?"

"They confined her to her room with no treatment for her injuries and said there would be none until the trap was sprung."

Armus stood. "Fetch the surgeon and meet us at the manor," he said to the Jor'ellian who found the medallion. "Take care of the lady while I free Lord Malcolm," he said to Roarke and Mona.

In the dungeon two guards played a game of dice. The door burst open, falling off the hinges. Armus' bulk filled the threshold, sword in hand, chestnut eyes deadly with intent. The guards gaped and paled in fear.

"Where is Lord Malcolm?"

"That one. We had no choice!" One pointed to a cell across the hall.

Armus opened the cell door by a flick of his wrist and speaking in the Ancient. Inside, Malcolm sat on the stone slab with his back against the corner, his eyes closed. Armus was uncertain if Malcolm was asleep or unconscious. "My lord?"

Malcolm's eyes snapped opened, startled and frazzled. "Armus? Is it really you, or is this a trick?"

"No trick, my lord. Hagley is safe."

"Ellis? He didn't come, did he?"

"No, he sent part of the army with General Barlow, Sir Roake and myself."

"My mother?"

"Sir Roarke and Mona are freeing her and a surgeon sent for."

"Thank Jor'el," he whimpered in relief. "I didn't want to do it."

Armus was sympathetic in feature and gentle in helping Malcolm stand. "I know. Come."

191

At the manor house a bruised, battered and weak Matrill was greatly distraught over the situation.

"Please! Tell the king we tried," she clamored.

"Easy, my lady," said Roarke. "You are not at fault and the king will not blame you."

"Malcolm tried. Oh, I fear for him."

"Armus went to free him," said Mona.

The door to the chamber opened. Malcolm rushed in. Armus and the surgeon accompanied him. Mother and son were overjoyed to see each other. Roarke moved beside Armus at seeing the Guardian's furrowed brow of compassion at sight of Matrill.

"It would have been far worse if you did not act."

"The general is dead," Armus said with no emotion on his face or in his voice.

"Malcolm and Matrill alive."

"No one needed to die." Armus turned on his heels and left.

Roarke did his best to keep pace with the Guardian. "What now?"

"Secure Hagley while I make certain the Dark Way is gone."

"I thought you said your declaration would bring out any remaining Shadow Warriors?"

Armus glared at Roarke, making the mortal stop in his tracks.

"Armus!" Malcolm called and he hurried on hobbling legs to join them. To him, the Guardian's features softened to placid.

"Thank you. I don't know what would have happened if you and the general hadn't arrived."

"The general is dead."

"Mona told me. I'm sorry yet glad Ellis didn't come. He could have suffered Barlow's fate."

"There is more at stake than you realize, my lord."

"I caught parts of conversation between the Shadow Warriors."

"Perhaps you should tell the king what happened," said Roarke.

With a look of resolve, Malcolm said, " I intend to do that."

"We'll leave when Hagley is secured." Armus departed, and Roarke chose not to follow him this time.

Outside Armus found the twins waiting and informed them of Lady Matril's condition and Malcolm's intent to accompany them and report to Ellis. While he was speaking, Mona arrived. "I'm going to search Hagley and when we leave, you three make certain it stays secure."

"We weren't anticipating trouble," said Daren in defense.

Armus rebuffed the argument. "Malcolm didn't inform you of the king's orders to ferret out the Dark Way?"

Mona stopped an irate Daren from speaking to reply in a calm voice. "Ay, and we found nothing to suggest any immediate danger, rather past activities, which Malcolm included in his report."

Daren could only stay quiet for so long, especially seeing the skepticism. "Armus, we know our duty."

"Lieutenant to you!"

Mona made a motion of restraint Armus didn't notice, so Darcy respectfully said, "Ay, Lieutenant."

Armus marched away, leaving the twins perplexed and asking Mona, "What was that about?"

"You heard how he wanted to handle the situation only to have his concerns rudely dismissed. Now the general is dead. A death that might have been prevented if Armus acted as he wanted."

"So why didn't he press the matter when Barlow resisted?" said Darcy.

She shrugged. "Heavenly authority doesn't persuade some mortals. Whatever his reason for not pressing the matter, my guess is the general's death is deeply troubling him. Along with being forced to use his power. I've not seen him gruff or moody very often, and I've known him since the Beginning."

"We didn't fail in our duty but he may tell Kell we did."

"Don't worry. I'll speak with Kell. For now, let's secure the city."

Chapter 13

THE ORANGE GLOW OF TWILIGHT gave way to night. A blanket of new snow covered the plain before Waldron. Iain lay on his stomach beneath a prickly hedge in the forest surrounding the castle using a spyglass for surveillance. Several tents and campsites stood outside the walls, smoke rising from warming fires.

Ferrell and Auriel joined him. She was a female Guardian warrior and Trio leader of the South Plains with strawberry blond hair and vibrant jade eyes. She wore a sword strapped to her back, a dagger at her right hip, and a chakram on her left hip.

Iain lowered the spyglass. "From all reports, I estimate two thousand soldiers in and around the castle."

"Not an overwhelming force," said Ferrell.

"Enough to take Waldron in a night. I wanted to leave five hundred, but Barlow insisted two hundred would be sufficient. How far are the sentry lines?"

"Not far. Just the camps you see." Ferrell motioned to the castle.

"Could Shadow Warriors be serving as lookout?" Iain asked Auriel.

"Possibly, but I didn't detect any on my reconnaissance."

"I thought Guardians could sense each other?"

194

"We can. Very few things prevent it. The first that comes to mind is a shielding medal. Dagar forced Rune to create them to give the Shadow Warriors stealth capabilities and avoid detection."

"Mahon reported Shadow Warriors among the invading force, but you didn't see any," he mused. "Using a shielding medal, they can be anywhere."

"Ay, and Shadow Warriors would not work voluntarily with a moral unless the mortal commanded the Dark Way."

Iain pursed his lips, staring at Waldron. "I doubt that's Owain. Although he could always be manipulated."

"If only someway could get inside and learn who," said Ferrell.

"I can go," said Auriel.

Iain shook his head. "Better to have you with us in case they do show up. Besides, Owain isn't thinking like a knight."

"How did he ever become one?" groused Ferrell.

Iain snorted a hollow chuckle. "His father bought the title shortly before he died. Marcellus didn't care who controlled Midessex or sat on the Council. They were immaterial to his plan, but money, he always needed." He turned to Auriel. "From what distance can Guardians sense each other's presence?"

"In relative mortal distance, a mile. Why?"

"Owain's present lack of thought may work to our advantage. The quicker Ellis gets here the better; say give or take a mile."

A cunning smile appeared. "I'll be back in a flash." She carefully crawled backwards before rising to her feet and dashing a short distance into the wood followed by a dim white flash of light.

Iain returned to his observation using the spyglass. Thus far he managed to maintain the calm exterior of a soldier. However, being at Waldron brought his deeply suppressed emotions to just beneath the surface. True, he was relieved to learn Wess and Bosley escaped with Avatar, but Hugh remained somewhere inside Waldron. Of course, that's providing he survived the attack.

His mind flashed back to the events bringing him to this point. Ellis rising to claim his birthright caused an unusual turn of events for his family.

When he learned of Latham blackmailing Hugh by threatening to kill the children, he had to act. Avatar arrived in answer to his prayer for help to rescue them. Now, Wess and Bosley were once again with Avatar. Under his breath, he spoke a prayer for their safety.

"Did you say something?" asked Ferrell.

Iain lowered the spyglass. "Just a quick prayer for my nephews."

"Avatar will keep them safe."

"He did so once before."

Ferrell smiled. "Ay. He charged me with their protection after you joined us."

Astonished, Iain gazed along his shoulder at Ferrell. "Why didn't you tell me that before?"

"You weren't in need of comfort until now. I volunteered to help you for when you did."

A look of gratitude with a hint of confusion passed over Iain's brow. "Thank you. Can I ask why?"

"Aside from the fact you are a brother Jor'ellian, I personally admire your courage and strength of character, along with Lord Hugh. What you both suffered and managed to survive is incredible."

"I can't judge how incredible, but after my sister's death and my wife's mysterious illness, I had to do something."

"Your wife? I knew Princess Lida was your sister."

Iain frowned at his miscue. "Only Hugh and Archimedes knew about Vera and I. Hugh secretly arranged it since Marcellus would not approve of his sister marrying a lowly general. We were in love and took the risk—until she confronted Marcellus about Latham."

"There were rumors her sudden ill-health was a result of the Dark Way."

Emotions crept into Iain's voice. "No rumor. If Latham could strike a royal princess, he could strike anyone. I tried to visit her in the Delta, only her illness became so advanced, she didn't remember me."

"Have you visited her since Ellis became king?"

"No," he somberly said. "I received word after the battle she died."

"I'm sorry."

Iain nodded and turned away, intent on returning to his observation and ending the depressing recollection, when Ferrell asked, "Did you and Vera have children?"

"No, thank Jor'el. I hate to think what Latham would have done if we did. He robbed me of my wife and my sister. I wasn't about to let him harm Hugh or the children." Iain raised the spyglass to his eye. "I told him Ellis' order to remain was given out of concern and for the best. Now this. I don't know if Hugh is alive."

"You couldn't have foreseen this."

"I feel responsible for telling him all would be well."

Ferrell's hand clapped Iain's shoulder. "It will be once Ellis arrives. Owain doesn't have the heart for battle. You said yourself his title was bought."

"Let's hope my assessment is correct and the Dark Way hasn't altered him like others."

At the royal encampment, Ellis paced inside his tent. He never liked waiting and since becoming king he had to wait all too often for those he dispatched to return. This time those errands were dangerous and may prove deadly. Each passing hour with no word from Darius vexed him. In hindsight, allowing the Council to act in daily administration of the provinces served well. However, when threats came to the welfare and stability of Allon, he had to take control. Despite the personal loss of a trusted and valued servant, Archimedes' reassurances convinced him of Owain's repentance. Yet Owain duped them all! The thought infuriated him, accompanied by a sense of foolishness at being so naïve to trust Owain a second time.

Now Allon stood on the verge of civil war if he couldn't get the support of the Council. True, he was marching to the North Plains at Malcolm's request but armed to the teeth. They encountered resistance from the people while reports told of finding evidence of the Dark Way in almost every province. If he's forced to put down rebellion throughout Allon, would the

Council tolerate it? Although Zebulon disliked Owain, he may refuse support to spite Ellis. Gareth would go along with his brother.

The waiting was almost intolerable. He couldn't move until he heard something, and if he made the wrong choice and moved too soon, the balance might tip.

Jor'el, give me wisdom and soon!

The arrival of supper briefly interrupted his pondering. Brief, in the fact he resumed pacing after seeing who arrived and why.

Kell ushered the servants out before approaching Ellis. He kept silent watch until now. "You must eat. The day is nearly done and you've taken no food."

"I can't eat. Not until my mind is at ease about Shannan and Nigel."

"I understand, and share your concern, but you must keep up your strength for when the time comes to act." When Ellis waved him aside, Kell laid hold of his arm. "It is your duty as king to be prepared physically, mentally and spiritually. You can't do that without eating."

Ellis yielded and allowed Kell to escort him to the table. For a moment he stared at the food. "Doesn't look or smell appetizing."

"But necessary."

"What about you? I would appreciate you joining me."

Together they sat, spoke a blessing and began to eat. Partway through the meal a flash of white light appeared in the tent. Ellis stood, reaching for his sword, but relaxed at seeing Auriel. Kell chuckled.

"Why didn't you say something, *Captain?*"

"By the time I spoke, you would have seen her."

"Well?" Ellis asked Auriel.

"We estimate two thousand soldiers, only no sentry lines, neither mortal nor Shadow Warriors. The general believes it's because Sir Owain isn't a soldier. He sent me to tell you that if you hasten to Waldron, we will have the element of surprise."

"I've not heard from anyone else. I don't know the state of Hagley or if Shannan and the Nigel are safe. I won't move until I know."

"We may lose the advantage, Sire."

198

He was firm in his regard of her. "That is a risk I'm willing to take to ensure my family's safety before fully committing to battle."

Auriel formally nodded. "Ay, Sire."

Raised voices came from outside and Kell went to investigate. "Armus is back." He held aside the flap for Armus and Roarke to enter. Malcolm accompanied them and fell to his knees before Ellis.

"Sire, forgive me!"

"What for?"

"We found Lord Malcolm in the dungeon and his mother badly injured. Shadow Warriors' way of persuading him to send to you for aid," said Roarke.

Ellis grew angry yet sympathetic. "They abused your mother?"

Malcolm nodded, his voice too choked to reply.

"Rise, Malcolm, you bear no blame." He took Malcolm's elbow to help him stand.

"My weakness prevented me from acting."

"You're not alone. They succeeded in taking Waldron and chasing my family into the wilderness."

"Sir Roarke told me everything, Sire. If my plea had not drawn you from Waldron, the queen and the prince would be safe."

Ellis glanced toward Roarke. In doing so, he noticed Armus. The Guardian appeared unusually grim, and avoided direct eye contact. Although curious to the reason of Armus' state, his focus went back to Malcolm. "If I were more forceful in stamping out the Dark Way, all of this might have been prevented. So, there is plenty of blame to go around."

"Owain also had a choice, Sire," said Kell.

"True, and it's because of him we are here."

Malcolm nodded, gathering his emotions. "Your orders, Sire?"

"I hope you didn't come unarmed."

"I brought a thousand men. All I could muster in a few hours."

"Good. Iain sends word I should return to Waldron and catch Owain with his guard down."

"We can be ready to leave at dawn."

"I will consider that."

"Any news concerning the queen and the prince, Sire?" asked Roarke.

"None yet." Since dealing with Malcolm, he didn't notice someone was missing. "Where is General Barlow?"

"Dead," said Roarke, soberly.

Shocked and dismayed, Ellis slightly rocked back. "Dead? How?"

"The Shadow Warriors laid a trap by using this to hide their presence." Roarke pulled the medallion from his belt.

"A shielding medal?" chided Kell, snatching it from Roarke. Auriel looked over his shoulder to see it.

The captain's fierce reaction did not go unnoticed by Ellis, but Roarke kept speaking.

"Twenty Shadow Warriors surrounded us. One cried out in the Ancient, *darkness strike* and we became incapacitated. Armus singlehandedly defeated them, saving the rest of us."

Kell, Auriel and Ellis all noticed Armus' set jaw, his lackluster expression, and he kept his focus straight ahead.

Roarke continued his report. "Afterwards we rescued Lord Malcolm and Lady Matrill, and secured the city. Hagley was the distraction, Sire."

Ellis's attention was slow to change from Armus. "Gentlemen, spread the word, we leave at dawn. Auriel, tell General Iain, we'll meet on the Plain of Herford in three days."

Roarke, Armus and Auriel saluted while Malcolm bowed. Auriel disappeared in white light, the others moved toward the entrance.

"Armus," said Ellis. The Guardian paused in the threshold, and for the first time he made eye contact with someone. The normal confidence and cockiness reflected in the bright chestnut eyes were dimmed and gloomy. Ellis found himself at a loss for words. Armus left.

"Failure isn't easy for a Guardian to accept," said Kell.

"Armus didn't fail. He defeated twenty Shadow Warriors."

"Perhaps not completely. Even when a single mortal dies under our charge we deeply feel it, especially one as powerful as Armus. You saw his fatigue and grim face. It took much energy to use his power."

"I remember you telling about those powers. He saved the others and secured Hagley. For that I am grateful." Ellis sighed, long and heavy. "If only I had some word from Darius I would make this move with a clear mind."

"Trust Jor'el for their safety. Besides, Elgin will return the moment he learns anything. I'd like to speak with Armus," said Kell, to which Ellis nodded and he left.

Under normal conditions Armus was impressive and intimidating to mortals who didn't know him. Add to his imposing stature, a sneering, brooding countenance and he was downright frightening. He wouldn't be hard to find. All Kell did was follow the scurrying, terrified mortal soldiers.

"Make sure to do it right this time!" shouted Armus.

Kell touched Armus' shoulder. He whirled about, drawing his sword. "Easy, old friend."

Angry, Armus slammed the sword back into the scabbard.

Kell pulled him aside to speak confidentially. "Now who's taking the blame?" Armus didn't reply, his glowering face said enough. "The medal prohibited you from sensing them. I realize it doesn't ease the burden, and Barlow's death is regrettable, but not your fault."

When Armus did speak, his voice was husky. "I sensed something wrong and tried twice to convince him to let me investigate. He refused by saying they needed to see the king's standard."

"He was right."

Armus growled in frustration. "It wasn't the fact of being right, rather dismissing my concerns, along with my ease of yielding. I should have insisted! He'd be alive if I had."

"You don't know that. When a mortal's appointed time comes, there isn't much we can do to prevent it."

"That's not helpful!"

"It's the truth. Take heart, Barlow's death will not be in vain." Kell tapped the shielding medal tuck in his belt. "I have a plan to learn who is behind this."

Armus drew to his full height, squaring his shoulders. "Tell me and it is done."

"Not this time, my friend. Your skills will be needed elsewhere." Kell closed his eyes, took a deep breath and became still. For several long moments he remained that way.

A flash of white light and Gresham appeared. "You summoned me, Captain?"

"Any word on Owain's family?"

"No. Whoever is hiding them is going to great lengths to conceal their whereabouts. I even tried several of the more remote Fortresses in the province along with obscure inns. They may be anywhere."

Kell looked directly at Gresham. "I wanted you to be the first to hear a dangerous plan crucial to uncovering whom is behind this, and be given the opportunity to accept or decline."

"You have my full attention, Captain."

Kell sent Armus a prompting nod. The lieutenant withdrew to let them speak in private.

Moving the army without receiving word from Darius was risky but imperative to secure Waldron and prevent the insurrection from spreading. Ellis told himself repeatedly of Avatar's presence and Darius' tenacity to find Shannan and Nigel, not to mention Arista. Only death would keep Vidar from Shannan and Kell assumed him he felt Vidar's essence.

Ellis didn't know what to think regarding Wess and Bosley. He knew of their escape from Ravendale, along with bits and pieces of family history from his occasional conversations with Hugh. Iain filled in some details left out, perhaps due to a father's protective nature. However, Ellis didn't know the brothers on a personal level. The few times they met the boys were amiable. Wess' determination and mind-set reminded him of Iain while Bosley seemed reticent. Small wonder after the trauma they experienced. Still, willingly going to protect Shannan and Nigel spoke to their credit, along with Hugh battling the invaders. Of all people who should harbor ill feelings towards him for disposing their family, they should.

Ellis could never find the words to express his feelings regarding Hugh's noble and tragic action in killing Marcellus. He couldn't imagine the depth of despair, personal agony and hopelessness to drive a man to such desperation and turn against his brother. Restoring the children to Hugh was a balm to his spirit. He hoped and prayed the outcome would be better for them this time.

After crossing the bridge to the town of Riverton, Ellis noticed the lengthening shadows of late afternoon. He considered traveling a few more miles before sundown, but why risk exposure? They moved closer to Waldron than he expected without causing alarm. Thus he called for a halt to make camp. Dressed in full armor, he slowly dismounted. Kell joined him

"A day's journey from Waldron and we still haven't been detected. Let's continue to hope Iain's assessment of Owain is correct and he doesn't start thinking like a soldier." Ellis removed his helmet and sighed in relief. "Standard camp and sentry procedures, Captain."

"Ay, Sire." Kell saluted and left to perform his duty.

A squire took the reins of Ellis' horse. "Rub him down good tonight."

"Ay, Sire."

By the time his tent and the picket lines were established, Ellis looked forward to getting out of his armor. Kell helped to remove the more cumbersome parts. "Amazing how light one feels when relieved of a burden."

Armus entered. He broadly smiled, the first smile Ellis seen from the Guardian in days. "The duke has returned."

Darius arrived, along with Jasper, Shannan, Arista, and the boys. Wren, Vidar, Mahon and Torin followed them. Kell bowed his head in prayerful relief

Ellis rushed to embrace his wife then anxiously glanced up and down at her. "You're not harmed?"

"No, nor is Nigel."

"Thank Jor'el. Where is he?"

"Melwynn with Avatar."

A wet nose and tongue licked Ellis' hand. He chuckled, kneeling to greet a playful Torin. Upon standing, he saw Arista and the boys. "My lady, I'm grateful for your safety also," then to the boys, "Mahon said you went to protect the queen."

Shannan moved to stand between Wess and Bosley, a hand on each shoulder. "They have done a job worthy of grown men, and earned my gratitude and respect."

"High praise indeed."

Darius grinned. "Master Wess is shrewd beyond his years. His suggestion of our route brought us on a direct course to intercept you in three days from Garwood."

"Really?"

"I have a head for calculations, Sire."

"And strategy." Jasper smiled and winked his good eye at Wess.

"Master Bosley showed uncommon bravery in confronting a Shadow Warrior threatening Nigel," said Shannan.

Ellis' brows rose in surprise. "He did what?"

Bosley heaved a sheepish shrug. "I wasn't thinking. I was charged with caring for the prince."

Ellis' glance passed between the brothers. Wess stood at attention while Bosley was more relaxed in posture only his face held a hint of apprehension. Ellis kindly smiled. "I owe you both a great debt."

"You own us nothing, Sire. It was our duty to keep the queen and prince safe," said Wess.

"Both are safe, so you have fulfilled your duty."

"If you please, Sire, I would ask my enlistment begin now, rather than waiting until this over."

"Your enlistment began the day we left Waldron," said Shannan.

"Ay," agreed Ellis. "Go with Jasper and get properly outfitted."

"This way, young master," said Jasper.

"And you, Bosley? Will you join your brother in my ranks?"

The question caught Bosley by surprise.

"I think Bosley's interests lie elsewhere." Darius smiled and clapped Bosley on the shoulder although his eyes direct on Ellis.

"If it pleases the king I will join the army."

Ellis noticed Darius' slight negative shake of the head and the hint of uncertainty returned to Bosley's eyes. "No," he said and softly smiled. "You bravely served the queen and prince when needed. You are under no obligation to become a soldier." A look of relief passed over Bosley's face. "Go and rest. No need to decide your future right now."

Bosley smiled. "Thank you, Sire."

Armus took charge of escorting Bosley from the tent.

"We had a heart-to-heart talk of politics," Darius said once Bosley was gone.

Ellis chuckled. "One more thing I need to hear about." He led Shannan to sit with him on the cot. Darius and Arista sat in chairs opposite them while Torin lay down beside the cot.

Armus returned. "Supper should be here shortly, Sire."

Ellis just nodded, more interested in Shannan. "What happened?"

Her face became set. "After midnight the alarm bell rang. Vidar said we were being invaded and went to hold them off. Mahon protected our departure while Avatar ushered us out. We could only run!"

He squeezed her hand. "You did the right thing."

She ignored his attempt of comfort and continued. "Once the shock wore off, we agreed it was safer to reach Garwood than the North Plains. I wanted Avatar to take Nigel to Melwynn then, but he refused to leave the rest of us vulnerable."

"He made the right decision," said Vidar.

"Ay. Although it nearly cost his life."

"What?" Kell asked in concern. Armus' face mirrored Kell's tone.

Arista spoke. "My feet were frostbitten, so he insisted on carrying me on his back through a clearing. Then the attack happened."

"Kelpies. Eight, at least," said Wren.

Arista continued, "Avatar tried to let me down easy when one leapt at us and we fell. It had him by the side." She motioned to her right side.

"We arrived," said Wren, indicating Vidar, and Torin, "and managed to kill about half the kelpies before a dozen Shadow Warriors surrounded us."

"Fighting proved difficult with both Avatar and I wounded," groused Vidar.

"You? How?" Kell took a quick survey of Vidar for any signs of injury.

"Crossbow darts from a Shadow Warrior at Waldron." He motioned to his right shoulder and side.

"Blindsided you the same they did Mahon?"

"Ay."

"Vidar gave me the Golden Bow, only one of them held Nigel and I couldn't shoot." Shannan fought back angry tears.

"The one Bosley charged?" asked Ellis.

"Ay. Nigel was crying."

Wren turned to Kell and Armus, her voice decidedly pointed. "Avatar used his power."

"After being wounded by a kelpie?" asked Armus in amazement.

"Ay," began Arista in awe. "He stood, spoke and thrust the sword over his head. Deafening thunder came from all around and blinding bolts of lightning shot from his sword. Soon, they were all gone. The creatures, the Shadow Warriors, and Nigel lying on the ground beside him."

"I thought you said Nigel wasn't hurt?" Ellis asked Shannan.

"He's not. Avatar collapsed and I feared he would succumb."

"Using so much of his power when wounded, it's a wonder he survived," Mahon said, and promptly received a hard jab from Wren.

"Vidar and I quickly got them to safety where I medicined his wound."

"And I'm sure you made certain he knew it was you who saved him."

"When he woke he couldn't feel his legs," Arista insisted to Mahon.

"A kelpie bite numbs a Guardian for hours," said Vidar at seeing Ellis' curiosity. "After some rest, he recovered enough to walk."

"Before leaving, I sensed someone in the forest. Sir Owain's men with orders to kill." said Wren.

"Which nearly happened because of that ... " Darius glanced to Vidar, "What did you called it, a tardundeen?"

206

"Ay."

Armus became astonished and Kell steely-eyed, features taut.

Mahon spoke in defense. "I thoroughly cleared the cavern, Captain."

Kell remained broodingly silent while Armus gave voice to their surprise. "The question is how did the it get out?"

"Out of where? And what is a tardundeen?" asked Ellis.

"A bull on two legs, twice the size of the largest Guardian and wields a giant axe," said Darius.

"A creature of Dagar's making," said Vidar.

"A creature of infrinn?" asked Ellis, sending an expectant glance to Kell. The captain still didn't speak. His glowering eyes said enough. This report was an unexpected, disturbing turn of events. "Avatar defeated it too?" he asked, his gaze slow to leave Kell.

"No, to use his power so soon would have killed him," said Armus.

"And spoil Wren's attempt at medicine," said Mahon quietly, only not low enough for Wren to hear, nor Kell. The captain's hot rebuking glare immediately made Mahon recoil with an apologetic nod.

"A combined effort of Shannan, Wren and myself," said Vidar taking note of his fellow Guardians' reactions, especially Kell.

Shannan voice was choked. "Not before losing Kato."

Ellis comforted her. "I'm so sorry."

Kell's pensive contemplation came out in words of sobriety. "Whoever is responsible must be well-trained in the Dark Way and has strong Guardian help to command the creatures of infrinn."

"Have you interrogated the prisoners I sent?" Darius asked Ellis.

"They just provided logistical information compliments of Guardian truth serum." Ellis confronted Kell. "You said you couldn't think of one who had the same desire as Dagar."

"That was before learning of the tardundeen."

"Don't forget the kelpies," said Arista.

Kell gave her tolerant smile. "No, any mortal skilled in the Dark Way can manipulate a kelpie. A tardundeen, wyvern or other such creatures spawned in the bowels of infrinn require a Guardian's strength and power to control. I sealed Dagar's nether dimension after the coronation and would have sensed a breech. Which means the tartundeen was taken before Mahon and his team cleared the cave and I sealed it," he said, tossing another glance to Mahon.

Shannan grew perplexed. "If Dagar created these creatures why didn't he use them against us?"

"He didn't create them, he enhanced them to unleash upon mortals. As for battle, he believed he killed Ellis and you were to marry Marcellus, preventing us from returning and thwarting his victory. Not until Lady Erin was revealed did he discover he had been duped. By then it was too late. We returned fully restored and Ellis alive. The battle became a fight for survival."

Ellis' eyes narrowed and he tugged at his chin. "So we could face some of these creatures at Waldron?"

"I didn't sense the presence of any creatures when they attacked," said Mahon.

"Nor did I," said Vidar.

"Auriel did not report any sensation of evil at Waldron," said Ellis.

"There may be none," said Darius, hopeful.

"What about Hagley?" Shannan asked Armus.

He grew uncomfortable at her question, but the food arrived, providing a brief interruption delaying his answer.

Ellis tossed a private encouraging glace to Armus before speaking to Shannan. "Hagely is secure. Now, let us enjoy a meal together."

Ellis' offered up a prayer filled with praise and thanks for the safety of his wife and son, along with Arista, the boys, and those Guardians involved. He noticed a spark of interest between Arista and Darius while eating. Shannan gave him a private smile and wink, turning the conversation to more light-hearted subjects. The more serious matter of taking back Allon could wait for a humorous respite at Darius' expense.

While the mortals engaged in a reprieve of merriment, Kell left. Deep in thought he wandered to a secluded spot. Hearing of Avatar's efforts and the danger confirmed the existence of the talisman. Did Owain possess it? That didn't seem likely knowing the mortal's feeble character. But Shadow

Warrior's would not work voluntarily with a mortal unless they possessed the talisman and were capable of using it.

No, not Owain. Someone else? The tardundeen …

Kell couldn't finish the disturbing thought since its appearance suggested the involvement of another Guardian. Against such forces he was grateful none were vanquished. Although it sounded like Avatar came the closest, and he would take the loss very personally.

"Seeing a tardundeen again was unexpected," said Vidar. He and Armus arrived.

"I should have expected something after not being able to find the talisman," complained Kell.

"The Dark Way can take many shapes and attack on fronts too numerous to account for. At least all are safe and unharmed."

Kell looked askew at the archer. "Avatar is nearly vanquished, you wounded and Mahon's skull cracked."

"I meant Shannan, Nigel and the others. What we suffered was in the line of duty."

When a piqued Kell stood to his full height, glaring at Vidar, Armus laid a heavy hold of Vidar's arm. "As captain, Kell is concerned for everyone's welfare, mortal and Guardian, you know that."

"Ay. I'm simply offering perspective."

"Which is why I withdrew, to consider the situation, not brood. However," said Kell, drawing closer to Vidar, the golden eyes intense in staring down at the shorter archer, "the perspective was too personal this time. Don't minimize that."

Vidar sympathetically grinned, meeting Kell's gaze. "I don't. And I'd hate to be the one to tell you ill news of either Shannan or Avatar."

Kell's intensity softened. "Ay. Now I must formulate a plan knowing the individual possesses the talisman rather than wondering."

"Against a mortal. But do you believe another Guardian is capable of Dagar's hate?" asked Armus.

Kell shook his head, his face and voice filled with sobriety. "I can't think of one. Shadow Warriors were Guardians who did not have the strength to resist Dagar, so I don't believe they are capable of such control."

"Roane had the tardundeen," said Vidar.

Baffled, Kell stared at him. "He commanded it? He has the talisman?"

"It was confined and he loosed it on us. I didn't see the talisman. Then again, I wasn't looking for it. I was more concerned with confronting the beast."

Kell was relieved. "Loosing a confined creature is different than being strong enough to control it or being capable of confining it."

"Not when it's bent on killing."

Kell couldn't help a low, wry chuckle. "No." The humor was short-lived and once again, he became deep in thought.

"We'll leave you to consider and plan." Armus pulled on Vidar's sleeve in a manner suggesting he would brook no opposition to leaving. The archer offered none.

Mahon arrived, contrite in tone and features. "Captain."

Kell said nothing, waiting for Mahon to continue.

"I'm sorry, my humor was out of line."

"There is enough rivalry between Wren and Avatar, it doesn't need prodding."

Mahon chuckled, yet stifled it at seeing Kell's arched brow. "No, but I do get caught up."

Kell pursued his lip in an attempt to quell a smile. The younger warrior was affable and easy-going; joined with his fresh-face youthfulness made it difficult to be angry with him. Mahon's similar personality to Avatar was why Kell paired them for training; he knew they would get along.

"Since Wren is too competitive with Avatar and Vidar trying to shield me from bad news, tell me truly, how is he?"

Mahon smiled, easy and wide. "Whole, perhaps a little worse for wear, but not as bad as expected after hearing that tale. Only they forgot to mention he also defeated a hunter-hawk."

"Hunter-hawk?" Kell repeated. He shook his head, befuddled. "That also must have been taken before you cleared the cave." The deep brooding settled anew in his mind and he gave Mahon a dismissive wave. "I have some hard thinking to do."

Chapter 14

THE DELTA REGION OF ALLON was known for its healing spas, wonderful fishing and tepid climate. Vast wetlands teamed with a marvelous variety of fish and wild fowl throughout the year. Rarely did snow or harsh winter weather affect the province; yet this winter bitter north winds and icy rain pelted the region.

Deltoria, home of Baron Erasmus, was splendid with spacious, open archways and lush, garden courtyards containing a cavalcade of colors during spring, summer and autumn. Sparkling pools and fountains flowed all year with the famed healing waters. The openness offered little protection from the unusual chill and smoke rose from almost every chimney. Servants were bundled in layers of clothes, scurrying about performing their daily chores before dashing inside to get warm.

Zebulon and Gareth sat upon their horses, impatiently waiting. Troops assembled several hundred yards behind them. Each brought six thousand men distinguished by their uniforms and standards. Across from them, two grooms in different liveries held the reins of two horses. These men represented Erasmus and Allard's forces. Allard's men numbered over four thousand with Erasmus' force totaling three thousand. Nearly twenty thousand mustered in front of Deltoria.

"Here they come." Gareth indicated Erasmus and Allard emerging from inside.

"My apologies for the delay but Ellis sent some last minute instructions." Erasmus mounted his horse and gave the signal to move out. Cavalry and foot soldiers fell in behind them in the order of Erasmus, Zebulon and Gareth with Allard's men in the rear.

Zebulon and Gareth pulled their horses between Erasmus and Allard. "Well?" demanded Zebulon.

"We're not going to the North Plains. Ellis is heading to Waldron. Hagley proved to be the distraction. Unfortunately, Barlow was killed in a trap created by Shadow Warriors in hopes of snaring Ellis," said Erasmus.

"Then Hagley has fallen."

"No. Armus and some Jor'ellians were with Barlow and freed the city, along with Malcolm and his mother. The cursed Shadow Warriors forced him to send for aid by abusing Matrill."

"Under those circumstances, any of us would have acted the same to protect our women," said Allard, directly looking at Zebulon.

The gruff older lord responded with a snorting grunt of agreement.

"The best news is Shannan and Nigel are safe," said Erasmus.

"So now he feels he can confront the enemy," chided Zebulon.

"You just agreed you would have acted the same as Malcolm, so how can you scorn Ellis for waiting to act until he knew about the safety of his family?" Allard rebuffed him.

"Malcolm isn't king, Ellis is."

"You find fault for him having the same feelings for his family that we do?"

"It's no use arguing with him," said Gareth.

The warning didn't please Allard so Erasmus quickly spoke. "The point is: Ellis is moving against the enemy and we are to meet him on the Plain of Herford, west of Waldron."

"The enemy we're talking about is a member of the Council."

"I never trusted Owain," groused Zebulon.

"I'm talking about Shadow Warriors and the person utilizing them. Once again Owain's weakness is being exploited," said Erasmus, sternly.

Allard shook his head. "Owain maybe weak but he can't claim ignorance. By aligning with the Dark Way, he's forced Ellis to take up arms, placed the lives of Shannan and Nigel in danger, seized Waldron, allowed the abuse of a fellow Council Member and compelled us to action. To back down is impossible. He will fight, and this time Ellis will not be merciful."

To this assessment no one offered dispute.

The nighttime temperatures dropped fifteen degrees, making it one of the coldest nights Iain, Ferrell and their group spent in surveillance of Waldron. The fires burned low in hopes of avoiding detection but hot enough to cook small game like a rabbit or fowl. Warm water was always available for tea, the only drink easily transportable for the secretive group. Eldric mixed one particular brew to help the mortals keep the night chill from their lungs. Each man drank a cup before retiring. Iain and Ferrell were drinking the prescribed tea when the sentries became alert. Auriel returned and Mahon accompanied her.

"Wasn't expecting to see you," Ferrell teased Mahon. He put up his sword and returned to his tea.

"What news? Did you find the boys?" asked Iain.

"Ay. They, Lady Arista, the queen and prince are safe. Avatar took Prince Nigel to Melwynn while the queen has joined the king and are on their way here."

Iain's shoulders sagged in relief. "Thank Jor'el. Where are they now?"

Mahon widely smiled. "With the king. For bravery, Wess' request to join the army was granted, while Bosley is still considering his future at the king's insistence."

Iain grinned. "Wess has the makings of a good leader. Bosley ... well, Ellis was wise. Hugh will be pleased, providing he's still alive," he droned the last part of his sentence.

"I pray he is, General. If by some misfortune he is not, remember he made his peace with forgiveness."

"For that, I will always be grateful to you, Mahon."

The Guardian modestly smiled and bowed his head in acknowledgement.

"Any movement yet?" asked Auriel, gesturing to the castle.

"None. Owain appears to be content in his present state—which is good for us," replied Iain.

Mahon was curious. "No sign of reinforcements?"

"No. Unless there is some Dark Way trick we're not aware of."

"Armus said they used shielding medals at Hagley."

"So you were right about them using the medals here," said Ferrell to Auriel.

"Possibly." She looked to Mahon. "You said Shadow Warriors were among those taking the castle, but I didn't detect any when we arrived."

"They may have gone to Hagley and not be here. Kell might be able to sense the medals once he arrives."

"Any word from the Council?" asked Ferrell.

Auriel replied, "Archimedes dispatched vassals commanding their forces to join the king. Which is why Mahon accompanied me, to escort you and the general to the rendezvous."

Mahon and Auriel led Iain and Ferrell from their surveillance to the Plain of Herford three miles from Waldron. Upon arriving at the royal camp, the army was noticeably larger.

"The Council forces have arrived," said Mahon.

"With this many troops Owain may reconsider," said Ferrell.

"If only it could be that simple," groused Iain.

"I said *may* reconsider."

At the royal tent a sentry admitted them. Erasmus, Allard, Zebulon, Gareth, Ranulf, Malcolm, Ned and Darius were with the king and queen. Ellis wore the less cumbersome parts of his armor. Shannan wore a blue and white uniform of a royal officer.

"General Iain, Sir Ferrell, welcome back."

"Sire," they replied.

"Majesty, it is good to see you unharmed and know the prince is safe."

"Thank you, General. I assume Mahon told you of your nephews and their invaluable service to the prince and I."

His smile held a hint of pride. "Ay, Majesty."

"Any change at Waldron?" asked Ellis.

"No, Sire. Sir Owain still appears ignorant of our presence and unconcerned about retaliation."

"He has not been reinforced?" asked Zebulon.

"No, my lord. Nor has he fortified Waldron's defenses."

"That's strange."

"Maybe for us who are trained in war, but not Sir Owain. He's not thinking like a soldier, which can work to our advantage, if we act swiftly."

"That is the plan, General," began Ellis. "Ranulf and Ned will take position in the north, Zebulon and Gareth the west, Malcolm and Allard the east, while the queen, Darius and I will confront Waldron head-on from the south. Erasmus will command the reserve should we need it."

"How many Guardians, Sire?" asked Ferrell, since only Kell, Armus, Vidar, Mahon and Auriel were present.

"One thousand. Kell formulated a plan to incorporate them."

Ferrell looked to Kell who said, "I will use their strategy against them." He held up the shielding medal.

"To your positions, and may Jor'el bless our venture," said Ellis.

"For Jor'el and Allon," said Darius. The Council members, Guardians, and Jor'ellians echoed his statement before beginning to disperse. He remained with Ellis and Shannan.

"General Iain," said Ellis. "I appreciate what the boys did more than I can say and I realize Wess is eager to do battle. However, now is not the time."

Iain grinned. "I'll find something for him to do." He saluted and left.

"Sire," said Mahon, to which Ellis smiled his understanding.

"Ay, go."

"Don't be too long. The Trio Leaders will be meeting shortly," said Kell.

Mahon hurried to find Iain and caught up to him just outside the tent where Bosley and Wess were staying. "I came to help, in case Wess isn't too happy with his reassignment."

"As his uncle and commander, I can pull rank."

Upon entering they saw Wess was in the midst of putting on pieces of infantry armor over his uniform. Bosley sat at a table, looking frustrated.

"Uncle," Bosley said in relief.

"General." Wess released the buckle of the arm strap he was fastening and snapped to attention.

Iain put on his military face. "Recruit."

"Wess says we're going to fight. But the king said I didn't have to join the army," Bosley complained. "Not that I wouldn't help to protect the queen," he added when Iain glanced side-ways at him.

"No one questions that. And you're right, you don't have the join the army, and I've already told Wess he has no place in this battle."

"But, Uncle ..." Wess began in protest.

"General!"

"General. The king gave permission ... "

"To join his service, not to fight. You're not skilled, and," he said, taking closer inspection of Wess' armor, "you are not familiar enough with the equipment to know how to properly dress for battle." He yanked the arm protector Wess was fastening and it fell off.

Bosley snickered, drawing a frustrated sneer from Wess.

Iain sent Bosley a warning glare, although continued speaking to Wess. "You could have lost your arm to a sword or pike." Without looking he tossed the arm-guard toward the cot, only Mahon was in the way and caught it. "However, I do have an assignment for you."

Wess went from dejection to curiosity. "What?"

"To continue the service you began upon leaving Waldron."

"Protect the queen? I thought she was joining the king in battle?"

"She is; Lady Arista is not. She is betrothed to the duke, and you would be doing a service by keeping her safe." Wess frowned, making Iain scold him. "You show displeasure for an assignment, Recruit? An assignment from the king?"

Wess again snapped to attention. "No, General." His brows furrowed in curiosity. "The king really wants me to guard the lady?"

Iain stood in front of Wess. "First, you show displeasure; now, you question your orders, Recruit? A soldier follows the orders of his superiors without question, dispute or offering an opinion unless asked. Did I ask?"

"No, General."

"Good. Now, when you are properly dressed, find the lady. Both of you." Iain turned and in doing saw Mahon held the arm protector. He gave a faint nod before passing the Guardian to leave only Bosley forestalled his departure.

"Uncle. What about Father?"

To this question, Iain's expression softened. "I'll find him."

"We'll find him," added Mahon.

"Ay. Now, be quick. We'll be leaving soon." Iain left.

Wess snatched the arm guard from Mahon. "I didn't put it on wrong, I hadn't finished fastening it."

Mahon smiled and left.

In a grove of trees just west of camp the Trio Leaders gathered.

"Gresham is probably hiding because he let things get out of hand," said Zadok to Derwin.

"That's not fair, Zadok," chided Mona. "I too was caught off-guard when they used a shielding medal to take Hagley; then abused Lady Matrill to force Malcolm to send for help. Unfortunately, they killed General Barlow."

"I'm sorry. I didn't know about the shielding medal."

Kell arrived with Armus, Vidar, Auriel and Mahon. "It will work to our advantage." Kell held up the medal. "We'll use it to get close enough to Waldron without being detected."

"You're going to use it to shield all sixty thousand?" asked Derwin.

"Kell, you can't. It will take more energy than you alone—" began Zadok in refute.

"He's not going to shield everyone, just the Guardians," said Armus.

"That's still one thousand of us," said Zadok, although not as forceful. He was promptly silenced by a reproving glare from Kell.

Zadok subdued, Kell gave instructions. "Ellis dispatched the Council and their forces around Waldron. Time for the Trio Leaders to join them. Wren and Auriel will go with Ranulf and Ned to secure the north. Zadok, Chase and Mona will join Zebulon and Gareth on the west flank. Egan and Priscilla will go with Malcolm and Allard to the east flank. Derwin, Barnum and Jedrek will hold in reserve with Erasmus. Armus, Vidar, Mahon and I will accompany Ellis and Shannan. Go quickly, the mortals want to be in position by dawn."

Mona held back waiting for the others to leave before approaching Kell. "Captain, where is Gresham?"

"He is taking care of something I asked of him."

"Will he be back in time to join us?"

Kell pursed his lips in uncertainty. "I'm not sure." Seeing her concern, he placed his hand on her shoulder. "Don't fret. Gresham knows what he's doing."

She flashed a retiring smile before leaving.

"Were you trying to convince her or yourself?" asked Armus.

"Both. I should have heard from him by now."

"Have you gotten any sense of him?"

"None. If they have more shielding medals, I may not."

"Perhaps when we get close enough to Waldron," said Mahon.

"I hope so. If anything happens to him, I will personally deal with the one responsible."

"Can you wait until then, or should you try sensing him now?" asked Armus.

Kell shook his head. "Doing so may alert them to our presence. I'll have to wait. Until then, we have work to do."

Owain normally didn't mind waiting. He enjoyed the slow pace of a quiet country life. All that changed. The waiting now was nerve racking and agonizing, especially in the still hours of the night. He tried to divert his mind to memories of pleasant unhurried days spent with his wife and daughters. However, reality came crashing in accompanied by the thought he may never see them again.

In one of his more lucid moments during the night, he found his way to the king's study. In this room Ellis chastised him about his past, practically accusing him of murder. He couldn't think about that now, he had to focus his thoughts for Lanay. If no one else, he owed her an explanation.

For several hours he composed, corrected and rewrote what became a lengthy six-page letter on both sides of the paper. Many times he spoke of his gratitude for her, his love for her and the girls, and hoped someday she would understand and forgive him. Even as he wrote, the explanation seemed surreal, yet these were his words, written in his hand. He scarcely believed he was capable of what he was writing, or even conceive of such exploits. If he were hardly recognizable to himself, how would Lanay feel when she read the letter? He dared not dwell too long on the thought, since every word was true and she deserved to know the truth.

He folded the letter. Using royal wax, he stamped three seals using his signet ring and wrote Lanay's name on it. Three seals marked a document of personal importance. If he were unable to deliver the letter in person, he hoped whoever found it would respect the seal and deliver it unopened to his wife. He put it in his pocket and left the study. Perhaps now he could get a few hours of sleep.

Nari stood in the shadow of an archway in the upper galleyway when Owain left the study. After he emerged, she considered following him, but wanted to know what he had been doing for so long, thus she entered the study. She made a quick visual search of the room. Wads of crumpled paper lay in the wastebasket. She straightened one piece enough to read only there were too many words etched out and numerous inkblots. She fetched another, only with the same result. By the fourth sheet of paper, she was fed up and left. Her fellow Shadow Warriors had taken to gathering in the family salon, so she joined them.

"About time you showed up. Owain retired hours ago," said Cletus.

"No, he got up and went to king's study."

"Why?

"I believe he was writing a letter to his wife. I found several wads of paper all scratched up and blotted out, but I did see her name in a few places."

"Some mortal males have weakness for their women and tend to write soppy love letters. Maybe that was it."

"We already know Owain is weak. That made him easy prey for our mistress to work her wiles," said Roane.

Cletus sneered. "While he sleeps would be a good time to kill him and rid ourselves of this wimpy mortal."

"Have you forgot the mistress said we need this wimpy and soppy mortal? His time will come."

"I don't see why we need any mortal."

"Because that's the way Dagar made the talisman."

"I don't know why."

"It has to do with our original creation," said Roane, growing bitter. "No matter our strength and power we are still subject to Jor'el and his mortals."

"Don't say that name!" Cletus angrily shoved Roane.

"Saying it or not doesn't change reality."

"I know. I'm just not comfortable hearing it."

"Has the mistress said any more about her plan?" asked Indigo, drawing Roane's attention from Cletus.

"No. Regardless of what Cletus thinks, the mortals are our major line of defense." He sent Cletus a withering glare.

Cletus snarled in rebuff. "Have they succeeded in capturing the queen and killing the prince?"

"There's been no word on that yet either."

"Then our status hasn't changed."

Roane reluctantly nodded. "Ay. Come morning, I'll try to speak with her again."

"Who's guarding her while she sleeps?" asked Bern.

"Lark. Keep to your rounds and we'll see what tomorrow brings."

Nari wasn't listening to them, her attention drawn aside by a sensation. "We may not have to wait until tomorrow." While she spoke, the others also became alert.

"Stay near the mistress," Roane instructed Bern and Indigo then motioned for Cletus and Nari to leave with him.

A dim light appeared in the wood outside the castle's postern gate. After the light of his arrival faded, Gresham carefully made his way along the tree line. A small camp of mortal soldiers stood outside the postern gate. They gathered around a fire to ward off the night's chill. He could use some of his power to avoid them and get inside, yet reports of possible Shadow Warriors around it was already risky arriving the way he did. However, time was short.

Whispering the Ancient, he made a tossing motion with his right hand. Noise came from the other side of the camp and the soldiers went to investigate. He dashed from the trees to the lowest point in the wall, four feet, and jumped over it. Seeing a nearby wagon, he darted behind it. From his concealment, he tried to get his bearings. Going right led to the rear terrace, directly behind the family's quarters. To the left were the barracks, armory and stables. His best bet would be the barracks and not the family quarters since that was too obvious. He headed left.

He only covered half the distance between the wagon and barracks when he sensed danger and heard voices from behind alert to his presence. He whipped out his dagger. They were not going to take him without a fight. He whirled about, dagger first, slashing and striking the closest assailant. Cletus staggered back and fell to his knees, a deep wound across his chest.

Roane and Nari closed in, keeping their distance, warily eyeing the bloody dagger. "It's useless, Guardian. You're no match for us," said Roane.

"He's not even a warrior! He's a vassal," spat Nari.

"Great. Wounded by a vassal," chided Cletus.

222

Roane feigned an attack and Gresham flinched. Nari lunged for his dagger arm but misjudged his speed and agility. His blade caught her in the arm, drawing blood. Roane came at Gresham from behind with a strong blow to back of the head sending him to his knees. Nari's foot came up under Gresham's chin, snapping his head back and laying him flat, knocking the wind out of his lungs and the dagger from his grasp.

She examined her arm. It was a flesh wound, but infuriated, she viciously kicked Gresham in the ribs.

Roane knelt, seized Gresham by the collar and held the dagger to his throat. "Who are you, vassal? And what are you doing here?"

"That's for me to know and you to find out. If you can," said Gresham between painful breaths. His head and ribs ached.

Roane pricked Gresham's throat with the blade, blood oozing from the wound. "I can cut the answers out of you."

Gresham winced in pain, yet held his tongue.

Nari went to help Cletus, examining his serious chest wound. "Be quick with him, there could be more."

"I'll take him where his cries can't be heard." Roane jerked Gresham to his feet. "How's Cletus?"

"He'll survive."

Cletus snarled in painful anger. "Cut him once for me!"

Roane obliged by making identical wound across Gresham's chest, the latter hissed in surprise yet didn't cry out loud. Roane held him up. "It'll get worse before it's over, vassal." He then spoke to Nari. "Inform the mistress and have Indigo and Bern search for others." He left, pulling Gresham toward the dungeon.

Another Shadow Warrior, Odell, stood outside the dungeon along with several mortal soldiers. "Who is this creature?"

"An insignificant vassal who dared to breech our security."

Odell snarled, glaring up and down with disproval. "He's tried to make himself appear important." He grabbed at Gresham's tunic, which made Gresham flinch in pain from his wound. Again he remained silent. "Rather fancy for you, isn't it, vassal?"

Gresham didn't reply, both for pain and determination. The stalwart gleam in his violet eyes received immediate disapproval.

"Don't raise your eyes to me!" Odell slapped Gresham.

The strength of the blow sent Gresham sideways, only Odell's grip held him up. The blow cut the corner of his mouth. Still, he didn't utter a word or sound.

"Stubborn."

Roane took possession of Gresham from Odell. "He won't be when I'm done with him. He'll be begging for the mercy of termination. Fetch the irons."

Odell wickedly smiled while Roane Gresham jerked inside the dungeon.

Even during his mistreatment, Gresham tried to take stock of his surroundings. Sooner or later he would have to leave and bring the information to Kell and the king. Only one cell of the dungeon was finished. Inside, Roane shoved Gresham back against the wall, pinning him. Gresham fiercely bit his lower lip to withstand the pain of impact radiating through his chest and tried to resist Roane, who wrestled to place his hand into the manacles. Once the manacles were secure, Gresham tugged on them and felt no pain or stinging sensation. Ordinary metal.

"Thinking of trying to escape?" asked Roane in a tone of high mockery.

Odell returned with a mortal soldier who held a pair of leg irons. "Put them on him," he said to the soldier.

At first touch of the leg irons, a sharp searing sensation shot up Gresham's legs making him loudly gasp in great pain. His knees buckled and he would have collapsed completely except the manacles held him up.

"You won't be going anywhere. And after I have my way with you, combined with the effect of the stygian irons, you'll talk," said Roane.

Gresham sneered at Roane, fighting back the desire to cry out from the burning now stretching the length of his body.

"Your stubbornness won't last long. I learned from Dagar. You will tell us what we want to know, or you will cease to exist."

Nari entered. She tossed an annoyed glance to Gresham then Roane. "Well?"

"I just started." He pointed to the leg irons. "Indigo and Bern?"

"Still looking, but he seems to be the only one so far."

Roane wasn't pleased and impatiently motioned for everyone to leave. When the door closed, he slammed Gresham against the wall. The sudden movement caused more sharp searing pain to rack his body and Gresham screwed his eyes closed and clapped his mouth shut. A whimpering moan escaped.

"You're determined, I'll say that. You can save yourself a needless end by telling me if there are others and what you are doing here?"

His eyes still closed, Gresham carefully shook his head. A surprised squeal escaped when Roane cut him across the abdomen, then more searing pain came from the irons upon movement in reaction to the wounding.

"I can keep this up all night. What about you?"

Gresham's eyes opened. His features were pale from pain and injury, but the look of obstinacy in his violet eyes unmistakable. "You'll get nothing from me."

Agitated by the news, Musetta paced the royal bedchamber, toying with the talisman and muttering under her breath. The last thing they needed was a Guardian infiltrating their defenses. Who is he and what did he want? She hoped Roane dealt with him quickly and sent Nari to find out. So much depended upon success and she waited so long already.

Although she had her own ambitions when initially becoming Latham's apprentice, she fell in love and became his mistress. She pleased him when becoming pregnant and he promised to marry her. However, dealing with the Son of Tristan and his claim to the throne came first. Despite the situation, they made plans to place their son on the throne. Then came the day she witnessed Latham's death at Ellis' hand. From that moment she vowed revenge. Until their son was born, she went into hiding. Since his birth, his resemblance to Latham served as a constant reminder of the promise and loss. She brooded and planned, dreaming of this day. Now the appearance of a lone Guardian threatened to disrupt her plans.

She stopped in anticipation of the door opening and Nari returned. "Well?"

"Roane put him in stygian irons. It shouldn't be too long before he talks."

"That's not good enough!"

"Mistress, Indigo and Bern searched the perimeter and found no one else."

She was irate. "You expect me to believe a Guardian just walked into the castle on his own?"

"What Guardian?" asked Owain, arriving unnoticed.

"I thought you went to bed?" chided Nari, caught off guard at seeing him.

"How would you know?"

Nari scowled at her miscue. "It's late. All mortals sleep."

"I, too, thought you retired," said Musetta.

"I've been occupied," he said with impatience. "Now what about this Guardian?"

"We captured him by the postern gate," said Nari.

"Who?"

"We didn't recognize him so Roane is trying to find out."

"What does he look like?"

"He's a mere vassal, who, by the look of his fancy uniform, tried to raise his status," she said with a prideful sneer on his lips.

"That doesn't tell me much, what about his face?"

"He has medium length white hair, violet eyes, strong chin—"

Owain grew uncomfortable at the description and asked, "Does he wear a green and red jeweled hilted dagger on his right hip?

"Ay. He gave me this," Nari snarled, indicating her wound.

He wasn't paying attention to her, his brows furrowed with recognition. "Gresham."

"How do you know him?" asked Musetta.

"He's the Trio Leader of Midessex. I've encountered him on occasion over the past few years."

"As a Trio Leader, he'll be stronger than Roane anticipates," said Nari.

Musetta wasn't listening to Nari, rather confronted Owain. "Why is he here?"

He heaved a partial shrug. "He probably came to try and talk to me."

"Or sent by Kell," said Nari.

To this statement, Musetta listened. Her hateful, withering stare shifted from Nari to Owain.

His whole body stiffened. "I will complete what I started."

"Oh, you will." Musetta drew close to him, her hand on the talisman. "I know where your family is."

His fists clenched into balls, glaring at her. "Leave them out of this."

"As long as you cooperate, they will remain unharmed," she said, releasing the talisman.

"What about Gresham?" asked Nari.

"Tell Roane to get what information he can. If he dies, that's one less Guardian to deal with."

Nari saluted and left. Owain began to follow her out when he heard Musetta say, "I hope we won't have this conversation again, my lord."

"We won't," he said over his shoulder before leaving.

Walking from Musetta's chamber to the Galleyway, Hugh's words, *"Kill the witch!"* echoed in Owain's mind. He believed he placed the thought aside; only when she threatened his family, it returned and he felt the impulse to lash out. *Kill the witch.* If he felt the impulse he did earlier, anything could happen under a moment of extreme distress.

He paused by a galleyway window and looked out at the Grand Courtyard. Most soldiers were asleep with a few on guard duty. All appeared quiet. *Like the calm before a storm,* he thought.

Whatever his inner turmoil regarding Musetta, he had to face the reality of what was to come. Absorbed in thought, he continued his trek around Waldron and ended up in the Council Chamber. The realization of where he wandered, staggered him and he backed away, practically falling into the Midessex chair. His gaze swept over the other chairs. His father considered his timid nature cowardice and scorned Owain until the day he died. He even purchased Owain's title for the family to retain control of Midessex and a seat on the Council. Now, ironically, by his uncharacteristically bold, treasonous actions he not only stood to lose Midessex and his seat on the Council, but cause his family more heartache than his cowardice. He accepted there was no turning back, no form of apology or excuse he could make. He must see it though to the end.

Chapter 15

A T THE ROYAL CAMP, Kell helped Ellis finish strapping on the Sword of Allon. He was now completely dressed in the Gold Armor. Shannan was outfitted with the Golden Bow, gauntlets and quiver. Ellis noticed she appeared distracted even when Vidar spoke to her about the tightness of the quiver strap.

"What is troubling you?"

"I was thinking about the boys. Iain made no mention of any news concerning Hugh."

"You think Wess' eagerness is a desire to rescue his father?"

"Wouldn't you?"

"Naturally. However, being unskilled, he could be more of a danger to himself and others."

"I realize that. I was only answering your question. Wess is eager, but Bosley is plain worried."

"We will reassure them the moment we know anything about Hugh."

"You believe he's still alive?"

"I have no reason to believe otherwise. Do you?" Ellis asked Kell.

"No. Lord Hugh is of the House of Unwin. With the Dark Way behind this, whoever is responsible may keep him alive and to use him to reclaim the throne."

In sudden, dreaded understanding she regarded Kell. "And it would be a more powerful claim if they succeeded in killing Nigel and me."

"They didn't," Ellis insisted, giving her a reassuring smile. "With Wess and Bosley exhibiting loyalty to the House of Tristan, the plan is also undermined by the heirs." He took his helmet from Kell. "Now we shall completely foil them by taking back Waldron and exposing the traitors." Ellis, Shannan, Kell and Vidar moved outside to where Darius, two Jor'ellians and Jasper waited with their horses.

Vidar held the stirrup for Shannan to mount while Kell helped Ellis. Darius and Jasper mounted unassisted. Darius saw Arista a short distance away seated upon a horse and accompanied by Wess and Bosley, both also mounted.

Ellis smiled. "Iain found the right task for them."

"If you'll excuse me for a moment." Darius didn't wait for a reply and moved his horse toward Arista. She smiled and blushed when he arrived. "I'm glad you agreed to stay back."

Her smile grew teasing. "I have some sense."

"Indeed." He chuckled then became serious.

Before he could speak, she spoke. "I'll be in the field hospital like before. I don't want to see you as a casualty."

He kissed her hand. "You won't." He addressed the boys. "I depend upon you gentlemen to continue your gallant service to *my* lady."

"We won't fail, Your Grace," said Bosley, willingly, while Wess looked a bit downcast.

"I'm in very capable hands," said Arista.

Darius moved his horse back to where Ellis and Shannan waited, both smiling. "Is something amusing?"

"Just enjoying the sight of you as a suitor."

"King or not, you can still be an irritating little brother."

Iain arrived, also mounted. "All parties report they are ready, Sire."

"Then give the signal, General."

Iain turned his horse around, stood in the stirrups and raised his right arm high above his head. With an open palm, he made a wide circular motion with his arm then quickly brought his arm down. Small flashes of white light disappeared before the troops began to move.

Darius looked over his shoulder to see Arista wave. He replied with a salute before moving off with Ellis and Shannan.

"All joking aside, you are well matched," said Shannan.

Darius simply smiled.

Since they had the least distance to travel, Zebulon and Gareth's forces were the first to take up position on the west flank. Zadok, Mona and Chase watched the mortals. Once they were done, each would place their Guardian forces among the mortal troops.

"I hate land battles," groused Chase. "Give me the wind at my back and a helm in my hand and I'll win the day."

"Zadok gets seasick at the thought of water," chided Mona, angrily eying Zadok.

"I already apologized what more do you want?"

"Something you don't understand, respect. Not just toward me, but Gresham." Her voice quivered making Zadok and Chase concerned.

"Has something happened to him?"

She heaved an uneven shrug. "Kell said he's doing a task asked of him."

"Kell is very careful in planning before asking one of us to do anything." Chase tried to assure her.

"I know, only when I asked if Gresham would return in time to join us, he didn't know and looked worried."

"For a vassal, Gresham can handle himself," said Zadok and promptly received a jab in the side from Mona. "What? I meant it as a compliment."

"We once served together as Trio Mates!"

"The mortals are settled. Time to move. Jor'el be with you both," said Chase before leaving with his group.

Zadok stopped her departure. "If Gresham hasn't returned after this we'll search for him together."

"Thank you."

Ranulf and Ned traveled north-by-east with Malcolm and Allard's forces. The latter group had the furthest to travel to reach the east flank and was prudent to combine the move before splitting and heading off alone. Wren led the combined groups through the forest: Auriel with her, while Torin accompanied them for added protection and security.

"So far, so good," said Auriel.

"Did you expect less from me?" said Wren in a challenging tone.

"No. And don't get touchy because I'm a warrior. I'm also female."

Wren wryly smirked. "Are they as irksome to you as rest of us?"

"You mean the males? A few, like Avatar and Zadok."

Wren's brows rose in surprise. "You lump Avatar and Zadok together? I don't think Avatar is as irritating as Zadok."

"He's not, but don't tell him I said so. Still, his clever teasing gets to me sometimes. His deadpan delivery and the way his goatee moves when he smirks."

Wren chuckled and nodded. "I was able to have the last laugh when I medicined his kelpie bite."

"I'm sure you let him know."

"Vidar witnessed my triumph."

Auriel heartily laughed. "Even better. He can't worm his way out of it."

Hearing Torin's low bark, Wren surveyed the surroundings. "Our position is up ahead about a quarter mile. Tell them while I secure the area."

Auriel ran to inform the mortal lords. At her arrival, Ranulf called for a halt. Egan and Priscilla joined them to hear Auriel's report. In appearance the wind Guardian and warrior stood in marked contrast. She was fair in hair and complexion with sky blue eyes, while he had black hair, ruddy complexion and light, translucent blue eyes.

"We're near the point of separation. Wren is securing the area," said Auriel.

"Not much night left. Can you make it before dawn?" Ned asked Allard only Egan replied.

"We have Daren and Darcy to ensure the cover of darkness remains long enough for troops to be securely in place."

"Then we bid you Jor'el's speed."

"Keep your head down, you stiff-neck, old Highlander," Allard spoke to Ranulf.

"Only if you keep your tongue in your head."

Allard laughed and signaled the group to separate.

Egan and Priscilla strategically placed Guardians at the front, middle and rear of Malcolm and Allard's mortal forces. Much to the night twins' chagrin, they were split between the front and rear of the column. This was critical because of the continued distance to travel undetected.

Priscilla glanced back at the mortals, tentative and unsure. "I hope Kell's plan works."

"It will." Egan kept his eyes straight ahead.

She crossly glared at him. "Why are warriors so arrogant and cocky?"

"How do you expect us to act? Flighty and uncertain?"

"That would be a refreshing change," she said, and a gust of wind ruffling his clothes and hair. "Such constant bravado is irritating."

"Irritating or intimidating?" he teased, his eyes direct on her.

Flustered at his amusement, she quickened her pace to get away from him, murmuring complaints about warriors under her breath. She was grabbed about the waist from behind and a hand covered her mouth. At that moment she heard the jingle of harness and spied a small patrol of enemy soldiers two hundred yards ahead moving toward Waldron. For several moments she remained held, until the patrol moved out of sight.

"You must be more careful," Egan warned in her ear. "If you kept going in your agitated state, they would have seen you and placed our mission in jeopardy." He released her.

She frowned in mild embarrassment and straightened her gown. "I suppose you want me to thank you for that."

"No. I want you to stop being cynical. I know you would have preferred Gresham, Chase or anyone other than a warrior, but you got paired with me."

"I'm beginning to think Kell did so on purpose."

"He did." When she glared at him, he continued, "You must learn to work with warriors whether you like it or not. Jor'el created us to serve. How we serve isn't the issue; it is that we serve and serve well according to our abilities."

"I know that."

"Then we are in agreement," he said, smiling.

"Is there a problem?" asked Malcolm. The troop caught up to them.

"A patrol heading toward the castle." Egan pointed in the direction the patrol passed.

"They didn't see us, thanks to Egan's quick thinking." She gave Egan a small friendly smile.

"Good. How much further?" asked Allard.

"A half-mile. I'll scout ahead." Egan returned Priscilla's smile before leaving.

Malcolm noticed the dark of night giving way to the gray light of pre-dawn. "It'll be day soon. Let's pray Owain hasn't completely lost his senses and this doesn't come to all out battle."

"If Kell's plan works, it won't," said Priscilla.

From the safety of the trees Ellis, Shannan, Darius and Jasper monitored the activity at Waldron. Ellis and Darius removed their helmets for easier observation.

Fret filled her face in observation. "Feels wrong to attack our home."

Ellis gave her hand a reassuring squeeze. "Waldron is Allon's seat of power. Whoever controls the castle, controls Allon."

"How can you think of it so coldly? Our son was born here."

"I must if we are to succeed." He again squeezed her hand. "Be assured, I will do all I can to preserve it intact and protect the innocent lives of those inside."

"Kell says his plan will insure Waldron does not suffer too greatly," said Darius.

Jasper glanced about. "By the way, where is Kell?"

"Getting ready," replied Ellis.

Shannan left on foot, heading east.

"Does it ever bother you?" Darius asked Ellis.

"Does what ever bother me?"

"The bond between Shannan and Kell."

Ellis cocked a curious brow then snickered. "No. She was appointed to help the Guardians and has a strong connection to many of them."

"I mean does it interfere between you two?"

"No, and I don't expect it ever will. Does it bother you?"

Darius heaved a shrug, frowning in uncertainty. "I'm not sure. There so many complexities in the way Guardians and mortals relate."

Ellis grinned and tossed an arm about Darius' shoulder. "Think of Kell as a second, hulking, older brother who hangs around all the time."

Jasper laughed, making Darius say to Ellis, "You've made your point."

Kell sat on a log about one hundred yards into the forest away from the main group. His eyes were closed and he held the shielding medal in both hands running over in his mind where each Guardian was positioned. He opened his eyes when someone sat beside him.

"Daughter of Allon."

"No need to be formal all the time, Kell."

He grinned. "It is your title and you are queen."

She held his arm, looking at the shielding medal. "Can you do it?"

"I'm ready to try."

"Try?"

"A thousand of us are scattered around the castle. I must be precise and selective." He softly smiled at seeing her concern. "But not beyond my capabilities if that is what troubles you."

"I saw what happened to Avatar when he used his power."

"He suffered from a kelpie bite, which was more debilitating than a drain of personal energy to use his power."

"That may be so, but I want the truth. What about you?"

"I'll feel a drain on my energy, but not life threatening."

"Are you certain?"

Kell looked directly at her. "Ay. And I appreciate your concern, Shannan," he said her name, which made her laugh. He noticed the first rays of dawn peaking through the trees. "The sun's nearly up. Return to Ellis, while I get into position."

When Shannan returned, Iain, Ferrell, Armus, and Mahon had joined the others. "Kell is getting into position."

"Good. The others are ready." Ellis put on his helmet. "Time to let Owain know the king and queen are back." He nodded to Armus and Mahon. Both saluted and ran eastward.

Ellis held the stirrup for Shannan. Jasper held Darius' horse. Iain aided Ellis to mount. Jasper, Iain and Ferrell then mounted to accompany them. Iain carried the royal standard, Ferrell the Jor'ellian banner. They moved forward and stopped at the tree line.

Ellis watched the eastern sky. "Once the sun is fully cleared of the horizon, Kell is to act and we advance."

"How will we know if he is successful?" asked Jasper.

"I will know, for if I can't sense him, they won't," said Shannan.

Ellis' eyes narrowed at seeing the last part of the sun clear the horizon. "Now!"

She took a deep breath and lowered her head. After a brief moment her head came up. "Nothing," she said, a hint of distress in her voice.

"He's done it." Ellis kicked his horse and moved out from the trees. Shannan rode to his right, Darius on his left, Iain, Jasper and Ferrell following.

Outside the main gate, the soldiers on duty spotted a group emerging from the trees. "Captain!" one shouted up to the rampart.

The captain's eyes widened with surprise when sunlight bounced off gold armor. "Sound the trumpet! The king is coming. To your positions!"

He ran in search of Owain and found him in the Council Chamber asleep in the Midessex chair. "My lord! The king comes!"

236

Startled, Owain bolted up. "Are you sure it is Ellis?"

"Ay. There is no mistaking the golden armor."

Owain rushed from the chamber. In the Grand Courtyard he met Musetta. He motioned the captain to continue to the battlement before confronting her. "Ellis comes. I hope your powers are up to the task, witch."

She narrowly eyed him. "Keep you wits and your courage and I'll take care to my responsibility." While he hurried toward the battlements she went to the dungeon and ordered Odell, "Fetch Roane."

Odell promptly complied and Musetta accosted Roane at first sight of him. "Ellis is coming."

"Without Guardians?"

"What do you mean without Guardians? You captured one."

"We haven't discovered any more and I don't sense any nearby."

She was extremely annoyed. "He's told you nothing?"

"No. As a Trio Leader, he is stronger than most vassals. I've done everything short of ending his existence but he is stubbornly silent."

"Then put an end to him. We don't need him summoning help."

"He's hardly capable of doing anything. It shall be as you command," he added at seeing her hot displeasure.

"Hold where you are! Come no further!" they heard Owain shout.

Musetta seized Roane's arm to stop his departure. "Learn what is happening. Maybe you can get a better sense of the situation."

Roane ran up the battlement steps. His brow furrowed at seeing the approaching group. "The Daughter of Allon," he growled under his breath.

Owain glared at Roane. "Witness what the failure of your kind has allowed to happen!"

"Beware, mortal. I can kill you where you stand."

Owain's brows furrowed and his face showed signs of wavering.

"Keep your wits, mortal. Remember what will happen to your family if you yield."

"You threaten me, but what price are you willing to pay, Guardian?"

Roane grew stiff and reached for his sword. "I am a Shadow Warrior, not a Guardian!"

"Roane!" Musetta shouted from the Courtyard. She held the talisman visible, which made Roane release his sword and Owain glare at her.

They heard Ellis shout, "This time, Owain, you have gone too far and will pay dearly for your insurrection!"

"Then I have no reason to yield, do I?"

"Perhaps not for yourself, but to spare your family and those you lead from further heartache and punishment."

Even at this moment of crisis, Owain's jowls flex in frustration and indecision.

Again Ellis called, "Well? What is your answer, Owain?"

Roane lowly growled and tapped is sword in warning.

Owain turned to fully face Ellis and shouted, "Come and take it!"

Ellis drew the Sword of Allon and held it over his head. "For Jor'el and Allon!"

Voices echoing Ellis' cry came from all directions and armed men emerge from the trees behind Ellis and along the horizon. Owain's eyes scanned the seemingly endless line of troops.

"My lord! Soldiers on the west!" shouted a guard from the courtyard

Owain moved to see where the man was pointing.

Another guard appeared in the courtyard and reported a sighting from the east.

"My lord! We're surrounded. There must be at last fifty thousand men," said the captain.

Visibly stunned to the core, Owain winced.

Musetta moved to the top of the stairs still hidden by the wall from outside view. "The number doesn't matter."

"That's easy for you to say!" snapped Owain. When she reached for the talisman, he drew his sword and ordered, "Prepare for battle!" He looked up and down the battlement. "Better to die fighting then at the end of a rope!"

The captain drew his sword. "To your posts!" he shouted to the men.

Musetta motioned to Roane and both descended to the Courtyard. "Kill the Guardian and be sure that none survive who know me."

Roane raced back toward barracks.

238

From the moment Roane left, Gresham tried to free himself and pulled on the manacles holding his arms. The numerous wounds and suffering the debilitating effects of stygian illness, made his efforts useless. He attempted to stretch out his senses in hopes of reaching Kell. A sudden pain hit his brain and he nearly fainted.

Even in his groggy state, he heard commotion outside. By the sounds, something was happening. Maybe he contacted Kell and didn't realize it in his feeble condition. Or maybe it was Ellis. With renewed determination, he pulled at the manacles, ignoring the pain from the stygian leg irons. He stopped when the door opened and Roane returned. Nothing was said rather Roane drew his sword.

Kell stood, his feet braced holding the shielding medal over his head. His lips moved but no sound came out. To shield them all, he recalled each individual Guardian by name. Suddenly the breath caught in his throat, his eyes snapped open, his whole body trembled and he almost dropped the shielding medal.

At the same time Armus and Mahon moved into position closer to the castle then anyone else. They were careful in approach, only when a mortal turned and said, "Hey! Stop!" they took cover and exchanged cautious glances.

The soldier appeared at the corner. They stood rock still, watching his head begin to turn toward them when— "Well?" someone called and he turned back. "I thought I saw someone. Guess I was wrong." He left the corner without seeing them.

"That was too close," whispered Mahon. He watched Armus, whose head was lowered, eyes shrouded and brow level. "Armus?"

Armus' head snapped up. "Something's wrong with Kell. Stay here, I'll be back." After a glance around the corner, he raced to Kell's position. Kell was breathing heavy, sneering, his eyes half-closed and armed locked above his head. "Kell?"

The golden eyes showed strain from the shielding while concern filled his voice. "Gresham! I sent him to Waldron. Find him before they kill him."

So sensing Gresham in trouble is what caused the wavering, not any wound or physical malady brought on by the shielding. Still, Armus didn't like the stress in Kell's eyes, nor the pale features. The effort was taking a great deal of energy. "What about you?"

Kell grunted, shaking his head. "Gresham may not have much time. I can hold until you get inside!"

Armus raced back to Mahon. "Gresham is inside and in danger. We have to find him fast."

"That could give us away."

"Can't be helped." Armus drew his sword and dashed from their position to enter through a low point in the wall with Mahon at his heels, armed and ready.

"Guardians!" shouted a soldier and nothing more as Mahon cut him down.

At that moment the shielding ended. Other Guardians pre-positioned around Waldron appeared out of nowhere.

"Where do we start looking?" asked Mahon.

"The dungeon, where else?" Armus headed toward the building. Egan and Zadok were at the barracks manhandling ten mortal soldiers. They wouldn't have mortals interfering with their search. However, Odell blocked the dungeon entrance.

"Going somewhere, Guardians?"

Armus snarled. "We haven't time for you, turncoat, so stand aside."

"How about us?" Four Shadow Warriors joined Odell.

Armus and Mahon were forced to fight. Egan and Zadok came to help. Armus dodged an attack and said, "Quickly! Gresham's in danger!" He motioned with his head toward the dungeon.

Zadok shouted in command, "*Luths ris buanachd!*" before finishing a Shadow Warrior, who vanished in a grey flash of light.

Finding the cell door locked Zadok kicked it open, making it crack and fall off the hinges. Gresham hung limply from the manacles, his torso a crisscross mess of savage cuts and a large wound in the middle of his abdomen. Gresham hadn't vanished meaning he was still alive.

Zadok sheathed his sword and lifted Gresham's head. The ashen features and cool skin temperature was not good. He positioned Gresham between the wall and himself then broke the wrist manacle. He caught Gresham before he completely fell to the floor. When he attempted to lift Gresham over one shoulder, a terrible and unexpected searing pain struck his left leg. So powerful and stunning was the sensation that his knee gave way. He managed to gently lower Gresham to the floor. The leg irons were a different color metal and he didn't need to touch them to realize what they were.

He drew his sword and stood. "By your will, Jor'el, let me free him." He raised the sword above his head and quickly brought it down on the leg irons. A terrific crash along with a brilliant flash of orange light knocked him off his feet. After shaking his head clear, he saw the leg irons in pieces and off Gresham's ankles. Sheathing his sword, he carried Gresham out of the dungeon.

Armus, Mahon, and Egan just defeated the Shadow Warriors when Zadok appeared, carrying Gresham. "He's in real bad shape."

Armus examined Gresham's face. "Take him to Melwynn."

Zadok stepped back and vanished.

Roane emerged from the barracks to see Guardians in the compound. One particular Guardian caught his attention, Barnum. In fact, the Highland Guardian saw him at same moment.

"Traitor!" shouted Barnum, baring his teeth.

Roane raised his sword in time to deflect Barnum's charging attack. Shadow Warriors were stronger than most Guardians, enhanced by the Dark Ways, but some Guardian warriors were exceptionally powerful, including Barnum. The attack sent Roane staggering sideways. A quick riposte, and several more attacks were exchanged.

"You can't defeat me, Barnum. I've been made your equal."

"Never. You turned your back on Jor'el and your companions. For that, you will always be inferior."

Roane roared in anger and slashed at Barnum then immediately waved his hand and sent a heavy crate hurling toward Barnum's head. Barnum dodged the crate. Roane vanished.

"Coward!" shouted Barnum.

"Whom were you talking to?"

The voice startled Barnum and he spun around with sword ready, and stopped at seeing Jedrek. He growled a low throaty answer, "Roane."

Jedrek's expression showed he understood. "Let's secure the postern gate."

Already wounded, Cletus wasn't fairing well against two Guardian warriors from the West Coast, Ewert and Bailey. Nari raced to his aid. Being an Enforcer, she was the strongest of Shadow Warriors and didn't require a sword.

Bailey didn't notice her arrival, rather felt a stunning punch to his lower back, paralyzing his legs. He fell hard to the ground with a cry of agony. Before Nari could bounce on him with her dagger there was a loud clap and everything went dark. She stumbled and fell face first to the cobblestone. Daren and Darcy grabbed Bailey under the arms and drug him to safety.

Ewert sent Cletus sideways before seeing the night twins secure Bailey. He heard footsteps to one side and turned in anticipation of Cletus' attack. Instead, Cletus scooped up Nari; both took a few steps and vanished. He went to check on his companion.

"How's Bailey?"

"Why don't you ask me, you big lummox," chided Bailey.

"Hold still," said Daren. He and Darcy leaned Bailey forward to work on his back. Together they struck on either side of where the initial blow landed. Bailey yowled in pain. "We had to unblock her blow."

"Did it work?" asked Ewert.

"Ay." Bailey gingerly moved his feet and legs.

"You'll be sore for awhile. Better let Eldric have a look to be sure," said Darcy.

"Come on." Ewert helped Bailey limp out the postern gate.

Iain gave the royal standard to a bearer before taking command of the troops in a frontal assault. He and Darius led the charge while Vidar and an appointed troop of Jor'ellians remained with Ellis and Shannan.

Upon their advance, a hail of arrows rained down them from the castle walls. Although out of range, she held her bow ready, watching with great distress on her face.

"Perhaps you should withdraw," said Ellis.

Suddenly she fired, the arrow whizzing past Ellis' face. His head snapped around to see her shot strike a Shadow Warrior, who vanished in the grey light of demise.

"Nice shot."

She wavered in the saddle, leaning on the pommel. He grabbed her arm to steady her. "Kell has abandoned the shielding. Gresham!"

"What about him?"

She shook her head, slightly pale. "Not good.

"What about you?"

"I'm well. Only fearful for Kell and Gresham."

At hearing a trumpet call, Ellis' attention returned to Waldron. "Our troops are inside."

Vidar came to stand beside Shannan's horse, which prompted her to speak to Ellis. "Go. I'll be fine."

Ellis turned to the Jor'ellians. "Time to reclaim Waldron." He drew his sword. "For Jor'el and for Allon!" He and the knights advanced.

Upon seeing the sudden appearance of Guardians, Musetta shrank back into a doorway. The realization struck her hard. Somehow Ellis managed to get a hold of the shielding medal she issued to the Shadow Warriors sent to wreak havoc at Hagley. With an overwhelming number of mortal soldiers and Guardians, defeat was imminent. There was only one thing left to do.

Owain moved along the battlement trying to give encouragement, only with each passing moment the futility of the situation sunk deeper into his brain. Guardians made short work of his men inside the compound. Peering over the wall, more of his men were being cut down or fleeing the king's army. He stepped back to reconsider. He noticed Musetta sulking in a doorway. *"Kill the witch!"* screamed in his brain. Impulsively, he felt for Lanay's letter.

At hearing a trumpet, he saw Ellis coming. The moment of reckoning arrived. There was no escape for him, but maybe he could save his family. He looked back to Musetta. She moved from the door, heading toward him. Snarling, he ran down the steps, raising his sword to strike.

She stopped at seeing him. There was no mistaking his intent. She seized the talisman. *"Bho neart gu neart.* You are dead!"

Owain paled, gasping for air. He fell to his knees in agony. Still, he lunged at her, collapsing to the ground, the contorted anguish of death on his face.

Seeing royal soldiers enter the main gate, she clenched the talisman harder and said, "Shadows veil this mortal frame, from the enemy back to whence I came." Unseen by mortal or Guardian, she dashed through the compound toward the postern gate.

Iain pulled his horse to a skidding halt in the Courtyard. "Arrest any of Sir Owain's men and secure the castle!"

Owain lay on the ground. By the look of him, he was dead. Still, Iain dismounted and checked for a pulse.

Ellis arrived and reined in his horse. "General?"

"He's dead."

Ellis' jowls flexed in anger, looking from Owain's body to survey the Courtyard. "We'll have to get answers from someone else."

"Have a detail secure the body," Iain ordered a soldier.

"Sire." Ferrell and Darius arrived on foot with Mahon and Armus holding the arms of a middle-aged man wearing Owain's livery. "This is Standish. He once tried to become a Jor'ellian and failed miserably."

Standish tossed an irate glance at Ferrell.

"What do you know of this?" demanded Ellis.

"Not much," said Standish impertinently.

Armus struck him to his knees. "Answer the king properly."

Woozy from the assault, Standish shrugged. "I told you, I don't know. I followed orders, that's all."

"Was Owain alone in this?"

"No, there was another. A pretty, blond young man, too pretty if you ask me. But then I didn't let my opinion be known because of the Shadow Warriors with him."

"Did he have a name?"

"Not that I heard. Although he and Sir Owain argued with Lord Hugh when we first arrived."

"Hugh?" Iain stepped closer. "Where is he?"

"Locked in the barracks."

Iain raced to the barracks. Mahon followed. Inside Iain grabbed a royal soldier. "Where is Lord Hugh?" The soldier couldn't answer, surprised by the seizure and question, so Iain repeated it.

"General." A Jor'ellian stood across the room in front of an open door.

In quick strides Iain crossed the dormitory. Mahon joined him when the Jor'ellian motioned inside the room. Hugh laid face to the floor in a pool of blood. Iain knelt and gently rolled Hugh unto his back. He was struck through the heart. Death was instantaneous. Mahon sagged against the threshold with a sigh of great lament.

Shannan again leaned on the saddle pommel in distress. Vidar kept her from falling. "What's wrong?"

She didn't answer, rather put up her bow, gathered the reins and turned her horse to gallop toward the eastern edge of the forest and Kell's position. Vidar easily kept pace on foot.

Kell lay on the ground. She abruptly drew rein and dismounted before the horse completely stopped. "Kell?"

He stirred to her touch. She and Vidar helped him sit up. He was very pale and the golden eyes weary. "That was more difficult than I thought. What's happened?"

"Ellis has taken Waldron."

Kell flashed a weak smile and motioned for Vidar to help him stand. He was unsteady, grabbing Vidar to keep from falling. Shannan supported him on the other side. After a brief moment, he began to walk. "I can make it."

She took the reins of her horse to walk beside Kell.

Now dismounted, Ellis was in the Courtyard along with Armus, Darius and Ferrell when they arrived. All took notice of Kell's tired and drained features.

"Your plan worked, Kell. Well done," said Ellis.

"You look like you can use a nap," said Darius.

Kell wearily grinned. "I'll rest when all is secure." He asked Armus, "Gresham?"

"Not good. Zadok took him to Melwynn."

Kell grimaced, both in distress at the news and the pain of exhaustion.

Iain and Mahon returned, grief visible on their faces.

"Hugh?" asked Ellis.

When Iain couldn't answer, Mahon droned, "Dead."

Shannan covered her mouth to stifle a sob. Ellis placed a comforting arm about her shoulder when she muttered, "Those poor boys."

Iain's voice was husky. "With your permission, Sire, I leave to take charge of Hugh and see to my nephews and nieces."

"Of course. Mahon, Ferrell, see to whatever is needed."

Jasper and royal soldiers escorted servants from the hall. Some women wept, others gladly greeted royal soldiers or Jor'ellians. One man fell to his knees before Ellis, taking the king's hand to kiss it.

"Bless you, Sire. We knew you'd come back to help us! Bless you. Bless Jor'el."

Ellis pulled him to his feet. "Indeed. Bless Jor'el for his victory. Now go and help those in need. There is much to do." Watching the man leave, Ellis stared at the Chapel and shivered. "We won back Waldron, but it is stained with blood by the enemy. We will not stay here."

"Are you sure? What will the servants think?" asked Shannan.

"The king is right. Waldron must be abandoned for the evil to be cleansed," said Kell.

Ellis told Darius, "After everything is secure spread the word for all to assemble on the front plain where I will address them."

Musetta ran as far from Waldron as she could. Exhausted, she collapsed to her hands and knees, laboring for breath, her mind a whirlwind of anger, frustration and anxiety. For years she longed to have what was promised and most desired, only to fail because of weak-minded sniveling coward! A coward she chose to use.

At hearing a nearby sound, her heart raced with fear. She gripped the talisman, her eyes shifting about. A hand touched her shoulder and she screamed, holding the talisman out, ready to speak. It was Roane.

"Easy, mistress. I made noise so I wouldn't frighten you."

She struggled to bring her emotions under control. "Where are the others?"

"Nari is tending Cletus and Lark while Indigo and Bern keep watch."

"Is that all who are left?"

"Ay, only six of sixty. Come. It isn't safe here." He helped her to where the others were hiding, two miles from Waldron.

Lark, a female Shadow Warrior, was more muscular and stout compared to Nari's lithesome frame. Her pale-blonde hair pulled back in a stark braid; the amethyst eyes dulled by pain. She suffered a deep wound to her left side.

"How are they doing?" asked Roane.

"They'll be fine in a day or two," replied Nari.

Lark snarled. "If Wren and I ever cross paths again, I'll finish her."

"You're lucky I jostled her aim," said Bern.

"Why didn't you finish her?"

"A female warrior cold-cocked him from behind," said Indigo to Bern's chagrin.

"What now, mistress?" asked Cletus.

Musetta sat on a flat boulder and shook her head, befuddled and upset. "I don't know. I moved too soon."

"Maybe, but they don't know about your son. He can be trained, you have the means, and I the strength to give you," said Roane, motioning to the talismans each wore.

"Ay," she agreed, sneering with new determination. "I shall tell him of his father, of his promise, and teach him to hate." With sudden thought she looked at Roane. "Have you located Owain's family yet?"

"No."

"We must and quickly! If he told them about me and all could be lost."

"We will, but you must go into hiding with your son."

"If you don't find them—"

"Mistress, we are bound to duty by the means Dagar used in altering us," Roane interrupted, indicating the talisman. "We will not fail. We cannot. Our fate lies completely with you. As such we will protect you and your son."

"Then I trust you to do what is necessary.

Chapter 16

ITTOOK THE REST OF THE DAY to secure Waldron, erect an encampment on the castle plain, tend to the wounded soldiers on both sides, and interrogate prisoners. Unfortunately, they were unable discover the identity of the blond man helping Owain.

Kell was fully recovered after a four-hour 'nap/meditation'. He ordered Jor'ellians and Guardians to prepare an area for the king's address. Although Iain was excused from duty, he and the boys attended the gathering. Mahon and Ferrell accompanied them. They stood beside Darius and Arista.

Torches illuminated the castle plain since night came early in winter. When all were assembled, Kell called for attention and announced the king and queen.

"People and Lords of Allon," began Ellis. "Today we liberated Waldron from those who raised insurrection in an attempt to destroy the royal family. Thankfully, with the aid of several Guardians, Lady Arista, and two brave young men," he said, looking directly at Wess and Bosley, "the queen and prince were rescued. For such bravery, they have the gratitude of their king."

"Here, here!" cheered Darius.

The boys were subdued and shy of the attention.

Ellis continued, "Unfortunately Sir Owain was aided by the Dark Way and defiled Waldron by staining it with blood. Because of that, Vicar

Archimedes will perform the cleansing rituals. Until such time he deems the evil is gone and the castle completed built, the royal family will not set foot inside. Court will again be held at Clifton Castle and Deltoria," he said looking at Ranulf and Erasmus. "Those of you summoned to Waldron as servants are free to return to your homes until you are recalled. And you will be recalled, for you also have the gratitude of the queen and myself for enduring captivity, and never wavering in your faith that Jor'el would hear your prayers for deliverance. Go now, with Jor'el's blessings and my thanks."

The moment Ellis and Shannan moved to leave, Darius, Allard, Erasmus and the rest of the Council applauded. Ellis caught part of a conversation in passing.

"For a lad wet behind the ears, he saved Allon again," said Allard to Mathias, only loud enough for Zebulon and Gareth to hear.

"You doubted he would?" said Zebulon.

Allard boomed with laughing at the unexpected yet welcomed retort.

Ellis fought to keep the smile from his face while Shannan appeared distracted. "Does Zebulon upset you?" he asked.

"No, the boys. Bosley looked lost; Wess stoic and hardened somehow." She glanced back to the dispersing crowd. "We should speak to them."

"I intend to as soon as I can." He stopped in front of the royal tent and took her hands to get her full attention. "I am most grateful to them, and although busy, I have not been idle where they are concerned."

"I know and I didn't mean to imply you were ungrateful or unfeeling."

Before Ellis replied, Darius and Jasper arrived.

"Jasper found something you need to see. In private." Darius motioned to the tent.

Once inside, Jasper handed the letter to Ellis. "This was found in Sir Owain's pocket."

Ellis took note of the three seals and soberly sighed. "It's addressed to Lanay," he said to Shannan then to all, "I will keep it until she can be notified."

"Will you keep it sealed?" asked Darius.

"What kind of question is that? Of course."

"He may name his accomplice."

Ellis pursed his lips and regarded the letter. "I will respect the seals and the person to whom it is addressed. I would not want the trust of my wife betrayed and will not do so to another man's wife. If after reading, she wishes to speak on the matter, then we will learn and not before." He gave the letter to Vidar. "Now, I think a good meal and rest is in order. Join us or are you helping Arista with the boys?"

"What kind of question is that?" teased Shannan, tossing a smiling glance at Darius. "Someday soon she'll be his accomplice."

"As if together we could corral such an incorrigible," said Darius.

She chuckled and took Darius' arm. "I'll come with you."

He hesitated. "I think you should wait."

"Why? Is there a problem?"

"No, they are shy of accepting Arista's help, so she sent for me. A manly quality of dealing unaided with grief."

Jasper added, "Teetering between manhood and childhood, boys want to prove they can handle themselves without female assistance."

"No matter how well intentioned the assistance is," Ellis said at seeing her vexation.

"That's foolish at time like this."

Darius, Ellis and Jasper just looked at her, which made her huff with exasperation.

"Very well." She waved a finger at Darius. "I want to know the moment I can visit."

Darius grinned and left with Jasper.

After the crowd dispersed, Kell left camp to inquire after Gresham. The lack of information from the interviews proved frustrating and he hoped Gresham could offer some insight.

Melwynn, Castle of the Guardians, was a large splendid palace built on a Highland plateau with part of the castle carved from the mountain itself. The terrace offered a magnificent view of the countryside. At night, numerous torches and oil lamps illuminated the castle, more for creating an impression for any visitors than to aid Guardians' visibility.

After the light of his arrival faded, Kell left the terrace to go inside. Other Guardians were about and didn't pay much attention to him since it was common to come and go in the performance of their duty. In the main hallway, he spotted Avatar walking away and carrying some folded white garments.

"Avatar!" he called, hurrying to catch his aide. He grinned while glancing up and down at Avatar. "You look better than I expected after hearing about your exploits."

"Thanks. I'm back to full strength and the bite marks are nearly gone."

"From the kelpie. What about the hunter-hawk?"

"No wounds, only a dunking. Which is how I disposed of it, by tossing it in the water so it couldn't be followed. In fact, what has happened? The last thing I knew Shannan planned on joining Ellis."

"She did, which is how we heard about your exploits." He sarcastically snorted and added, "Although Wren wasn't too gracious when Mahon commented on her medical treatment of your wounds. Still, hearing of the hunter-hawk and tartundeen was disturbing."

"Hearing? Try facing them."

Kell motioned to cloths and asked, "Bandages?"

"Eh, no. These are for Nigel."

Kell grew concerned at Avatar's hesitation. "Is he not well?"

"No, he's fine. Just eating, sleeping, and doing what mortal infants do after they've eaten and slept, regardless of the time of day or night."

Kell heartily laughed. "You're changing diapers."

"No," Avatar stammered in embarrassment. "Fetching them. I don't know what became of Faline so Yolanda found a mortal nurse."

Kell still laughed. "She was among those liberated at Waldron." His humor faded. "However, because of the Dark Way, Ellis instructed Archimedes to begin the cleansing rituals. And there is sad news. Lord Hugh is dead."

"Oh, no. Such news must be hard on the boys. They were of great help."

"So it was reported and acknowledged in public by Ellis."

"That is some compensation, I suppose."

Kell grinned. "There will be more. Ellis will not let their service go unrewarded."

"What about Owain? Did he have the talisman?"

Kell shook his head. "He's dead and we still don't know who aided him. In fact, I sent Gresham to infiltrate Waldron to discover the identity, only he was captured. Armus said Zadok brought him here for treatment of his wounds. I thought those were for him," he said of the cloths. "Have you seen him?"

"No, but bad news would have spread by now."

"Avatar!" an impatient female called from a doorway down the hall.

Avatar cast a hapless look at Kell. "Please tell me I can return with Nigel. Faline is far more agreeable."

Kell chuckled. "Sorry. You're both to stay here until Ellis sends for you."

"Avatar!"

While Avatar made his way down the hall, Kell went to the infirmary. Phoebe sat in a chair beside Gresham's bed. His concern grew at seeing Gresham's condition. Armus' vague description of "not looking good" was a severe understatement. Blood soaked through the bandage around his torso and he was ashen.

"How is he?"

"By Jor'el's will he lives. I don't know of many warriors who could have survived the torture he did."

"Can he talk?"

"Not until morning. I gave him something for the pain and help him sleep."

"I'll wait."

"He may wake, but the injuries and stygian metal drained a significant amount of his lifeforce. It'll take at least a week of strengthening tonics and rest for him to fully recover."

He simply stared at her, which caused her to vacate the chair, although not pleased to do so. He sat and spoke, "Don't trouble Eldric. He won't make me leave either."

"Ay, Captain. I'll be nearby." She crossed to her desk near the examination area.

Kell's focused on Gresham. Owain dead and his men speaking of a young blond man with Shadow Warriors, Gresham was the only one capable of shedding light on the mystery.

During those hours Kell considered each mortal connected to the Dark Way during Marcellus' reign. Most were dealt with after the battle. Did Latham have a protégé or unknown accomplice? Or perhaps some secret plot Dagar devised and planted years ago finally came into being? How were the tartundeen and hunter-hawk removed without notice? Mahon did a thorough job of which he approved, so whoever retrieved the creatures was able to obtain them without arousing suspicion. This pointed to the possibility of a secret plan by Dagar. Ellis' question plagued him because he couldn't think of another Guardian who bore such hatred toward Jor'el and the mortals as Dagar. He hoped Gresham discovered the identity of those involved, mortal and Guardian.

Past midnight, Kell noticed Gresham stir, only his eyes remained closed. He gently touched Gresham's forehead and spoke his name.

Gresham stirred and his eyes fluttered open. He looked baffled for a moment. "Kell? Where am I?"

"Melwynn."

"How did I get here?"

"Zadok brought you."

Gresham lowly groaned. "I don't remember much past getting into Waldron."

"Nothing?"

He sighed in painful annoyance. "No. Roane caught me before I could begin reconnaissance."

Kell's brows knitted, both concerned that Gresham didn't remember and anger at his condition. "Is Roane responsible for your injuries?"

Gresham nodded, swallowing back fatigue and pain. "I told him nothing. I'm sorry, Kell. I failed."

Kell gripped Gresham's shoulder, compassion in voice and face. "No. The blame is mine. I asked you to risk your life. I'm glad you survived for me to say thank you."

Gresham grinned, small and weak. "It had to be done. What about Owain?"

Kell took a deep deliberate breath before replying. "The rebellion is put down and he is dead. No wounds or marks of any kind. By the look of his distorted face, the Dark Way killed him."

Gresham grimaced in remorse. "Any clue of who?"

"All we know is a blond young man with Shadow Warriors helped him. It's still a mystery."

Worried filled Gresham face. "What will become of his family?"

"Depends if they were involved or not."

"I've got to find them." He tried to sit up, ignoring the pain.

"Easy. I understand your concern, but you're in no condition." Kell eased Gresham to lie back down.

Gresham seized Kell's hand. "Promise me you will see they are found and treated fairly."

"I will. And Ellis isn't heartless."

"Enough, Captain. He needs rest," said Phoebe. She gently removed Gresham's hand from Kell.

"Take care, Gresham."

Gresham grunted and closed his eyes. Phoebe pulled the blanket over him.

Back at camp, Kell entered the royal tent. Ellis and Shannan slept and Vidar stood beside the entrance. "Something wrong?" asked Vidar.

"I need to speak to Ellis." Kell approached the bed and gently woke Ellis, whose eyes snapped open and quickly became alert.

"Kell."

"What?" Shannan sleepily asked.

"Sorry to wake you both. I just returned from Melwynn."

Concerned, her fatigue vanished and she sat up. "Has something happened to Nigel?"

"No," said Kell with an impulsive chuckle. "He is well taken care of. In fact, Avatar is learning to deal with diapers."

Vidar coughed to cover his laughing.

Ellis propped himself on his elbow, smiling curiously. "Then what is it?"

"Gresham?" asked Shannan.

"Alive. Unfortunately, he was captured and tortured before he could discover who aided Owain."

Ellis' brows leveled in anger and some discomposure. "Our arrival took them by surprise, meaning he told them nothing and suffered for it."

"Gresham would have died before speaking."

"Oh, dear Gresham," she murmured.

"Be assured, he will fully recover. However, he is distressed about Owain's fate and feels he is to blame for not stopping him."

"He shouldn't," said Ellis.

"All the same, he asked me to find his family and see they are treated fairly."

"He thinks I would do otherwise?"

Kell shook his head. "No, but whoever killed Owain maybe looking for them, or know where they are. It would be best if we found them first and time is of importance."

Ellis agreed with a nod while trying to stifle yawn. "Who will you take?"

"Wren, Armus, and Mahon."

In consideration, Ellis regarded Kell. "Do not tell Lanay the full story, just enough to satisfy her. I want to judge for myself by her reaction if she knew of his plan or was involved in any way."

"As you wish." Kell bowed and left.

Chapter 17

THE GUARDIANS ARRIVED on the road two miles from Presley then cautiously moved to within a mile before stopping to observe the house. All seemed quiet.

Kell's eyes narrowed in observation of the manor house. "I still can't sense any evil."

"You really think they'd leave his home unguarded?" asked Armus.

"No, and I'm surprised we've not sensed any presence." He pulled out the shielding medal from inside his belt. "I brought this so we can search the manor freely without leaving any essence. If we stay together and are careful, we can all be masked."

Wren snatched it from Kell. "No, one is better than all. And this requires the stealth of a huntress not warrior boldness. Wait for my signal." She placed the medal around her neck and dashed off.

"And you wonder why she and Avatar clash?" Mahon asked Kell.

Using the shielding medal, Wren boldly approached the house. Once there, she crouched down at the west corner. With all quiet and everyone asleep, she could dimension travel inside; but why risk chances if any undetected Shadow Warriors were present? True, the shielding medal hid her essence, but touching something and using too much power could be detected. Small, incremental uses of power were masked, but dimension travel required a great deal of energy.

She approached the back door and whispered, *"Fosgail."* The locked door clicked open. She paused, listening for any signs that someone heard. Nothing. She silently slipped inside. Since day or night did not affect a Guardian's eyesight, she moved easily in the darkened house.

The search of the bottom floor yielded no one. She was so nimble and careful on her feet not a single floorboard creaked when she went upstairs. Again, she found no one. She left the way she came and whispered the lock closed before dashing back to the others.

"Nothing. The house is abandoned."

"Well, they went somewhere," said Mahon.

"Ay, but on foot or—" began Armus.

"Armus, you're a genius!" she cheered.

"What did I say?" he asked, but was ignored as she ran back to the house.

Wren found the stable empty of horses. Two carriages remained. In this case, she could not be so careful and had to touch the carriage to get a sense of, or if, the mortals used them to travel. First she placed a hand on the smaller carriage and closed her eyes. Nothing. She moved to the larger one and did the same. She flinched, opened her eyes and smiled. She was still smiling when she returned to the others.

"They took a long journey southeast."

"How did you learn that?" asked Kell.

She motioned to Armus. "Genius here. Noble families don't travel on foot but ..."

"In carriages," said Armus the same time she did.

"Ay. The horses are gone but the largest carriage transported his family."

"To sense that, you had to touch the carriage," said Kell.

"It only required the barest use of power. However, this will interfere with tracking." She took off the medal and gave it back to Kell. "This way." She took the lead, heading southeast.

Shortly after the Guardians left, the Shadow Warriors arrived. They were not cautious in their approach or search of the manor. Bern and Indigo threw open the front door and entered. Nari and Lark went in the back while Roane and Cletus searched the carriage house and stable.

"Nothing," complained Nari when they gathered outside. "The house is empty."

"That's not the half of it. Wren was here," said Roane.

"How do you know? I don't sense her presence, or any Guardian," said Lark.

"She left a faint impression on the carriages."

"So she knows which way the mortals went," said Indigo.

Roane nodded with a sly smile. "All we have to do is follow her and she'll lead us right to them."

"You realize we need to keep our distance so she doesn't sense us?" said Nari.

"There are six of us," said Cletus.

"You're assuming she's alone."

"We only sensed her. And she's heading southeast," said Roane.

By daybreak Wren led them across the border of Midessex and into the Meadowlands, eighty miles from the manor. Guardians covered great distances in a short period of time. Stopping at a crossroads, she knelt to inspect the ground for signs of travel.

"This is as far as the carriage went," she said.

"You mean they continued on foot? A noble family?" teased Armus.

She made no immediate reply to his sarcastic humor, rather turned onto a short secondary road. It ended at a post house where carriages arrive to exchange horses or passengers. She triumphantly smirked at Armus before knocking on the door.

A man near the age of thirty answered. "Ay? Oh," he said, surprised at seeing Wren. She stood a foot taller than he. He briefly noticed the other Guardians behind her. The voices of small children came from the house.

Wren gave him a friendly smile. "Have no fear. We were told Lady Lanay was here."

"Who?"

"Lady Lanay. A noblewoman traveling with three girls."

"Oh, ay. I never knew the name and that was about two weeks ago."

Kell stepped forward. "Can you tell us which way she went?"

The man gaped in awe of Kell, whose appearance was both impressive and intimidating. "Toward the east coast," he nervously replied.

"Post house or a certain destination?"

"The next post house is at Carson. She never mentioned any place specific."

"Thank you." Wren nudged Kell away from the door. The man remained in the threshold anxiously watching them leave. She smiled and said to him, "By the way, there's a rabbit in your trap."

"My trap? I haven't set ..." He went around the side of his house to a small shed and saw a rabbit hanging in the trap he had yet to set. "Thank you!" he called after her. When he turned back to take the rabbit down a large hand pinned him against the shed. The hulking form of Bern made his speechless with fright.

"Interesting way to catch a rabbit. What did you tell them?"

"They asked where Lady Lanay went so I told them."

"Where?" Bern tightened his grip, making him gasp in pain.

"East, toward Carson. Please! Don't hurt me!"

Wren was speaking as they turned onto the main road. "Why did you frighten him, he was answering me."

"I didn't mean to—" Kell stopped. The others also became alert to trouble. He waved Wren to go right, Mahon left. He and Armus drew their swords and ran back toward the post house. They heard the man say, "Don't hurt me!"

Twang! Whiz! A crossbow dart impaled Bern's hand before he could strike the man with a dagger. Bern yowled in pain and dropped the dagger. He turned in the direction the dart came and saw Kell and Armus racing up the road. He retreated into the forest.

Kell stopped beside the man while Armus pursued Bern. "Are you hurt?"

"No. Who was that?"

"A Shadow Warrior. Did he say anything?"

"He asked what you did about Lady Lanay."

"And you told him?" asked Kell, irate.

He spoke in defensive. "What else was I to do?"

Kell guided the man toward the house. "Quickly, fetch your family. We must get you to safety."

"What? Why?"

"I am Kell, Captain of Jor'el's Guardians. Trust us," he said, looking directly at the man. This time the man obeyed and ran to the house.

Armus returned, and with Mahon and Wren. "Gone. He dimension travelled before we could catch him."

"He also asked about Lanay and was told," said Kell in annoyance.

"You can't blame him for protecting himself," said Mahon.

"I don't. Only the Warrior may return to finish what he started, and perhaps with others. We must take them to safety before going to Carson which delays us in finding Lanay." Kell pursed his lip in momentary thought. "There's a Fortress between here and Mylton."

The man emerged from the house with his wife and two young sons ages five and eight. "I'll hitch up the wagon."

"Too slow," said Kell to the man, then to his companions. "Four. One each."

"One each, what?" asked the wife. She held the youngest boy.

"I'll take him. He'll be safe with me," said Wren, and took the boy.

Mahon held the oldest son. Armus stood beside the wife, taking her arm, while Kell placed an arm about the man's shoulders. "Hold on to us."

"But, Captain ..." was all he said before disappearing in white light.

At the Fortress several priests were in the courtyard tending to their morning duties when bright light blinded them. From the light emerged four Guardians, each holding a mortal who fainted.

"Captain Kell?" asked a tall, lean older priest.

Kell didn't immediately answer since the family was regaining their senses and stunned at where they were. "We are at a Fortress for your safety," he said to the man, then to the priest, "Master Averil, this family is in need of sanctuary."

"Of course, Captain."

"But the post-house, my duties," the man protested.

"Trust us," said Kell.

The golden eyes were reassuring and the man nodded. Averil led them to a room on the second floor of the dormitory. Wren, Mahon and Armus waited in the hall while Averil and Kell accompanied the family inside. The room was nice size with modest furniture.

"These are adjoining rooms," Averil said of the connecting door. "Have you eaten breakfast?"

"No, we just woke when it happened," replied the man.

"I'll have the cook prepare you food."

"Captain Kell," he began when Averil and Kell turned to leave. "Thank you. But how long will we have to remain here?"

"Hopefully not too long. Once the situation is put right, I'll return to escort you home. Any income or lose you suffer will be recompensed. In the meantime, enjoy the hospitality of these good priests."

With that said, the Guardians left the Fortress.

<hr />

The post house at Carson was in an upheaval when the Guardians arrived. A middle-aged man knelt on the ground beside an unconscious younger man. Both showed signs of injury, the older man with a bloody forehead and bruised face. The younger man sustained a severe head injury and large, gaping stab wound to his abdomen.

Kell knelt beside them. "What happened?"

The older man angrily lashed out at seeing them. "Get away! Your kind is all alike."

"The Shadow Warrior," said Armus.

"Which way did he go?" Kell asked the man.

"I don't care, they just went. You also! Go!"

Kell caught the use of the plural *they* and glanced at his companions. By their expressions they also heard.

"He'll die if you don't let us medicine him." Wren started to take supplies out of her pouch.

"No! Take your foul remedies and leave."

Kell seized the man by the shoulders, forcing him to look at him. "Believe in Jor'el and your son will live."

"How do you know he's my son?"

"I know many things. Release your anger, Bayden, and trust Jor'el like you once did and Malick will live." Kell's golden gaze went deep and probing

Bayden's shoulders sagged and a sob caught in his throat when Kell spoke his son's name. "Don't let him die."

Kell released Bayden and placed one hand on Malick's forehead and other over the wound. "By the power of Jor'el let the darkness be gone, heal the wounds and bind the heart." The undersides of Kell's hands began to glow and the Malick's injuries began to fade until finally they were gone. Malick took a sudden deep gulp of air and he eyes snapped open with bewilderment. Bayden helped Malick sit up.

Malick's confused focus shifted from his father to Kell. The captain was slightly pale. "What happened?"

"You and your father were attacked by Shadow Warriors," said Kell.

"Ay," he said in remembrance. "Who are you?"

"I am Kell."

"Jor'el's captain. That's how you knew my name and Malick."

Kell kindly smiled. "Now, which way did they go?"

"Toward Pickford. They asked about a lady and her daughters."

"There's a Fortress at Pickford. Did she mention going there?"

ALLON ~ BOOK 2 ~ INSURRECTION

"No. She just wanted a ride to the town so I sent them with Jaron, my eldest son who is a driver. He might know, or my brother. He runs the Two Roads Inn that serves as Pickford's way station."

"For the rest of the day, go fishing."

"I can't fish. I must run the post house."

Kell helped Bayden to stand. "Take your sword."

Bayden lightly frowned but nodded. "Come, Malick."

"What sword, Papa?" asked Malick, following Bayden.

"You expect them to spear fish?" asked Wren in her usual dry wit.

Kell ignored the comment and motioned for them to leave. "They'll be safe for now."

"What about you? Your color still hasn't returned," said Armus.

"I'll be fine."

Mahon appeared skeptical. "I thought such healings were limited to physicians."

Kell smirked. "They usually are. I'm grateful Jor'el answered me. Perhaps because Bayden was once a Jor'ellian knight who became disillusioned when his wife died during Malick's birth." He wearily rubbed his neck and rotated his shoulders. "I've not done a healing in centuries. Too taxing on my lifeforce."

Wren chuckled. "I'm sure Eldric will enjoy hearing that."

"I depend upon you to tell him."

***

At the Fortress of Pickord, the day was underway. Priests were up and about seeing to their daily chores. The front gate stood open for ease of passage in performing daily chores and to welcome any travelers.

"The gate's open," said Katlyn. She rushed from the hall.

"Katlyn! We're not supposed to go outside," Candice called and ran after Katlyn, catching her at the gate.

"Just for a few moments to play in the snow. We've been shut up for days. I'm so bored."

"So am I, but remember how Mother punished you for going outside last time."

Katlyn sneered. "She wouldn't have known if you didn't tell her."

"I didn't! The priests did."

Katlyn rolled her eyes and stomped her foot. They heard the jingling of harness and a voice calling to the priests working outside the gate. Katlyn became excited. "A peddler! Oh, and look at his wagon. He has ribbons and cloth."

"Ay," Candice agreed. When Katlyn bolted for the wagon, she grabbed for her, but missed. "Katlyn, get back here!" Frustrated at being ignored, she picked up her skirt and ran after Katlyn.

"Candice! Where are they going?" Lanay hurried to the gate. She saw both girls at the peddler's wagon and angrily scowled. "Grounding won't be good enough this time."

On a bluff overlooking the Fortress the Shadow Warriors appeared. They watched the peddler call a greeting to the priests.

"The Fortress is about to have a visitor," said Roane.

"Look." Nari indicated the girls showing interest in the peddler. "Must be them."

"If they step outside, we'll grab them. Get ready to move."

One girl made her way toward the peddler's wagon, the second following.

"Now!" said Roane and vanished.

The sudden appearance of six Shadow Warriors startled everyone. Roane seized Katlyn and Nari snatched Candice. Both girls desperately fought to get free. Lanay screamed from the gate at watching the priests try to protect the girls only to be tossed aside by the Warriors.

"Leave off!" came a commanding shout.

Indigo, Cletus, Bern, and Lark moved to intercept the Guardians. Kell was not about to be stopped and swung his sword, catching Cletus with the flat of the blade and sent him sideways. By the time Cletus got his balance, Kell reached Roane. He grabbed Katlyn with one hand while clouting

Roane's head using the hilt of his sword. Roane dropped to his knees, releasing Katlyn.

"Back to the Fortress!" Kell shoved her toward the gate before engaging Roane.

Katlyn didn't need any further prompting. A priest aided her back to Lanay, who gladly received her. Both fearfully watched for Candice.

Armus headed for Nari when Bern swung at him. They were equal in size. Seeing Bern's wound, Armus made a quick parry and brought the flat of his blade hard against the back of Bern's wounded hand. Bern yowled and dropped his sword, exposing his back. Armus sent a needed, savage slash to the Warrior's back.

Nari was busy subduing Candice when Bern fell at her feet, startling both her and the girl. Candice screamed. When Nari looked up, Armus' fist crashed into her face sending her backwards. He snatched Candice from Nari when she fell.

"Go back inside!" said Armus. Candice raced to join Katlyn and her mother.

When Armus turned to deal with Nari and Bern, "*Siuthad!*" they said together and vanished in a bright flash of white light. Temporarily blinded, Armus didn't see the blow that knocked him sideways. In fact, his vision was slow to return, but he saw enough to clumsily parry Cletus' next attack.

Wren aimed at Cletus to protect Armus. Lark's sword knocked the crossbow from her. Unarmed, she dodged Lark's next swing. Her dagger wasn't much use against a Shadow Warrior. Her best defense was to retrieve her crossbow. Lark blocked her path to the crossbow and with a mocking sneer, attacked. Wren again dodged Lark's blade, only to be clouted by a pommel between the shoulder blades and sent sprawling.

Seeing Wren down, Mahon made a quick feint to Indigo's body. When Indigo parried, Mahon ducked under the sword, came up from behind and threw an elbow jab into Indigo's back. Indigo stumbled into Lark and both Warriors fell. Mahon pulled Wren to her feet, only to release her when Indigo came up swinging at them. Lark moved to blindside Mahon. Wren dove for her crossbow and fired off a quick shot, striking Lark between the shoulder blades. Lark vanished in grey light.

The blinding light from Lark's demise distracted Kell and Roane. Kell recovered first and wounded Roane in the left side. It was a modest wound, still not good to be opened against the captain. Roane sent blast from his hand to Kell's head making the captain duck to one side. Roane vanished in dimension travel.

With the others gone, Cletus and Indigo stood alone against four Guardians. Not for long. They swiftly disengaged and disappeared.

"Should we track them?" asked Wren.

"No. We must to see to the lady," said Kell.

By now the Fortress gate was closed. The fight outside and appearance of four Guardians in the compound brought the Fortress Master hastening from the chapel to meet them in the courtyard.

"Peace, Master Quentin," said Kell.

"That's a difficult greeting to accept after what just happen, Captain."

"Are they safe?"

"Ay, they are in the chapel and very frightened."

"No doubt. I must speak with the lady."

Quentin stepped in front of Kell to block his advance. "She came here seeking sanctuary."

"Do you know why?"

Quentin answered with discretion. "It is confidential."

"In this case, the confidentially of the Fortress is waved, Master Quentin."

Quentin stared at Kell, the seriousness evident in the captain's face. "Let us first speak in private." He motioned for them to follow him to his study adjacent to the chapel and accessible by a private entrance. "Close the door," he said, and Mahon obliged. "Since you are Jor'el's Captain, I know you would not wave the confidence without good reason. Can you tell me why before I break my vow?"

"Those Shadow Warriors were in league with an individual who helped Sir Owain lead a rebellion against the king."

Stunned at first, Quentin shook his head. "For their sake I hoped and prayed he was not involved. Did you learn the identity of the individual?"

"No. However, we believe whomever it is possesses Dagar's talisman. They captured Waldron when the king was away answering a call for help from the North Plains. The queen and prince escaped and are safe and unharmed while the rebellion put down."

"And Owain?"

"Dead."

Quentin had to sit. A somber moment passed before he spoke again. "You believe she knew about his plan?"

"The king sent us to fetch her for an interview to gauge her knowledge or involvement."

"Perhaps being his wife, but the girls …" Quentin stopped, his brows furrowed in thought.

"What about them?"

He shook his head in mild confusion. "I'm not sure. The eldest, Gwen, is angry and bitter over the situation. Her attitude since arriving was worrisome, but what she said and did deeply disturbed me."

"How so?"

For a moment of consideration, Quentin regarded Kell before speaking. "She tried to leave the Fortress and in doing so, assaulted Captain Durant. When I confronted her, she admitted she does not fear Jor'el. Although she denied embracing the Dark Way, she doesn't fear it either. To ensure the safety of all and protect the Fortress, I placed her under locked guard. Lady Lanay was greatly upset."

"Has Lanay also expressed such sentiments?" When Quentin hesitated to answer, Kell became steadfast in regard and pressed the issue. "This is a matter of treason against the king and Jor'el. Has Lanay spoken similar sentiments to those of her daughter?"

Quentin sighed in resignation. "She never said anything specific, rather was cryptic, but it is clear she doubts him and fears repercussions."

"She must know," said Armus to Kell.

"That is for the king to determine." Kell then spoke to Quentin, "Fetch the eldest to join the others in the chapel."

In the chapel, Lanay, Katlyn and Candice sat on the front pew, all very upset. Lanay sniffled back new tears upon seeing Gwen arrive escorted by Durant. She hurried to her mother and they embraced.

"Are you well?"

"Ay. What of you and the girls?"

"Nearly kidnapped!" Candice sobbed.

"What?"

The conversation stopped when Quentin entered accompanied by the Guardians. "My lady, this is Captain Kell."

"I'm aware of who he is. Do you bring news of my husband, Captain?"

"We are to escort you and your daughters to the king."

Lanay gasped in alarm and nearly fainted, catching herself on the pew to sit.

"Mother?" Gwen asked in concern then lashed out at Kell. "What has the king done to our father?"

"Nothing, miss."

"Liar! The king wouldn't want to see us if he hadn't done something to Father."

Kell stiffened, golden eyes flashing in anger at the insult. "You know nothing of the king to make such a statement, nor to accuse me of lying."

His rebuke had no effect on curbing her brashness. "I know he doesn't trust my father, none on the Council do. If everything were well, he would send for us rather than the king, and not by way of heartless Guardians!" she chided, sneering at Kell and the others.

The fury rising on Kell's face prompted Quentin to scold Gwen. "You are speaking to the Captain of Jor'el's Guardians!"

"And he is as callous now as he was last time!"

Lanay hastily rose to stand beside Gwen to plead with Kell, "Forgive her, Captain. She is very upset. We all are."

269

Gwen again lashed out. "I maybe upset, but I know what is happening and so do you, Mother. I don't care who he is. He is a cold-hearted, dishonest creature."

"Enough!" Kell commanded, his voice startling the mortals. Even fiber of his being was taut and voice strident in the effort it took to control his temper at being continually insulted. His eyes narrowed upon Gwen. "You will not speak another word until I, Kell, Jor'el's Captain, give you leave."

To this, Gwen showed the greatest concern and chewed angrily on her lower lip, glaring at him for being forced into silence.

Lanay watched in apprehension. "Gwen? Captain?"

His patience exhausted, he put up a stiff hand to Lanay, his focus still intent on Gwen. She did not flinch from his scrutiny, rather remained stubbornly fixed in expression and posture despite being made silent. Indeed, she showed no fear or respect for Jor'el or his servants. He said at length, "By heavenly authority, I commanded her mute. Time is pressing and we must leave." He motioned to the other Guardians who each stood beside a mortal, while he took hold of Gwen. She stiffened with resistance, but he was stronger and held her secure. They vanished.

<hr />

In a nether dimension hideout, Musetta was startled by the appearance of a badly wounded Bern and battered Nari. In quick succession, Roane, Cletus and Indigo arrived, increasing her anxiety.

"What happened?"

"Kell," replied Roane.

Her anxiety turned to fear. "Did you learn if she knows about me?"

He shook his head, which made her strike him on the chest in quaking, almost uncontrollable anger. He didn't retaliate rather spoke when she finished assaulted him. "In time, we'll learn the answer. You and your son are safe here. Dagar made certain it is secure, even from Kell's astute sense.

Vexed and concerned she crossed to an iron rail separating the upper part of the room from a lower part. In the middle of the floor sat a brown-haired boy of four playing with wooden toys.

Roane joined her at the rail. "There is the future, mistress."

She sent him an irked side-glance and fingered the talisman. "Serve him well and I may forget your failure."

"I live only to serve. The day I stop, is the day I cease to exist."

Chapter 18

ARISTA JOINED DARIUS, SHANNAN AND ELLIS, who sat in large canvas chairs leisurely partaking of late afternoon tea beside a warm fire outside the royal tent.

"How are the boys?" asked Shannan.

Arista didn't immediately answer, more intent on pouring tea from a pot near the fire into a cup. Once settled in a chair, she replied, "They seem to be managing. At least according to Iain, neither of them has spoken to me."

"I told you," Darius said to Shannan.

Ellis changed the subject. "When will the big day be?" he asked Darius, his smiling glance shifting between Darius and Arista.

"Once Court is settled at Deltoria. Is that acceptable?" Darius asked Arista.

She nodded, since she was drinking tea.

"Will you be ready?" Ellis asked her.

"Why not? I've faced Shadow Warriors and all manner of beasts. Marrying Darius on short notice should be easy."

Ellis chuckled. Although she tried to speak with levity her features were melancholy. "You say that, but you do mean it? You seem distracted."

"I'm sorry, Sire."

"Ellis. You may want to start calling me Ellis, at least in private. You are marrying my incorrigible brother."

Her smile was plaintive, the humor not reaching her eyes. "Very well, Ellis."

"Come. What disturbs you?"

"The boys, of course," said Shannan since Arista was drinking.

Ellis swallowed his drink before speaking to Arista. "Don't fret too much. From what I've seen of Wess, he'll be fine."

"And Bosley?"

Ellis smiled, tossing a pleased glance at Darius. "He'll have a good deal of support. Besides, after the appropriate time of mourning, Darius will begin his education. So, come, what else troubles you?"

She was reluctant but Shannan gave a nod of encouragement so she replied. "I understand you are within your rights and duty to take charge of Midessex and do with it as you will. What of Lanay and her daughters? Will you punish them for Owain's actions?"

Stalling to consider, Ellis took a sip of tea before answering. "That depends upon whether she knew of his plan or not. The extent of her involvement will determine the punishment. That is the best answer I can give you." Seeing her distress, he asked, "Why does their fate concern you? Owain gave orders to kill."

"Sire ... Ellis," she demurely began, "it is a little known fact that one of my uncles fathered a child out of wedlock."

"Lanay?"

"Ay, she is my cousin. Although the family didn't publicly acknowledge the relationship, contact was frequent and provision made for her marriage to Owain."

"You're asking me for mercy."

She met his gaze. "Only as much as lies within royal law. Those poor girls lost their father, I would hate to see them lose their mother also."

Ellis stirred in his seat, pursing his lips. "You ask a great deal."

"She asks mercy only if Lanay was involved," said Shannan.

"You too? He nearly killed you and Nigel."

"Arista came to me troubled and we spoke at length. As a parent I understand the wisdom in her request. What if we had failed, who would raise Nigel? True, Darius would take the role, but he would be deprived of his parents."

"I appreciate your argument; however, I was an orphan raised by another family."

"You never knew your parents or bore the stigma of traitor."

Ellis sighed, looking across to Darius. The latter shrugged and said, "The argument can go either way. The answer won't come until we learn of her involvement or not."

Vidar arrived. "Sire, Kell has returned successfully."

Ellis tossed a glance to the women, then Darius. "We'll learn soon enough. Where are they?" he asked Vidar.

"The lady is with Kell and Armus in the duke's tent while the girls remain with Wren and Mahon in another tent."

Ellis spoke to Shannan. "You and Arista wait, Darius will come—"

"No!" Arista bolted up. "Please, Ellis. I want to be there." Warring consideration furrowed his brow so she pressed her case. "I won't say a word, I promise. I need to be there."

Darius stood beside Arista to support her yet spoke to Ellis. "It may be for the best."

"Lanay may not appreciate having a audience since I need to break the news to her of Owain death before determining her involvement."

Shannan also moved to stand beside Arista, assuming a staunch brow and firm voice. "We were the ones pursued," she spoke of herself and Arista. "We have a right to know."

To this argument, Ellis yielded. "Very well."

Kell and Armus waited at the entrance outside the tent. The captain raised a warning hand, prompting Ellis to ask, "Is there a problem?"

"The Shadow Warriors?" added Darius.

Kell replied, "We fought, but only one was vanquished, the rest escaped. We didn't pursue because our task was to bring the lady and her daughters here. However, I had a contentious confrontation with the eldest daughter, Gwen."

"She was at Court last time, wasn't she?" asked Ellis in recollection.

"Ay. She is very angry and holds you to blame."

"She told you this?"

"Adamantly. She called me a liar and a cold, heartless creature."

Arista gasped in alarm. Neither Ellis nor Darius looked pleased. Shannan warily eyed Kell and asked, "What did you do?"

"Commanded her to be silent until I give her leave to speak. Bound by royal orders and my station, I could do nothing else." He then spoke to Ellis. "She is clever and perceived something is wrong because you sent Guardians to fetch them."

"Also Master Quentin was forced to confine her for attempting to leave the Fortress and join her father," said Armus.

"She admitted to this?" asked Arista in disturbed astonishment.

"Ay, my lady."

Arista pressed Kell asking, "What about Lanay? Did she condone the behavior or express support for Owain?"

"She begged me to excuse Gwen's behavior, claiming she is upset. However, this goes beyond upset. Master Quentin told us she confessed no fear of Jor'el and I the truth saw in her eyes."

"And confirmed her feelings by continuing to confront you even after you were identified as Jor'el's Captain," said Armus.

"Ay. Her anger and bitterness are very deep."

Arista's distress grew. Shannan placed an arm of support and comfort about Arista's shoulders, while Ellis said to her, "Your presence may not be a good idea."

"No. Armed with this knowledge, I can be better prepared. Gwen is more impulsive and temperamental than Lanay."

Ellis pursed his lips, his gaze shifting between Arista and Kell. "I should speak to Gwen first."

"Why?"

"I'll explain later. Armus, stay with Lanay. You and Arista wait out here for our return, and I won't take no for answer," he said sternly to Shannan. "Kell."

Kell led Ellis and Darius to the tent where Mahon and Wren kept watch of the girls. The two younger girls sat at a table with food and drink while Gwen paced.

"Sire," said Mahon. His address made the girls pause in eating and Gwen to stop.

"The king!" Candice nervously whispered to Katlyn, who quickly wiped her mouth, trying not to gape at Ellis.

Ellis kindly smiled at Katlyn and Candice. "I hope you are enjoying your meal."

"Ay, Sire," said Candice.

He turned to Gwen. She warily regarded him, and when their eyes met, she stiffened and her lips pressed together. Indeed, she bore hostility towards him. "Wren," he began, his eyes slow to leave Gwen, "would you see the younger girls are taken to Master Burton with my compliments. They have food and drink, but none of his prize desserts."

"Of course, Sire." Wren took the girls cloaks off a nearby chair and for the time it took her to usher them out nothing was said.

Ellis continued his regard of Gwen. She returned his stare then shifted her glance to Kell, a small snarl appearing. She moved her mouth, but again pressed her lips.

"The king wishes to speak to you, so I release you from my command."

Far from being grateful, Ellis became the focus of her displeasure. "Sire. Why was I excluded from your generous offer?"

The patronizing tone and obstinate look were something Ellis was not about to tolerate. "Mistress Gwen, I heard you called Captain Kell a liar. That is something I take great exception to. He is the King's Champion, but foremost the Captain of Jor'el's Guardians and not to be questioned by you!"

Gwen gripped her hands at the rebuke, but did not back down. "I meant in reference to my father. What the captain said could not possibly be true."

"Oh? What makes you so certain?"

276

"Because I know my father. He is a mild-mannered man and, although given to occasional bouts of weakness, has no stomach for outright rebellion."

Ellis drew to his full height and squared his shoulders, fury on his face. "Tell that to the dead and wounded! His act of insurrection forced me to take up arms and liberate my own castle."

Gwen was taken back and paled in fright. "That can't be." She stiffened with new resolve. "No, I don't believe he did as you claim."

"Are you now calling the king a liar?" Kell demanded, his golden eyes flashing in anger.

Gwen bit her lower lip, which trembled at Kell's hostile look.

"Well?" Kell pressed, taking a step closer to Gwen.

She fearfully recoiled and blurted out, "No! It's just hard to believe."

"You told Master Quentin you do not fear Jor'el, but you have no idea the power of the Dark Way."

"I also told him I don't embraced the Dark Way," she lashed back.

Ellis laid hold of Kell's arm to draw the captain back from Gwen. He stared at her, adding his own rebuke. "You can't take both sides. Where good and evil are concerned, there is no middle ground."

She set her chin and stubbornly turned away.

Although Ellis suspected the answer, he asked the most important question. "What would you have done if you succeeded in leaving the Fortress?"

She glanced at him along her shoulder and replied, "Joined my father."

"Then you would have been a party to his rebellion," said Darius.

Despite the tears swelling in her eyes, she straightened and faced them. "I support him because I love him. If you consider that rebellion, so be it."

Ellis winced at her declaration. "You don't realize what you just said." He turned on his heels and left, Darius following.

Kell sent a warning glance to Mahon concerning Gwen before following the others. They briskly crossed camp back to where Shannan and Arista waited.

"By your expression, I say you found out what you wanted," Shannan said to Ellis.

He took a few deep, calming breaths before speaking to Arista. "I hope you are up to this."

Arista set her chin. "I am."

Meanwhile, Lanay paced the tent, the wait nerve racking. Armus stood inside the entrance keeping watch of her every move. She clenched her hands together when the flap opened. Kell appeared first then came Ellis, Darius, Shannan and Arista, and lastly Vidar.

"Sire." Her voice quivered and her curtsey unsteady.

"Lady Lanay, please be seated," he spoke in a thick formal tone.

She remained standing. "Sire, I know something dreadful has happened, please don't keep me waiting with courtesies."

"Very well." Ellis proceeded, direct in his look and speech. "A rebellion endangered the life of the queen and prince, forcing them to make a desperate escape from Waldron in the middle of the night."

In horror, she turned to Shannan. "The prince?"

"He is safe, thank Jor'el."

Lanay relaxed. "Thank goodness. You are unharmed, Majesty?"

"I am. Lady Arista suffered frostbite."

Lanay's surprise glance shifted to Arista. A slight look of wariness passed over Arista's brow when their eyes met. "You are recovered now?" Instead of a verbal answer, Arista nodded.

Ellis continued, drawing Lanay's attention back to him. "You noticed the army. I had to call upon the Council forces and attack Waldron to free it from the evil which seized it." His face grew stern and his speech become bitter.

"My husband told me about your orders concerning the Dark Way, Sire."

"What else did he tell you?"

She shrugged, her manner growing uneasy at the questioning and rising tension. "Nothing. He was agitated when he returned from presenting his report. He woke me during the night and told me to take the girls and flee to the Fortress at Pickford. He acted so strangely."

"How so?"

"Forceful and gruff, not like himself. He commanded me to leave."

Ellis pursed his lips in mild frustration, looking across to Darius. "He told you nothing about the report?"

"No, Sire, except," she grew hesitant.

"Except what? It is very important you answer me truthfully."

She stared at him a moment. The deep seriousness on his face frightened her. "Sire, Owain can more answer you than I."

"Except what?"

The knuckles of her clenched her hands turned white at his forceful insistence. Indeed something was terribly wrong, not just by his demeanor and behavior, but also evident on the faces of the others.

"Answer the king," said Shannan, with great insistence.

Lanay held Shannan's steady gaze for a brief moment before complying. "Erasmus arrived to relay your orders, Sire. He told how some suspected Owain was behind the trouble." She grew defensive. "He couldn't be. He has no connection to the Dark Way."

"Owain led the rebellion," said Ellis, his voice thick and declarative.

Thunderstruck and speechless, she gaped at Ellis. "No, it can't true," she weakly refuted. Ellis stared at her, harsh and unsympathetic and she grew annoyed. "No, I don't believe it."

"Are you calling the king a liar?" asked Darius.

Lanay regarded Darius. He too was grim and fierce then she glanced to Shannan and Arista. There was no sympathy to be found. "No, but …" On the verge of tears, she turned back to Ellis. "Sire, there must be a mistake. He wouldn't do that again to us."

Ellis held out his hand and Vidar gave him the letter. "This will answer you better than I."

Lanay stared at it. The three seals only meant one thing; Owain's will. Her hands trembled when she took the letter. Opening it was difficult due to the shaking, but she managed and began reading. By the time she finished, she had to sit, her sobs uncontrollable.

Ellis motioned Kell toward the side table upon which sat food and drink. Kell offered Lanay a cup of wine, which she initially refused, pushing it away.

"You must regain your composure," he said in a firm yet soothing voice. She took the cup and drank.

"I did not intend to break the news of Owain's death so abruptly. However, there may be some clue in his letter as to why and who influenced him."

She shook her head. "He speaks only of his love for his family and his deep regret of what will become of the girls and me."

"He doesn't name an accomplice?" asked Darius.

"Here! Read for yourselves." She flung the pages at Darius.

Darius picked them up and scanned the pages. Arista moved to his side, also reading. After a moment, he shook his head at Ellis.

"How unfortunate," said Ellis, somberly.

"Unfortunate? My husband is dead! Branded a traitor and accused of leading rebellion. Why? I don't know," she cried. "What will become of us?"

Arista seized Darius' arm, fretful in watching Ellis, who focused on Lanay.

"Do you swear in Jor'el's name you had no knowledge of Owain's plans?"

"I told you, he had us flee to a Fortress for safety."

Kell stepped forward to get Lanay's attention. "Answer the king."

The Guardian's eyes were unnerving yet compelling and she swallowed back her emotions before replying. "I suspected something was wrong, only afraid to ask him. Afraid of what he would tell me." She wept again.

Kell gave Ellis a short nod to indicate truthfulness.

"I believe you," said Ellis. "Armus will take you to your daughters while I make arrangements for your future."

Darius held the letter out to Lanay. She took the letter and fought to maintain her composure while leaving.

Arista leaned against Darius and softly wept. "I'm so sorry," he said.

"As am I," said Ellis. "I hoped it was otherwise with Lanay—for your sake."

Arista nodded, wiping her eyes. "What will you do?"

"They cannot stay in Allon," said Kell.

She gaped at Kell in dreadful surprise. "Banishment?"

"For the good of all," he said, his voice and eyes certain yet sympathetic.

Arista tightened her hold on Darius, but looked to, "Ellis?"

Compassionate consideration weighed on his face. "I realize this is difficult, but I cannot make the same mistake I did last time and let this rebellion go unpunished."

"Last time was done out of compassion in hopes of winning him over," said Darius.

"Which nearly cost the lives of my family and the throne."

"To punish them could inflame anger into hate."

Kell intervened. "That happened by Gwen's attempted escape, assault upon a Fortress officer, confrontation with me and then the king. It can't remain here to be fully expressed again. They must be banished."

Seeing Darius' frustration and Arista's pain, Ellis kindly spoke to her. "I will not leave them desolate. An annual pension from the estate's revenues will be established, at least until the girls are married. This way Lanay can focus her attention on raising them and not worrying about provision. Afterwards, she is on her own."

"Why? Gwen showed anger not Lanay," her voice was choked.

Ellis shook his head and tried to contain his rising emotions for her sake. "Lanay admitted to Owain's strange and out of character behavior. And that she was afraid to ask him why because she knew the answer. If she contacted Erasmus, Allard or someone else on the Council with her concern perhaps some intervention could have prevented this. For keeping silent, she does bear responsibility." Emotions surfaced as told by Darius's level brow at him and quick side-glance to Arista. He turned to Kell and in a near whisper said, "Make the arrangements for their deportation."

Dejected, Arista sat. Shannan knelt beside the chair. "You know Ellis does this with a heavy heart."

"I know."

"Sire." Jasper called a moment before he entered.

"Is there a problem?"

"General Iain and the boys will be leaving shortly. This would be a good time to speak to them."

"Are you up to seeing them before they leave?" Shannan asked Arista.

"Oh, ay." She wiped the tears from her eyes and face.

Ellis, Shannan, Darius and Arista found Ian, Wess and Bosley in a tent on the west side of camp gathered around a plain closed casket. Ferrell remained with the boys and was the first to notice their arrival.

"Sire. Majesty."

Ellis waved aside the address and approached Wess and Bosley. Wess was pale and grim and Bosley's eyes were red and sorrowful. "I'm so sorry."

He barely spoke when Bosley started crying and Shannan comforted him. "Hugh would have been proud," she said to Bosley, then to Wess, "Proud of both of you."

Wess' expression didn't alter.

"As I am." Iain clapped Wess on the shoulder.

Wess challenged Ellis. "All for what, if you plan to abandon Waldron?"

"Wess," scolded Iain, "You're speaking to the king."

Ellis was kind in the reply. "No, it is a fair question, and he deserves an answer." For a moment he regarded Wess who didn't retreat or flinch at royal scrutiny. Why should he? He too was of royal blood. Since Wess was nearly six feet tall, Ellis looked him in the eyes. In a few more years he could reach or exceed Ellis' height of six feet two inches. The recent dangers aged Wess, making him appear more astute than his sixteen years. The eagerness of seeing battle was tempered, replaced by experience and gained wisdom. In fact, a thought struck Ellis. Wess was just six years younger, not a vast age difference between them. "We are not abandoning Waldron forever, only until the evil is cleansed. You should be familiar with the stench and stain the Dark Way leaves behind."

"And why you ordered Ravendale destroyed because it couldn't be cleansed."

"Exactly. Waldron is not so polluted. This will only be temporary."

Wess' voice softened, but he remained fixed in feature and posture. "How long will it take to cleanse Waldron?"

"It will be for the Vicar to decide. Until then, the queen and I would appreciate your continued service. We owe you, your brother and your father a great deal." Ellis gazed at the coffin, a twinge of distress crossing his face. "I'm glad Mahon said he finally forgave himself and accepted mercy, because I do not have the words to express my gratitude and admiration. He helped saved Allon; much like you and your brother did by protecting the queen and prince." He took hold of Wess' shoulder and with all conviction and purpose said, "You will be my personal squire."

Wess was stunned. "Sire."

"You earned it by your bravery, and it is your birthright to serve in the royal house."

Wess clasped the hilt of his sword and bowed his head.

Ellis softly smiled. "Two brothers displayed uncommon valor."

Bosley grew apprehensive. "I too am to be a squire?"

Ellis chuckled and shook his head. "No, something more to your liking. I am in need of advisors also. The duke will be your tutor and mentor in politics, if you are agreeable."

"You mean to someday sit on the Council?" asked Bosley, surprised.

"Midessex is now under royal oversight until I can find someone trustworthy and loyal to take responsibility for the province," he said in a knowing tone.

Bosley widely smiled, yet tried to curb his pleasure to give a serious answer. "I would be honored, Sire."

Ellis laughed. "I have named your sisters as royal wards and they shall continue to receive their pension and a dowry upon marriage."

"Sire, you overwhelm us with such generosity," said Iain.

"General, I am honored to have been so faithfully served by a family that in the eyes of the world should be my enemy."

"I look forward to seeing both of you upon your return to Court," said Shannan.

"We both do," said Arista in tender agreement.

"As do we, Majesty. My lady," said Wess. He made a deep bow, Bosley agreed and mimicked his formality.

Ellis, Shannan, Arista and Darius. Outside Ellis gazed at the tent while wondering aloud. "Of all the people who should hold a grudge against me, they should."

"Despite Wess' outburst, he doesn't hold a grudge," said Arista.

He grinned and took her arm to begin the trek back toward the royal tent. "I admit when you, Shannan and Darius told of their heroics, I was very surprised. Throughout this ordeal you witnessed first-hand the mettle of Hugh's sons. In their young lives, Wess, Bosley and their sisters endured more upheaval than Owain's daughters. They lost their parents, endured captivity, a coup and, while comfortably provided for, were reduced in station from a royal life to live as commoners in the country. Owain and his family continued a normal life even during his probation. However, he allowed anger, bitterness and resentment to become manifest, throwing Allon into turmoil." He paused in speech and step to fully face her. "That is why I went to speak to Gwen first. By her own words she confirmed what Kell and Armus said regarding her personal sentiments. What a stark contrast between the families. And with both, I initially granted mercy, only to be betrayed by one. Mercy a second time won't change Gwen's heart but gained loyalty of a family who should be my enemy."

Arista nodded her understanding. "I suspected something like that. Hearing it expressed brings your response to them into perspective. You had no choice. Ellis."

Relieved and grateful, he embraced her about the shoulders. "Dealing with them was hard enough, but having it affect you was distressing."

"Well, I suspect more times like this now that she'll be your sister," said Darius, tossing a wink at the women.

"Oh, heaven forbid."

"What, that I'll be your sister?" Arista picked up on Darius' teasing.

"No!" said Ellis, flushed in embarrassment.

"That he has to think more before he speaks, or the three of us will let him know when he doesn't," said Shannan.

"Is this what is going to be like? Three against one?" Ellis playfully chided.

Widely grinning, Shannan locked arms with Arista. "No, two against two. Us keeping you two in line." She turned Arista to continue on their original course. "Come, we have a wedding to plan."

Ellis glanced askew to Darius. "You still have time to reconsider."

Darius just laughed and followed after the women.

Explore the Kingdom of Allon

www.allonbooks.com

Featuring

- Original Character Art
- Interactive Map of Allon
- News and Events
- Photo and Video Gallery
- Links to:
  - Facebook – Allon Group Page
  - The Kingdom of Allon blog
  - Contact Shawn Lamb

Made in the USA
Middletown, DE
15 January 2022

58749887R00159